THE MELTING

Lize Spit gained a master's degree in screenplay writing and has also written prose and poetry, published in several magazines. In 2013 she won both the Jury Prize and the Readers' Prize at WriteNow!, a prestigious writing competition. Her debut novel *The Melting* was published to widespread acclaim, became an instant bestseller and has been sold in ten languages. She lives in Brussels.

LIZE SPIT

THE MELTING

Translated from the Dutch by Kristen Gehrman

PICADOR

First published 2021 by Picador
an imprint of Pan Macmillan
The Smithson, 6 Briset Street, London EC1M 5NR
EU representative: Macmillan Publishers Ireland Limited,
Mallard Lodge, Lansdowne Village, Dublin 4
Associated companies throughout the world
www.panmacmillan.com

ISBN 978-1-5098-3869-1

Originally published in Dutch 2016 as *Het smelt* by Das Mag Uitgevers.

This book was published with the support of Flanders Literature (flandersliterature.be).

Typeset in Bembo MT Pro by Palimpsest Book Production Limited, Falkirk, Stirlingshire
Printed and bound by CPI Group (UK) Ltd, Croydon, CR0 4YY

MIX
Paper from
responsible sources
FSC
www.fsc.org   FSC® C116313

Visit **www.picador.com** to read more about all our books
and to buy them. You will also find features, author interviews and
news of any author events, and you can sign up for e-newsletters
so that you're always first to hear about our new releases.

For Tilde, Jornt & Saar

9:00 a.m.

THE INVITATION ARRIVED three weeks ago with way too many stamps on it. The weight of the stamps must have required even more postage, which made me hopeful at first: apparently there are still things that perpetuate their own existence.

I found the envelope lying on top of the rest of the mail, which consisted of a dozen or so letters and flyers stacked in two equal piles in front of my door. Clearly my neighbor's work; one stack for each favor that would have to be returned. Under the overly stamped envelope was a special offer for a French psychic and a toy-store ad intended for the upstairs neighbors—my mailbox often serves as a vanishing pit for the kind of mail that makes children whine. Other than that, there were bills and four brochures from a discount supermarket advertising skimpily stuffed turkeys, mocha logs, cheap wine. Come to think of it, I still didn't have any plans for New Year's Eve.

I gathered up the attempted barricade and went inside. I made the usual rounds, mail in hand, opening every door in the apartment, not knowing which was worse: actually catching an intruder one day or always finding empty rooms.

I hung up my coat and mittens and started making dinner. I peeled a potato and snipped off the long antlers that had sprouted in the sun. I filled the electric kettle to the brim and lit the gas under an empty pan on the stove so the kettle would know it needed to hurry.

While waiting, I examined the letter.

My name and address were written in black pen in a

handwriting that I recognized but couldn't quite place. I tore it open along the edge with the tip of the potato peeler. Inside was a white card, a baby photo and a name. I didn't have to look at the face, name or date to know that it was a picture of Jan and that this was not a birth announcement. This year, on December 30th, he would have been thirty years old.

I looked at my address again, the street name. The scribbles had been pressed deep into the paper; the loops sprang just out of the lines. It was Pim's handwriting all right. I sat next to him in school for years and saw how he filled in the answers on tests. I never understood why he pressed down so hard with his pen. It wasn't going to make his answers any more right.

Pim must have looked up my address. He had written it perfectly, letter by letter. The invitation itself was pre-printed. On the inside was a bit of text.

"Dear . . ." My name had been written in on the dotted line.

"As you know, Jan would have been thirty this month, and we're also celebrating the inauguration of our almost fully automatic dairy farm. Let's get together and raise a glass in honor of this special occasion."

I took off my shoes so I could feel the smooth parquet floor under my feet. Jan's posthumous party was being used as a marketing stunt, an attempt to get as many people together as possible to launch a new business.

I didn't read any further. I threw the card into the trash along with the potato peels and the rest of the mail. I turned on the tap, thrust my wrists under the cold water and splashed some in my face.

The empty cast-iron pot crackled, begging for water. Even though the kettle had just started to boil, I turned off the gas. I wasn't hungry anymore.

Of course, even before I was drying my cheeks on the kitchen towel, I knew I couldn't just leave it at that.

I pulled the card out of the trash.

Jan's photo had been smeared by the potato starch. There was a black smudge that started at his mouth, stretching his lips out past his forehead. I tried to dab the smile back into place with the corner of the towel.

"3:00: stall doors open. 3:15: short milking machine demonstration and party to follow. P.S. Be sure to wear warm clothes. Please no flowers, but feel free to share a photo or a good memory of my brother. These can be emailed to info@dairyfarmvisit.be or posted on Jan's Facebook page. See opposite side for directions."

On the other side of the card, under a rudimentary road map, was a sappy quote. I read it aloud a few times, as Pim would've intended. But no matter how I read the sentences, they were still trying too hard.

Now it's a little after nine. I've just driven past Vilvoorde. The clock in my car flickers every few seconds and runs a few minutes ahead of my cell phone. Maybe it's because of the cold. As I drive down the highway, Jan's expressionless face gazes up at me from the passenger seat.

I didn't bring the card with me for the photo. Nor do I need to it to check the exact times or directions again.

All I need is the thick layer of postage stamps on the envelope. Those stamps are proof that Pim really wanted this invitation to reach me. I realize that it's not addressed to the person I am now, but to who I was back when we were still speaking, to the Eva from before the summer of 2002. Which is why I am going to do exactly what I would have done back then: show up even though I don't want to.

July 4, 2002

THE NEWSCASTER'S VOICE is coming from the yard. It's Thursday. There are so many traffic jams they'd be better off giving a summary of where the traffic is moving. The next few days are going to be hot, the voice warns. After the weather, "The Ketchup Song" comes on. The music is drowned out by the sound of flapping birds taking flight.

Maybe it's because I've finally got a good night's sleep or because the hand movements go so well with the song, but for the first time since winter, it feels like I've woken up in the right place. There's still an untouched summer before me. The church bells will guard the duration of each hour. No one can speed up or slow down the hands of the clock, not even Laurens and Pim. For the first time since Jan's funeral, the thought of it is calming. All I have to do is keep the set pace, and everything will be fine.

I sit up in my lofted bed. Only now do I notice Tessie standing beside hers. Her short, spiky hair is plastered against her sweaty head. She's inspecting her bedsheet, checking to make sure the flaps are exactly the same length on either side.

"Did you sleep okay?" I ask.

She nods.

It's a perfect day for jawbreakers.

On my way out to my bike, I run into Dad. He smokes a ciga-rette as he listens with pride to the eleven o'clock news blasting loud and clear from the radio he's just hung in the top of the cherry tree to scare away the crows. He leans against the shed, which we all call "the workshop", though no one ever does any work in there.

The traffic towards the coast is still backed up due to two major accidents on the E40; in the meantime, I shove a 50-cent coin into each of my socks. With every step, they slide down a little bit further.

Dad smokes the cigarette down to the filter, takes the butt from his lips, stomps it out with his slipper and picks it back up again.

He's got his black jeans on. There was a time when these were the pants he wore to work, but they've long since lost their shape. There are two bulges in the fabric just above the knees, an impression left behind by all his squatting next to the beer crate.

"Eva," he says.

He turns around and motions for me to follow him. When he says my name, it sometimes sounds like a command, sometimes like a question, but rarely like anything that's mine.

I follow him into the workshop. The coins slip down my ankles and under my feet.

It was Mom who came up with the term "workshop", back when they first bought this house, when every empty room could be anything if they repeated it enough. Dad had big plans for the place. He was going to fix up the garden, trim the hedges, make a compost pile, renovate the bathroom. The latter was used by the previous owners as a children's bedroom and came covered in teddy bear wallpaper. In the middle of the room, Dad had built a half wall out of hollow bricks and planned to install a sink. The sides would be tiled as soon as there was enough money for it. Jolan discovered that the holes in the bricks made excellent toothbrush holders.

"So handy in the meantime," Mom declared. But Jolan had already figured it out—there's no time in meantime.

The workshop is littered with empty beer cans and other junk. The interior walls are sprouting with mushrooms. Most of them grow sideways on their stems so they can peek out from under their little caps and see for themselves what actually goes on in here all those hours.

Dad drops his cigarette butt into a can with a slosh left in the bottom.

"Otherwise, that woman'll complain." He motions towards the door leading into the kitchen.

His shoulders have a dent in the top as if his armpits are too heavy. We stand there for a moment looking at each other, in the middle of the workshop, surrounded by all kinds of freebies that Peter's Liquor Store gives away with crates of Maes Pils—blue hats, blue inflatable beer trays, blue beach balls.

Does Dad see what I see? That this place has become a warehouse full of potential raffle prizes?

My eyes land on the drill. It isn't hanging from the ceiling with the other tools but lying on a rack that has been recently screwed together and anchored into the wall. It's the only time the machine has ever been used, and it's hard to say which enabled which: the drill the rack or the rack the drill.

All these tools didn't end up here by chance. We live close to Aldi—it's just a little too far away to walk to, but well within biking distance. Every year, they've got some new gadget that fathers don't have yet. On the bridge over the highway separating our village from the next, it's not unusual to see mothers trying to balance jigsaws, Medion massagers, hedge clippers and barbecue tongs on their handlebars.

We gave Dad this drill a year ago as a present. He seemed to like it best when it was still in the box sitting on the sideboard. After he unwrapped it, he left it on top of a pile of ironed dishtowels, where it remained until the preparations for his next birthday couldn't be put off any longer.

"The average drill will be only used for about eleven minutes in its entire lifetime," Dad says.

"That's not very long," I say.

I check whether there's still a price tag on the box so I can calculate the price per second. This is something I can tell Pim and Laurens later. They might find it interesting.

"Look, Evie. I wanted to show you this."

He points up to a loop hanging from the center beam at the peak of the roof, next to the hedge clippers.

"You can't tell by looking at it how hard it is to hang something like that, now can you?"

I reply with a shrug. People shrug their shoulders when they don't care, but also when they care a lot but can't find the words. Surely another body part could be chosen, or even another gesture. The anatomy of the shoulders, unlike the eyebrows, offers little room for nuance.

"Not just anybody can tie a knot like this," he said, "it's got to hang at just the right height."

"I can see that," I say. "So, what's the right height then?"

But my question goes unheard.

"With the wrong knot, you'd suffer. You don't want me to suffer, do you?"

I look at the noose again and shake my head.

"If you don't fall from high enough, your neck won't break. Then it takes a long time. But if you fall from too high, your neck will snap. And you wouldn't want to do that to the people who are going to find you, now would you?"

"No, I wouldn't," I say.

Dad is wearing a baseball cap on his head. The sweat of the past few days has soaked up into the fabric and dried, leaving behind white, wavy lines of salt across his forehead. The hotter the day, the higher the streak.

He looks at me in silence, takes off the cap and checks to see if there is anything unusual about it. He doesn't see it. It lands back on top of his head, backwards this time.

I can't help but think: this man is my father. He is older than most dads because it took him so long to find someone who wanted to have children with him. He works for a bank, where he does things that he never goes into detail about, and no one ever asks questions because they just assume that as long as no one brings it up, there's nothing to tell. To get to his job, he has to bike—rain or shine—to a bus stop and then sit on a bus for half an hour. During the week, he earns just enough to feed his family, no questions asked, and to pay for the roof over their heads from which he can hang the presents they buy for him with his money that he didn't want in the first place.

I am this man's oldest daughter, so really, I shouldn't just nod or reply without knowing exactly what he's up to.

I force a look onto my face. Not a smile. Not pity. Understanding perhaps, although I don't really know how that looks in grimace-form.

"You think—just like your mother—that this old prick doesn't mean a word he says. That this old prick doesn't have the guts to go through with it?"

Dad always says "your mother", and Mom does the same when she talks about him, "your father". This isn't really fair. It's a way of letting themselves off the hook by acting like I'm the one who chose them.

"You want me to show you how it works?"

He unfolds a rickety ladder right under the noose and climbs up. On the third step, the ladder starts to wobble dangerously. I come closer to it and position myself on the side for support. The coins sink down even lower until they are under the soles of my feet. The eleven o'clock news is over, and the radio switches to commercials.

"Why pay more? If you find the same appliance for less, we'll refund the difference!"

Dad reaches the top of the ladder. He balances both feet on the top step so he's standing right below the loop. He bumps the rope to the side, and it swings around and hits him in the back of the head, almost knocking him off balance. I grip the ladder and hold it steady. All I can do is keep him from falling. There's nothing I can do to stop him from jumping. I feel the coins burning under my feet. King Albert II's head will be engraved into my soles for the rest of my life.

Dad gives the noose a little tug—it's strong enough. He slips it around his neck and gazes out over his blue empire. He nods, looking satisfied.

"People who hang themselves often end up clawing the skin off their neck. That's regret. You should have no regrets," he says.

I nod.

"Did you hear me, Eva?"

I nod again.

"What did I say?"

"You should have no regrets," I say.

"I can't hear you."

"No regrets," I repeat, louder.

Only now does he look down and see me standing there holding the ladder.

For a moment, he falls silent.

Then he says, "You've got to do something about your hair, Eva. It doesn't do anything for you."

If you ask me my hair is just the right length: short enough to wear down when it's cold and long enough to pull back into a ponytail when it's hot. Dad will just have to get used to it. Last week, I trimmed off a few centimeters myself because the ends were splitting. I did it in our moldy bathroom in front of the mirror, over the old-fashioned washstand, with a pair of scissors my mom sometimes uses to cut fabric.

"Thanks for holding the ladder, Eva," Dad says. He's removed the noose and already taken two steps down. "You're the only one who knows about this. Not even your mother knows. Let's keep it that way."

He reaches into his pocket, leans his lower back against the middle of the ladder and lights up another cigarette. "The fact that I even let you see it is probably a good sign."

He sucks his cheeks into his jaws and carefully climbs down the remaining steps. Back on the ground, he punches me so hard against the shoulder that I lose my balance, the kind of punch that fathers are supposed to give their sons.

"Smoking's bad for you," I say.

In the window of the Corner Store are a few Raider bars displayed on plastic grass. Actually, they're not called Raiders anymore—now they're Twixes—but no one dares to tell Agnes. She's been running the place for longer than anyone can remember.

The deep, narrow house has pretty much anything that you'd find in a grocery store. Though most people only come here for products that can't expire, shrivel or dry out. Once, Laurens's cousin had the nerve to bring back a pack of noodles that were past their sell-by date.

"That's not the expiration date, kid," Agnes barked. "It's the date the product was made." After a short debate, the pasta was exchanged for a pack of permanent markers. A few hours later her sign outside read: FOR ALL YOUR DRY GOODS *that still have to be made*. Agnes never tried to wash it off. On the contrary. She's become a specialist in manipulating expiration dates. With a fine-tip pen, she transforms threes into eights and nines; all it takes is a little horizontal line to turn January into July. She knows the locals will keep coming anyway: anyone who wants to be picky can drive ten minutes to the next town for a pack of flour. Principles always have their limits. Even Laurens's cousin would still come back again for noodles.

I go in. This day got off to a good start. I still owe it some jaw-breakers. A bell rings as I walk in; it's not the same one as in the butcher shop. This one sounds more like a shriek.

The shutters are almost completely rolled down, casting a dusky light over the store. A musty coolness lingers among the shelves, like a morning kept too long. I wait, keeping an eye on the office at the back of the shop. That's where Agnes hides out doing photocopies of crossword puzzles. Maybe she's got a table and chair in there, a kitchen too. No one can confirm this.

I keep waiting; Agnes doesn't like customers nosing around when she's not there. I untie my shoelaces and fish the coins out of my socks. I didn't really need to hide the money this morning. Mom didn't see me leave.

"Hi, Eva," a voice says. I finish tying my shoes and stand back up.

Agnes hurries to the counter; she walks with a slight hunch. Her back has grown crooked, like a side table. Laurens once made a joke about how many beers she could carry on her shoulder blades without spilling. Today I count eight. I have to remember this, maybe I can tell him later.

I follow Agnes between the gray shelves laden with sponges, toothpicks, sanitary pads and plastic flowers. She knows what I'm here for. The candy is in the centermost aisle.

"Where are the other two musketeers—the butcher's boy and the farmer's boy?" she asks. I shrug.

Ever since her husband ran off with another man, ever since the new slogan appeared on her sign, she's stopped letting customers scoop their own candy, including me.

I politely ask for twenty satellite wafers, five sour belts and two packs of jawbreakers. She drops the candy into the cone-shaped paper bag.

"Are you hanging out with Jan's brother today? You going to share this with him?" she asks.

I nod convincingly, though I'm not sure.

She gives me a little extra of everything.

I pedal through town with the bag swinging from my handlebars. I scan the empty streets, hoping that if I look long enough, Laurens and Pim will emerge from the collages of old memories. After an hour, the candy is gone. My mouth burns from the sourness. My stomach feels heavy. I should have stayed home. Maybe they tried to call me.

I bike past the butcher shop.

Laurens's bike isn't leaning against the front of the house. Maybe he's got new friends or hobbies he hasn't told me about, maybe he's not home. Maybe his bike is just in the garage today or he'd rather watch TV in this heat than hang out with me.

I peer in through the big shop window. Inside, the priest is picking out cold cuts. He points to the ring bologna. Laurens's mother swings the log onto the meat slicer. Through the open door, I can hear the slow movement of the blade. Slicing meat doesn't make a chopping sound, it's more like unravelling.

Laurens was right. "A cow is made up of a million threads," he once said during lunch at school as he rolled the spongy center of his bread into little balls, divided his meat into strips and laid each strip on a separate bread ball. "Once you know this, you don't mind cutting it up anymore." This didn't sound like something he thought up himself, but still, I was impressed by the fact that he'd remembered it.

Watching Laurens's mom has a calming effect on me. I can tell by the way she's moving her hands that she's talking about the weather. Then she stacks cool, loose slices of salami on the scale.

Here, watching the priest nod approvingly and pay for his meat, I'm overwhelmed by a gloomy feeling that's left me alone for a little while, a feeling that I had thought, I had hoped, was maybe gone for good.

I now know that nothing can protect me from this feeling, even when I'm in my seat in the right class on time, wearing an outfit that everyone is used to seeing me in, even when I'm looking at meat, even when I'm not looking at meat. Suddenly, it's as if something, everything, is missing inside me, as if I used to be more whole and a part of me still remembers how that felt.

The feeling also strikes me when I'm standing in the bathtub, washing. Suddenly, I'll feel something on my skin. It closes me in, tightens around me, reminding me that I'm in the wrong place.

Maybe, I thought recently, it's because I was born shortly after twins, from a womb that was all stretched out. Maybe Mom was just too loose around me in those first nine months.

Before Laurens's mom sees me standing there watching her, I slip out of sight.

The storm hits before I make it home. The first raindrops are lukewarm. I guess it was inevitable, even the cold taps have been running hot these past few days. I look for a tree to take shelter under and end up under a pine at the edge of our yard. I watch the storm rage around me. Gusts of wind whip through the pouring rain.

We never should have given Dad tools as gifts, and definitely not hedge clippers. That thing has been hanging from the roof with its two handles towards the ground for two years now.

Whenever the wind blows, it starts to sway. Maybe that's where he got his ideas.

At first, the tree's branches are able to keep out the rain, but after a few minutes, thick, irregular drops start leaking through. I'm getting wet, but it doesn't matter.

Four Shadows

WE WERE THREE, but we had four shadows. Jolan, my oldest brother, would have had a healthy twin sister had his umbilical cord not been wrapped around her neck.

They were born four weeks early in '85, and there are endless photos of their birth, all of which have been stuck into an album with double-sided tape. Under each one is a date, exact time, names of unknown uncles, notes about big dreams—attainable because they would only ever have to be partially achieved.

JOLAN DE WOLF and TES DE WOLF. There was a little cross next to the second name on the birth announcement, which saved the cost of a death announcement.

As soon as Jolan was out of the incubator—as my dad liked to exaggerate—I was born.

That was somewhere in the middle of '88, at midnight. I was a girl. My name was Eva. I too arrived alone. Dad had just stepped out for a smoke.

Compared to Jolan, who was small and slow to develop, I was stronger from the start. Of my first year of life, there are fifty photos at most. None of them have a time written under them; no unknown uncles and aunts came to visit.

"Elephant feet", Dad wrote under a picture of me using the potty for the first time. The other captions must have been written in hindsight because they all describe something temporary and include an evaluation of the situation. "Eva, still a little towhead." Or: "January, when she could still smile."

Three years later, in '91, Tessie was born. Dad only took a

handful of photos of her, none of which landed in an album. From a young age, Tessie was smaller and more fragile than we were. She had thin, veiny skin and fine blond hair.

"What did you expect? After two kids there just wasn't enough material left over," Dad joked after she was born, or that's how my mom would tell it. Maybe he was proud, maybe he was overcome with emotion. But to the nurses, it must have sounded like an apology, the kind of apology women make when a recipe doesn't turn out quite right.

"That's something my own goddamn father would have said. And you have four kids, by the way, not three," Mom replied. I could tell by the way she would bring it up from time to time, the way she always included that "goddamn", that this was where it all started. This was her ultimate grievance.

The choice of a name led to a long debate: Mom wanted Tessie, Dad wanted some other name, preferably Charlotte—Lottie, if necessary. But maybe, in an effort to make amends, he finally gave in and agreed to my mom's choice. Tessie became an homage.

By the time she was two years old, they'd started calling her "the little runt". In the household my mom grew up in, where she was the oldest child of a tyrannical father, Little Runt was the nickname for the youngest in a family. There was something tragic to the name—it reminded me of a guinea pig that shits on one side of its cage and sleeps on the other. We were pretty sure the nickname wasn't given out of nostalgia, but out of regret for the name Tessie, a regret that Mom didn't want to admit to Dad. Either way, it stuck. Language was the one thing from Mom's childhood that she still talked about with pride.

Tessie's arrival made me the middle child. This meant that whenever sides were being taken, I got to pick which one I wanted to be on, depending on whether I wanted to form a coalition or an opposition.

Before Jolan was born, Mom and Dad moved from a larger town nearby to the three-bedroom house in Bovenmeer.

Bovenmeer was the type of place where, in order to keep the

balance between supply and demand, there had to be either one or none of everything: one store, one hair salon, one bakery, one butcher, no bike shop, one library (whose entire collection could be read in a single sitting) and one primary school.

For years, we would refer to every place in town as the something, as if it all belonged to us, as if we could pinch it between our thumb and forefinger. It was if, after a long war with the big cities and surrounding towns, we had won the prototypes of a store and a butcher shop and firmly anchored them around the church and parish hall, within walking distance of pretty much everything and in reach of everyone.

The shop owners took advantage of this; whether it was out of laziness or arrogance, they didn't bother to come up with more original names for their businesses than "the Corner Store" or "the Butcher Shop", except for a few cases where the owner's last name was tagged on like a kind of subtitle.

Bovenmeer had a few exceptions, though. There were two bars, for example. Men were known to stumble out of the Night, steady themselves against the doorframe, and head over to the Welcome, where they served beer until the early hours of the morning.

Certain names were given over and over again: Tim, Jan, Ann. Both Pim and Laurens had a brother named Jan, but from the winter of 2001 onwards, they each had one in a different way. Laurens still had a brother; Pim used to have one.

There was also an empty henhouse between the Welcome and the parish hall called Kosovo. An Albanian refugee family had lived in it for months, and after they were deported, various local clubs started using it to store their junk.

I had no idea what Mom and Dad had hoped to find in Bovenmeer. Whether they had ever thought about how they would survive in a town with an annual parish festival, where no one thinks it's strange to send someone to Kosovo for a pack of napkins.

9:30 a.m.

SIX DAYS AGO, two weeks after the invitation arrived, I took a plastic Curver tub over to my neighbor's and asked if I could fill it up with water and stick it in his freezer. He lives one floor below me, so I guess he's more of a downstairs neighbor than a neighbor-neighbor. He's twelve years older than I am. We both happen to be teachers: he teaches geography and biology at a French-speaking middle school, and I teach art at a Dutch-speaking one.

We lived in the same building for four years without ever saying a word to each other. The first time we spoke was about a year ago; he was carrying a clear plastic bag full of large hunks of raw meat—a heart, a sirloin steak, tenderloin, tongue, spareribs, beef tips. I was carrying a few collages left behind by my students. I'd given them a bunch of old atlases to cut up and told them to use the pieces to assemble their ideal world. The razor blades and Styrofoam were barely touched; most of the students were content with ripping up the atlases and slapping a few scraps on a sheet of paper. Most of them hadn't even bothered to pick up their work at the end of the school year.

The neighbor felt the need to address me about this. He said I'd be better off teaching my students to value facts and respect history.

I pretended not to understand French. The smell coming from his bag was making me nauseous.

Since it would have taken him far too much effort to reprimand me in Dutch, he started explaining how he acquired such a large amount of raw flesh: every year, his mother had an entire cow butchered at an organic farm and shared the meat with her three sons. They could each pick out the pieces they wanted. This was the only time the family got together all year.

As I turned towards the stairs, he said that my heels made a lot of noise on the wood floor in my apartment, but he didn't mind because I seemed like the type of person who knew what she wanted.

This led me to two conclusions: this guy has a very large freezer and very little understanding of people, especially women.

Half a year later, he wanted me to indulge him in more than just small talk. I wouldn't say I considered this a plus, but it didn't bother me as long as he washed up beforehand and let me keep my clothes on.

After I received the invitation, I cooked us a piece of organic beef from his freezer every night for two weeks. Once there was enough room, I brought over the empty Curver and filled it up with water from the sink. It just barely fit in the freezer.

The neighbor allowed it and didn't ask any questions. He just cleaned his dick with the water sprayer, using his thumb and fore-finger, as if screwing off a lid. After I'd sucked him off—he with his bare butt on the corner of the tub, me with my knees on the bath-mat—we sat in silence, sipping fresh mint tea. I put a lot of sugar in mine, as usual.

An hour ago he helped me carry the heavy block of ice from his freezer to my car. It was still dark out. Just as we were about to load it into the trunk, he paused and asked in broken Dutch where I was planning to go. He ran his eyes over my legs, which looked more bronzed and attractive than they actually were in the panty-hose I was wearing, over my hair that I'd tied back in a bun, over the mascara on my lashes. I could sense that he found me prettier than usual but had no idea if that was because I'd done my best or because I was about to drive away with a big block of ice in my trunk without specifying where I was going.

"To my parents," I said.

"Your parents," he repeated, as if it had just dawned on him that I wasn't born in a cabbage patch.

"How long do you think a block of ice like this'll last?" I asked.

"Depends which is the temperature of the car and for what you need it," he said.

I let the grammar errors slide so as to avoid discussing the matter any further.

"Will you come over again tonight for tea?" he asked, as he heaved the block of ice into the trunk in one swift motion.

"Sure," I said.

I watched him walk back to the building, his skinny legs, his back. I stood there watching until long after he was gone.

Before I started the car, I called Tessie but hung up before the call went through so it wouldn't show up on her phone. I double-checked the event's Facebook page. Pim had set it up a few days after the invitation arrived—a sure sign that he, and not his parents, was behind the whole thing. The information on Facebook was different than that on the card: the event description said that we were welcome any time from three o'clock onwards, but the card said the party started at three o'clock. That was typical Pim. By encouraging people not to show up on time, he was already creating an excuse for the empty chip bowls.

The cover photo was the same baby picture as on the invitation. Most people marked themselves "Going" right away. After a few days, I changed my status to "Maybe."

At first, there was a surge of activity on the page. Friends posted all kinds of anecdotes and photos. I followed every post. Jan had never had a Facebook profile himself—he was dead before he ever had a place to make himself look better than he was. So now other people were doing it for him. Only attractive, happy photos of Jan appeared on the page—photos I didn't even know existed.

I think everyone turned off the notifications early on. Once the event was off the ground, the page died out within a few days. All the good photos had been shared.

"Hello, my name is Karin Peters. I'm 39 years old and from Belgium. The reason I'm telling you all this is that I have a product I think you might be intrusted in. Just the thing you need!!!! Pay now. Send me your contact info and I'll send pics!!" That was the last post—right there at the top of the page. Last night, I thought about flagging it as offensive, but in the end I didn't because I wasn't sure what was so bad about it.

I'm now halfway to my destination. The traffic is slowly easing up. I keep checking on the block of ice in the rear-view mirror. The frozen mass has lowered the temperature in the car considerably. I don't drive too fast and keep the heating off so as not to speed up the melting process.

The Facebook page is still open on my phone. Forty-five people are going. Jolan was invited, Tessie too, but neither has said they're coming.

I'm still the only "Maybe".

July 6, 2002

I CHECK UNDER the covers to see if they're still there. My two breasts could have just packed up and left in the middle of the night while no one was watching and gone off in search of a better, more credible body. My tank top got twisted up in my sleep, and now my nipples are peeping out of the armpit holes.

These breasts make me think of Uncle Raf, my dad's brother, who, whenever he arrives somewhere, always remains standing, even after someone has pulled up a chair for him. When he finally does sit down, he never rests his weight on the back of the chair. That way he can disappear halfway through the family gathering without saying goodbye.

My breasts aren't round and heavy like the other girls'. They're pointy and stick out straight. How can I let them know they're welcome to stay?

I wrangle the tank top back into place and lie in bed until ten-thirty. I hear lawnmowers, church bells, the neighbors coming home from shopping, an airplane, a scrap-metal collector so wrapped up in roaring unintelligible announcements into an over-powered megaphone that he doesn't even notice the riches flying overhead.

As I glance over at Tessie's bed, at her thin bedsheet folded symmetrically in the shape of an open envelope, I feel indecisive and shapeless.

Before I walk into the kitchen, I can already tell Dad's in there. The smell of tobacco follows him wherever he goes.

Recently, I read that the amount of money a smoker spends on cigarettes each year is enough to pay for an entire vacation. No one had researched whether some people smoke so as not to have to take the family on vacation.

The remnants of breakfast are still on the table. Bread, chocolate spread, syrup.

"Your mother went to the Farmers' Union to get dog food. Jolan left early to go bird-watching," Dad says without looking up. He's sitting at the table reading the newspaper with a ballpoint pen. There's nothing worth underlining today.

I can choose not to have breakfast, but it won't make any difference; Dad won't mention what happened the other day, he's not one to bring up the past the next morning. He always needs a little push.

I pull up a chair. He doesn't even look up. Beside him on the table is a neon-green lice comb and an open tissue covered in brownish red spots—little squished bodies and a couple of wiry hairs with nits on them.

"Where's Tessie?" I ask.

Dad clicks his dentures in and out of his mouth. "Somewhere," he mutters, but without his front teeth, it sounds more like "nowhere". I take a slice of bread and slather it with syrup. Still, Dad doesn't ask what I'm having: "Bread with syrup or syrup with bread?"

He stops fiddling with his teeth and looks at my hair and neck. I lay down my knife and pick up the bread; the soft center sags under the weight of the syrup. His eyes sink down lower and rest on my arms. The longer he looks, the heavier they get.

Even on the hottest days, I still wear long sleeves. The only people who never say anything about it are Laurens and Pim. I haven't worn short sleeves in three years. The last time I did, I didn't feel light and free—I just felt naked.

Dad's eyes sink even lower, to my midsection, then climb back up to his newspaper. He takes a sip of lukewarm tea.

"That sweater shows off those little titties you're getting," he says.

I fold the bread in half. The next bite sticks to the top of my mouth. It doesn't taste like pear syrup anymore. I don't dare to swallow it until the phone rings.

I can tell by the three-second delay that it's Pim. Those three seconds have always been there, giving me just enough time to feel ashamed of everything I've ever told him about myself. Three seconds is long enough to remember anything you want. Though it's probably just the amount of time it takes for the sound to travel through the long, thin telephone cables connecting our houses.

"Hi, Pim," I say, before he can get a word out.

"Me and Laurens are going to go check out the old school today," he says. His voice sounds hoarse. I don't know if that's because it's changing or because there's a lump in his throat. "It was Laurens's idea, but you can come if you want."

"When?" I ask.

"Right now," he says.

"Want me to stop by your house on the way?" I ask. "Oh and Laurens said you got a Honda? Is that true?"

Pim doesn't answer for a moment.

"The Honda's not running," he says finally. "Come by if you want, whatever."

I head to the primary school, following the same route I used to take two years ago, with the little detour along the farm. Pim lives on the edge of town like me, but on the other side. If you were to draw a line between our houses, you'd see that it actually runs perpendicular to the axis between Laurens's butcher shop and the school, but I don't mind the detour. It makes more sense for me than it does for Pim.

When I was younger, I had to fill up a whole water bottle just to bike these two kilometers. Now that I have to pedal twenty-four kilometers a day to and from my new high school, our town seems laughably small and the primary school ridiculously close by.

As I'm leaving the Bulksteeg, I pass a sign Dad made that reads NO PUBLIC URINATION PROHIBITED.

Of course, they know it's not right, that the NO cancels out the PROHIBITED. They aren't stupid, I know that, but every time I bike by it, I hope that the neighbors will give them the same benefit of the doubt.

When my parents bought this house, the Bulksteeg was nothing but a dirt road along the edge of three backyards that also happened to connect the highway exit to the town. The path runs right between our hedged garden and the neighbors' field. Not long ago, when they were repaving the main roads, the city workers started dumping the leftover tar here. Meter by meter, the path became hard and permanent, good enough for cut-through traffic. Even though there are three perfectly good backyards along the road, people still prefer to piss in our hedge.

Once I've reached the end of the Bulksteeg, I have to bike down the busiest road in town. The speed limit is seventy kilometers an hour, but hardly anyone sticks to it. By now I can guess how fast the cars are going from my bed. When school's out, people tend to drive slower.

Beside me, on the surface of the road, is my shadow, a ghost that never leaves my side and is slowly taking on a different shape. I already started noticing it last school year. Certain clothes were getting too tight, my tops didn't fit anymore, pants were getting harder and harder to button. For a while, my nipples were red and hot. Hard disks emerged beneath them. Eventually they let go of my ribs to make room for something to grow in between, something softer. I could feel things changing from one day to the next and didn't know what order it was happening in: was it that they suddenly showed up or that I was suddenly aware of them? Now, thanks to Dad's comment, they're not just mine anymore; they symbolize a major, lasting change.

I've almost reached Pim's house. The farm is set back from the street. The driveway is about twenty meters long and leads to the main barn, which is big enough for the heavy machinery, combines, horse carts, and herds of cows.

Nearly lost in the wide strip of asphalt is a doormat. The word "Welcome" is almost completely worn away. Maybe I can still read it because this house used to be like a second home to me.

I've barely spoken to Pim since Jan's funeral. He hasn't come to any of the parish parties, and no one has birthday parties anymore. I've walked past the farm a few times with our dog, but I never dared to ring the doorbell. I'd always end up walking away, telling myself that the silence between us didn't have to mean anything. We couldn't talk about an end until at least the summer was over.

I gaze down the long driveway looking for a sign of life.

For the first time, the path doesn't bridge a distance but an emptiness. Pim isn't waiting with his bike in the front yard like he used to, when I'd come get him for school. I don't dare to just walk up to the back door, so I follow the stone path to the front door, which, until last summer, I'd always assumed was purely ornamental, a door that was never meant to be opened and had thus been installed without hinges. The front yard is overgrown with those purplish white flowers that smell like pee. I could already smell them three houses away. The paving stones from the street to the front door were laid so haphazardly that the path might as well have been created by nature itself.

Just as I ring the doorbell, Pim appears in the driveway. First his front wheel, then his head.

"The doorbell doesn't work," he shouts. "You should know that by now."

He stands up on his pedals and bikes slowly until I'm back on my bike. Before I can catch up with him, he puts all his weight into the pedals and shoots off ahead of me onto the street.

The distance is exactly one kilometer. We knew that because one of our primary school teachers, Miss Ria, had demonstrated it once in a geography lesson. She marched us all out to the playground with a meterstick, and, after a thousand spins of the stick, we ended up at the farm. This left a deep impression on me. After that, for every distance I travelled, I'd count how many meterstick spins would fit into it, and after every kilometer I thought, I could have been at the farm by now.

Bike rides are always faster with Pim. He stays right in front of me, and whenever I try to catch up, he pulls ahead again.

His thick blond curls flutter in the wind. Pim has the kind of hair that everyone wants. Whether that's because people always want someone else's hair or because it's actually handsome is hard to say.

Pim isn't carrying a backpack. Neither am I. He's the type of person who makes sure that other people bring whatever he needs. He was already like that in primary school, always asking me for sheets of graph paper and borrowing Laurens's markers. I watch his wiry ankles crank up and down on either side of his chain guard. Suddenly, I notice he's wearing his socks inside out; the print is an indiscernible tangle of threads. It's possible he's been wearing them for a few days now, that he's turned them inside out to avoid having to wash them.

The back of Pim's head doesn't betray his thoughts or feelings. He just keeps pedaling. Perhaps with a bit too much determination for someone who just lost his brother six months ago.

After a few minutes, I stop trying to keep up with him.

It would take a while to catch up anyway. Maybe it doesn't matter. We've still got the whole summer ahead of us. Off in the distance, I see Laurens, the savior and spoilsport. He's waiting in the butcher shop parking lot with his bike next to a sign that says, "Summer deal—all BBQ meat buy 2 get 1 free!"

Laurens is easy to spot from afar: broad shoulders, big nose, a prime filet. He moves clumsily. There's a certain sloppiness about him, like a kid stuck with a tedious chore who tries to do it as badly as possible in the hope that his mother will eventually just take over.

"Hey guys," he says. He's wearing socks with the days of the week embroidered on the cuffs. On the right foot it's only Monday, and on the left foot it's already Friday. He shifts his gears, searching for the slowest, heaviest gear possible.

Pim doesn't slow down, so Laurens pedals at top speed until he catches up to us. In the meantime, I've caught up to Pim as well, but when Laurens gets there our formation changes. We no longer fit on the narrow bike path with all the low-hanging branches. We're an odd number, so somebody's got to fall back. Pim doesn't care who he bikes with, he'd rather bike alone. We can see that—he was that way before too, which is why he'd always end up in the middle, as long as the road was wide enough. He accelerates once again so he can pass us. Laurens chases after him. I follow behind.

On the left, Pim pedals in the lowest gear; on the right, Laurens, in the highest. It's almost as if they're communicating, even without words.

Every time Laurens turns his head to look at Pim, I can see the cut under his nose where the bungee cord around the rear rack of his bike smacked him in the face the day I left him behind at school last week. It seems to be healing up nicely. The scab has come off on one side. It's almost perpendicular on his face, like a misplaced wing.

Pim slaloms out ahead of us across the playground; the loose paving stones clatter under his tires. He tries not to touch the lines on the hopscotch grids. I maneuver around the sewer that used to serve as a two-dimensional jail.

Pim manages to stop without hitting the brakes by running his front wheel into the red brick wall under the awning.

Without any kids, the school is nothing more than a building. One of the wings is home to two nuns, who, as the school's original founders, are allowed to keep living on the premises. Other than watering the purple flowers on the playground, they don't serve much purpose anymore.

Back when we went to school here, there was a third, over-zealous nun living on the property. She used to make sandwiches for the kids who forgot their lunch, so we would all forget our lunch on purpose just to keep her busy—even Laurens, who was extremely attached to the bag lunches his mother prepared for him. His mom always packed cookies in threes, probably thinking that Laurens would share them with me and Pim, but he never did.

Laurens and I do more or less the same tricks as Pim and then pull up on either side of him on our bikes, right in front of the big front window. Through the frosted glass we can make out our empty sixth-grade classroom.

The furniture has been sorted: desks pushed to the left, chairs stacked on the right. I recognize my old desk, with its battered top, a little lighter than the other ones, safely tucked away beside Miss Emma's dark, heavy teacher's desk, leg to leg.

The classroom looks just like it did on our last day of school. Someone had tried their best to transform it into a dance floor. It pains me to see it because I can't help but think of how Miss Emma presented the goodbye party to us—"a one-time privilege for three musketeers she was really going to miss"—and how I subsequently managed to ruin her life.

Pim quickly discovers that the gym door is unlocked, which isn't that unusual—in Bovenmeer burglars are scared off with hospitality. We walk right into the building, without sneaking through any windows, without scaling any walls, without really knowing what we're doing here.

Laurens skips sideways around the room, pulling his knees up one after the other in sharp movements, like we used to do in Mr. Joris's gym class. Mr. Joris was this demanding old man in a tracksuit who no one believed could actually do the exercises he assigned, so we never bothered to perform them to the expected level of perfection.

Pim breaks into a run and hurls himself into the thick mats propped up sideways against the wall. They fall to the floor with a loud smack, first the soft middle, then the edges with a few seconds' delay, like the corners of a mouth after flashing a fake smile.

We set up a game using the most dangerous equipment we can find, the stuff Mr. Joris never let us use. We run and jump on the springboard, over the leather pommel horse, onto one trampoline, onto another trampoline, finishing with a flip onto the soft, thick mat.

"Cool, an obstacle course," I say.

"No, this is way cooler than an obstacle course," Pim says.

All of a sudden, the bell rings. Long and shrill, scaring us to death. If this were a school day, this would be the start of a fifteen-minute recess. Today we could hang out in the halls forever; no one, not even a nun, would catch us.

Pim flops onto the mat and stays there. I launch a failed cart-wheel and land next to him. He plucks his sweaty T-shirt with his thumb and forefinger, releasing a breeze as the cotton falls to his chest. I love the sour smell of his sweat. This is what Jan's must have smelled like too.

I lie on my back, my T-shirt clinging to my body as well. I see Pim eyeing the bulges under my shirt, which doesn't really bother me, but then I remember how Dad described them this morning—as "titties" not "breasts"—and in Pim's eyes, I suddenly realize what he meant: I don't actually have breasts yet. These are just half-breasts, putting me somewhere between having and not having.

"What do you guys wanna do?" I ask. I glance at Laurens, but I'm not hoping for an answer from him.

"I gotta go home," Pim says. "I'm going to Lier."

"What are you going do in Lier?" Laurens asks.

"Visit my mom at my aunt's."

"How is your mom?" I ask.

"Bad."

Even Laurens shuts up after that.

Pim gets up without a word and heads outside to his bike. He speeds off across the playground. Laurens and I watch him until he reaches the old monastery and the back of his head shrinks to a dot and disappears.

"You can't tell by looking at him," Laurens says.

"No," I reply. "What did you expect to see?"

"Just . . . you know."

The set-up in the gym that had seemed so dangerous a half-hour ago now looks like a pile of junk.

For a split second, but just long enough, I'm able to get a good look at the cut on Laurens's face. From a certain angle, I can see what's under the scab. I take a quick, cautious look, like when you're somewhere you're not supposed to be.

The healed skin is pink and shiny.

We push the pommel horse against the wall and put all the other stuff back where it belongs.

"I'm gonna head home too," Laurens says.

I lean against a wooden bench propped up on the wall bars like a slide and watch him shuffle across the playground, throw his leg over his bike, and pedal away. I stay there until he too has shrunk to a dot—only because I'd feel bad if he somehow found out that I'd watched Pim and not him.

After Laurens is finally gone, I wander around the room. Everything has been returned to its place, as if this afternoon never happened. The sky above the playground drifts by angrily. The clock on the wall in the gym ticks tirelessly on. The bell rings again. I don't know whether it's announcing the beginning or the end of something.

Three Musketeers

IN THE SUMMER of 1993, right before Laurens, Pim and I finished pre-school and started kindergarten, a letter was sent around to all of the teachers at the primary school and our six parents: a meeting had been planned, and their presence was required.

In the meeting, Beatrice, the school principal, got right to the point: How was it possible that only three babies were born in 1988? Was it the cold winter, the hot summer, the black Monday the previous October that made couples take it easy in the bedroom for a while? Why were so few children born that year? Her school was the smallest in the region, with an average class size of ten (one of its greatest assets in her opinion), but—and perhaps she pushed her glasses up her nose to show there was no point fighting it—no one was going to lift a finger for so few children.

The only solution was "a side class": three extra desks in the back of the classroom. The teachers would simply adapt the day's lessons for the three additional students, making them easier or harder depending on the level of the rest of the class.

"Your father didn't put up much of a fight, and Laurens's and Pim's parents didn't have any better ideas," Mom told me six years later. I was eleven at the time. We were doing the dishes. The hot water on her hands always made her open up, but most of the time she just complained about all the things she'd missed out on in life, and all I could do was listen.

I could tell by the way she said "better ideas", proud and uncertain at the same time, that she'd been intimidated by the imposing presence of Laurens's mom and decided out of self-preservation not to get along with her.

Maybe it was something her own mother had whispered to her with her hands in the dishwater: the people you get along with are the same ones who will stab you in the back.

As for me, Pim, Laurens, we all thought the side class was a great idea. It was either that or be sent to another school and have to bike a lot farther every morning.

The lessons we got were easier than those designed for our age group. We'd hear the older kids whining about all their homework and tests, which made us feel like we'd been spared something.

Since the other kids started calling us "the three parasites", Pim came up with the name "the three musketeers" in second grade. We didn't know exactly what the name was supposed to mean, but the motto "all for one and one for all" that he chanted loudly as we walked onto the playground had a positive effect. We started using the name all the time—as we charged for a goal, when we got good grades, when we got bad grades, every time we popped a bottle of Kidibul sparkling grape juice—until we believed that there'd never be anything more important than our friendship. We thought the history books were based on us, not the other way around.

Together, we played soccer against the boys from the other classes, and even they didn't seem to mind as long as I stayed in the goal and didn't accidentally score for the wrong team: winning because your opponent scored an own goal was pretty much the same thing as losing, but not nearly as bad as losing to a girl.

It wasn't my dribbling that set me apart from the average girl, but my competitiveness and my clothes. From first to fifth grade, I wore dark blue jeans and either Jolan's old soccer jersey or a green Mickey Mouse sweater.

After tackling a boy who called me a cheater for being offside, I wasn't invited to Laurens's and Pim's birthday parties anymore, but I did get invited to the other boys'. I kept showing up at every party until they were surprised I didn't pee standing up with them too.

I wasn't so easily accepted among the girls. It was always up to me to let them know I wanted to be included. Then they'd form a wall and ask me for the password, which was constantly changing. I never guessed it right, so they'd make me answer a difficult question or a riddle, and even if I actually figured it out and was allowed to play flagpole or hairdresser with them for the last two minutes of recess, I still became indebted to them, and three recesses later they could still seize my wafer cookies.

With the younger girls, I just assumed they just didn't get me. But that didn't explain why the older girls wouldn't let me talk to them either.

"Being a Spice Girl" required tremendous attention to detail. They were always changing their mind about what they liked, and the differences between cool and uncool became increasingly subtle—one day your scrunchie was supposed to match your shoelaces, and the next day it wasn't; one day Jimmy was the cutest band member in Get Ready!, and the next day he wasn't; one day you had to have a Polly Pocket in your bookbag, and the next day you didn't. Compared to the boys, there were a lot more hoops to jump through to become popular.

At first, I thought my friendship with Laurens came with certain benefits. But when the girls started parading around the playground arm in arm, they only let me walk behind them, never beside them. I'd see their long ponytails bouncing from shoulder to shoulder, their clean fingernails, their slim thighs under their skirts, and I knew: these girls have spent their entire lives hanging out with other girls. They're finely sharpened knives. Not like me, I've got a dull tip.

10:00 a.m.

NINE YEARS AGO, when I moved to Brussels, every middle-aged Arabic man looked the same to me. Now, on the highway back to the town I grew up in, every white man behind the wheel looks like my father.

I didn't want to live in the capital per se. I just wanted to live in a city I didn't know. Because whenever I was in a familiar place, I had the same problem: I couldn't stop looking down at myself from above. Shopping centers, department stores, libraries—they were all the types of places where, from a bird's eye perspective, I could see the top of my chestnut-brown head brushing past thousands of people without touching them.

I ultimately decided to study architecture so I could use what I had long considered a weakness as a strength. I moved into an all-girls student house with a shared kitchen. The bathroom was shared too. For the first few months, things went pretty well. On Tuesdays, I made pasta for everybody. We didn't tell each other where we were from, what high school we went to, what our parents did for a living. There was no point. All that mattered was who we were in that moment, together, sitting around a table with our mouths full of pesto.

I never skipped a class, and at the end of the day, I went straight back to my room. When my housemates went home to their parents for the weekend with all their dirty laundry, I stayed behind to study and cleaned the common areas. I got the best grades and was under the impression that, with each design and scale model, I was making something possible.

But eventually things changed. Fewer people came to the Tuesday-night dinners. No one bothered to say they weren't coming, they just stopped showing up. People preferred to hang out with friends who were studying the same thing they were—medicine, law, communication. They went out to bars, to the Fuse. I realized that the reason why we didn't ask about each other's backgrounds was not because we wanted to give each other the chance for a fresh start, but because it wasn't worth the effort. Our friendship was only ever meant to bridge a gap.

I kept on cutting cardboard, working out plans, studying materials, but I couldn't see what I was making possible anymore. All I could see was what I was making impossible by trying to give it physical form. By the end of the school year, the only thing I still enjoyed was searching the internet for tiny figurines to use in my models. I looked for silhouettes in various positions: walking, sitting, swimming, jumping, chatting, bending, cycling. Trees, airplanes, bicycles, staircases, chairs, umbrellas, Christmas trees. They weren't cheap; I ended up spending a significant portion of my student loan on them. Some of the figurines reminded me of Tessie or Jolan. I didn't use those ones in my models; I set them on my nightstand instead.

When my models were displayed in the auditorium with all the other ones, they were easy to spot because of the copious amounts of tiny people.

It wasn't until my second year, when I overheard a teacher make a comment about it to another teacher, that I saw what they meant, why I would never be invited to the Fuse.

It took a few more weeks before I stopped cleaning the common areas, and another three months before I finally moved out of the house.

It wasn't as cold in Brussels as it is here. There, the raindrops were feathery and delicate, the kind of rain that stops a few centimeters above the ground and forms a thick, low-hanging mist. Here, there's no mist to cover the wide-open landscape, and it's almost below freezing.

I don't have any anecdotes about Jan to share, and I didn't send Pim a photo or post something on the Facebook page, even though I probably knew Jan better than all the others put together. They'll all come with the same clichés: that he was born just a little too late to be a Christmas baby, that he was left-handed, that he was extremely shy and good with the cows.

Back when Jan was still alive, he and Pim would get a disposable camera from their mom every summer. At the start of the fall, they'd have the film developed and printed in doubles. Then came our ritual, the claiming of memories: Pim would spread all the photos out on the kitchen table, we'd pour the River Cola and divvy up the sour belts. Pim's mom paid for everything, so her son always got a copy of every picture; Laurens and I had to share the doubles. We took turns taking our pick. There were never very many photos of all three of us—the few there were must've been taken by somebody in town or Pim's parents.

In the early days, we used to fight over the group photos, but as we got older, we only wanted the ones that we looked good in ourselves. Once, when I claimed one of the good photos of Laurens, I could tell by the way he shrugged his shoulders that he didn't appreciate it.

There were always a few photos that me and Laurens weren't in, taken on days when we weren't out at the farm—Jan with a brush or a pitchfork in his hand or a bad shot of Pim and Jan together holding the camera out in front of them, or Pim, Jan and their mom on a rare trip to the zoo.

Me and Laurens never claimed these photos. Laurens didn't want them, and I was afraid I didn't have a right to them.

After Jan's accident, Pim's mom didn't buy the disposable cameras anymore. I could see it in her eyes—she expected Jan to come back at any moment, to walk across the farm and start sweeping the stalls. That's why no memories could be captured until he returned. Otherwise the pictures, the representation of the brief period when he was dead, wouldn't make sense.

At the end of the first summer I spent alone in the empty

student house in Brussels, I was mostly sorry that there weren't any photos to spread out on the table anymore. I understood that, once you're out on your own, there are fewer photo-worthy moments.

July 8, 2002

"ARE YOU GOING to ask if we can set up the pool?" Tessie asks. "There's a bigger chance they'll say yes if you want it too." She's got a scar around her lips. Actually, her whole mouth is a scar. On a warm summer evening, when she was three years old, she tried to catch up to me and Jolan on her tricycle. She went tearing down the Bulksteeg behind us in her bathing suit. A pebble got caught in her front wheel and jammed it. She flew over the handlebars and landed on her face. Her lips served as brake pads. They were left hanging on her face by a thread.

As always after these kinds of things happened—as if there were ever a better time for such an accident—Mom and Dad claimed that they were just about ready to go out that night. They were even wearing new clothes. Anne, the babysitter, wasn't there yet. The neighbor, Anne's dad, brought Tessie home with a necktie tied around her chin to hold everything in place.

Tessie's mouth was sewn back on in the ER. The plastic surgeon was trying to make it to a party herself—or that's what Mom said—she was in a hurry and ended up sewing the lower lip on crooked. The kind of crooked you'd only notice if you knew to look for it.

Tessie sits up straight, shakes the snow globe on her nightstand, lies back down and waits for all the glitter to fall to the bottom.

The snow globe is her snooze button. Every morning she wakes up with a fixed number of blizzards.

I've been waiting in the kitchen for an hour, in the chair Mom usually sits in. Out of the corner of my right eye, in the back of the yard, I see Jolan starting to dig up the old turtle. It's overcast but still oppressively hot. I can tell by the pearls of sweat on his back. He's wearing the black jeans that he keeps in a separate pile in the closet for the weekends, just like Dad does. The big neon work gloves make him look particularly pale.

Dad buried the turtle out there three years ago in the winter under the cherry tree, between the bike shed and the chicken coop. He claimed that it would decompose into a beautiful skeleton, a real "collector's item" as he called it. He marked the spot with one of the hollow bricks from the bathroom wall. "Now you have to wait six years to dig it up again. The more often you ask about it, the longer it'll take."

For a while, we waited in silence for the worms and insects to finish their God-given task. Eventually the grass grew back over the hole. Every time we passed the cherry tree, we'd pause to inspect the brick and imagine the turtle carcass being gnawed away bit by bit.

But the longer we waited, the more patient we became. It's been months since I've thought once about how the turtle was faring underground. Maybe Jolan hadn't thought about it much either, until this morning, that is. I had no idea where all this brute force was coming from. He already had Dad's gloves on and a shovel in hand when I woke up that morning.

"You coming, Eva?" he asked excitedly. "It's the perfect day for an excavation!"

He ran into the kitchen with the shovel in hand and started fixing himself a piece of toast. He couldn't spread the butter with the work gloves on, so he asked Tessie for help. He marched back out to the garden, leaving a trail of sand through the house. Tessie hurried off behind him with the toast. She desperately wanted to help in my place, but Jolan shooed her away.

"Excavation isn't for girls!" he shouted.

"Eva's a girl, isn't she?"

Jolan stuffed the entire piece of bread into his mouth to avoid answering the question. So Tessie started digging random holes on the other side of the yard. That way, at the very least, Jolan would have to share his tools with her.

I watch them closely. They both dig at top speed. Sand starts piling up next to Jolan's hole. The handle of Tessie's shovel is thicker than the cross-section of her wrists. She keeps starting new holes in different spots, leaving little mole hills all over the garden.

I could stand up, walk out into the yard and help Jolan with the excavation or help Tessie catch up to him. There's no one stopping me. But it would be a waste to dig up a carcass without Laurens and Pim, the waste of an adventure.

I get up, fill a glass of water and sit back down.

This is the most profound boredom I've ever felt. I no longer exist as one body, but as an entire group of people who've all run off in different directions. And the table doesn't help. It's not just for sitting, like this chair, it calls for some higher purpose.

I could scoot back a little, into the middle of the room, so it won't feel like I have to make a decision anymore. But sitting in a chair in the middle of the room is something you only do on your birthday so people can sing to you. If only it was somebody's birthday. I lay my arms out in front of me on the table.

There are sighs coming from the living room. I don't need to go in there to see what's going on. Mom is sitting in the armchair with the pear-shaped kitchen timer we got her for her fortieth birthday on the coffee table.

When she unwrapped it, she held it up and said resentfully, "These types of presents are the reason they invented Mother's Day."

The timer is used solely by her. She sets it to the maximum of fifty-five minutes and leans back in the armchair. If she has to get up for some reason in the meantime, to go to the bathroom or something, she turns it back to the max. The only minutes that count are those filled with uninterrupted sleep.

In front of me on the patio is our husky, Nanook. She's sleeping too. Mom tied the end of her leash to one of the table legs. Now, she's so tangled up she can barely move. She's just lying there with her head on her front paws. Every once in a while, she lets out a sigh that sends the sand around her nose into the air.

Ever since Jolan came home from school with a terrarium full of walking sticks, we've had pets that are allowed to sleep in the house at night too. We put the terrarium in the corner of the living room. At first the insects didn't do very well, but once we took the electric bug zapper out of the room, they perked up a bit.

Somehow, those walking sticks reminded me of Mom.

No one cried when they finally croaked. The confirmation of death was spread out over the course of a few days. It was more of a process of elimination, really. We ruled out every possible sign of life until only the opposite remained. When walking sticks die, they dry out. Their bodies transform into these yellow-brown rolled-up leaves. As long as fall is around the corner, no one makes a big deal out of it.

I head out into the garden. With every step, it's as if two knitting needles are digging into my lower back. I sit down on an overturned bucket near Jolan's archaeological site, far enough away so that I can't see down into the hole. Judging by the giant pile of dug-up sand, it's pretty deep by now.

"Eva, when I reach the skeleton, I'm going to brush away the sand with a paintbrush. Otherwise it might break."

Tessie sits down beside me. The sky overhead is getting darker. The landscape is parched and dry. I watch how the storm rolls in. It starts with rumbling in the distance, until the clouds merge like a bruise forming in reverse: first light gray, then dark blue with patches of purple. We're winding up for the blow; there's a knockout coming.

There's a sticky feeling in my underwear. I need to go to the bathroom. Maybe that's it. I stand up to go inside.

"Can you bring me a plastic bag?" Jolan asks without looking up. "And a raincoat, one that can get dirty." He tosses the shovel aside and takes up the paintbrush.

Although there are no windows in the bathroom, I can still tell when it starts to rain. Even windowless rooms get darker, the mood changes. The thunder rolls in from far away and ripples through the entire house, into the tiniest corners.

I look down at the blood. It's everywhere, in my underwear, between my open thighs, on the toilet seat.

My vagina is no longer a hole that leads to nowhere, like a stitched-shut pocket that turns out to be fake after purchase. I have a uterus. I'm no different from the other girls. Elisa was right.

The toilet seat is warm from my thighs. I only notice because it feels cold when I shift my weight. As soon as I become aware of my own body heat, the nausea hits.

Someone's coming down the hall. The door doesn't have a lock, but there is a ventilation system that starts humming when the light's turned on, so everyone knows it's occupied.

"Who's on the toilet?" Mom asks.

"Me," I say.

"Who's me?"

"Eva."

"You've got a phone call."

"I'm coming."

"She's coming."

I can hear Pim's voice blaring on the other end of the phone.

"Pim wants to know if you want to go swimming," Mom says.

"Now?"

"Now?" Mom repeats the question into the phone.

I didn't know Pim had a pool. It's crazy to think that someone who just lost his brother suddenly has a swimming pool. An unfair trade that no one should have ever signed off on.

"Not now, tomorrow."

Mom turns back down the hall and shuts the living-room door behind her. I hear her fiddling with the handle, mumbling to herself. I hope she's at least remembered to hang up the phone.

Pim's probably already called Laurens anyway. Maybe they're swimming right now, without me. Nothing is more fun than splashing around in the middle of a thunderstorm as the vibrations ripple through the water. I should have taken his call, then maybe I could have joined them.

But if I want to go swimming, I have to figure out how to insert a tampon.

After a half-hour of poking and wriggling, I go back into the kitchen. The tampon hurts, making it hard to walk normally. I can feel how deep it is; I could point to the exact spot on my lower abdomen.

On the table is a shoebox without a lid. Lying at the bottom is a stinky, muddy turtle carcass, the flesh greedily eaten away. It reminds me of beef stew. The shell rests crooked on what's left of the legs. If this were a meal, Mom would put it back on our plate and say, "There's still some work to be done here." Next to the box is a bottle of glass cleaner and a pile of cotton balls. Lying on a piece of newspaper are two clean feet. It's easy to tell which one was cleaned by Tessie and which one was cleaned by Jolan.

The garden is empty. The piles of sand have shrunk and turned into mud. The day's not over yet. Only now does it occur to me that Tessie never got her swimming pool.

I have no idea where everyone's gone. I open all the windows in the house, but the smell won't budge.

Windows 95

JUST LIKE EVERYBODY else in town, we could split our childhood into two periods: before Windows 95 and after Windows 95. In all the other families, that split came in '95 and was marked by the sudden appearance of English words.

Games. Points. Levels. Winner.

Everybody did their best. But Jolan and I couldn't help but notice that the round English sounds didn't fit very well in their sharp, dialect-formed mouths. We were practically the only kids in Bovenmeer who didn't have a TV or Windows and still called "cornflakes" "breakfast grains" or Quakies, because that's what was written on the Aldi box.

In our family, the split came a few years later and had nothing to do with the development of Windows but with the start of Tessie's strange behavior, which was, in its own way, related to the introduction of an operating system.

In '97, a few days after Laurens beat Tomb Raider for the first time and called me on the landline to brag about his victory during a time of day that was reserved for calls from grandparents, Dad decided it was high time we entered the digital age too.

Tessie was already asleep, but I wasn't. I did what I had to do—be a lighthouse, but without light. I listened to every sound from my lofted bed but didn't move out of fear that I played some kind of crucial role and all hell would break loose if I did, that Dad would never come home again.

After a few minutes, there were noises in the hall. Someone was coming up the stairs with shoes on. It was a walk I didn't recognize, quick and determined. The footsteps reached the creaky top step.

Both the stairs and landing were covered with cardboard, perfectly measured to fit into all the nooks and crannies and secured with masking tape. Underneath the cardboard was a light parquet floor and an oak staircase. The floor had been covered for so long that it might as well not have been there at all. Every morning we walked over the wood grain that Mom and Dad were so desperately trying to preserve. It should have been comforting—the thought of something not getting destroyed—but the longer I thought about it, the more ridiculous it seemed. The parquet floor was being preserved for some other, more important life.

The light switched on in the hallway. I rolled over so my back was facing the bedroom door. The door opened and the bright light from the hall landed right on my pillow, slicing my head in half at the temples. I let my mouth hang open a little, closed my eyes and didn't react to the sound of my name. Still, I was ousted out of bed. That's what lofted beds were for—to put children at eye level so it's easier to wake them up in the middle of the night.

I followed Dad downstairs, watched his head drop fifteen centimeters with every step.

I couldn't help but think back on the night Dad dragged me out of bed because Mom had announced that she was going to "end it once and for all". End what exactly—her life, their relationship or the cherries waiting to be made into jam—Dad probably didn't know. He made us race around the house in the middle of the night and confiscate anything that might make it easier for her.

We had to take the certain for the uncertain.

"Trust me, if you really want to end it and have enough imagination, even the garlic press is dangerous," he said.

We collected everything in a big cardboard box: compasses, sharp cutlery, toothpicks, fountain pens. The next morning, Mom woke up to a plundered house. The medicine cabinet was empty except for a box of waterproof Band-Aids and a small, blunt pair of scissors. For three days, we ate with a spoon and fork. We weren't allowed to cut paper anymore.

In hindsight, I think I was more worried that if she didn't have a death wish already, our ransacking of the cutlery drawer might have been enough to give her one.

We reached the bottom step. Dad walked down the hall ahead of me into the living room and shut the door behind us. Even after I saw the big empty cardboard box with handles cut into the sides sitting in the middle of the living room, I still thought he was planning to hurt me.

"Look."

He turned the light off in the room. In the opposite corner, on a little table, was our brand-new, second-hand computer. The screen emitted a cold, white glow.

"Evie, the time has come. We now own a Windows 95," said Dad solemnly. Together, we stared at the feeble light in the room for at least a whole minute. Then he switched on a lamp, went into the kitchen, and came back with four open beers in his drink carrier. "I scored it at work."

He massaged the neck of the first bottle, as if he wanted to put it at ease before gulping it down.

"Windows 95. What an operating system."

Even with the white screen, the giant humming tower, the keyboard, mouse and mouse pad right there in front of me, I didn't really get it. I just stood there shivering.

"Go put your bathrobe on," Dad said.

After that, he let me stand next to his chair and watch him play five rounds of solitaire in a row.

For about three years, the second-hand computer remained in the same spot, between the wall and the marble fireplace, beside one of the fancy dining-room chairs that had been in Mom's eyes downgraded and in Dad's eyes upgraded into a computer chair.

It was the most high-traffic area in the house, which allowed us to keep a close eye on each other's computer use. Not only was it on the way from the back door to the hallway and from the kitchen to the bathroom, it was also exactly halfway between the basement door and the kitchen, two rooms in the house where Mom had a lot of power. Her many trips back and forth led to a tacit disagreement: she thought we were spending too much time on the computer. We started noticing how often she went down to the basement with the same can of tomatoes, even when we weren't having spaghetti or any other kind of red sauce for dinner.

After the arrival of Windows 95, it took us a little while to work out who could use the computer and when. Jolan decided that we could each play for an hour every night and that we'd take turns from oldest to youngest. As long as the person playing didn't mind, we could watch over their shoulder.

Jolan and I discovered the "Fun stuff" folder on the desktop, which contained two video clips: Weezer's "Buddy Holly" and "Good Times" by Edie Brickell. We played the clips over and over again—never had we been so close to having MTV. "Good Times" became the soundtrack of '97.

After we got bored with the songs, everyone chose their own specialty. I started making drawings in Paint, which never worked—the stiff mouse was too hard to maneuver; Jolan devoted himself to Hover!, ramming flags into pixelated backgrounds while the compass spun around arbitrarily on the dashboard; Tessie, who was only six at the time, liked staring at screen savers. Her favorite was Starfield. She'd ask me to set it to the maximum number of stars at the minimum speed, and she'd just sit there traveling through time for hours. The wicker seat on the fancy chair left a red grid on the back of her legs, making it easy to see when she'd been on a particularly long space voyage.

It wasn't until a few months later, when Tessie was seven and had gotten good at Minesweeper, that I started noticing her odd behavior. Every time a bomb exploded under her mouse, she had to win two games.

Sometimes, when I came to take her place at the computer, I'd find her in tears because she hadn't managed to sweep away all the mines. As long as the number of explosions was higher than the number of dismantled mines, it was all for nothing. Oftentimes, I'd end up giving up my computer hour to sit beside her and listen to her nervous clicking. Maybe that's when it happened—as I sat eye to eye with the controlled rage inside of her—maybe that's when my love for her started to grow.

10:15 a.m.

THE EXACT DECOMPOSITION time of a pair of panties was nowhere to be found. Though I did learn how long it takes for other types of litter to decompose—cardboard, cigarette butts, plastic bottles, banana peels. I estimated the time it would take for a piece of cotton fabric with a light blue embroidered edge, size Small, to disappear into nature to be somewhere between a newspaper and a banana peel—at least one month and no more than three years, depending on the weather conditions.

Even today, the roadside from Brussels to Bovenmeer is lined with trash—the kinds of things that make you wonder how anyone could have lost them without noticing. A shoe, a bra, a refrigerator door, half a ping-pong table.

Chances are the loss eventually was noticed, but the owners never came back to claim their possessions—out of shame, guilt, or a lack thereof.

I hadn't planned on leaving so early this morning. I woke up before sunrise, got dressed and sat at the edge of my bed waiting for my downstairs neighbor to wake up, for the sputtering sound of his coffee machine, so I could go down and pick up my block of ice. Rather than waiting to start the process of waiting, it seemed more bearable to at least be in the car until three o'clock, to keep moving.

Bovenmeer still hasn't made it onto the signs yet. The town is locked in between the Albert Canal and the highway, with only two roads in and out. I'm not going to take the shortest route, though that would make the most sense. I don't want to drive past the pollard willows.

In the summer of 2002, I lost my panties at the foot of those trees. They landed alongside the bike path, the only route to the high school. The loss didn't go unnoticed, but I wasn't completely aware of it at the time either.

When school started again, I had to bike along the pollard willows every day, and each time my eyes would fall on the triangular piece of fabric with the little bow on the front, waiting defenselessly on the side of the road. Week after week, the passing trucks blew life into it. The rain pushed it a few meters downhill. It became dirty and colorless, like a flattened animal.

I could've jumped off my bike and picked it up. But as long as I could deny that the panties were mine, I could go on pretending the summer never happened.

July 11, 2002

I'VE NEVER MANAGED to show up late for anything. Pim can do it no problem, and he always has a good excuse: the barn had to be swept, the extra milk had to be poured into plastic bottles, one of the cows gave birth to a backwards calf. Now he's got Jan. After a loss, people don't ask too many questions.

While biking, sometimes I pass through alternating streams of warm and cold air. If I were in a swimming pool instead of biking between houses, I would think somebody just peed in the pool.

I've got my bathing suit on under my clothes. It's an old one. I've had it since primary school, and now it's too tight. The straps cut into the skin on my shoulders, which puts me under a tension so strong that, if I let it, it could fold me in half.

The more I wriggle back and forth on the saddle, the more crooked the tampon becomes. I put in a new one right before I left the house. We were out of the ones with the cardboard applicators, so I had to use one of my mother's thick, bullet-shaped ones. My finger turned out to be much shorter than the applicators I'd just gotten used to, so I didn't manage to get it in very deep. I pulled back the little string and tucked it between my butt cheeks like a bookmark.

The church bell gongs. Four o'clock is a strange time to pass through town on your way to something. Most people are headed home around this time of day, which makes the thought of starting something seem pointless. This is why I left a half-hour earlier than Pim asked.

I cycle past the houses in the center of town, past the cemetery wall, the parish hall.

The carnival has arrived. Six massive trucks rolled into town at the beginning of the week and are now parked on the street corners, waiting to be opened and unpacked. Since we don't have a town square, the stands are set up around the church in the streets, which have been closed off to all but local traffic—though there's hardly any traffic here that's not local.

I recognize all six of them: the shooting range, the bumper cars, the flying planes, the duck-pond game, the raffle stand and the fries stand. Bovenmeer is the only town that considers French fries an attraction.

Now it's just a matter of waiting until tomorrow. The balloons will be inflated, the guns loaded, the ducks launched, the prizes displayed, the potatoes pre-fried. At six o'clock sharp, the headlights of the bumper cars will switch on, chasing away the daylight. Friday night will kick off with "No Limit" blasting from the loudspeakers until each stand eventually switches over to its own CD, giving way to a cacophony of sirens and pumped-up jams.

I bike up Pim's driveway to the house. The geese follow me in their pen until the wire fence stops them from going any further. I see Laurens's blue bicycle parked in front of the milk house. He's early today too.

It's the first time since Jan's funeral that I've been invited to hang out at the farm. These last few months, I've only looked at it from afar.

Pim's dad appears at the milk-house door to see what the geese are honking about. Either his overalls are too big or his body is too thin. His pants hang down over the heels of his wooden clogs and are frayed at the edges. Without a word, he points to the hayloft and ducks back inside.

Pim's dad was never much of a talker. Sometimes I wondered whether introverts became farmers or farmers became introverts. If I knew the answer, I might be able to guess what Pim would become.

The hayloft is in the barn, next to a big silo full of dry feed and a manure spreader parked on the left side of the property. On my way there, I immediately spot the new swimming pool. It's under a homemade roof with a clear tarp over it. The pool is five meters in diameter and has a bright blue serrated edge and a white collapsible ladder hanging over the side. There's an inflatable dolphin floating around in the water. Sticking out of the black roof of the barn are several pipes connected to the pool's filtration system, pumping heated water into the pool. Pim learns how to make these kinds of things at school.

There used to be nothing out here. It was just a barn surrounded by pristine concrete, room for the tractors to maneuver. The pool is an ugly scar.

The heavy barn doors are open just enough that I can sneak in without having to slide them open any further. In the back is the blue Honda; it's missing the rear wheel and the engine is exposed.

I climb up the narrow, free-standing ladder. Once I reach the top, I see the musty curtains, the entrance to the fort we built up here two years ago. Before we started stacking the hay bales, we laid out the whole floorplan. It would be in the shape of a snail, with a secret hideout in the middle. We built three entrances on the outside, two of which were dead ends, booby-trapped with sticky fly catchers to stop intruders. It took us several long summer days to build it. When it was all done, we spent one night up here. The fact that Pim hasn't dismantled it is a good sign.

Coming from inside the straw is the sound of hushed voices. I can't quite make out what they're saying. I crawl under the curtain. The tunnel is darker, mustier and narrower than I expected, or maybe I've just gotten wider. I can just barely crawl through it on my hands and knees. The closer I get to the center, where the voices are coming from, the harder it is to breathe. Right before the end of the tunnel, just outside the entrance to the hideout, is a gap between two hay bales with a ray of light shining through it. Suddenly, I can hear Laurens's voice loud and clear.

"Rita is the one with the okay body. But her face is super-ugly. And with Kim, it's the other way around. She's got an okay face, but between you and me, she's flat as a pancake." Most likely Pim had asked him to hypothetically choose between two girls.

"Did you know that a girl's clam tastes like salt?" Pim asks.

"How do you know that?"

"Like a mouthful of seawater. Sometimes the North Sea, sometimes the Atlantic."

Neither Pim nor Laurens has ever swum in the Atlantic Ocean. I know that for a fact. None of us have ever been farther than the Netherlands or France. It was something we used to be proud of—since we'd never been anywhere, we were allowed to use the school computers to search for images.

In fifth grade, we had a pop quiz in geography. I couldn't identify Belgium on a map of Europe and got a zero. I was the only one in the class who didn't have a TV at home. The teacher decided to give me a second chance. She gave me two weeks to learn all the European countries and capitals by heart. Since I assumed that Europe was everything except America, I studied all of Africa and Asia too. The fact that I had once been so far behind means that there are certain things I know now, like that the North Sea borders the Atlantic Ocean and that it's all the same water.

I crawl a bit closer so I can peer through the gap. Laurens and Pim are sitting side by side with their backs against the wall, across from me.

So this is what Laurens meant by "guy stuff".

I try to be as quiet as possible, breathing softly so as not to disrupt the spectacle.

Pim looks around for a moment, then pulls a plastic bag out of a crack in the wall behind them. It's full of magazines. One by one, he tosses them onto Laurens's lap.

"Where did you get these?" Laurens slides his eyes down the covers and starts greedily flipping through the pages like he used to do with the toy catalogues that showed up in the mail around Christmastime.

"Does it matter? Did you bring what I told you to?"

There's a rustling sound as Laurens digs around in the backpack beside him in the straw. He pulls out a towel and a pair of swimming trunks, a bar of chocolate and finally a small package from the butcher shop. He unwraps it carefully. Inside is a slice of dark pink pâté.

"Perfect." Pim takes it and breaks off a piece.

"Close your eyes and open up," he says. "Eva'll be here at four o'clock. We have to hurry."

"Did you really have to call her?" Laurens sighs with his eyes closed.

A knot forms in my stomach. Pim doesn't respond.

"Open your mouth, man."

Laurens squeezes his eyes tighter and constricts his neck, waiting for a blow. Then he opens wide. Pim places a small lump of pâté on his tongue. Then he takes the magazine on the top of the pile into his lap, flips through it until he finds the right picture, folds it in half and holds it up in front of Laurens's face.

"What're you doing?" Laurens mumbles with his mouth half open.

Pim presses the magazine even closer to Laurens's lips, smothering the sound. I can't see his face anymore.

"Let the pâté melt in your mouth, then open your eyes and move your tongue."

Laurens does as he's told—judging by the way he's sitting, he's slightly uncomfortable. He makes quiet, smacking sounds. His face is still hidden behind the magazine. The photo on the back side shows the top half of what Laurens is licking: a black woman on an orange couch.

Pim starts to laugh.

The page becomes wet and limp from all the saliva. Pim lowers it and selects a new page. Laurens pulls his tongue back in his mouth.

"Want more?"

Laurens shrugs.

"You hold it, then." Pim drops a lump of pâté into his own mouth and chooses a page from another magazine. "So, now you know. That's exactly how it tastes, except without the peppercorns."

"How do you know all this?" Laurens asks.

Pim can't quite answer the question. Probably not from his own experience.

There's a long silence, filled with a lot of slurping and smacking. They've still got more than half the pâté to go, and I don't feel like watching much more. I crawl the last few meters around the corner into the hideout. I greet the boys with the enthusiasm of someone who has just arrived.

Laurens jumps. He swallows the big chunk of pâté he's just laid on his tongue in one gulp. He closes the magazine on his lap. Pim leaves his lying open.

"You're early," he says.

"Do you guys have your bathing suits on already?"

I glance at the slice of pâté. What would be less suspicious: saying something about it or ignoring it completely? I'm not sure whether the fact that they don't feel embarrassed about it in front of me is a good sign or a bad sign. But if they really aren't embarrassed, why hadn't they invited me to hang out with them? I take the remaining pâté and stick it in my mouth. It tastes grainier than usual. I swallow it as fast as I can.

I pick up one of the magazines and flip through it. I stare at each photo just long enough—but not too long—though to be honest I've never seen anything like it up close. I get to the wet, saliva-covered page with the orange couch.

"They don't call it a clam for nothing," I say. "You really shouldn't look inside though. It won't taste so good anymore."

Laurens is dying to rip the magazine out of my hands, but I take my time folding back the dog-eared page. Then I toss it back on the pile.

"I'm going swimming," I announce. I crawl out of the fort and back down the ladder.

I wait by the barn doors, heart pounding, listening for them to come down after me.

I float around in the swimming pool. It's awfully quiet around here for a dairy farm.

In the farthest stall to the right, Jan would often take a break from shoveling cow feed, one hand on the end of the shovel, the other picking at pimples on his face. I could always feel him watching me, which I liked and didn't like at the same time, the way I feel when somebody points a camera at me. I never know what about me is worth taking a picture of, or if I should pose differently.

One time he said to me, "Who'd have thought you'd turn out so pretty."

I didn't know how to respond. Should I take a compliment from an ugly boy in overalls as an insult? What did he know about pretty?

If only I'd flashed him a smile and asked about his favorite cow.

Somebody taps me on the arm. I jump. For a second I think it's Jan, but it's just the nose of the inflatable dolphin floating around in the pool.

After a while, enough time to stash all the evidence in the hayloft, the boys come down the ladder. They're laughing. They've got their swimming trunks on their heads. They each duck behind a different tractor to change clothes.

Maybe things aren't so bad between us after all.

"I invented a new game," shouts Pim. "It's called Rodeo Dolphin." He climbs up the ladder on the side of the pool and sticks his toes into the water. Since Laurens considers himself too old for rules, we just start playing. We take turns trying to mount the dolphin floating in the pool. It's not so easy. The animal tips back and forth as we try to clamber on top of it, creating wild waves. Liters of water splash over the edge of the pool. I'm the last one to give it a go. When I push up off the bottom, the tip of my tampon slides out, and it immediately fills up with water. Even still, I manage to tame the dolphin—probably not because I'm any good at it, but because Laurens and Pim are already bored with the game.

"Time to go home." Laurens's family eats dinner earlier than mine and Pim's. It's always been that way. The kids in primary school were always divided into two categories. The ones who could only play from two to five, and the ones who could stay out until six.

Pim and I always had to be home by six, Laurens by five-thirty. That's when his mom was done with work. Laurens would pick out something from the display case, and she'd cook it for dinner.

The rule was: six o'clock kids play with other six o'clock kids, that way no time was wasted. But Pim and I didn't abandon Laurens. Most of the time we followed him home so we could spend the last half-hour together. If we were lucky, his mom would toss a steak in the pan for us too.

Today, Pim has no intention of spending the last half-hour with Laurens, and Laurens doesn't ask him to. I dry off and pull my clothes on over my bathing suit. Pim stays in the water. His chest hairs have lost their curl. They're straight on his chest, as if they've been combed down with gel.

Laurens and I bike home side by side. You can see the outline of my wet bathing suit on my clothes.

Little drops run down my bike seat and thighs. I hope it's water, not blood. It must be, otherwise Laurens would have given me a weird look.

"Do you remember when we used to go swimming at the Pit with Jan?" he asks.

I'm glad he's bringing up Jan. It's strange that Pim didn't say a single word about his brother all day.

Of course I remember. When they built the E313 twenty years ago, they dug a deep pit, roughly two hundred meters in diameter, on the edge of town so they could raise the highway. Over time, it filled up with rainwater and the trees and ferns grew around it. It was the perfect place to cool off on a hot day.

Pim's mom wouldn't let Pim go swimming there by himself until he'd earned his fifteen-hundred-meter swim certificate, so she sent Jan with us.

In third grade, after all three of us had passed the two-hundred-meter test, Laurens and Pim insisted we swim across the Pit. I reminded them of what Pim's mom said: "There might be whirlpools that will suck you down."

But the boys were undeterred. Jan dove in after them, and I

couldn't stand to be left behind. The first hundred meters were no problem—I even pulled ahead a few times.

"Now we're officially in the deepest part," Laurens said when we reached the halfway point.

"If you built a four-story building on the bottom here, the roof would still be under water. No one has ever touched the bottom before."

At that, Jan took two deep breaths and disappeared under the water. I held my breath too.

We waited, treading water. I counted the seconds, the number of strokes he had to make: the height of an attic, a bedroom, a living room, a basement.

The surface of the water was completely still, except for the pond skaters and the ripples we created. Pim's eyes darted skittishly back and forth. In the distance, we saw something move.

"A flesh-eating turtle," Pim said.

Laurens swam between us.

My legs started to feel heavy. Both banks were equally far away. At this point, giving up would be as hard as persevering. Suddenly two hands emerged from the water. Then, Jan's curls, his forehead. He shot out of the water with a huge splash, clutching a fistful of sand from the bottom. His heart pounding in his fingertips.

I was so relieved that my muscles stopped aching for a moment.

"Ready for the second half?" Jan asked. The question was primarily addressed to me. I didn't react. I had to save my strength. Jan swam ahead of us, trying to keep the handful of sand above the water. Pretty soon, the boys were way ahead of us. The faster I tried to swim, the farther away the shore seemed. Laurens and Pim were ten meters ahead of me, and Jan was between us. I focused on my breaststroke, on opening and closing my fingers at the right moment. The others were swimming farther and farther away. I couldn't tell whether the water was cold or warm anymore. It started to feel less and less necessary to keep going.

When I was about fifty meters from the first branches hanging over the water, I lost sight of everything around me. I heard murmuring and splashing and thought about all the things at home I'd leave behind. The sandwich box that had been sitting in my backpack all summer. My seat at the kitchen table. My underwear in the laundry basket. Which of the three boys would remember to pick up my towel and clothes on the other side and take them home tonight? Water splashes into my mouth, I start choking. My ears fill with water.

Suddenly, something pulls me down. For a second, the force works against me, but then it propels me forward a few meters. At first, I thought I was caught in a whirlpool or had been bitten by a flesh-eating turtle. Where was Jan? I sputtered and flailed until two big hands grabbed me by the ankles and a wave of calm came over me.

Jan was swimming behind me, pushing me along. His skin was warmer than the water. I didn't resist.

Laurens and Pim were way ahead of us, going for the final sprint. When they reached the shore, Jan let go of me and swam ahead. But Laurens and Pim didn't look back. I ended in last place but hadn't lost anything.

Clam

CONTRARY TO EVERYONE'S expectations, the side class worked out pretty well for four years. Teachers found ways to teach two grade levels at the same time. Usually they'd go over the material and put the rest of the class to work and then come over to me, Laurens and Pim to explain what we needed to know and what we had to do extra, which was usually some kind of additional reading sheet with adapted assignments and questions.

We spent a lot of time waiting around for instructions, but we never complained because it gave us time to chat. It was me who turned it into a kind of motto: "down time at school is more time together". But this one never caught on like "one for all".

It was on a Friday afternoon in fourth grade that the side class became a problem for the first time. On our way back from the playground, we sauntered back into class. The room looked like it always did after recess, like a bomb had gone off but no one had been hurt. Pens, crayons, open bookbags, cookie wrappers, piles of notebooks, sloppily folded paper planes. But on this particular day, the chalkboard at the front of the classroom next to the map of Belgium was smaller than usual. It had been folded shut and standing beside it with his back against the white wall was Mr. Rudy, his face bright red. It didn't take long for the class to start whispering.

Mr. Rudy ordered everyone to have a seat, and contrary to habit, he turned to us, the side class, first. He sent us over to the reading corner, behind the bookcase, and told us to sit down and keep quiet. We were each given a book and a set of headphones.

All the other students waited around bored until Mr. Rudy was done explaining our assignment. For the first time, the order of operations was reversed. Thus, when Mr. Rudy tried to explain the difference between not needing to absorb something and not being supposed to absorb something, we pretended not to understand. As the noise in the classroom increased, he repeated the instructions three times.

"Listen to the story, then complete the crossword puzzle. This will be graded."

"How many points?" Pim asked.

Rudy glanced at the worksheet he had just given us.

"Thirty. It won't count on your report card."

"What does it count for, then?" Laurens asked.

"Just complete the assignment the best you can and hand it in by the end of the day." Rudy returned to the front of the class, urging the rest of the students to quiet down. We put on the headphones, pressed play, and hunched over our worksheets—but kept our eyes glued to the chalkboard.

Back at the front of the class, Rudy nonchalantly unfolded the side panels. Inside was a drawing of a diagram shaped like a half-open clam.

Behind the voice reading into our ears, we heard the class grow quiet. Laurens and Pim stopped taking notes and exchanged looks.

"Who knows where the urethra is located? That's where your pee comes out. Who can circle it here on the board?" Rudy handed the chalk to the first girl who dared to look up. Pim and Laurens turned the volume on their headphones all the way down.

That afternoon, on our way home from school, they rattled on in high, excited voices.

"Just because we're a year younger doesn't mean we don't know how things work!"

"What does that *Miss* Rudy think? That we don't know what a pee hole is for?" Laurens exclaimed.

"Come on, you've eaten clams before." After a prudish childhood out on the farm, Pim had only recently discovered that women didn't have udders.

The rest of the way home, they laughed about how when Rudy asked the class who had ever used a tampon to light a campfire, he was the only one to raise his hand.

I biked alongside them, following their conversation, but had nothing to add. The lesson about the male reproductive organs wasn't until next week.

I felt dirty. Mr. Rudy had touched the thing I'd kept hidden all those years at least twenty times with his chalk.

10:30 a.m.

THE EXIT TO Bovenmeer consists of a dangerously sharp hairpin turn, marked with blinking red arrows. Before they installed these arrows in '98, there were all kinds of accidents here. They happened so often that the people who lived behind the curve, a couple who raised pigeons, would come out on icy days with their folding chairs and a thermos full of coffee in the hopes of becoming the first people since World War II to witness something truly tragic.

As I turn off the exit ramp, the Curver slides to one side. The handle breaks off, catapulting a shard of plastic against my windshield. I can't lose control of the car now, not today. I'd end up the subject of some sensational headline in the *Antwerp Gazette*. "Young Bovenmeer woman crashes with block of ice in trunk."

That would be a real head-scratcher for the people waiting in line at the supermarket. They'd then proceed to fill in the story with half-truths. I can picture them, those people, their faces, I can just hear the self-satisfaction in their voices.

"Eva had been living in Brussels for years, but she was always one of us." "Her sister wasn't all there either." "Her brother sent her money every month that she never did anything with, y'know, she should've spent it on winter tires." "Nine years, that's how long it'd been since she last visited her parents, and then, right before the family was reunited—bam!" And: "The ice hit the back of her head so hard that they needed a passport to identify the person in the vehicle."

Then they'd take their groceries home, where they'd press their forks into a plastic container full of meat salad for the third time even though it had already lost its flavor.

Once I've made it safely off the exit ramp, I let out a sigh of relief. I follow the bridge back over the highway and across the Albert Canal.

The town sprawled out before me is completely unaware of the world around it. Laundry hangs out to dry, smoke drifts up from the chimneys. Some of the hedges are decorated with Christmas lights. But the streets are empty. There's no one around, not even an approaching car. Maybe everyone has already arrived where they need to be. Maybe they're all waiting in line at the bakery, pushing and shoving for the last dinner rolls.

There must be someone around to witness the fact that I'm back for the first time in nine years. Someone, anyone, by chance, out of sight even. A little girl taking a selfie, perhaps. In the corner of the photo, through her bedroom window, would be my little car—that would be enough. She wouldn't even have to know who I am.

I could call Tessie, just to hear her voice. Then maybe the two of us could make a stand together today.

I'm down to the last kilometer. From above, the scene feels familiar: my car is a tiny speck, slow but driven with purpose. Along the busy road between the highway exit and my parents' house are mostly old houses. They were built in the first half of the twentieth century, but I still wonder whether they were actually there when I was a teenager. Most of the facades I never even looked at. They were like decorations, concrete houseplants, on the road between the house I grew up in and the places where I truly felt at home.

It turns out that there are families living behind those facades, with well-organized parents who order new moon boots for their offspring every year and remember to wrap the little trees in front of their door in plastic against the frost.

July 12, 2002

LAURENS CALLED THIS morning to ask if I wanted to go swimming out at the farm. "We'll have to ask Pim first, but if we both like the idea, he'll say yes." I'm wearing my bathing suit under my clothes— the same old one that's too small. Yesterday, my shoulders were sore where the straps had been. My periods stopped coming as suddenly as they arrived.

Laurens and Pim aren't in the new pool, but next to the barn on one of the mounds covered in white plastic. They're standing at the very top. When I squint so I can see them against the glare, the blurred mound reminds me of a wedding cake, with Laurens and Pim as the two little figurines on top.

Pim's parents always let us play anywhere we wanted on the farm, but there were four places that were off-limits: the left side of the hayloft (the hay was too thin there, and we might fall through), the garage with the floor pit (the wood cover was rotten and dangerous), the septic tank grates in the old cowshed (no longer reliable) and the white mounds. They'd never given us a reason for that last one. We were simply told that they were forbidden territory, even though they looked so innocent and inviting.

Once at a birthday party, Laurens rested his foot on the white plastic. Pim yanked him to the ground by the hood of his jacket so hard that it ripped off the snaps.

"What's under there that's so dangerous?" Laurens squeaked after a whole minute of choking and spluttering.

Pim offered no explanation. He just turned around and walked away. For the rest of the afternoon, he and Laurens acted like two cats that had just had kittens.

On the way to school, Laurens and I exchanged theories. Under that plastic were dead animals that had succumbed to mad-cow disease. Or even worse—drugs, grown in the stalls or nearby fields. We concluded that Pim's parents had been the cause of the mad-cow epidemic that broke out in the nineties. They were the Mafiosi of the agricultural industry.

I crawl up the mound on the least steep side, carefully placing the tips of my ballet flats in the grooves of the rubber tires to avoid stepping on the contaminated cows potentially lying below. Warm rainwater sloshes up with every step.

When I reach the top, my ballet flats are soaked. Pim and Laurens have sat down in a tractor tire lying flat on the top of the mound like a swimming pool, their legs hanging over the edge. Their hair is tousled from the wind that, even in today's sweltering heat, is still blowing through the open barn.

"What are you guys up to?" I ask.

"Nothing," Laurens says.

"Doing nothing is doing something too, y'know," Pim says.

A strand of hair keeps sticking to one of the corners of my mouth. It tastes like chemicals. I sprayed on some hairspray this morning, hoping that it might help to add a bit of volume. Instead, it made my hair sticky and heavy, and now it's hanging down in stiff spikes on my forehead. I'd assumed that I'd be able to wash it out with pool water right away.

"You decide what we're going to do."

I take a seat in a smaller tire a little ways away. There isn't anywhere to sit closer to them. No one says anything for a while.

"What was always so dangerous about all this?" I ask, motioning to the sea of hot plastic around us.

"I know!" Laurens exclaims, taking my side because Pim doesn't react. "Why weren't we ever allowed to climb up here, and now all of a sudden it's okay?"

We look at Pim. It most likely has something to do with Jan.

But maybe in our eyes all of the recent changes on this farm have to do with Jan's death.

"There's silage underneath," Pim explains. "In the months when grass grows fast, but the field isn't dry enough to make hay, we shred it and store it as cattle feed. This is the farm's most important product—cow feed. Climbing on the plastic could cause it to tear, which would let in light and moisture. Then, the feed will rot, and you have to throw it all away."

Laurens and I listen, nodding. How many times had we called Pim on summer days to ask if he wanted to go swimming in the Pit? How many times had Pim's mother said that her boys were helping out in the field, that we'd have to call back another time? All those hours that Laurens and I were forced to hang out just the two of us, all for two mounds of grass.

Of course, we're capable of understanding how important they are. But the question remained: why were we climbing on them today?

"So all of a sudden it's okay to climb on it?" I ask.

"No, but do you see anyone around here who's going to try to stop us?" Pim asks.

No one says anything for a few seconds.

"What did you guys come over here to do anyway?" he asks then. It sounds more hostile than he intended, I think.

"Swim?" Laurens glances in my direction.

"Okay," I say.

Pim divides his gaze equally between the two of us.

"Or play truth or dare? We could do that too," Laurens adds quickly.

Pim gives him a thumbs up. A cloud moves in front of the sun, and the temperature instantly drops a few degrees.

Laurens gives me a look—this is all your fault.

"You first," Pim says, slapping Laurens on the knee.

"Truth," he says in a spooky voice.

"A little question to get started, then," Pim says. "What's the most embarrassing thing that you, Laurens Torfs, have ever done?"

Laurens ponders the question, hums and haws a bit to let us

know that he's thinking about his answer. To me, it's also a sign that he's not thinking about the most embarrassing thing he's ever done. That he'd be able to tell us right away. The longer someone has to think about their answer the less truth you can expect. He's going to tell us something that's a bit less embarrassing, but still embarrassing enough.

Pim stares up at the sky above the barn. He must be thinking about what kind of answer he'd make up if someone asked him this question. Whatever you ask in this game has a way of coming back in your face like a boomerang.

"Once I caught my mom and dad in the store after closing," Laurens says.

"Caught them doing what?" I ask.

He rolls his eyes.

Pim smirks, unimpressed. It's his turn. Not to be outdone, he goes for a dare.

"Drink from one of the tires." Laurens points to the big tractor tire with a puddle of green slime at the bottom.

Pim doesn't hesitate for a second. He drops to his knees, presses his lips against the rubber and takes a big gulp. I see a small army of tadpoles squirm out of the way. Pim drinks it up and manages to keep it down. Then he turns towards me.

"Your turn."

"Truth," I say.

"What's the worst thing you've ever experienced?" Pim asks.

Following Laurens's lead, I don't tell them the worst thing—my mom and dad standing across from each other in the kitchen wielding potato knives at each other, neither one of them brave enough to take the first swing—but something just bad enough.

"One time we had to carry my mom home in a wheelbarrow after trivia night at the club," I say.

Laurens doesn't say anything. Pim lets out a snort, at which Laurens bursts into laughter. I don't dare to tell them the rest of the story. They're laughing so hard they're almost crying. Even I start dabbing the corners of my eyes.

"That's all well and good," Pim finally says, "but it sounds more like the worst thing your mom's ever experienced. Tell us something about yourself."

I think about it for a moment, but all I can come up with is other people's misery. Suffering I saw happen, that I just kept watching, until it became my own. Sharing it would reduce its density, making it more bearable for both of us.

"Isn't Jan's accident the worst thing you've ever experienced, even though you're not the one who died?" I ask.

The silence that falls over us is filled by farm sounds: the clickety-clack against the iron troughs, the rumbling of the refrigerator engine in the milk house, mooing. Cows always sound like they're in pain.

"That's different," Pim snaps. "And who says Jan's death is the worst thing I've ever experienced?"

"At least Jan's not suffering anymore," Laurens says.

I look at Pim to see how he will respond, but he doesn't. White clouds float by overhead, behind him the horizon is still a clear shade of blue.

"Okay, for real." I decide to make something up. "The worst thing I've ever experienced myself—one time, on the way to my grandparents' house, we were stuck in traffic, and I had to go so bad that I went in my pants."

"Pee or poop?" Laurens asks.

"Both," I say.

That does the trick. The boys nod, offering their condolences.

"That's bad, Eva."

The top of the mound offers an incredible view of the land behind the farm. If this were a painting, somebody would pay a lot of money for it. To the right are the fields, and to the left, I can look out over the top of the barn.

This panorama might be the real reason we were never allowed to climb on this pile of grass. Up here, we have a view of the whole property, of the grime on the roof of the barn, and can see it for what it truly is, a dirty old dairy farm.

Pim's dad is down below, absorbed in his chores, withdrawn. He glances up at us. Why doesn't he say anything about us sitting on the mound of grass silage, threatening to destroy all of his hard work? He briefly makes eye contact with me.

"What base are you at, by the way?" Pim asks Laurens. "Be honest."

"What do you mean by 'base'?"

"At my school, they call them bases. There are six of them: making out, feeling up, fingering, going down. Then, there's fifth base, sex, and then a homerun."

"So what's the homerun?"

"If you have to ask, you clearly haven't gotten to it yet."

Laurens and Pim are sitting across from each other. Their pant legs catch the wind, inflating their calves.

"Who said I wanted truth?" Laurens says.

It falls quiet for a moment.

"Come on, just say it," Pim urges.

"I'm at third base," he claims. "Where are you?"

"Fifth. Gradually inching my way towards a homerun." Pim holds up five fingers, then makes a fist and slams it into his other hand.

Again, a cloud moves in front of the sun. A shadow glides across the roof of the barn.

"What's the worst thing you've ever done to someone?" I ask Pim after he asks for truth. "Jan's accident doesn't count," I add, "because there was nothing you could do."

He doesn't need long to think. The grateful look on his face breaks into a grin.

"I put a ping-pong ball up a cow's ass."

"And . . . ?" Laurens asks.

"And what?"

"Did she fart it back out?"

Pim furrows his brows conspiratorially.

"Nope. I put it in there pretty deep."

"Why would you do something like that?" I ask.

"Why wouldn't I? Nobody ever found out."

I gaze off in the distance. Pim's dad is nowhere in sight. The man who knows all the spots on his cows' backs has a blind spot for his own son.

"Your turn, Eva," he says.

Again, I choose truth.

"What's the worst thing you've ever done?" Pim asks, hurling my own question back in my face.

I think about it for a moment and say the first thing that pops into my head.

"I killed Elisa's horse."

Pim's eyes widen. "How?"

"I gave Twinkle sugar. Apparently, it kills them instantly."

"Who told you that? Animals don't die from sugar. In the meat industry, they pump them up with way worse stuff than that. You didn't poison her—at most you helped her put on an extra pound or two." Laurens gives me a wink, like his father would do. "Butcher's sons know these kinds of things, trust me."

Is he trying to put my mind at ease or is he dissatisfied with my answer again?

The sun breaks through the clouds, illuminating the white plastic. As if realizing on their way down that they're about to be beamed back up, the rays seem to make a sharp turn towards a spot of bare skin on my neck. It smells like burning rubber. I want to stand up, but my tight bathing suit keeps me down.

"Laurens, go for a dare."

"Okay, fine. Dare," he says.

"I've got the perfect task for you . . ." Pim pauses for a moment to let the tension build. "I'll tell you which cow it was, and you pull the ping-pong ball out."

Laurens shakes his head.

"Come on, are you a butcher's son or not?"

Pim climbs out of the tractor wheel; the wind whooshes out of his pant legs. His butt looks smaller than ever.

Before we enter the cowshed, Laurens and I each pull on one

of the pairs of boots lined up outside the giant door. I take the biggest pair. They're so big that I can wear them without having to take off my ballet flats. The stalls are made of cinderblocks and covered with corrugated metal. In here, there's no breeze at all. As we wander around, the cows pull back their slimy noses. Their heads bang against the iron bars, which makes an infernal clacking noise that echoes across the entire farm.

We climb over the fence and walk between the animals. We trample over cow droppings, releasing the smell of rotten grass and musty earth. The closer we get to the cows, the bigger they seem. Laurens, who confidently followed Pim into the barn, slows his pace. The cow we're headed towards is rubbing her back on a giant brush. She whips her tail around, flicking the flies off her hind legs. Her hip bones jut up out of her back. Pim positions himself behind her and takes a wooden broomstick. The other cows make a run for it, their udders sloshing back and forth as they scramble out of the way. Pim beckons Laurens to come closer.

"This is a heifer," he says. "Something between a mother and a child. In other words—a sweet young piece of meat."

The heifer shakes her head nervously back and forth. Pim directs her to the side with the broom, to where the cows are normally held when they are pregnant. The animal has no choice but to saunter forward, shifting her weight from one hind leg to another, her limp udders swinging back and forth.

Pim takes a step back. Laurens looks around helplessly. He doesn't know what to do. Then, he pulls himself together and walks forward, stopping thirty centimeters from the animal. The cow's anus bulges out.

"You've got to reach into the top hole!" Pim says. "Otherwise, you'll be in her uterus."

Laurens rolls up his right sleeve and rubs his hands together. The cow becomes nervous, shifting her weight faster and faster from one leg to the other. She can't reach us with her tail. She knows what's coming. Over at the fence, a couple of cows are huddled together; one of them moos encouragingly.

"You'd be better off doing it with your left arm. It's going to stink for a while," Pim says.

Laurens looks at me. I say nothing. Pim points to a bottle on a nearby stool. "Put some of that stuff on your hand."

"Are you sure he has to do this?" I ask.

"Here." Pim squirts the slimy substance on the cow's butthole. He grabs Laurens by his left wrist and pulls him closer. Laurens doesn't stop him. Pim pushes Laurens's fingertips in about a half a centimeter. They do not go in easily. Laurens's hand falls limply against the hole. He can't bring himself to push.

"Don't make a fist. Do like this." Pim motions with his arm, making a kind of slow-motion forward crawl. "Don't be too gentle."

Laurens slowly wriggles his hand until it slowly disappears into the hole, followed by his wrist and then his lower arm.

"See what I mean?" Pim says. "The ball is in about shoulder deep."

He winks at me, finishes pantomiming the job, this time doing the forward crawl motion with two arms. Suddenly, it occurs to me: there's nothing in there. At first, I'd hoped that Pim wasn't capable of doing something so barbaric. But what he's putting Laurens through right now is just as bad.

Laurens works his way in deeper, until he's in the animal up to his neck. He'd have to stand on his tiptoes to go any further.

"I think I got it! I feel something," he shouts. The animal puffs up her belly, her udders swing. She could easily absorb Laurens into her intestinal tract with a reverse fart.

At first, Pim just stands there, grinning.

"There's no ping-pong ball," I say softly.

Pim smacks me on the upper arm. Then, all of a sudden, he freezes. He's staring at the boots on my feet. He looks up at me, then back at my feet. I can tell by the way he walks away: I'm wearing Jan's boots.

I want to run after him, but Laurens, still halfway inside the cow, hasn't noticed Pim's departure yet.

"There's no ping-pong ball!" My voice sounds shrill.

It takes a few seconds for the message to sink in. Laurens pulls his arm out. What would upset him more: that there's no ball or that Pim isn't even watching?

The animal's butthole contracts and releases. As Laurens withdraws his hand, a stream of shit comes out with it, plopping down between his legs. Some of it splashes against his shin, dripping into his boot. The cow sways anxiously. The mucus dripping from her anus forms a bubble.

I try to pull off the boots, but they won't give. My shoes are stuck inside.

Even Laurens is rattled. He starts fidgeting. He wipes off his arm on the first straw he can get his hands on. I pass him a towel hanging on a nearby railing. He looks at the boots in my hands, at my socked feet. I wrench my ballet flats out of the boots.

"I had no idea these were Jan's," I say.

Laurens's anger quickly dissolves into anxiety.

"Which way did Pim go?"

He heads off in the direction I indicate. Against the light, I see him holding his left arm away from his body. His skin has that strange orange glow that people get after applying self-tanning lotion without reading the instructions.

I put Jan's boots back outside the door just like I found them, with one leaning against the other. In the distance, I see Laurens and Pim at the base of the mound, both sitting on an upright tire.

What is Pim saying to him? Are they talking about Jan? Is he finally letting it all out? I move closer.

"Okay, fine. This is the last one. Dare," says Pim.

I can't hear what Laurens tells him to do. Pim stands up. He brushes off his pants even though there's no dust or dirt on them. It's a movement I often make myself, a reflex left over from all the afternoons we spent together on our knees in the hay.

He climbs a few meters up the mound and stops. For a moment, he gazes off in the distance in the direction where I saw his dad driving the tractor back and forth a little while ago leaving trails of manure behind him.

"C'mon, what are you waiting for?" Laurens comes over and stands beside me.

Pim looks straight at us. Then he bends down and punctures the plastic with his finger.

Elisa

ELISA WAS A new student in the fifth-grade class that we were parasiting off of that year. She showed up right after summer vacation. We saw her coming down the hall before she was introduced to the class. As she followed the principal to our classroom, her ponytail swung up over the top edge of the classroom windows with every step. Principal Beatrice entered without knocking and proudly pushed Elisa forward.

"This is Elisa. Her father has been working abroad as a representative. She was homeschooled for a little while, but now her dad doesn't have to travel for his job anymore. They live in Hoogstraten, but Elisa will be attending school here, twenty-six-point-nine kilometers from home," she boasted, as if this said something about her qualities as school principal. "She is living with her grandmother on Lijsterweg. We'll see how far along she is with the lesson material—it's possible that she'll be able to move up to the sixth grade in a few months."

Elisa was a little on the ugly side, but the kind of ugly you knew would turn out pretty as long as she fixed her eyebrows. They had grown dark and crooked across her face, making everything she said seem calculating, malicious. She had tanned skin, and her long, skinny legs had been squeezed into a pair of tight black pants with white tennis shoes at the ends. Over her shirt she wore a short, square black puffer vest that accentuated her slim hips. She wore it zipped up to the bottom of her breasts, making them look like two half-popped chestnuts.

Elisa was born in 1986, so she was a year older than everyone else in the class, and two years older than Pim, Laurens and me. She listened to what Principal Beatrice said about her, looking modestly down at her shoes.

"Who here has ever been to Hoogstraten?" asked Mr. Rudy, in an effort to warm us up to the new student. As long as Principal Beatrice was standing there, he did his best not to stare at her puffed chestnuts.

Nobody raised their hand.

Nothing was said about Elisa's mother. Before the bell had even rung for recess, rumors were flying around that she died giving birth, when she had to push out Elisa's long legs and puffer vest. Somebody even made a drawing of it—the crumpled paper was passed around the class after recess. It was the first time that me, Laurens and Pim ever got to see one of their notes.

Elisa didn't take off her vest that whole first day, or the days after that. She always had it on. She must've been used to the idea of always having to be ready to leave in a hurry. To make matters worse, she made the same mistake I did of claiming that, even if she could choose from all four, she wouldn't want to go out with any of the guys from Get Ready!. After that, no one wanted to be seen with her on the playground anymore.

Every day at noon, she'd walk home to her grandma's for a hot lunch and to visit her mare, Twinkle, who was out grazing in the fields near the Bulksteeg, across from my house. A few weeks before Elisa moved in, they delivered the horse in the middle of the night. It whinnied until the sun rose. Every time Elisa came back to school after lunch, she had little seeds between her teeth.

A few days after Elisa arrived, our class went swimming at the Pulderbos Aquatic Center. A Verhoeven coach picked us up at the school gate. The bus had to make three trips between the school and the pool so that every class would have a chance to swim that day.

On the bus, I spoke to Elisa for the first time. Pim was sitting next to Laurens, even though it wasn't my turn to sit alone. Elisa was in the seat in front of me. As soon as the bus got going, she turned around and rested her chin on the back of her seat.

"Guess what?" she asked, then paused dramatically to make me curious.

"What?"

"My mimi has the same name as you."

She'd hung her swimming bag on the hook next to her seat. It swung back and forth with every sharp turn on our way out of town. The bag was covered with rhinestones and glitter and dangling from all the zippers were these little neon plastic pacifiers. The thing wasn't ugly per se. Like her shiny puffer vest, it wasn't a matter of taste, it was just something she was used to. We'd never seen anything like it before in Bovenmeer.

"I call my grandma 'grandma'. Not 'mimi'," I said.

"Same thing," she replied.

"No, it's not." I immediately started explaining the difference. It took almost the entire route to the Aquatic Center for me to make my case. Every once in a while, I'd look out the window at the autumn leaves to give myself time to come up with new arguments. Elisa just sat there staring at me, her chin resting on the top of the seat in front of me. Her uninterrupted gaze gave me a warm feeling inside: I existed in the eyes of a girl from Hoogstraten.

When we arrived in the large gray parking lot outside the pool, Elisa finally lifted her chin off the seat. "So 'mimi' sounds like some kind of baby toy to you," she summarized, "but in my opinion, a baby toy is still better than a grandma you only see two times a year because she lives in West Flanders." Then she laid her chin back down on the top of the seat and pushed down on the handle on the side of the chair, which made it recline until her face was nearly pressed against mine. She pouted her lips and laughed. I could feel the warmth of her odorless breath.

Pim and Laurens were sitting two rows up, watching us in silence. I hadn't heard them laugh once the whole trip.

"Mind telling us what's so funny?" Pim asked.

"Girl stuff," Elisa said.

The Aquatic Center smelled like chlorine. I took deep breaths, trying to extract a bit of oxygen from the hot, sticky air. The

building didn't have enough changing rooms for everybody, and
boys and girls weren't allowed to go in together. Anyone who wasn't
quick enough to grab a partner of the same sex and duck into one
of the cubicles had to change in the family locker room where the
toddlers were being helped by the volunteer moms.

Elisa immediately grabbed me by the arm and pulled me into
one of the cubicles.

This had never happened to me before. I'd always been forced
to use the family changing room. No one ever stared in there. The
naked little kids weren't too picky about other people's bodies. They
clung to the backsides of the volunteers, all unshaven women with
blunt edges. At the start of the swim lesson, the moms would wade
into the shallow water like a herd of hippos to watch—with their
eyes just above the water—the children's first cautious breaststrokes
and somersaults.

I never had an extra set of eyes on me. I never learned to do
somersaults.

Elisa sat down on the little bench that also served as a door
blocker. First, she took off her shoes, then her puffer vest.

"You first," she said.

I'd never seen her without the vest. She looked even skinnier.
For once, she didn't seem concerned about the fact that she might
have to leave again in a hurry.

She didn't check the cracks around the cubicle very carefully;
she didn't check for boy's noses or little mirrors. She just looked at
me, curious about what she was going to see. I took off my pants
and top. I already had my bathing suit on under my clothes. Apparently, they hadn't discovered this trick in Hoogstraten yet.

Then I watched as Elisa changed her clothes. I did check the
edges of the cubicle walls, vigilantly in fact, but there were no
prying eyes, no one wanted to look at us.

Out of the corner of my eye, I watched Elisa shimmy into her
suit. I could count her ribs, at least four on each side. Her labia
hung down like the little curtains in the Verhoeven coach, open
with gray and pink pleats. On her back was a brown mole the size

of a small grape. She could just barely tuck it under the edge of her high-cut bathing suit.

Without a word, she'd told me all her secrets.

One week later, I was invited to go home with her to Mimi's for lunch. Her house was at the start of the Lijsterweg, next to a big chestnut tree. Mimi was one of the few people in town that nobody knew much about. All we knew was the color of her facade, that she had a doorbell in the shape of a lion's head and that she made jam from the berries that grew in her garden.

I followed Elisa on my bike as she walked in front of me at a brisk pace, the plastic pacifiers on her backpack bouncing happily from side to side.

I tried to figure out what kind of person Mimi was based on her front yard. The garden wasn't perfectly manicured. The grass hadn't been patiently mowed in circles like a squeezed-out dog turd. There were a couple of postcards in the mailbox.

Apparently, she didn't have much time for gardening, which meant she must have a social life and friends who sent her cards from their cruises to faraway destinations—so she couldn't be all that bad.

Inside, it was actually pretty cozy. The floors weren't covered in carpet, it didn't smell like a dead animal, her cola was still fizzy, she didn't carry giant burlap bags—every time Mimi didn't fit my description on the bus, Elisa flashed me a triumphant smile.

The only thing I'd been right about was the furniture: none of it matched.

"You don't get to choose who dies when, and you can't say no to heirlooms," Mimi said, wiping away bit of dust on a massive wooden wardrobe.

After a while, I didn't dare to take my eyes off my plate.

We had baked endives with ham on top. They were still nice and crispy.

"Well, is it edible?" Mimi asked me.

I nodded. Endives were the one thing my mother excelled in. But Mimi's were even better. I decided not to mention this at home.

I watched Elisa wolf down her food. She finished before I did and motioned for me to hurry up. I brought the fork to my mouth as quick as possible, but still gave myself the time to savor each bite.

"I'm gonna go to the bathroom. Then we can go." Elisa disappeared into the bathroom.

For the first time in my life, I understood the secret to getting along with a girl: don't want it too much.

I laid down my fork and knife.

"Elisa is just crazy about horses. You better watch out," Mimi whispered and dumped all the food I hadn't eaten into the trash.

11:00 a.m.

IF SNOW ON a day like today were an added feature on a car, like air-conditioning, somebody would've thought to make it prohibitively expensive.

The first flakes flutter and swirl, defying gravity, disappearing at the slightest touch. But pretty soon it's snowing harder—boxy, determined flakes. They pile up on the road, in the empty lots between houses, on the poles separating pastures, on the hideous light-up Santa Clauses trying to sneak in through the windows, on the mailbox of the dilapidated house that can't possibly swallow any more advertisements.

You can see the mossy black roof of my parents' house peeking out above the trees from a hundred meters away.

I park my car on the side of the road, behind the big pine trees doing their best to shield our yard from strange looks. The trees are thinner at the bottom than they are on the top. Between the trunks, I can see our patio. There's the cracked aquarium with a puddle of green rainwater at the bottom, a couple of iron tubs, a big pile of sand that we used to call the sandbox, a sawed-off tree trunk, a row of planted Christmas trees. The garden looks exactly the same as it did nine years ago. Leaning against the side of the house is the broken plastic bucket we kept our turtle in for a while.

Mom got the turtle, along with the aquarium, as a present when Tessie was born. Eight years later, in 1999, the tank cracked while the water was being changed, so we transferred the turtle into the orange bucket. It lived there, in a corner on the patio, for the entire summer and fall, far enough away that we couldn't really see it.

On the first cold winter morning, the bright orange plastic caught my eye against the white frost.

I went outside. I knew it was too late to save the turtle. Even the bucket had cracked. The last bit of water had tried to trickle out the bottom, but it didn't get very far.

Without looking over the rim of the bucket, I flipped it upside down in one fell swoop. I tapped the bottom and the block of ice broke free and slid to the ground. I carefully lifted off the mold, as if the block underneath were an almost-failed cake. The turtle was stuck upside down in the ice, its belly looked like the slice of an apple.

If you ask me, drowning and being buried alive are the two worst ways to die. The turtle had been successful in both. Jan's death was a pretty good combination of the two as well.

Now that the car has stopped, the flakes start piling up. I pull the key out of the ignition, step out and check the trunk. I have to cross the Bulksteeg to reach the backyard. To the right is Mimi's field, where Elisa's horse used to graze. There's no horse out there now, and it's not Mimi's field anymore either. The land has been sold off into lots.

I walk on, to where our driveway meets the street.

As usual, the backyard is empty. Other than the broken freezer, there's nothing but the doghouse, its door hanging crooked on its hinges.

Now I remember. Nanook is dead.

The news came via email about a year ago, sent from the new domain Dad had set up for the whole family with a separate address for each person and a link to a website he planned to use to post weekly family updates.

Dad was good at feeding us highly detailed, but totally un-necessary information: a history of paella plucked off of Wikipedia, news about current events that would have been impossible to miss, even without his help. He wasn't trying to inform us about the earthquake in Haiti per se, he just wanted us to know that he had heard about it.

His last email came about ten months ago with the subject line "Pa died." The email confirmed that Grandpa, my mother's father, had passed away. It stated his date and place of birth and offered a limited timeline of his achievements, again, like something from Wikipedia. At the end was a P.S.: "the dog has been peeing in the house a lot lately—if it's okay we're going to put her to sleep."

Half question, half announcement—his way of covering himself in advance for the lack of answers.

The time the email was sent, the fact that Dad had CC'ed Mom (when the news about Grandpa had most certainly come from her), the inaccurate but elaborate descriptions—it all suggested that he was as drunk as he was the time he started responding to his own posts on the family website.

I didn't reply to the email, mainly because Jolan and Tessie didn't either. Answering would mean we'd have to go to Grandpa's funeral.

That was, as far as I can remember, the last I heard from my parents.

Behind me, the car is slowly disappearing under the snow. I could turn around and head back to Brussels while the roads are still clear enough to drive on. But I keep walking, down the path to the back door.

On the side of the house, there are bedsheets hanging out to dry. One double sheet and three single sheets—Jolan's with the cars on it, mine with Babar, and Tessie's with Barbie. Either Mom still changes the sheets on our unused beds regularly, or she and Dad no longer sleep together and take turns sleeping in our rooms. The bedding has collected a lot of snow in a short amount of time. The back door is unlocked. I'm getting covered in snow, but still I hesitate to go inside. With the doorknob in my hand, I gaze up at the back facade.

This house is way too big for what's left of our family.

July 15, 2002

FOR THE FIRST time I hope that something relatively terrible will happen to a mutual but distant acquaintance, something only I know about, so I'll have a story to tell Pim and Laurens that's worthy of their full attention.

A story like the one about the drunk tourist who, after a party at the Pulse Pallieterzaal, walked out into the cemetery next door to take a piss, steadied herself on a loose headstone and ended up crushed by "Josepha Louis, 1856–1924", surely something Josepha wouldn't have wanted either. Or like the one about the local policeman who was accused of killing his own wife, or the man who climbed into a tree with a chainsaw to trim the branches, accidentally cut off his own head and went unnoticed by the postman for several days.

My urge to tell these kinds of stories is stronger than I am. It's kind of like needing to pee. I can postpone it for a little while, but I can't make it go away. If you want to be somebody in this town, you've got to know something about someone else worth blabbing.

The carnival is all folded up in the center of town, exactly how they left it yesterday evening. There was a short but heavy downpour during the night. The cardboard French-fry holders have become soggy boats.

And here we are, summoned by Pim. He called this morning. After the usual three-second delay, he told me to meet him here. He didn't say why. Judging by the solemn tone of his voice, we were going to have some kind of meeting.

We nab the best spot in town: the wooden bench against the low churchyard wall right in the middle of the carnival.

Tomorrow is Tuesday. The carnies will be up early to pack up their stands and travel on to the next village. Like anything you look forward to, the carnival takes a lot longer to set up than to break down. Tonight will be the last night I'll be able to lie in bed and listen to the airplanes going around and around. I'll hear them whizzing by one by one. If the wind is right, I'll be able to hear the crack of bullets hitting chalk, too. And I'll wonder why I wasn't born in Lier, or in Zandhoven, or in some other town with more than one bakery, some place with fifteen carnival stands and two annual markets, where you learn from a young age that you can't be everywhere at the same time. Kids from Lier and Zandhoven are—unlike us—used to choosing and losing.

I sit on the wall between the two boys. They keep giving each other looks as if I'm not there. When Laurens first showed up, Pim grabbed his arm and sniffed it. Laurens punched him in the gut, and that was the end of it. We rest our feet on the old plank where the bench seat is supposed to be.

"What are you guys looking at?" I watch Laurens try to roll up the sleeve he's just used to wipe off the wet bench. It's hard to do with one hand. I stand up, facing him, and help him roll it up. He doesn't object. I fold back the sleeve slowly, buying time.

"Laurens and I have a plan," Pim confesses. Laurens gives him a look to try to shut him up. Pim doesn't see it.

"And when did you two come up with this plan?" I ask.

"Does it matter?" says Pim.

I shrug.

"It's a really great plan, but we need you to come up with a riddle," Laurens explains.

"What kind of riddle?" I sit back down between the two of them.

"A riddle that nobody can solve," he says.

"And why do you need that?"

"We'll tell you later. Just try to think of one. Laurens and I will work out the rest. Right, man?" Pim has been asking Laurens for his opinion more often lately. Or briefly summarizing for Laurens what he's just told me, as if there's some special code between guys that requires fewer letters.

"Okay, Laurens, it all starts with a good scoreboard." Pim picks up a piece of soft white limestone, jumps over the cemetery wall and struts between the graves of unknown soldiers. He hastily draws a few lines on the stucco wall, forming an off-kilter grid. Laurens jumps down from the wall and follows him.

I pretend to be thinking hard about my riddle, but I'm straining my ears to hear what they're saying.

"Your girls first, Laurens."

They think quietly for a moment.

From where I'm sitting, I can just make out the fields to the right of our backyard. Between the fields and the house, parked on the narrow Bulksteeg, is a Jeep pulling a trailer. Its brake lights are on. Just as it catches my eye, the lights go out and the Jeep starts moving. It turns into the field, the trailer bouncing along behind it. Somewhere in the middle of the field, it comes to a stop. A man steps out and opens the trailer. A giant brown horse jumps out the back. It's not Twinkle. She had to be put down. I think this one is a stallion. As it romps around the field, I notice something swing-ing back and forth beneath its sleek brown silhouette.

"Melissa, Ann, Indira . . ." Laurens rattles off the names of a few girls, and not just ones from the class we were tacked onto last year.

The man that just stepped out of the Jeep could be Elisa's dad. Then a girl with a long ponytail steps out too. They turn around and walk across the field to check the barbed wire. Now I know for sure—Elisa is back.

After that late-summer school day four years ago, when we shared a changing room at the pool, Elisa and I were best friends for four months. I listened to her go on and on about horseback riding and wondered if she ever talked to her horse about me.

Every day except Wednesday, when school let out early, I'd go home with her to Mimi's during the lunch break for a hot meal. The sandwiches I'd made for myself that morning would end up thrown away in the trash can on the playground.

Elisa always made me scarf down my lunch so she could spend more time with Twinkle, but I didn't mind. I could tell she liked sharing her horse with me. Sometimes during the lunch break, she'd ride a few laps bareback. I'd watch her ponytail swing back and forth from one shoulder to the other in the same rhythm as the horse's tail.

Oftentimes I wasn't really focusing on her, but on the house off in the distance, my house, where Tessie and Jolan were eating sandwiches—the butter dish in the middle of the table, Mom slouched sideways in her chair, three sandwich fillings laid out neatly on a wooden cutting board, cheddar, monkey head, ringwurst. I wondered if I could really see it all, or if I only saw those details because I knew they were there.

One day, Elisa started talking about her mother.

"Does being with animals ever make you think of someone who's no longer here? And then you treat the animal like you treated that person?" she asked.

I nodded, though I'd never lost anybody before, and in my case the opposite was true: people made me think of animals.

"Does Twinkle look like your mom?" I asked.

"No, stupid." She shot me a dirty look. "Poor thing."

"Who's a poor thing?"

"My horse!"

Later that afternoon, without my asking, she told me the truth. Her mom had walked out on her and her dad right after she was born. Now she ran a hotel somewhere in Ireland. Elisa had never missed her because she'd never known her. She hugged her horse's neck as she told me.

Afterwards she ran the horse through a few drills. I watched their two tails swing back and forth in unison. For the first time, I started to dislike her. I knew more about Elisa than she would ever want to know about me.

A few days later, four months after arriving at our school, she was bumped up to the sixth grade because she got such good grades on her first report card. The sixth-grade girls welcomed her with open arms, and soon enough they were all slathering their lips with glittery lip gloss, wearing puffer vests and plastic pacifier necklaces and filling in their eyebrows with pencil. It turned out every single member of Get Ready! was gay. Elisa was the only one who saw it coming.

I had lunch with her at Mimi's a few more times, but we hardly talked. I was the scab that needed time to come off on its own without scratching.

It wasn't long before Elisa started having lunch at school.

"Mimi packed me sandwiches. She even put some of her home-made jam in a little jar to keep the bread from getting soggy," she announced one morning without any advance notice. I had already thrown my sandwiches away, maybe because I was hoping it might still sway Elisa's decision.

If you wanted to sit at the girls' table, you had to answer a question: "Who would you least like to be fingered by? Leonardo DiCaprio or Tom Cruise?"

Since I didn't know who Cruise or DiCaprio was, they didn't ask me who I wanted to be fingered by, but how. Elisa opened her jar of jam and pushed it across the table at me.

"First, demonstrate. After that, you can sit."

Later on it occurred to me that none of the girls knew how fingering worked. I should've just given it a go.

That afternoon, Twinkle and I met the same fate. Elisa stopped visiting the horse at lunchtime. She got invited to all kinds of birthday parties and let her new friends talk her into getting her hair crimped. After school, I'd wander out into the pasture and share what was left of my lunch with her horse.

One time, Jolan spotted me and told me I'd better stop. At school, he learned that sugar wasn't good for animals, that it made them sick.

"Forget Elisa," he said with a faint smile. "She's not that great." But his tone suggested otherwise.

After school that day, I spent my entire allowance on sour belts and jawbreakers at the Corner Store. Agnes even gave me a discount because it was almost my birthday. That afternoon, Twinkle and I ate candy until my stomach hurt.

"What does it mean when a horse lies on its side in the grass and starts foaming at the mouth?" Tessie asked at dinner that night. I almost choked on my meatball.

"Oh, he's just taking a nap," Jolan replied.

Elisa hasn't been around these last two years. Our four-month friendship is fading further and further into the past, but the memories are more vivid than ever.

Pim and Laurens are too busy making their lists to notice the trailer off in the distance.

In the months I was friends with Elisa, they were obsessed with Lara Croft and addicted to that game where you have to take her through the Lost Valley. They never knew Elisa as well as I did. Maybe that's when it happened, while I wasn't around—maybe that's when they started shutting me out.

"I pick Evelien, Heleen, Amber, Penny and Elisa," Pim says.

The piece of limestone he's writing with has gotten so small that he has to pinch it between his fingernails to avoid scraping his fingertips on the wall.

"Who's Amber?" Laurens asks.

"A girl from my school. She's really good with the laser cutter. She doesn't know she's a lesbian yet," Pim says.

"So why'd you pick her?" Laurens asks.

"She's got huge tits."

A gray cloud rolls over the town. The light falls down in slanted rays, streaming through the emptiness between the top and bottom of the cloud.

I turn my gaze from Elisa to the cemetery.

"Eva, since you're listening to everything we're saying anyway, why don't you tell us which girls you like?"

I pretend not to hear him.

"Okay, Eva doesn't like anybody," concludes Pim, and he goes to add this information to the wall.

"What do you mean by 'like'?" I ask, looking them square in the eye. "There are different categories of 'like'."

"Say you're having a party, and you're allowed to invite a few girls. Who would you invite? Who would come?"

I take my time thinking it over, though there aren't too many possible answers. "Tessie. And Elisa."

"No," Pim says, "family doesn't count."

I can't just invite Laurens's mom.

"Okay, Elisa then," I say.

"That's all?" Laurens asks. "Pim's already got her on the list. Small party."

I don't say anything about Elisa being off in the distance. I don't know why. I can't tell who I don't want to share with who.

"You got that riddle yet?" Laurens asks.

I shake my head. I haven't thought beyond the fact that I'm supposed to come up with a riddle.

"We'll start by giving points, then," Pim says to Laurens. "We don't need the riddle for that."

They've had their point system for years. They came up with it one night while we were camping out in a tent in Laurens's back-yard. They gave girls points based on individual aspects of their appearance. My role was not to give scores but to make sure Laurens and Pim remained objective enough, that they weren't blinded by a crush. They used practically the same scoring system as everybody else in and outside of town; they were just the only ones to actually write it down, in black and white.

I was the secretary. My job was to keep quiet and take notes.

Before we started, we would calibrate the scale by identifying the ugliest and the prettiest girl in town. Everyone in between got a score between 0.5 and 9.5. Each girl started at zero. Points were given for each attractive physical attribute, and scores were carefully rounded to the first decimal point.

Laurens and Pim were mostly interested in using the point system to figure out their own worth. They never discussed their own scores out loud. All they had were vague suspicions based on the girls they saw as equals.

Over two summers, 1999 and 2000, the most relevant girls in town were scored. There were only two groups that Laurens and Pim didn't discuss: the uppermost layer (too old) and the bottommost layer (too young). Everyone else—every girl of a relevant age—was examined in detail.

I can't remember when the last evaluation took place. The upper and lower layers seem to be shrinking. The older Laurens and Pim get, the more girls they're interested in. Age also obliges them to act differently. Today, they don't calibrate the scale. Instead of zero, each girl starts at ten. Rather than adding points for pretty features, they subtract them for ugly ones. Whether this is kinder or not, I have no idea.

One by one, Pim and Laurens go down the list of names they've just written on the cemetery wall. Birthmarks, crooked front teeth, flat in the front, flat in the back. No detail is spared. They don't go any lower than one because anyone with a clam is at least worth that.

I look out at Elisa, at the distance between us that can be counted in steps—about three hundred. But now that I'm standing still, it seems unbridgeable.

Oddly enough, Laurens and Pim have nothing but positive things to say about her.

"Come on, no girl is perfect," I say.

"We need a ten," Pim says, "so we can separate the tens from the fives."

"So you're saying there's no girl prettier than Elisa?"

The boys look at each other and shrug.

Three years ago, she just left town, without a word, without owing anybody anything. Her sudden disappearance is what makes her so attractive now.

"All she talks about is her horse. I'd subtract points for that."

"That may be, Eva, but we're talking about looks here." Pim

picks up a new rock. He numbers the names on the wall based on the score behind the name.

In the end, Elisa doesn't get a ten. But her score is still the highest at 9.5, a half-point from perfection. The deduction was just for good measure, some kind of concession to me.

"Now all we need is a good riddle," Laurens says.

"Come on, Eva. You gonna help us out or what?"

The harder I try, the harder it is to think of a good riddle. Off in the distance, Elisa and her dad are getting ready to leave.

"Can't I get one night to come up with something?"

Laurens lets out a deep sigh and looks at Pim.

"Okay by me," Pim says.

The church bells ring twelve times. The patio outside the Welcome is empty, except for two old men waiting to order their first pint of the day. They eye each other as if each one is sitting in the other's spot.

The carnival slowly starts to wake up. At the sound of the buzzer signaling the first unmanned test drive, two people show up in the street: a grandfather and grandson. I don't know them. They don't live here in town. They climb into a bumper car together and drive around the empty rink. I watch them make the same loops over and over, nobody in their way. It's a beautiful sight.

Laurens carefully pulls two fifties out of his pocket. I don't have any money on me. Pim takes out two fifties too.

"Who's gonna be the treasurer?" Pim asks.

The two boys fall silent and exchange a rehearsed look.

"How about Eva?" they say in unison.

They pool their money and hand it over.

"Which ride do you want to go on first?" I ask.

"This isn't for the carnival," Laurens says. "It's an investment."

"An investment in what?"

"You'll find out tomorrow," Pim says.

We sit there for a while. The carnival is starting to fill up. My parents didn't give me any money. I just assumed Laurens and Pim would let me ride shotgun with them. That's our tradition.

"I'm going home," Pim says. "All you've got to do is show up tomorrow with the money and a riddle. We'll handle the rest."

"Let's meet at my house tomorrow at 1:45," Laurens says. "And Eva, if you can't come up with anything, call me beforehand."

They two boys walk off in opposite directions. I watch them leave, looking from left to right, until I realize I'm shaking my head no.

The Air Salesmen

IT WAS IN '99, the day the salesmen showed up at our door, that I first realized that Tessie wasn't okay. I'd already had a vague suspicion. In addition to her excessive desire to win at Minesweeper, it was taking her longer and longer to get home from school. It never took me more than two minutes to put away my bike and take off my shoes.

A little after four, the doorbell rang. I opened it to find two men in suits. At first glance, there was very little about them that made sense. One was short and squatty and had a big head. The other was tall and gangly with a small head. Apparently, these types always come in this combination and were the reason why houses in towns like Bovenmeer still had a doorbell.

Little Head tried to peek over my shoulder into the hall. There was no one there, just the sideboard full of junk. Big Head was carrying a collapsible whiteboard on his back that stuck out over his shoulders; it was clearly hard for him to walk without letting the three legs drag on the ground. In his breast pocket was a pack of markers.

"We're Rob and Steven," he said without offering any clarification with his body language as to who was who.

"Is anyone home?" asked the one who looked most like a Steven. He had elongated freckles on his face and was wearing a shirt with an oval pattern. Everything on his body seemed just a little bit stretched. He reminded me of a Play-Doh sausage that was pressed too hard while being rolled.

"I am," I said. Just then Jolan entered the scene with a pair of tweezers and a magnifying glass and announced that we shouldn't wait for him for dinner. Tessie trampled in behind him wearing boots way too big for her feet. Mom had gone out to the chicken coop for the third time to check for eggs.

I could've just shut the door in the men's face. Let the neighbors listen to their sales pitch for once. There was this salesman with a fat album full of aerial house photos who came to our door every year. A few weeks ago, I let him into the hallway—not out of interest, but because it was raining. I didn't even look at the photo of our house. If I did, he would force me to buy it, I could feel it. But out of the corner of my eye, I could tell that, even from above, our yard was nothing more than a collection of half-finished projects. The white spot in the garden wasn't a swimming pool, it was a broken freezer. Nobody in our family even noticed it anymore, including me—except from above.

A lot of people in town had these photos hanging in their entrance hall, usually for the same reason that people kept Red Cross stickers on their windshield for years to ward off vendors at stoplights. Only Laurens's family had their aerial photo framed and proudly displayed over the meat counter. Laurens's dad believed that the bird's eye view of his business instilled trust. They had nothing to hide.

"Unfortunately, we can't sell you a picture of someone else's property," the man replied when I asked him how much the photo of Pim's farm would cost. Then he stomped out of the house and tore our house photos to shreds. Right before he crossed the busy road, he ran back to pick up a little scrap he'd dropped. As if I were someone who might be able to do something with it.

This time it was the whiteboard in the stocky one's hands that compelled me to let them in, mainly because I wanted to know what he was planning to draw and whether he was the one named Rob.

"My mom's out back," I said, "but she'll be in any minute." It sounded like a lie. And it was, but it wasn't my lie.

We had five chickens. Everybody knew that Mom knew that

chickens only lay one egg every twenty-four hours, and early in the morning. Still, she went out to check on them several times a day, and every time she came back with a fresh egg in her hand. She must have a pack of store-bought eggs hidden out there somewhere, next to her box of wine.

I opened the door a little wider. The men squeezed in sideways between the wall and the sideboard, bringing the cold in with them. They pulled their pant legs forward so the pleats wouldn't get caught on anything.

We stood in the middle of the veranda, patiently waiting for my mom. It wasn't really a veranda. It was just a room my dad called a veranda because my mom always wanted one.

Big Head, presumably Rob, set up the whiteboard.

From where we were standing, we had a perfect view of the path leading from the back door to the garden. Nobody installed the path, it had just been trampled into the grass over time, the shortest line between two points. Our yard extended back about a hundred meters and had the same clumsy shape as Belgium, but with four bulges instead of three. In each bulge was a different kind of fruit tree, each one planted when one of us was born. They were all about two meters tall now. The fourth bulge didn't have a tree, but it did have a bush with berries on it.

Pretty soon, Mom would show up with an egg. I pointed to the door of the chicken coop, an asphalt-plate house of cards where we used to store our bikes until the weasels and foxes became a bigger threat than bicycle thieves.

Instead of Mom, it was Tessie who appeared at the end of my index finger. Lost in thought, she walked to the back door, stopped and turned her profile in our direction. She pushed down the handle without opening the door, and then proceeded to repeat this motion several times.

Suddenly, she spit on the handle, rubbed it dry with her sleeve and started to sing. I could just make out a few of the words through the window. It was a summary of everything she'd done that day.

Big Head cleared his throat nervously.

At that, Tessie turned around. She froze at the sight of the two men in suits standing next to me in front of the window. She ran away to the farthest corner of the garden, towards the rabbit pen.

All of a sudden, I remembered a day when something similar had happened, when I went to take a couple of dripping teabags out to the compost pile and noticed the back door handle jiggling up and down, but no one came inside. I jumped to open the door, only to find it unlocked. On the other side was Tessie, gathering spit.

"Can I get anyone a glass of water?" I asked in an attempt to distract the men from Tessie's strange behavior. They followed me into the kitchen.

I blew the dog hairs out of two empty glasses and filled them with tap water. They wouldn't drink it, but it would give them something to do with their hands. Steven examined the water's quality. The shorter one glanced at the pile of shoes next to the door.

Maybe that's why I let them in—so I could see the disapproval on their faces, the confirmation that there was something fundamentally wrong with us. Men in suits always gave the impression that they had the power to change things, that they had been sent by some higher authority. The whiteboard, the aerial photographs, they were just the necessary props.

"How many people live here?" Big Head asked, though it was a question I would have expected from Steven, who, given his height, was probably more used to being in charge.

"Five," I replied.

"Do you have other brothers or sisters?"

"Yeah, I have a brother."

"How old are you guys?"

"Fourteen, eleven and eight."

The man nodded. It seemed like he wanted to write it down but was too polite to pull the little notebook out of his pocket.

"What are you selling, by the way?" I asked.

The room got quiet. The two men looked at each other.

"Are you sure your mother's home?" the Steven-looking one asked.

I nodded.

Until the age of nine, I believed there was a hatch in the back-yard where Mom kept her second family. I wondered what she said when she left that other family to come back to us, if she told them she was going to check on the eggs too. Would she tell them bad stuff about our family? Did she try harder with them? Did she dread coming back to us?

The back door opened. All three of us looked up. Tessie had finally come inside. She placed her boots neatly under the radiator. At first the right one was on the left, but she quickly noticed and corrected it immediately.

"Catch any rare bugs?" I asked.

"Jolan wouldn't let me get close, the sound of my boots was scaring them away," she said.

"Where's Mom?"

"She's coming," Tessie replied.

"What time is it, by the way?" Little Head asked Big Head.

"Quarter past four." I nodded at the digital clock on the micro-wave right in front of him.

"It's four-fourteen," Big Head said. He held up his shiny watch in front of Steven's face. I could tell by the way he let his sleeve fall down over the hands of the watch that they weren't here to help us. All door-to-door salesmen wore watches—the clock was always ticking, time was money.

Mom walked in at four-sixteen, her hair full of cleavers.

"Hello, madam, can we ask you a few questions?"

Big Head reached out his hand. Mom tried to shake it, but an egg slipped out from under her arm and splattered on the floor. Egg white went all over the place, but the yolk remained intact, landing a few inches away from the shell and slime. We all just stared at it, an orange dot on the black tiles.

"Leave it," Mom said when I jumped to clean it up. Tessie tried to fish the cleavers out of her hair, but Mom swatted her hand away.

"Why don't you girls go play," said Little Head.

We only obeyed because we didn't know him and retreated into the hall. But being told to "go play" was like that beautiful drop of the egg, it couldn't be executed on command.

We listened to their voices. Their shapes were distorted in the textured glass in the veranda door, but we could still make out their strange proportions. The little one pulled the whiteboard closer while the big one began his pitch, making all kinds of drawings as he talked. Whenever door-to-door salesmen work in pairs—even nowadays—there's always one who speaks firmly while the other nods his head and occasionally repeats things in a gentler tone.

No cars passed by outside. I gathered up my courage and asked Tessie what she was doing when she came in.

"That's between me and the back door," she said.

After fifteen minutes, the shadows behind the glass packed up the whiteboard. It got quiet. The door opened and Big Head stepped out into the hallway first. One after the other, they squeezed past the sideboard full of junk.

"I always remember how I got myself in, that way I'll know how to get myself out," Steven said with a wink. He forgot to pull back the legs of his pants this time, but the nails sticking out didn't get caught on his shiny tailored suit.

"What did you guys come here to sell anyway?" I asked.

"Air."

I could tell by the way they walked away that Mom had promised to buy something just to get rid of them.

Me and Tessie stood in the doorway and watched them stop in front of the next house, wipe the board with a handkerchief, punch each other in the shoulder and walk up to the door. We watched until the need to switch the heads from their bodies, just for good measure, disappeared. Tessie let the heavy front door slam into the lock. No help was ever sent.

11:15 a.m.

I TIPTOE THROUGH the empty house, inspecting the rooms one by one as I used to do on mornings when I woke up early—the first cop to show up at a crime scene.

I pass through the hallway full of shoes, the kitchen, the veranda.

Nobody. My parents are probably still in bed, which comes as no surprise. You have to have something to get up for in the morning. Clearly, they weren't invited to Jan's posthumous party, otherwise the invitation would be tacked up on the bulletin board like a trophy.

Scattered on the side tables are the remains of any given evening: an empty bag of peanuts, opened beer bottles, a box of wine under a kitchen towel on the windowsill.

The hallway in the middle of the house is dark. The only way for light to enter is through the front door, but the winter rays are too weak to penetrate the dirty window. I feel around for the light switch, the entrance to the basement, the handle on the bathroom door.

I knock on the wood panels with my knuckles. No answer. I count to three before opening the door.

I try to imagine, just like I used to, the worst thing I could possibly find, so whatever I actually do find won't seem as bad. My mom doubled over on a chair, empty pill strips on the floor around her, an empty can of disinfectant, a half-drunk bottle of nail-polish remover, her head between her knees, foam on her lips, blood dripping from her nose, the effervescent tablets she greedily tried to swallow still fizzing in her open mouth. My dad lying in cold bathwater, a thin layer of coagulated blood on the surface like a pot of old black tea, his crotch a desert island sticking out of the water, brown and filthy. Beside him, on the edge of the tub, the manicure set. His forearm torn open down to his wrist, the scissors stabbed straight into the artery.

On the count of three, I push open the door. The tub is empty. The bathroom is deserted. The bottle of nail-polish remover is right there at eye level on the shelf next to the nail polish. My father's shirt is hanging on the back of the chair shrugging its shoulders. On the white wall above it is a giant black mildew stain that Jolan once said was the shape of the European Union. Both the Union and the stain have expanded since then.

I push the door open further. It bounces back.

This could be my dad too, behind the door, in the corner of the bathroom, dangling from the sash of his bathrobe. Heart pounding, I peek around the door. The obstruction turns out to be a bunch of unwashed pajamas and bathrobes divided over two coat racks. The smell of sleep hangs over the entire ground floor, except in the spots where the stench of old, wet dog has seeped into the fabric.

The more I made these rounds around my own house, the more I felt at home at other people's. Laurens's butcher shop was full of sharp knives, intestines and dead bodies hanging from the ceiling, but at least there I didn't have to walk around in fear. Even if something bad were to happen there, it wouldn't be my fault because it wouldn't have been my job to prevent it.

The fact that my parents aren't up yet is probably best for all of us. Now that I survey everything that hasn't changed, each piece of furniture, I realize I've got nothing to say to them, nothing to forgive.

I walk over to the window and roll up the aluminum shutters. There are little perforations between the slats that oblige the faint winter light to dance around the bathroom, on the laundry basket, on the sloppy brick wall with two toothbrushes standing like soldiers in the holes, on the towel cabinet in the corner of the room.

In my earliest memory of my mother, I'm lying on this

cabinet. I was sick, and she launched a "poop rocket" up my butt. She laid her cold hand on my backside to block the light from entering my butthole so the bullet-shaped suppository wouldn't find its way out.

For a long time, we all used the cabinet to display the contents of our toiletry bags. Stuff that didn't fit in the drawers anymore that we didn't want anybody else to use. Even as a kid, the sight of all those bags gave me a gloomy feeling: everyone had their own bar of soap, their own toothpaste, their own toothbrush. As if we were all slowly packing to leave, each of us dreaming of a different destination.

I need to hear Tessie's voice. One hand fishes my phone out of my pocket, the other puts it back.

I open the drawer that used to be mine. Inside is a shoebox full of stuff I wanted to keep forever. A plastic container containing years-old lemon juice I used to rub on my face every night to prevent pimples. Two folded notes from Elisa I would read over and over again at night: "Kisses, Elisa" and "HAHAHA", both replies to notes I'd passed to her. I saved them because she so rarely laughed at my jokes in real life. A piece of straw from Pim's hayloft. A couple of screws from Laurens's bike rack. A pile of bras with big and small cups that I used to wear one on top of the other. A Chance card: GO DIRECTLY TO JAIL. DO NOT PASS GO, DO NOT COLLECT 4,000 FRANCS.

Behind the shoebox I find a pair of crumpled, unwashed pajamas that have retained the shape of my former body. A splotch of cereal is caked on the collar. I don't dare to touch them; I'm afraid I'll wake up something. Whatever I wake up, I won't be able to leave behind.

I head to the back of the house, to the kitchen. There, I sit down at the glass table overlooking the garden, which is now covered in a blanket of snow. The house is still freezing even though the heating's on.

I fill a glass with water to wash out my mouth and then take a few sips. I have to stay for few minutes at least, so my parents can't say I came to town without stopping by. Now it's up to them to wake up.

On the blue wall above the table are two drawings of the house and garden. The one on the right is mine; the one on the left is Tessie's. The day we made these drawings started out sunny. I had received a big box of colored pencils for my birthday and finally caved in and told Tessie she could draw with me. We dragged the patio table out to a shady spot in the back of the yard, where we had a good view of the entire house. I flipped open the brand-new box, put two pencils—tent poles—in the corners to hold up the lid, and set to work. I held up my ruler to the roof and the doghouse and did my best to capture the right proportions. I pressed down hard on the pencils to bring out every detail. Tessie wanted to use all the same colors I did; she snatched up every pencil I set down but wasn't finished with yet and carefully sharpened the dull tips to perfection. In an effort to preserve as much of the pencils as possible, she barely pressed down on the paper. Her sky looked like a veil; her roof was far from watertight. Only after we were all done and our drawings were lying side by side on the table did I notice how different they were. In her picture, the electric wires, the birds, the flowerpots next to the front door, the door handle and the dog were all missing—not because she hadn't noticed them but because she hadn't had time to work them in. She didn't mind though. All she'd wanted was to be with me.

When we showed the drawings to our parents, Dad didn't try very hard to hide the fact that mine was better. The only reason Tessie's picture ended up on the wall next to mine was because Mom had handed him eight thumbtacks instead of four.

From then on, the drawings hung over our heads at every meal, and every time I looked up at them, I wished I hadn't tried so hard.

July 17, 2002

IT'S NOT THE song that kicked off the carnival last weekend that's running through my head but the riddle I have to deliver to Laurens and Pim. They made such a big deal about it that now I'm afraid I'm going to forget it, and without a riddle they won't let me into the barn.

Most of the time I don't have any trouble remembering a joke or riddle, as long as I can remember the face of the person who told it to me, their tone, the rhythm of the sentences and pauses used to build up suspense, how their tongue moved in their mouth, whether they'd just drunk milk and still had white threads of saliva on their lips.

The riddle came to me yesterday—no face, no voice, no emphatic pauses or milk threads. That's what worries me now. A riddle's weakest point is its origin. Who knows, maybe Pim or Laurens told it to me once, maybe I read it in a book. Once a riddle has been published in the local paper, it can't be used again for years.

I bike through town at lightning speed. In the pocket of my faded jeans are the four fifty-euro bills. It's the first time I've ever had so much money in my pocket, and the first time I've ever been late. My delay has nothing to do with the two hundred euros, but if Pim or Laurens asks, I'll say I forgot the money and had to turn back halfway. I actually do have a valid excuse, but it's useless because I can't tell anyone: Tessie spent over an hour in the shower this afternoon. Probably because she kept making mistakes—didn't step in right over left, didn't rub in the shampoo the right way. In the end, she must've had to scrub herself ten times before she got it right, because when she finally came out the skin on her neck and arms was bright red. Of course, I shouldn't have waited until the bathroom was empty to brush my teeth, but I wanted to make sure she got clean.

Laurens's mother looks up in surprise as I lock my bike in the butcher shop parking lot. I haven't been here in a while.

She smiles over a customer's shoulder and points to the side of the house. I don't have to enter through the shop. I'm still allowed to use the side door.

She almost always smiles when she sees me. Not the quick, grateful smile she flashes Pim or the priest and other customers for hanging out with her son or consuming her meat. No, her smile forms more slowly for me; it's more rigid and a little bit sad and wrinkles her face, as if her lips weren't really made for it.

I know why she does it, what I did to deserve this special grimace.

She told me herself, confessed it really, at Laurens's tenth birthday party. We were too old for a bouncy castle, but I think she wanted to see us little one last time. She rented the biggest inflatable palace they had.

I was sitting off to the side taking a break and watching Pim do perfect back flips. Laurens's mom came up beside me.

"You okay?" she asked. I just said "yeah" because I didn't know what she was getting at.

"You want to jump with us?" I asked her.

"Oh, I can't do that," she said. "Have you seen the size of me?"

"Yes," I said.

For a moment she looked at me insulted.

"I'm no good either," I said, "I've got elephant feet." I pressed my finger over one of the tiny holes in one of the seams to stop the air from leaking out.

"You don't have elephant feet," she said.

I shrugged.

She plopped down beside me, her butt sinking halfway down into the slowly deflating castle. I slid into her and ended up with my arm pressed against her right side. She didn't squirm or try to push me off her or anything.

Then she just started talking.

"You know, Eva, when you and Laurens were still in kindergarten, your Mom and I used to chat outside the school. One time, I was watching her pedal away, and all of a sudden, she just fell over, bike and all. You guys were little. Tessie was in the front, buckled into the child seat on the handlebars, legs forward. She was fine. But you were sitting on the saddlebags with your legs hanging on either side."

Every time Laurens and Pim landed a flip, we bounced up a bit and gently knocked into each other.

"I went over to help her, but she pushed me away. She was upset and told me to mind my own business. Jolan had been riding out in front on his BMX bike. He helped get your mom and her bike upright again. Tessie was crying, and he calmed her down. But you, Eva, you didn't make a peep. You just sat there, clinging to the seat."

Laurens's mom pursed her lips, like she did when she sniffed her salads to make sure they were still fresh. Next to us, Laurens broke into an overconfident run. She waited a few seconds until he had safely landed.

"I'll tell you, Eva, I couldn't eat a bite that night. I just kept seeing Jolan helping your mom and her bike disappearing into the distance with your little legs dangling on either side of the saddle-bags. Your right foot was twisted at a weird angle."

She looked at me and for the first time gave me that smile, loving but filled with regret. She took my right ankle between her hands and petted my leg, longer than necessary, like I sometimes did to street cats, with firm strokes, hoping to charge them up with happiness so they would go on purring for hours after I was gone.

"These things happen," I said. And I meant it. It was good Mom fell off her bike that day because it got me this: the smile she didn't give to anybody else, that came from far away.

Laurens shot us a quizzical look but didn't interrupt. As long as his mom was sitting there, the castle had more air in it, which meant that there were still more somersaults to be made.

I don't think Laurens's mom knows what happened between me and her son three weeks ago on our last day of school. Maybe she didn't ask any questions when Laurens came home with the scratch on his face, maybe he didn't dare to tell her what really happened.

I walk along the window display, open the gate on the side of the building, and pass by the door to the back of the shop. That's Laurens's dad's domain. We were never allowed to go in there. Laurens's mom always said there were knives so sharp in there that we could cut our eyes just looking at them. We knew this was unlikely, but still we never looked in for more than a few seconds.

I head into the courtyard. Under the awning are doors leading to various places: one to the old kitchen, one to the workshop, one to the giant walk-in freezer they installed during the first renovation.

The last time we played hide-and-seek, Pim hid in the walk-in freezer while I was counting to a hundred. The door locked behind him. It took a while before I dared to look for him among all the hanging carcasses. I found him balled up in a corner, lips blue, face pale. For the rest of the day, he smelled like death.

Behind the courtyard is a long narrow backyard with a wooden swing set and an old shed where they used to boil the hams and dry the salamis. It also contained a machine for vacuum-packing meat, which is why we called it the vacuum shed. Nobody ever goes in there anymore, but for some reason it's where we're meeting today.

The door's already open. Laurens is sitting on a chair behind a desk with only three legs—it must be leaning on something I can't see in the dark. The barn is full of cast-off furniture. A family from Kosovo could live in it, no problem. There are old bookshelves, a recliner with an old pair of reading glasses on top, a washstand, an old TV and a discarded heat blower. It's really hot inside. Hanging above Laurens's head is a strand of dark red, speckled sausages. They'd almost look festive if they weren't made of meat.

"Is Pim here yet?" I ask.

"What does it look like?" Laurens eyes dart emphatically around the empty room. To his left is a dark imprint on the floor where the oven used to be.

I don't dare to ask any more questions. I plop down on a wheelie office chair and roll myself around the room.

Laurens nervously opens and closes a desk drawer. I can't blame him for not talking. I don't have anything to say either. We keep a close eye on the door.

Pim hasn't been here in a while. Maybe Laurens isn't sure if he's really coming, if he still knows how to get here.

"So," I say. "What's the plan?"

Laurens looks at the door again and sighs.

"Pim's not coming alone. He's bringing a girl. You're going to recite your riddle, and she'll try to solve it. And if she can't, then . . ." He raises his eyebrows three times in sharp arches.

"Then we'll make sausages out of her?" I ask, my eyes fixed on a drum of flour. But Laurens looks dead serious.

"You've got some imagination, you know that?" he says, trying to sound as offended as possible.

Outside, the gate clatters. Laurens jumps to his feet. Pim walks in. Behind him is a girl I immediately recognize: Buffalo Ann.

There are two Anns in Bovenmeer. One of them lives next door to me—she used to be our babysitter. The other Ann, the one standing in front of me, owes her nickname to the fact that she once showed up to track practice wearing Buffalo platform sneakers, thinking the heavy soles would make her legs move faster. Before the starting gun was even fired, she'd twisted both her ankles in all the pushing and shoving before the race. But that didn't stop her from wearing those shoes. She wore them all the time.

Ann is a year younger than we are, but she tries to make up for it with the way she dresses. In addition to her Buffalos, she's wearing a short black skirt, a yellow top, and a plastic tattoo necklace around her neck that reminds me of those nets they sell lemons in. The black-and-yellow color scheme is no coincidence; her dad is the president of the Lier soccer fan club.

She moves swiftly through the shed over to Laurens and doesn't leave his side. She used to have a crush on Pim until it became clear that he was out of her league, so she set her sights on Laurens instead.

"Friends," Pim says ceremoniously. He steps up onto a can of breadcrumbs so he's a head taller than the rest of us. Laurens glances at the lid sagging under Pim's weight but doesn't say anything.

"I already explained the rules to Ann on the way here, didn't I, Ann?"

She nods enthusiastically.

"Can you repeat them for us, please?" he asks.

"There's a riddle. And a chance to win two hundred euros. I can guess as many times as I want, but each guess costs an item of clothing." Ann pulls three pieces of chewing gum out of her pocket and grinds them down with her front teeth. I watch the white chunk morph into a different shape with every time she opens her mouth.

"Any questions?" Laurens asks.

"No," she smacks.

"All right, Eva, over to you," Pim says. "Let's hear the riddle. Ann will start guessing. If she's right, nod your head yes; if she's wrong, shake your head no."

"Did you hear that, Ann?" Laurens chimes in. "Eva is the only one here who knows the answer."

I clear my throat and recite the riddle without looking at the boys. While I'm speaking, Ann pushes the gum between her front teeth with her tongue and lets it sit there, like putty between her upper and lower jaw.

"How am I supposed to know what happened to the guy?" she blurts out, letting the gum go.

"That's why they call it a riddle," Laurens says. "Start asking yes or no questions, so you can figure it out." The look on his face suggests that he has no idea where to start either.

"Okay, okay, give me a second to think." She tugs at her plastic choker, loosening it up so that it's even more obvious that it's not a real tattoo.

It's so quiet that we can hear the bell over the shop door in the distance. I try to imagine how the sound reached us all the way from the front of the house, what it had to hit and dodge along the way.

"You want me to tell another riddle?"

Pim motions for me to shut up.

"Did he wet his pants? Is that how the water got there?" Ann tries.

Pim and Laurens look at me. This is what they would have guessed too. I let the suspense build up for a second, then shake my head.

"No, he didn't wet his pants."

Ann lets out a deep sigh and pulls the choker over her head.

"That thing doesn't count," Pim says immediately. "It's not an item of clothing."

Without protest, Ann pulls her underwear down under her tight miniskirt. It's a thong. She folds it into a square and stuffs it into her pocket. Maybe she's thinking about leaving it at that. Whether she starts with her underwear or not, she's only got four guesses. But apparently she's not worried.

"Was there a chair or a ladder in the room?"

"That was already given in the riddle," I reply. "I said the room was empty."

Ann's already reaching for the bottom of her yellow top. Arms crossed, she lifts up the lower edge, revealing a pale belly and sports bra. She tosses the shirt on the ground.

"You can stop, you know," I say.

Ann chews her gum at full speed.

"Did he fall through the ceiling?" she blurts out in the hope that it might only count for half a piece of clothing. She's looking only at Pim. This isn't about winning two hundred euros.

I shake my head.

Ann reaches behind her back and unfastens her bra. She slides down the straps, and it lands on the floor next to her top. She has small, average breasts. Exactly what you'd expect from her.

Laurens and Pim look at her without flinching—as if they can't believe someone's actually going along with this. They stare at her belly button. Laurens doesn't know what to do with his hands. He wants to shove them into his pockets, but he doesn't have any, so he sticks them under the edges of his pants.

Standing there under the sausage bunting, with only two Buffalos and a short skirt left, Ann becomes awkward and vulnerable, like a newborn calf with oversized hooves. Pim takes a step closer.

"You've got one shot left," he says. "Shoes count for one guess."

Suddenly, Ann's embarrassed. She covers her upper body with her arm. The thought of taking off her shoes suddenly makes her feel naked.

"I'll stop," she says.

"Okay, shoes count for two then," says Laurens.

"No." Ann bends over and wraps her arms around her knees. She scoops up her clothes. There's nothing sadder than a pile of recently removed clothing on the floor. She wrenches her T-shirt back on.

"Too bad," says Pim.

Ann takes the thong out of her pocket, unfolds it and holds it up to see which side is the front. She pushes her feet through the holes. One of the platform sneakers gets caught on the fabric and she stumbles. Laurens catches her.

No one says a word.

I don't know what else to say except sorry, but I can't say that because I'm one of the guys.

As she's walking out of the courtyard, Pim and Laurens high-five.

"Not bad for a five-pointer," Pim says.

"But she's definitely not a six," Laurens says. He looks at his watch. "So far our system is spot on."

"So we'll leave it on the cemetery wall as-is. Buffalo Ann, five out of ten." Pim nods.

I sit back down in the chair and roll myself over to them. Only then do they notice I'm still here.

"You came up with the best riddle ever," Pim says.

"So, what did you think?" Laurens asks me. "You can talk now, by the way."

I shrug and check to make sure I still have the money. I pull it out and pass it to them.

"No, you hold onto it," Laurens says. "It's for you. Not really for you, but for the bank. You're the secretary."

"Why am I the secretary?"

"We need one for sampling purposes." Pim steps back up onto the can of breadcrumbs. "You should know that. All these years we've been making rough estimates. Now we're making sure we haven't been wrong all along. A sampling only counts when it's done properly." At the word "sampling", he licks his finger, forms a circle with his thumb and forefinger and punches the wet finger through the hole.

Laurens forces a loud laugh but stops when he sees the worried look on my face. "We need you. Without a bank, no one will play. It's like the lottery—it's not valid without an official." He reaches up and grabs one of the sausages, yanks it off the line and snaps it in half. A clot of coagulated fat lands on his chin.

Conscience

IN FOURTH GRADE, I gave my conscience a name and a face. Miss Emma was left-handed and wore her hair in a bun that, even after looking at it for a really long time, you still couldn't figure out how it stayed so firmly in place. On her forehead were three parallel wrinkles. She reminded me of a picture from the Miffy memory game we played at home sometimes—not a lot of lines were needed to draw her.

Miss Emma wasn't married. In addition to teaching at the primary school, she volunteered at the White and Yellow Cross and gave first-aid courses to local clubs. Students could go to her with their more embarrassing problems: girls who got their chin or boys who got their foreskin stuck in a zipper. She had small, soft hands and could provide resuscitation if necessary.

In third grade—when we were all in our Roald Dahl phase—I noticed that the tip of Miss Emma's right pinky was missing. She saw me staring at it. "Oh, I've tried watching it grow back," she said, "but so far it hasn't helped."

It was her "so far" that left just enough room for hope. During the afternoon recess, while the rest of the class was whizzpopping, conjuring Snozzcumbers out of lunchboxes, and slurping Frobscottle through a straw, I watched Miss Emma monitoring the playground. I narrowed my eyes like Matilda and tried to make her little finger grow back. After a while, I stopped, mostly because I started to doubt what I was trying to achieve. Did I want to fix her finger so she would adopt me? That would be sad for my parents, I thought. They weren't nearly as bad as the ones in the book—they at least had better intentions. They weren't crooks.

How exactly Miss Emma became my conscience the next year, I don't know. I only know when it happened: it was on a Thursday afternoon during arts and crafts. Usually, she only taught sixth-graders, but that day some of the teachers got shifted around, and she ended up in charge of our class for a few hours.

She gave me, Laurens and Pim the same assignment she gave everyone else. There was a storybook cassette playing in the background, but we never got past the first side of the tape because arts and crafts only lasted forty minutes. After recess, we still had to do an hour of religion. Miss Emma walked around the classroom while we were working. She stood behind my chair the longest.

As far as I could tell, there wasn't anything about what I was making to be worried about. The assignment didn't leave much room for it: our task was to color the inside of a plastic folder with markers, sprinkle it with salt and let it absorb the ink. Then we carefully drained the colored crystals into a glass jar, layer by layer. It was the kind of craft that didn't require any specific talent, just two hands, patience and a mom that was easily satisfied.

Pim kept things easy for himself. He brought in one of those tiny capers jars from home. He finished quickly, and the teacher said he could help others. Laurens showed up with a giant pickle jar. The sweet and sour gherkins label hadn't been peeled off completely. He made sloppy work of it—after all, he only had forty minutes to color an entire kilo of salt. After two hundred grams, his markers were all dried out, so he confiscated mine. He put too much salt in the folder at once and ended up with pink instead of red.

We all wanted to do a good job because at the end of the day we'd have to walk out the gate carrying our works of art, past all the parents waiting to pick up their kids. There were some kids who would make a parade of it, proudly displaying their jars in front of them. Others, like us, would toss the masterpieces into our book-bags and make a run for it.

Laurens reached forward and tried to nab Pim's jar so he could shake it until all the layers turned brown. Miss Emma didn't call Laurens out. She was still standing there, watching me. Her presence made me nervous. The plastic folder in my hands started quivering.

Right before recess, just as everyone was getting ready to bolt out at the sound of the bell, she asked me to stay behind for a moment.

The bell rang.

"Soccer time!" Pim exclaimed.

The room emptied out, the playground filled up, and left behind on every desk was a jar filled with colorful layers of salt—except in the back, where the side class sat. Three desks, three jars: one with a black lid, one jumbo gherkin jar filled halfway with light brown salt and mine—a small bottle with a short, elegant neck, filled to the top with yellow and blue layers that blended into green when they touched. I'd been happy with my work before—at least it was prettier than Laurens's big brown flop. But now, from a distance, all I could see was the shape: it was a miniature wine bottle.

A lump started rising in my throat. I swallowed hard.

"Maybe there's something you'd like to get off your chest?" Miss Emma asked. She sat down on the corner of her desk.

I couldn't tell her what I was feeling, what she wanted to hear. If the things I wanted to get off my chest had anywhere else to go, they wouldn't be weighing on me in the first place.

Twice, Miss Emma started to say something and then stopped, as if she wanted to tell me a secret but was waiting for me to tell her mine first. I picked the raisins out of my cookie and ate them one by one. I tried not to stare at her pinky and focused my gaze on the crumbs that fell between my feet. A few minutes before the bell rang, she said it was okay if I didn't want to talk about it and told me I could go play soccer.

Right before she opened the door, she held up her hand with the cut-off finger and said, "I've never told anyone how this happened."

"Do you want to tell me?" I asked.

"It will stay between us, right?"

"Of course."

Miss Emma shifted her weight on the desk, searching for a more comfortable position.

"I was born this way. My umbilical cord got twisted around some of my limbs, cutting off blood circulation to certain parts of my body. As I grew, it got tighter and left scars."

She bent down and pulled up the leg of her pants. On her lower leg was a deep impression, all the way down to the bone, a wrinkled scar, as if the leg were being constricted by an invisible rope.

On my way out to the playground, in the hall, where nobody could see, I suddenly felt nauseous. I checked my reflection in the window to see if you could tell by looking at me. I shook my shoulders and tried to walk like Laurens, then like Pim, then like other random people who I assumed never had anything they wanted to get off their chest.

I played soccer more aggressively than usual, hoping that one of the boys would knock me down, and I'd have to go back in to Miss Emma to get patched up.

This just led to more points for the other team.

At the end of the school day, something strange happened. When I left the schoolyard, Miss Emma followed me home. I saw it with my own eyes: not her entire body, just her head and neck. All the way home, her head hovered above me in the blue sky, floating in the wind, like a helium balloon attached to my wrist by a string. She was watching me from above—a power that, until then, I thought only Sinterklaas had. There was nothing gruesome about it. I hadn't decapitated her or anything, her body just wasn't there. All I needed were her eyes.

I didn't have to explain to Miss Emma where I lived, which room in the house was mine. She followed me all evening and stayed with me until I fell asleep. Her face hovered at the foot of my bed until I closed my eyes. The next morning, before I opened them, I could feel her watching me again.

Miss Emma stayed with me for weeks, months, years. I knew

she wasn't real, but she didn't let me out of her sight for a second. She could see through ceilings, walls and roofs, through steel, wood, through multiple floors. If necessary, she'd even travel a hundred kilometers with me to family gatherings in West Flanders.

I only put two restrictions on her: she wasn't allowed to look through clothes or blankets, and at school, when I was with the real Miss Emma, she couldn't be the face of my conscience at the same time.

Because of her presence, I was seldom alone. Still, I felt lonelier than ever before because I couldn't tell Laurens and Pim my big secret. Not only was I afraid they'd laugh at me, I was worried they might ask Miss Emma to watch over them too.

After a few months, things got more complicated. Laurens and Pim didn't have anyone watching over them. They seemed freer to me, less and less inhibited. I couldn't do anything without thinking about what it might look like from above. I followed myself everywhere: cycling through the streets, swimming across the Pit, sitting at a table, leaning over a book, lying in my bed: the girl with the elephant feet, always on the move.

The day Miss Emma raised her voice at me on the playground, it became even harder. When I got home, I had to make it up to her. I didn't dare to do anything that might make her angry for fear that she wouldn't want to watch over me anymore. I tried to be perfect. I helped with the dishes, I stopped bingeing on chocolate, I stopped secretly using Mom's expensive anti-wrinkle cream, I stopped farting. And just in case she could read my mind, I didn't think any bad thoughts about anyone, or fantasize about naked people. That would disgust her. On the toilet, I wiped my butt in such a way that she couldn't see, I didn't lie in bed in the morning, I didn't pick my nose, I didn't look at breasts in the women's clothing catalogues. It became harder and harder to sleep. When taking tests, I couldn't help but watch myself from above. I got bad grades on everything.

Hiding from someone who could see through walls and ceilings turned out to be nearly impossible.

In the months that followed, I looked at Miss Emma as little as possible during class. On the playground, I no longer watched her watching us, I just kept track of which kids she talked to and who she took care of. Every time I looked at her, I worried about her head following me home that afternoon, and at the same time, I dreaded the day it would suddenly disappear.

12:30 p.m.

THE SKY IS completely gray. There are no visible edges where a cloud could tear itself away and let a bit of sunlight in. Fresh snowflakes cover the birdhouse, the flowerpots, the roofs on the surrounding houses. Every car that exits the highway seems lost.

I lay my hands on the kitchen table with my fingers spread wide. There's a cat pacing back and forth on the windowsill. Meowing, she tries to wriggle herself through the closed sliding door. She stops and looks at me, concerned. Who is this person, what is she doing here, why is she sitting in my spot? I'm wondering the same thing.

In my old student house, everyone had a fixed place at the table. It's hard to say when this seating arrangement was made, who decided that my place was not at the head.

After I moved out, I rented a flat in Schaerbeek for a few months. It was the first time I'd ever lived alone. Not once did I sit at the head of the empty table.

Without a degree, I couldn't work as an architect. To fill my evenings, I signed up for figure-drawing classes at the academy.

Bodies are kind of like buildings. I went to class every week, until one day the teacher asked me why I never drew the models truthfully, naked. "This is an observational drawing course, after all," he said.

I couldn't tell him that when I got home, I pinned my sketches to the wall across from the table, and it was hard to eat with limp genitalia in your face.

After his comment, I started going to class less often, and my walls became barer. There was one drawing I left up, because the model reminded me of Tessie. The veins running through the temples, the short spiky hair, the protruding collarbones. I had drawn her exactly as I remembered Tessie, with the red wool sweater she used to wear all the time. This was the only drawing that moved with me to my current apartment. I had it framed and hung it in the bedroom.

I've been sitting here for half an hour. I haven't left the chair. When I finally do stand up, it will be to leave. But it's still too early to show up at Pim's.

I look at my phone. No emails, no messages, no missed calls. I turn on airplane mode, turn it off again, hoping it will bring something new: a message, a Facebook tag, a roundabout question from someone who needs something, even a bill or bank spam would be okay.

Nothing. I'm not surprised. Those who don't sow don't reap. I didn't give the neighbor my cell-phone number. I never responded to the last emails about the drawing class.

I send myself a message: "TEST".

My phone makes a loud beep. I immediately put it on silent. It would be stupid to wake Mom and Dad up myself. A message appears: "TESSIE". It lands in the folder under my own number. It takes me a second to figure out it was just autocorrect. Her name ends up among all the other unanswered tests.

I call her again. This time I actually let the phone ring. Three times. I hang up right before it goes to voicemail.

I'm sitting in Mom's spot at the table. She could stare blankly into the garden for hours without ever really seeing what was going on out there. People who stare would rather their eyes be turned towards the inside of their skull. This chair was the perfect spot for her to reflect on all the things that never happened: the sandbox that never arrived, the diapers that never made it onto the line, the twins she'd never walked down the Bulksteeg to school, the mother she never became.

July 18, 2002

"IT's MELISSA'S TURN today. We'd like the same riddle," Pim commands over the phone, like someone ordering a pizza.

"Which Melissa?" I ask.

"Do you know more than one?"

"You don't mean Nancy Soap's niece?"

"She's coming to the vacuum shed at two."

Nancy Soap, a widow with six dogs, runs a wet mop through the parish hall every week, but never a dry one afterwards, so the floor always has this sticky film on it, as if it were polished with lemonade. Really, her name should be "Nancy Fanta", but nobody would ever dare to call her that. You can't really question volunteer work.

After mopping the hall, Nancy doesn't have much energy left over for her own household. She lives across from the presbytery, on Kerkstraat, in a small house with steel shutters that are almost always rolled shut. The last time they were up, I tried to peek into her house, but the windows were so filthy that you couldn't see inside.

During the summer, Nancy Soap takes care of one of her nieces, Melissa, who mostly comes to pet the dogs and take them for a walk. Every time I see Melissa walking down the Bulksteeg carrying six bags of poop, I feel the urge to wash my hands.

"Okay, two o'clock, then. I'll bring a wet washcloth," I say bluntly.

Pim laughs. "Oh, that's right. It's gonna be a hot one. She won't be wearing a lot of clothes. It'll be a quick game, and if you're lucky we can go for a swim afterwards."

Before I've even hung up the phone, a thick cloud has slipped between the town and the sun. Everything looks a shade dirtier.

On the way to the butcher shop, I see Elisa riding her stallion. Her ponytail swishes around in perky figure eights behind her head. Mimi's big ugly kitchen chairs have been set up in the field for her to maneuver the horse around. I have just enough time to turn off the Bulksteeg before Elisa turns the horse around to repeat the exercise in the opposite direction.

Before Elisa was moved up to the sixth grade, she spent another three weeks trying to make contact with Pim and Laurens. The first time was on a field trip. We were on the bus. Pim and Laurens were sitting in the seat behind me and Elisa. I didn't feel like talking about Twinkle's mane and horseshoes again, so I didn't ask any questions. After a few minutes of silence, Elisa turned around to the boys and rested her chin on the back of her seat. That was exactly how she first made contact with me three and a half months earlier.

"You guys wanna know something?" she asked.

"No," Pim replied.

She continued anyway. "If you've got a pen and paper, I can tell you your fortunes."

Despite her scary eyebrows, Pim was flattered by the proposal.

"Eva, you got a pen and paper?" he asked.

I handed him a ballpoint pen and notepad over the back of my seat, which he passed back to Elisa.

"I need someone to write for me," she said and shoved the paper and pen back into my hands.

"Draw a grid with six rows and number them one to six in random order. Don't let us see it." Then she whispered in my ear—"Write 'boys' names' over the first column, 'girls' names' over the second, 'number of kids' over the third, 'honeymoon' over the fourth, 'jobs' over the fifth and 'cause of death' over the sixth."

I turned the paper away from her and did as I was told.

"Now I'm going to say six boys' names, and you write them in the first column."

Elisa named six random boys, ones we liked and ones we didn't, including Pim and Laurens.

"Okay, Pim, now give us six girls' names. They can be girls you like and girls you wouldn't be caught dead with."

Pim gave six names, including Elisa's and mine.

"No, Eva doesn't count," Elisa said. "She's the fortuneteller. She could rig things in her favor—then it wouldn't be random."

My name was replaced with Melissa Soap's.

"Now the number of children, honeymoon destinations, jobs and causes of death." Elisa held up six fingers for each category.

I filled in the grid with the information, in the given order.

"Alrighty," Elisa said when I was done, "now Eva can tell us the future. First you read all the ones, then all the twos, and so on."

She reclined her chair, so her face was even closer to Pim's.

"Laurens marries Elisa, they go to America on their honeymoon, have eighteen children, run a strip club and die in a plane crash," I read.

Elisa laughs in Laurens's face.

"Pim marries Melissa Soap, they go to Bobbejaanland on their honeymoon, have two kids, live on a houseboat, work as door-to-door salespeople and choke to death on a peppermint." This made Elisa laugh harder than I thought possible. I hoped she had bad breath.

After that, whenever they got bored on the playground, Laurens and Pim would ask her to tell their fortunes again. And every time, I had to be the fortuneteller. I didn't mind so much at first. I was proud: my random numbers determined their fate. Until one day, Elisa offered to take over the job, and Pim sprang up in protest. Only then did I understand—Elisa was the whole point of the game. Without the chance of being matched with her, there wasn't much hope for the future. Pim and Laurens kept insisting that I play the fortuneteller, not because I carried out the task dutifully and honestly, but because there was no way they wanted to get stuck having eighteen children with me.

Not long after that, Elisa was transferred to the sixth grade and the jam-fingering incident occurred. From then on, she went swimming at a different time than we did, and the future no longer needed to be predicted.

It was a loss, of course—after all those lunches with her at Mimi's, I thought I knew all her secrets. But when I saw how Pim would look in Elisa's direction every time he scored a goal at recess to see if she was watching, how she couldn't care less, I figured that her transfer was probably the best thing for all three of us musketeers.

Melissa's bike is already parked in front of the butcher shop when I arrive. I'm late because I stopped at the cemetery on the way to have a look at the names and scores on the wall. As long as we don't get a heavy rain, they should remain readable.

I head straight for the shed without waiting for Laurens's mom to point me in the right direction. She's busy mixing the meat salad. Every few hours the discolored top layer has to be scraped away.

As soon as I walk into the shed, Pim locks the door behind me.

Melissa is a six-pointer, or at least that's what was written on the wall. It's not hard to see what cost her those four points. Her scarred, pale face reminds me of my old Mickey Mouse sweater that I once tried to repair by pushing the loose threads back in with a knitting needle. Her shoulders are so wide that her armpits, once closed, form horizontal stripes. She's wearing a tight top with a glittery thread woven into it. Her breasts are small for the width of her body and way too far apart, as if they were only temporary.

I'm surprised they gave her a six. There's something wrong with their new point system. Anyone who starts with the assumption that every girl has at least ten positive features, and then subtracts the ugly ones from there, could actually end up more off than someone who starts at zero and adds a point for every asset.

"Where do you live again, Melissa?" I position myself as far away from her as possible.

Laurens's places a finger over his lips—it's four o'clock, the game has started, time for the secretary to zip it.

"Do you sleep at Nancy's too?" Pim asked. "Where do your parents live again?"

"Why do you want to know?" Melissa quips back.

"I don't. But our secretary does," Laurens replies.

"My parents have a news stand near the church in Kessel. I only come to Aunt Nancy's for the dogs." Melissa fishes a pack of cigarettes out of her pocket. She's wearing sweatpants that aren't meant to be so tight. The legs are covered in dog hair. She passes around the cigarettes. Pim takes one. She puts the pack away.

All three of us watch Pim light the cigarette. He's clearly done this before. He inhales deeply without coughing. He breathes out the smoke so that it hangs between us, forming shapeless figures. He passes the cigarette to Laurens. He inhales deeply too, then coughs, emitting three perfect smoke rings. He acts like that was exactly what he meant to do

"How much does your aunt pay you?"

"One euro per hour per dog," she says. "But I'd do it for free. They're sweet pups."

Pim cuts to the chase. "We're giving you the chance to win two hundred euros here. That's the equivalent of walking two hundred dogs for an hour. All you have to do is solve a riddle. For every wrong answer, you take off a piece of clothing. You in?"

"Okay, fine. But I'm not giving up the dogs."

"We're not asking you to. See this as a bonus."

Pim looks at me. That's my cue, time for my one and only contribution to the afternoon. I'd better make it quick, before Melissa changes her mind.

I recite the riddle slowly and clearly. I still don't remember where I got it from or if it took me a long time to figure it out myself. I didn't have to pay for guesses in clothes though—that I would remember. Maybe somebody just told me the riddle and gave me the answer for free.

"So Eva's question for you is this," Pim says. "What happened to the man? How did he end up like that?"

"He broke his neck," Melissa blurts out almost immediately.

"That would make sense," Pim says, "the guy did hang himself."
Still, he looks at me. I'm supposed to confirm this, just for good
measure.

"You could still slowly choke to death without your neck breaking," I say.

"Is she right or not, Eva?"

"It's not wrong, but it's not quite right."

"Take something off, Melissa."

Unlike Ann, Melissa starts with her shoes.

"Two shoes count for one guess," Pim adds quickly. Without
bothering to negotiate, Melissa takes off her shoes. After that, her
guesses are more or less the same as Buffalo Ann's.

"Did he wet himself?"

"Was he a swimmer?"

I shake my head without offering any further elaboration.

The sweater falls on the floor between us. Melissa starts wring-
ing her hands. The grease on her skin from petting the dogs forms
pale coiled flakes that float down to the floor, landing among the
sand and other filth.

After the third guess, she lowers her pants down to her ankles.
Melissa was Laurens's choice. Pim blinks suspiciously. This wasn't at
all what he'd hoped to see.

I understand why they're doing the lowest-scoring girls first. We
weren't raised like our parents were with the they-can't-take-what's-
already-yours mentality. We're saving the best for last, which means
we've got to stomach the worst of it first, because everything tastes
better when you're hungry. That said, there are some things you just
don't want to eat, even when you're starving.

Was he hoping that Melissa would have some kind of hidden
beauty? That she'd be one of those girls that gets prettier the closer
you look?

Laurens has been staring at her bare thighs for a while now, but
the look on his face doesn't seem any more excited. I don't feel
sorry for anybody, not even for the pile of clothes on the floor
between us. We could've just gone swimming.

"Laurens?" a voice calls from the garden. It's his dad.

There's a knock on the shed door. A shadow appears behind the blinds. Melissa scrambles back into her clothes.

Pim puts out the cigarette. Laurens snatches her sweater off the ground and waves it around, but the smoke doesn't go anywhere.

Only after Melissa has her T-shirt back on does he open the door a crack. His dad walks in. He's wearing a white apron caked in dried blood and a hairnet on his head. He looks at us one by one.

Laurens's dad is the spitting image of what Laurens will look like later on in life.

"What are you guys up to?"

"Nothing."

"Have you been smoking?"

"No," Pim says.

"I think it's time for your friends to go home," Laurens's dad says in his usual polite way.

Laurens nods apologetically in our direction.

When he tries to slip out of the shed behind us, his dad grabs him by the earlobe. None of us says a word. We don't even dare to look at each other. Melissa's sweater is on inside out.

Right before leaving the courtyard, I turn around. Laurens's dad is still holding his son by the ear, dragging him through the yard, probably to his mother.

Ears are more firmly attached to the head than you might think.

Camping

I KNEW BEFORE the summer was even over that these months would stay with me for a long time. There was more sunlight on everything we did, allowing the memories to develop more sharply.

In '98, there was a new trend in town—especially popular among the older boys—of camping out in each other's backyards and sneaking out to commit minor acts of vandalism in the night. Stuff like knocking letters off of gravestones to make dirty words, graffitiing the sidewalks, covering people's stoops and facades with chalk, pissing in free-standing mailboxes, getting the school nuns all riled up.

Laurens's parents wouldn't let him camp out at anybody's house.

"Our Laurens snores. He'll keep you up all night," his mom said when we first came to her with the idea.

In her opinion, her son already spent enough time with us between the hours of two and five. As long as there wasn't a blizzard or a war, Laurens had to be home well before dark.

"Don't worry, we're not going to pee in any mailboxes," Pim pressed.

"If your parents are okay with this whole camping thing, then you two are more than welcome to set up a tent in our backyard," she replied.

Of course, she didn't get it. If she said no to something her son wanted, Pim's parents would say no too. Musketeers are only as adventurous as their weakest link.

We spent the longest, hottest summer afternoon of '98 brainstorming how to get Laurens's parents to let us go camping. Pim didn't have to help out on the farm, and Laurens was relieved of his duties in the shop because the weatherman, Frank Deboosere, had warned of a heightened risk of dehydration. We sat on Laurens's swing set in the shade of the neighbor's big oak trees.

From the top of the swing set, Pim threw pebbles at a pigeon that was trying to steal our shade. Laurens picked his nose, fished out a few boogers and wiped them on the trapeze ropes while swinging back and forth. I sat cross-legged in the grass, occasionally taking a sip from the two-liter bottle of water that Laurens's mom had insisted we drink empty.

Laurens was in charge. They were, after all, his parents.

"We can't ask three times. That'll make them mad, I can already feel it." Every time he shoved his index finger up his nose, his voice sounded nasal.

After a lot of discussion, I was sent in to try and convince Laurens's mom "woman to woman". In all our deliberations, it never became clear to me what women would actually say in such situations.

The shop was closed from twelve to two, but it was open again now. There were no customers inside. According to Laurens, nobody ever came in until six or so, until you'd just started running a bucket of water to soak the knives, tongs and spoons. Filling the bucket around three o'clock so people might come earlier didn't work, he said.

Laurens's mom was standing with her back to the lowered window shades, sideways to me. Her swollen belly swallowed up half the counter she was working at. She carried out quick, routine movements. She arranged the green, oval-shaped papers between chunks of freshly chopped meat, which she then pushed into a machine with a big handle and started cranking. She arranged the freshly ground lumps into two stacks on black plastic trays. There was still an entire bowl of meatballs waiting on the counter; a bunch of hamburgers had already been made.

I repeated one of Pim's arguments from our brainstorming session. My voice sounded shakier than I would've liked.

"Camping out with friends is a basic right that no child should be denied."

Without stopping the grinder, Laurens's mom looked me straight in the eyes. She was at least impressed.

"What is so interesting that you can't do it during the daytime?" she asked. "You're going to have to explain that one to me, Eva."

The longer she looked at me, the bigger the lump in my throat got. After a while she stopped the routine motions. All the meat had been run through the machine. But the two piles of ground beef weren't the same height. It looked funny. Apparently, she didn't like it either. She took some meat off one pile and transferred it to the other, but that just shifted the problem.

"Have you ever made hamburger patties before?" Her voice sounded less severe than her face suggested.

She made room for me at the counter. I stood between her and the meat grinder, shaping the balls of fresh meat she handed to me into perfect oval hamburgers. I kept going until I thought she wasn't mad at me anymore. We barely said a word as we carried out the task, but we understood each other again.

I made forty-three hamburgers. Laurens's mom arranged them on the tray. Sometimes I heard her apron rubbing against me, and I'd lean back ever so slightly so I could feel her giant body through the fabric. Within fifteen minutes, we'd worked our way through the second load of ground beef, but the stacks were still uneven. Laurens's mother sighed, peeled a patty off the top and tossed it in the trash. Then she placed the tray in the display case and wiped the counter with a damp rag. All of a sudden, she stopped, looked at me, and said, "You know Eva, if there's ever anything going on at home, you're welcome here, day and night. Tessie too. But camping? Laurens's father comes from a strict Catholic family. He's not going to like the idea of two boys and a girl sharing a tent. And I can't stand the thought of Laurens and Pim camping without you. That just wouldn't be right."

She walked over to the sign on the front door and checked to make sure the "Closed" side was facing out. It'd been hanging the right way all along. She opened the door wide.

"It's still too hot to even think about barbecuing," I said. "People won't come until after they've had their siesta."

That made her smile.

I washed my hands in the back room and headed out to the swing set. Laurens and Pim were exactly where I'd left them, only the pigeon had disappeared. Their enthusiastic gestures were a clear indication that they'd already started making plans for the camping trip they assumed was now on.

I made sure they saw me shaking my head from afar, that their disappointment would have already subsided by the time I reached the swing set. That way they wouldn't ask too many questions and figure out that camping without me could have been an option.

While I was still a few meters away from them, I threw my empty hands in the air—that's what I'd seen soccer players do when they wanted to deny having done anything wrong and avoid getting a yellow card. I had a right to keep Laurens's mom's words to myself. I kept shaking my head until I was standing right in front of them.

"Stop shaking your head. We get it, she said no," Laurens said.

"What did she say exactly?" Pim asked.

"Not much," I replied.

"I told you guys," Laurens sighed.

"If she didn't have much to say, then what took you so long?" Pim picked up a pebble and threw it with a slight curve so that it whizzed right over my head.

"She put you to work, didn't she? What did you have to do— make patties or split eggs?" Laurens asked.

I shrugged.

"We're all going to go home and pack a knapsack," declares Pim. "In a half-hour, we'll meet at the church. From there, we'll head to the Pit."

"Fine with me. Who's bringing the gas burner and who's bring- ing the food?" asks Laurens.

"You bring the food. Eva brings the burner," Pim delegated. The way he said it, it sounded binding, full of promise.

We nodded.

"And if they come looking for us, we won't give away our position. Even if they start combing the woods with dogs. Do we need anything besides the burner and food?"

"Knives, rope and a tarp," I said. "And a shovel."

"A shovel?" Laurens asks.

"We have to make camp, don't we?" I say. "And dig a hole for our you-know-what."

"Anybody got a tent?" Laurens asks.

"You do. What else would you sleep in when you go camping in the South of France?" Pim asks.

"No way we're using ours."

We had a tent at home too. Actually it was Jolan's. But now that there was a rip in it, it belonged to everybody. A ripped tent was better than no tent. But I didn't mention it. Offering up our tent would mean falling out of favor with Laurens's mom. That would be a dumb trade-off.

Nobody said a word.

"No tent then. That's real camping," Pim declared. The plan was already sounding less promising.

By five o'clock Laurens had listed all the delicious one-pan meals we could make over a gas burner, but it still wasn't clear who was bringing the tarp and who was bringing the shovel. We started getting hungry.

"Should we just have dinner here?" Laurens asked.

"Did we not just spend the whole afternoon brainstorming?" Pim stood up to leave—apparently, mom's cooking was still the best.

"Eva, are you coming or staying here?"

I went with them and made a detour to Pim's house. I thought about asking him if he and I could camp out in my backyard in the ripped tent—as long as we didn't involve Laurens, I could stay in his mom's good graces.

The closer we got to the farm, the shabbier the little tent became in my memory and the more ridiculous the idea sounded. Still, right before he turned up his driveway, I asked. Not very loud.

"Macaroni with ham and cheese—you smell that?" Pim replied.

He stuck his nose in the air and climbed off his bike. I tried to convince myself that he hadn't heard my question, but I didn't smell any macaroni. All I smelled was cow dung.

It wasn't until we were in fifth grade, in '99, that both circumstances and Aldi finally decided to cooperate: Laurens's dad was away for the weekend at a trade show to buy a new machine for the shop, and all of a sudden these cheap three-person tents appeared in the flyers of the German supermarket chain. Pim and Jan got one from their parents at the beginning of the summer as a reward for a variety of things: they had helped a cow give birth with their own hands, they made hay bales for a whole week without complaining, Jan's end-of-the-year report card was good and Pim's wasn't so bad either.

Pim came biking over with the tent on his handlebars. On the package was a picture of a dome with a point on top set up in the middle of a lawn not much bigger than Laurens's backyard next to a barbecue, with a child playing football, a camping chair and a happy couple around it.

Aldi cornflakes always looked worse on the box than they actually were. If this was true for the tent, then it was a pretty promising acquisition.

Now that our camping plans felt within reach, our strategies for convincing Laurens's mom became increasingly bold. We spouted off ideas as we set up the tent in Laurens's backyard, well out of her line of sight. The outer shell had a camo print, just like in the picture. Once it was pitched, we plopped down inside of it. It smelled like new. And kind of like sausage, but that was probably because the door of the vacuum shed was open.

"I think I got it," Laurens said suddenly. "I don't know why I didn't tell you this before!"

Pim and I turned towards him.

"My mom hates her knees. If you stare at her lower half while whining for something, she's more likely to say yes."

We walked into the butcher shop and stood behind the display case, at the back of the line. We waited our turn, hoping she'd have as much patience for us as for the customers.

"Sir, madam, how may I help you?" Laurens's mom said, banging open a new roll of coins on the edge of the display case. She distributed the contents into the little slots in the cash register.

"Look, Mom." Laurens took the empty tent bag and waved it in the air. His mom stepped out from behind the counter to inspect it. She was wearing a white shirt with the shop logo on it and a pair of flowery shorts. Exactly what we needed.

"Pim got this tent. It would be such a pity if we weren't allowed to use it."

"I don't see any tent," she replied, "all I see is an empty bag."

Her eyes moved from the bag to us, then to the window and out at the gray clouds forming in the distance. All three of us fixed our eyes on her pale, clumsy knees. They were covered in mosquito bites.

"Bugs in the bedroom?" Pim asked without batting an eye.

It was the first time I'd ever seen Laurens's mom shrink. It made her look even chubbier.

Just then, the doorbell jingled, and the youth priest walked in.

"Fine," she said quickly, "but you'll do it here, in our backyard. After midnight it's lights out. And don't make too much noise, and don't tell your father." She gave the instructions to Laurens only. She didn't dare to look at me and Pim.

We left the shop through the back door. The boys high-fived. I felt sick to my stomach. We hurried to the back of the yard so we could put in the stakes and tie down the lines. The thing needed to be firmly anchored before she could change her mind.

The three-person Aldi tent was just big enough for two air mattresses. Pim got to sleep in the middle. Not because it was his tent, but because he was Pim.

Before bedtime, Laurens's mom came out to say good night. I'd never seen her in her nightgown with her hair down before. She brought us dinosaur cookies and insect repellent.

"You can always come sleep in the house if you want," she said. "I made up the spare bed, and Eva can sleep with me since Dad's out of town."

She walked back through the dark garden and into the house with the empty made-up beds. Pim drew circles on her back with his flashlight. She stumbled on a loose clod of grass. I grabbed the flashlight out of his hands.

Laurens didn't watch his mother leave. He was rustling around in the dark with the pack of cookies.

"We have to be good tonight," he said. "No going into town, no leaving the tent. We have to make a good impression. We've got one night to win her over. It's like in the shop—if a promotion catches on, she'll leave it up on the board for months."

For a second, I wanted to tell them the truth. That it wasn't up to Laurens's mom, it was his dad who decided. But then Pim started reading the safety instructions printed on the inside of the tent out loud in his best German.

After we'd had enough of watching the shadows of the dinosaur cookies mate with each other on the wall of the tent, we started smearing ourselves with insect repellent. This required more light, which attracted more mosquitoes. I didn't dare ask Pim or Laurens to help me spread it between my shoulder blades.

The rest of the night, they talked about all the things we could do in town. The darkness offered all kinds of new possibilities. I thought about the empty beds. The spot next to Laurens's mom. My lofted bed in Tessie's room. I wondered if they were asleep yet. If they were thinking about me.

There were mosquitoes everywhere. I dug my shoulder blades as deep as I could into the air mattress. After an eternity, it started getting light again outside.

12:45 p.m.

I'M STILL SITTING at the kitchen table. In front of me, parallel to the hedge around the garden and almost perpendicular to my line of sight, is a row of evergreen trees. Planted from left to right, neatly arranged by size, waiting for orders to make a quarter turn and march away, out of the frozen ground and into the snowy fields.

This row is the result of our annual trip to the garden center to pick out a Christmas tree. The trees with roots were a bit more expensive than the ones on a stand, but Mom saved up. After Christmas, we'd plant it in the garden with the intention of using it again the next year. But when it came down to it, Dad would put his foot down and say it was ridiculous to uproot a healthy tree. Mom's plan became his pretext—year after year, he bought a Christmas tree with roots.

The blue spruce on the far left has been there for twenty-five years now. By now, it wouldn't look out of place in the center of a big shopping mall, but if what Jolan had once claimed is true, that a tree's roots can grow as long as its trunk, there's no way we could ever dig it up. Only the smallest one on the right would still fit into a pot; this Christmas tree hadn't survived the return to solid ground and refused to grow an inch.

The trees were planted in their order of use, and I can still remember the holiday celebrations that went with them. It's not that hard, really: we always ate fondue, always on the same tablecloth with the gold dots, Mom would always get up early to get the house in a perfect state—folding napkins, polishing silverware, hollowing out tomatoes, making sauces, building up expectations that we'd never be able to meet.

Around five o'clock, the sun would go down, and the neighbors would retreat into their homes to gather around their own Christmas trees, and Mom would start to sigh—she'd been hoping that somehow she wouldn't be left alone with us. In tears, she'd put the finishing touches on dinner, fill the tomatoes with shrimp, and make one last effort to get the rest of the meal on the table in a decent state.

Once the salad had been mixed, everybody had a boiled potato on their plate and we'd decided who got which color fondue stick, it was up to Mom to try to keep up with Dad. It was the only way to avoid having to blame each other later—they both had to stay equally drunk the entire evening.

Mom drank from two glasses at the same time. One was next to her plate and constantly topped off by Dad; the other was in the kitchen, which she stumbled into with every empty basket and dish. She was always stingy about seconds on meat and bread.

We let it happen right under our nose. Jolan made himself the lifeguard of the simmering pot of oil—anyone who let a piece of meat drown would be on dish duty later that week. Tessie didn't eat much. She worried about the colors of the food on her plate and the fact that it wasn't going to be a white Christmas. They were both counting on me to take over for Mom and Dad halfway through the evening.

Between fondue and dessert, we went to midnight mass, which actually didn't take place at midnight at all. It was at nine o'clock. The church was a safe, calming place—always the same Christmas pageant, the same reading, the same hymns, the same widows who came for the hot chocolate and mulled wine served afterwards.

Laurens's parents always came too, mostly to receive compliments from parishioners in grease-stained shirts on the quality of their gourmet meat. After the hymns and the pageant, no matter how far away I was, whether I was dressed as an angel or a shepherd, Laurens's mom would search for my eyes during the "peace-be-with-you".

I check my phone. It's almost afternoon. It's still too early to show up at Pim's, but I have to get out of here. I've given Mom and Dad enough chances to wake up.

Something stirs in the garden. A bird lands on the smallest Christmas tree, right where the star goes. I'm not surprised the tree didn't survive. Dad waited months to plant it. It was mid-summer by the time it was returned to the earth. This little tree is all that's left of our last real Christmas, in 2001. We set up the electric griddle on the table for the second year in a row. For every load of meat that was dumped onto it, Dad filled Mom's glass with more wine than she should've been able to drink. In no time, she gained an insurmountable advantage—not just over Dad, but over all of us, over the entire room—until she was practically cutting next to her meat.

"Anyone who can't handle a knife and fork can go eat with the dog," Dad declared, as he moved her and her plate towards the dog bowl in a corner of the kitchen. He let go before it was on the ground, just like he did with the dog food. The porcelain clattered on the tiles. Nanook jumped out of the way.

He sat back down in his chair and threw back his glass. It was already empty. He slammed it back down on the table. A blob appeared on the surface of the homemade garlic sauce, right in the middle, as if some invisible creature had just come up for air.

"That sauce is way too runny," he said.

Mom's meat was burning on the griddle. We didn't dare to take it off.

"I'm never bending over backwards for you again," she sobbed in the corner.

"C'mon. Those aren't tears. That's just all the wine coming back out," Dad scowled. His eyes were glassy too. He looked from Jolan to Tessie, but he didn't dare to look at me.

For the first time, we crawled into bed without going to midnight mass. Christmas felt unfinished—I hadn't been a shepherd or an angel, I hadn't received a peace-be-with-you from Laurens's mom.

Later I learned that Pim and his family hadn't shown up at church that night either; two cows had given birth. In retrospect, I wondered whether the absences at that church service determined which families would survive and which ones wouldn't.

After midnight, Dad appeared at the edge of my bed, groping around in the dark for something he could use to sleep in the armchair. I went and got him a sleeping bag and a bucket. It was the first and only time that I followed him down the stairs and thought: one push and he's gone.

July 19, 2002

No one's home but Tessie. Dad's at work, Jolan is out back in the fields and all that's left of Mom is what she can't wipe out with sleeping pills. The tops of the trees in the garden are still, but the colorful ribbons in the open doorway are rustling. Someone must have ordered them to keep dancing, wind or no wind.

Outside on the green plastic garden table Tessie is playing Monopoly. Two of the five chairs are pushed halfway under the table, the rest are tilted on two legs so rain can slide off. She's got the bank set up in the lid of the cardboard box. The properties are lined up on either side of the table. The bills are stacked small to large, their corners tucked under the edge of the game board. It's an old version of the game, still with Belgian francs.

Tessie doesn't see me watching. She gets up, switches places and sets two thousand francs in the middle of the table. Then she changes seats again to collect the money on behalf of the other player.

If anyone can play Monopoly against themselves, it's Tessie. She recently told me she counts her steps on certain routes.

"One of my feet shouldn't get more exercise than the other," she said.

I tried it once. On my way to the Corner Store, I counted the steps on each foot separately. I didn't have enough brain halves to keep track and ended up tripping. But Tessie apparently finds it calming.

She still hasn't noticed my presence. She rolls the dice, moves the piece the right number of squares and draws a Community Chest card. She reads it in silence.

In our bedroom, Tessie's bed is closest to the door. When we were little and got wound up at night because we couldn't or wouldn't go to sleep, Dad would storm in, rip off Tessie's bedsheet, jerk up her nightgown, pull down her underwear and spank her bare behind with the palm of his hand. After he'd turned off the hallway light and was walking down the stairs, Tessie would switch on the nightlight and check her backside to see how long it took for the bright red hand with five outstretched fingers to fade. We both knew that even if my bed had been closer to the door than Tessie's, Dad would have taken those few extra steps to be able to hit her.

I move closer to the sliding window to get a better look at Tessie's strategy, to see if she favors one of the two players. The conquered streets are neatly arranged by color on either side of the board. Apparently, she doesn't make the game easy for herself: each player has bought up the exact streets the other player needed. The left player has bet on the railroads, the electric company, the water works and the cheap streets; the right player has gone after the grand boulevards in Ghent and Brussels.

Her hair is about three inches long now. Under the short spikes, her scalp is red and flaky from all the washing.

Jolan looked up why her hair grows so slowly. It could be because she eats so little; on most days she eats only green foods and has to chew every bite a fixed number of times. Sixteen, to be exact. I think I'm the only one who ever counts along with her.

I can tell by the look on her face that the next card she draws is bad news. She counts her houses and pays what's owed to the bank then switches places. She still doesn't see me. She rolls the dice, balls her fist and triumphantly moves her piece to Station Zuid. She buys it. Four thousand francs, four gray notes in the pot.

"The money for railroads and property taxes goes to the bank," I say.

Tessie jumps at the sound of my voice. Even the dog is startled. She hoists herself up and shuffles across the patio, but her chain is too short. Since she can't reach me, she lies back down under the plastic patio table, pressing her wet snout against Tessie's calf bones.

"Wanna play?" she asks. "We can start over."

"I've already got plans with the musketeers."

"What are you guys going to do?"

I don't know what to tell her. Laurens called this morning and said that we were meeting at Pim's hayloft, not the vacuum shed. I can't tell Tessie what we're going to do there. I don't exactly know myself, and I don't want to give her the feeling that somewhere, outside this Monopoly game, outside our backyard, there's something better or more fun going on, because she's definitely going to be stuck here for the rest of the afternoon.

"Just hang out at Pim's," I say with a shrug.

"Are you going swimming in the Pit? Or are you gonna play in the hayloft?"

"No."

"Then stay home and play Monopoly with me," she says.

I don't say no right away. She latches onto the silence.

"Can't Laurens and Pim come here?"

I shake my head.

"Or we can play some other game. That works too."

"Tonight, I promise." I better go now, otherwise I'll have no choice but to stay. My throat is tight. Every time I leave Tessie at home alone, I regret not having said a more proper goodbye, because by the time I get home she might be gone. Her spiky hair, her skeletal frame, the constant washing. She is slowly scrubbing herself away, like a stain on the counter: you soak it, then scrape it off.

I bike off in a hurry. I'll talk to Mom or Jolan about it tonight. Or am I just feeling brave because from here I can cover the house with the tip of my little finger?

When I get to the farm, I see Laurens's and Pim's bikes already there. I park mine in between, as close to Pim's as possible. For a moment, I linger outside the barn. I can't remember the last time I saw the doors closed.

I make a lot of noise sliding them open, just like Pim's dad does, pushing them back as carelessly as possible in the hope that Laurens and Pim will be startled and stop whatever it is they're doing because they think I'm him.

I climb the ladder up to the hayloft and find them sitting at the entrance to our fort with their hands on their knees, waiting for me. No cigarettes. No pâté mustaches. No dirty magazines. Laurens is wearing blue pants, a blue shirt and matching shoes. Had they not put so much thought into their outfits, they could almost be the boys I used to know.

"You got the money?" Pim asks before I've even reached the landing.

"Of course."

"Sorry, but we really couldn't meet at my house this time," Laurens says, styling his shoelaces. "We need a system where we take turns at each other's houses, so we don't get caught. You guys don't know my dad. My earlobes are still burning."

I don't mention that I could feel his earlobes burning last night too.

Pim shakes his head defiantly. "My dad's keeping an eye on us too."

"You've got more hideouts around here than anybody, Pim. Be happy we don't always do it here," Laurens says.

"Eva's got a shed too, you know," Pim says.

"It's not a shed, it's just a chicken coop," I say.

"You're not getting off the hook just because you have chickens," Laurens says. "Here's what we're gonna do. We'll take turns, follow the hands of the clock."

"The hands of the clock?" Pim asks.

"My house is twelve. We started with me. Your house is five, Eva's is nine, so we're headed in the right direction. Next time we're at Eva's."

"Who says your house is twelve?" Pim sticks up his finger to check the direction of the wind. "It's not at the top of town."

"Yeah it is. Depends how you look at it."

"Who's coming today, anyway?" I ask, even though I know perfectly well who's coming. I know who it'll be next time when we're at my house in the chicken coop—I know the list on the cemetery wall like the two times table.

"Evelien," Pim says. "One of my girls."

"One of your girls?" Laurens retorts.

"Melissa was one of yours, wasn't she?" Pim says.

Laurens turns up his nose. Pim slaps him on the knee. I watch his fingerprints fade from Laurens's skin.

"So what's her score?" I ask.

"Seven," Pim says at lightning speed. "We're done with all the six-pointers now, thank god. Those were just warm-ups. We weren't expecting much. But now it's on. From here on out, it only gets better."

"Melissa was not my girl," Laurens insists.

"Okay, whatever. You can still look at Evelien's tits," Pim grins.

"I vote we go swimming," I say.

Pim gives me a dead look.

"Good idea, Eva," he says loudly and jumps to his feet. "I'm in."

Laurens hesitates, but then slowly clambers to his feet.

I turn around and start climbing down the ladder. Halfway down, I realize they're not following me. Still, I keep going until my feet are on solid ground. Laurens peers over the edge of the platform.

"If you're going home, you're gonna have to give us our money back," he calls.

"And the answer to the riddle," I hear Pim whisper.

"And the riddle!" Laurens echoes.

I march out of the barn. The lump in my throat returns. No matter how much distance I put between us, everyone will still think they left me.

I stand at the edge of the pool and run my hand through the murky green water. The filtration system has stopped working. I'm not even wearing a bathing suit. Next to my feet, on dry land, is the grinning inflatable dolphin.

I could go home to Tessie, play a board game with her. Instead I walk back to the barn and grab a pitchfork. I press it into the belly of the inflatable animal. The plastic goes in but with my weight evenly distributed across the three prongs, it doesn't pop. What am I waiting for? I've seen Jan and Pim's dad stab tools into mice plenty of times. In a few seconds, all the life drains out.

The sharp, penetrating stench of cow shit overpowers the smell of chlorine. Pim's father is driving the full manure spreader across the property, and every time it hits a bump, some of the slurry escapes from the nozzle. He waves at me and steers the rig towards the other side of the farm.

I take one hand off the pitchfork to wave back, and when I do, my weight shifts and the right prong slowly punctures the plastic. There's no pop, I just feel something sighing against the leg of my pants. The air that comes out smells like waking up next to Pim in a very hot tent. The dolphin's grin slowly fades.

I keep waving and smiling until the prongs of the pitchfork hit solid ground and Pim's dad is out of sight. Why do tractors move so slowly? Why do farmers suspect so little?

I climb back up the ladder with my head held high and take a seat next to Laurens and Pim. I pull the four fifty-euro bills out of my pocket, smooth them out and lay them in Pim's lap.

"The water's too gross to swim in."

Pim picks up the money and gives it back to me. He pats me gently on the knee and leaves his hand there. I can feel the blood pumping in his fingertips through the fabric of my pants. Three heartbeats. Three sorrys.

Suddenly we hear voices outside the barn. He pulls his hand back. I jump up and look out through a hole in the roof. Two girls are parking their bicycles next to ours. One is Evelien, who was a year behind us in primary school. But over the last two years, I haven't seen her, I've just heard other people's stories about her. People say she's got an eating disorder—that there's always this sour smell around her. Still, she was always surrounded by a flock of girls at school. They all wanted to be close to her, as if they hoped her skinniness was contagious.

Rumor had it she was in some kind of rehab in Lier, but that might be an exaggeration, because today, from where I'm standing, she doesn't look like someone who's been through treatment.

Hesitantly, their shadows pass by the silage mounds. They stop for a moment, maybe trying to figure out exactly where Jan died. That's not so easy though: the police tape, the flowers, the candles—Pim's mom got rid of it all right away.

A few seconds later, the barn doors slide open, their wheels groaning under the weight of the iron.

"Pim?" a girl's voice calls.

"Up here! We're in the hayloft."

Laurens and Pim stare at the top rung of the ladder, their eyes full of expectation.

Two small hands appear, then a face. Not Evelien's. This girl is small and chunky, with a round head, narrow blue eyes and a wide grin. She's carrying a swim bag on her back, the straps digging into her shoulders. She hoists her leg over the final steps and climbs up onto the platform. She's wearing tight leggings with an op art pattern that reminds me of a screen saver. They're all out of shape from climbing the ladder, the crotch is hanging halfway down her thighs. She spreads her legs wide and hikes them up as high as possible. A camel toe forms at the top. Laurens and Pim exchange glances. The girl keeps smiling.

Evelien arrives at the top of the ladder. She looks as waifish close up as she does from afar. She's wearing a jean jacket with long sleeves and boots with the laces loose around her narrow ankles.

"This is my cousin, Nelle," Evelien says. "I'm supposed to keep an eye on her today. She loves swimming. I heard you've got a pool now, Pim."

Nelle's older than we are. It wouldn't surprise me if she was going on thirty.

"I work at Mivas in Lier. I have three cats at home. I love swimming." Her voice sounds hoarse, and every "I" has a different tone, as if she's referring to three different people.

"Mivas is a special-needs workshop," explains Evelien.

"I pack LU cookies," Nelle says. "Dinosaur cookies, and other cookies. A lot of them get messed up. You can order a whole bag of messed-up cookies from me for two euros."

Pim gives her a faint smile. Then he turns to Evelien.

"We were just about to play a game. You in?"

"You want to play, Nelle?" Evelien asks.

Nelle nods.

Pim explains the rules to Evelien—for the first time, apparently. He doesn't look at Nelle, hoping they won't apply to her.

Evelien listens in silence. Then, she puts her hand on Nelle's shoulder.

"Did you hear that, cuz?" she says. "Two hundred euros! We could ride roller coasters at Bobbejaanland, buy a ton of popcorn." She takes off her jean jacket and ties it around her waist. The sides flap down over her narrow hips.

"Yeah, or a swimming pool even," Pim says.

"Can we work together?" Evelien asks.

Laurens looks at Pim, waiting for him to answer.

"We only have two hundred euros. You can team up, but you'll have to share the prize money."

I count their layers of clothing. There's at least ten between the two of them. They've got the best chances of anybody yet.

I recite the riddle.

Why didn't I come up with something simpler and less serious, something like "it's green and slides down a mountain" or "what's black-white-black-white-black-white-boom"? A skiwi, a nun falling down the stairs—answers that aren't impossible to figure out. Then the girls would at least stand a chance.

"Now you can ask questions and try to figure out the answer," I explain.

"Okay. Did the guy slip on something and fall?" Evelien ties the sleeves of her coat around her waist again, tighter this time.

"No," I say.

"Damn." She gestures at her cousin and points at her shoes. Nelle bends down and pulls them off. Evelien doesn't give her a chance to ask the next question.

"Was there a second person involved who left the room?" she asks.

"No," I say.

Evelien helps Nelle take off her jacket.

"Did he drown?"

"No."

Nelle pulls her sweater over her head. Underneath is a boxy gray T-shirt.

"Was his death his own fault?"

"Yes."

Pim presses his fingernails into his palm impatiently. Evelien points to the next item of clothing Nelle has to remove—her pants. Nelle immediately does as she's told, pulling down her leggings with a smile. Maybe she's used to Evelien bossing her around. She stands there in her T-shirt, the downy hair on her thighs standing on end.

"Does the water in the room have anything to do with his death?"

"Yes."

Once Nelle's T-shirt comes off, you can see her overall composition. Her upper body is a lot narrower than her lower body, yet both parts meet nicely in the middle.

Nelle puts her hands on her hips and wiggles them around like a lady in a shower-gel commercial.

"She would've been good for that game where you draw half a picture and pass it on," says Pim. Nelle lowers her hands. Evelien isn't laughing.

"Come on, Nelle, that's enough. Time to go." Evelien unbuttons her jean jacket from her waist and uses it to shield her cousin.

"What about the swimming pool?" Nelle protests. She takes off her underwear and tosses it over Evelien's shoulder. "Here you go, guess again."

The floral cotton panties land on the floor in front of us. Laurens tries not to look at them.

"Put your clothes back on, I have to pee." Evelien pushes the pile of clothes into her cousin's arms. Nelle looks down and hurries to get dressed. She doesn't dare to fetch her underwear. She puts her leggings on backwards. The seat of the pants, which is stretched to the shape of her behind, sags in her lap.

"We never would have figured it out, I take it?" Evelien asks, looking only at me. I catch a whiff of that sour smell. It reminds me of Tessie.

"You guys still have five chances!" Pim says. "Don't give up now."

I shake my head.

"Bye, Eva," Evelien says.

She snatches up the panties, stuffs them in her coat pocket and climbs down the ladder ahead of Nelle. Once her head is out of sight, Pim sinks down on a hay bale, thoroughly pissed. He pulls out a few pieces of straw and throws them over the edge of the platform. They swirl down to the ground.

"There's something wrong with the rules," Laurens says. He sits down next to Pim, hawks a loogie and spits it behind the straw.

"Why do they always give mongols bowl cuts?" Pim crosses his eyes and sticks out rabbit teeth. "Makes them even uglier. I'm never eating dinosaur cookies again, by the way."

Suddenly I remember very clearly the intention I'd set for myself at the start of high school: at my new school, I would be someone new, someone better, a different Eva. What intention had Pim set for himself when he found out he wasn't going to be stuck with Laurens and me all day? Who was he trying to become?

"Nelle, Evelien, wait!" I shout. Nelle stops at the door, about ten meters from the foot of the ladder.

I stand up and pull the cash out of my pocket.

"Don't, Eva!" Pim moves between me and the edge of the loft and watches me fold the four bills together. "Okay, okay fine. Give her one. Fifty's more than enough."

I throw down the entire wad of cash.

"What the hell are you doing?" Pim roars. He gives me a shove. I stumble to the side into a hay bale.

Laurens leans recklessly over the edge of the loft.

"Don't just stare at it," Pim cries. "Do something!"

Judging by the slow speed at which Laurens shuffles through the straw to the ladder, Nelle has already picked up the money. Before he's even touched the ground, the cousins have left the farm.

"You didn't owe them anything! That was all we had!" Pim shouts, spit spraying from his mouth. "Why did you do that?" He pushes me again, but I'm already seated. I don't have an answer for him.

Laurens kicks over an upright bale half-indignantly. The dust makes all three of us sneeze.

When I get home, Tessie's done playing Monopoly. I don't ask who won.

Millennium Bug

THE MILLENNIUM BUG was all over the news. Even at Laurens's butcher shop, they hung a sign in the window weeks before the end of the year that read DUE TO MILLENNIUM, NO CARDS!!, out of fear that every cent they had would evaporate into thin air.

"Better safe than sorry," I heard Laurens's mom say to customers before they left the store with change rattling in their pockets. She didn't say anything to me. Maybe she wanted to prevent me from being sorry—not that I was all that safe at home anyway.

At the table on New Year's Eve Jolan finally explained in layman's terms what a "bug" was. To him, "layman's terms" just meant that after every question he paused to flip his meat on the griddle.

"When computers were first invented in the sixties and seventies, they were much slower and had almost no memory. Right?"

Tessie and I hummed in agreement. But Jolan wanted to make eye contact with Dad.

"So there wasn't much space to store data. To keep the costs down, all the dates were recorded in six digits, which turned out to be a pretty stupid idea."

"Really? Why?" I asked.

"It was then, at that moment, that the bug became possible. Tonight, when everything switches to the twenty-first century, the computers are going to think that we're back at nineteen hundred. Get it?"

Tessie cast a worried look at the computer in the corner of the room.

Dad, who had given no indication whatsoever that he had any

idea what Jolan was talking about, suddenly interrupted in a boom-
ing voice.

"When the clock strikes twelve, nuclear power stations will
explode, chemical companies will release clouds of gas, nuclear
missiles will shoot off automatically—and, I hate to tell you this, but
those rockets in the Eastern bloc, they're aimed straight at us. Thermo-
stats will jam, planes will fall out of the sky, respirators and other
medical equipment will fail: in short," he said, like a minister reading from a script, "at least one percent of all companies will go
bankrupt."

He took another sip of wine. "Eva, will you pass the pearl
onions?"

Tessie put down her fork and passed him the jar because she was
closer to it. Jolan removed his carefully grilled filets and offered one
to Dad, but he turned it down.

"What about our computer?" Tessie asked softly. Mom took the
jar of onions after Dad. She fiddled around in the vinegar with her
little fork. The yellow whites of her eyes glistened. I came to her
rescue, placing three little onions on the edge of her plate.

"We'll have to wait and see," Dad said. He refilled his own glass,
no one else's.

"How much longer, Jolan?" I asked.

Jolan kept a close eye on his new waterproof G-Shock watch,
which was sitting in a glass of water in front of him on the table.

"Thirty-five minutes and thirteen seconds. Twelve seconds.
Eleven."

For days, Jolan had been saying he wasn't going to eat with us
this New Year's Eve. Mom didn't raise any objections until she came
home from the supermarket this morning with other people's ideals.

"No child should spend New Year's Eve with a watch and a
diving mask in the bathtub," she declared. "This is family time."

Jolan tried to resist. Didn't she understand? This was the only
chance he would ever have to experience the turn of the century
under water with his G-Shock. He had to seize the opportunity.

"I gave you that watch. I get the last word," Mom declared.

Jolan opened his mouth to retaliate but stopped short and turned around.

I knew what he wanted to say. Anyone who goes to bed claiming that a chicken can lay three eggs a day doesn't get to wake up the next morning and suddenly get the last word.

Fortunately, Jolan knew how to handle disappointment. By noon, he had a new plan. He spent hours synchronizing his watch with the world clock online, down to the second, timing how long it took to walk from the kitchen table to the backyard so he could tell us exactly when we had to go out to catch the fireworks or the first crashing planes.

At eleven o'clock, he carefully lowered the watch into the glass of water so he could still have his submerged countdown.

After Dad's Millennium bug explanation, Tessie didn't touch her food anymore. She just kept looking anxiously at the computer in the living room.

Nobody said anything, but we all knew it. She was fond of the thing. Or maybe "fond" wasn't the right word, it was more sickening than that. In the months following the air salesmen's visit, her strange back-door ritual became more elaborate.

She developed a little door-opening routine for every room in the house, a few innocent, barely noticeable steps, like tapping the little iron swing figurine on the sideboard in the hallway or turning over the soap in the bathroom.

In the living room, the most important thruway in the house, the ritual involved the computer: every time Tessie walked by it, she had to type something on the keyboard. Most of the time it was just a few quick keystrokes, sometimes more. She did it every time, whether the computer was on or not. In the morning, when no one was using it, it wasn't such a problem. It seemed harmless and, most of the time, no one saw it. But after school, when the computer was in use, she'd take a detour around the veranda to avoid the living room.

A few weeks ago, I locked the veranda door and spent the entire morning on the computer. Not to trap Tessie, but in the hope of understanding her. If she was going to stick to her ritual, she'd have no choice but to walk through the kitchen and type on the keyboard.

During my thirteenth game of Minesweeper, I finally heard her coming down the stairs. She entered the living room, saw me sitting there, and immediately turned back into the hallway without setting foot in the room. She softly closed the door behind her. Then I heard her rattling the door handle to the veranda nervously. A few minutes later, she was back in the living room, waiting in the corner.

"Do you know where the key to the door in the hallway is?"

"No," I reply.

The shame of having to admit that she needed to borrow the computer keyboard was greater than her haste. I lost my game again, opened a new twenty-by-twenty minefield with only three mines and clicked around at random because I didn't know the rules.

"Are you done, Eva?"

"I just want to win one game," I say.

Tessie took a few steps closer so she could see the screen.

"The numbers tell you how many mines are bordering the square."

Tessie took over the mouse for a moment. She clicked three times, which set off a chain reaction, safe area revealed. She smiled.

I looked down at her bony hand; her skin was almost as gray as the mouse. "Look. Like this," she said. "Maybe try it with flags. They help in the beginning." Then she retreated to a corner of the room and waited for me to leave.

"Do you need the computer?" I asked.

"No, you can finish," she said.

After a few minutes, her presence became more compelling. She cleared her throat, sniffed, paced back and forth. I got up to go to the bathroom, and when I came back, the keyboard was neatly placed in the center of the table, and Tessie had disappeared into the kitchen.

In the days that followed, I kept my eyes and ears open, hiding in the living room in the hope of deciphering what she typed when no one was looking. I counted more and more keystrokes, more than the letters in her name but not enough for a whole sentence. I didn't ask questions. Maybe it was like with the door: as soon as she knew someone was watching, she'd have to start all over again.

"Time for the countdown," Jolan announced. "We've got five minutes and thirty seconds to assume our positions in the backyard, so if anyone needs to pee, now's the time."

"Who cares about peeing when there are nuclear missiles on the way?" Mom mumbled.

She stood up and gripped the back of the chair.

Jolan looked at his watch. "It's almost two o'clock in Russia. The missiles would've arrived by now."

Tessie stood up, walked to the corner of the room and unplugged the computer; that way it wouldn't know the year had changed. She walked out to the backyard in front of us.

While we waited for Jolan to start the ten-second countdown and the fireworks to start, I thought about how Tessie and I used to leave notes to each other when we were little. I'd write her a message in invisible ink on a Post-it note and stick it to our bedroom door. She'd color in the entire square with a marker to find out what it said.

Maybe typing on the keyboard was a new, more sophisticated version of the Post-it notes? Maybe she was hoping I'd make an effort to decipher her secret code like she used to do for me?

At one minute before midnight, the neighbors began a loud countdown and the alarm on the submerged G-Shock started beeping. As with all disasters predicted way in advance, nothing happened when the clock struck twelve. A few bottle rockets were fired, but not many.

Behind me Mom let out her typical burps. Dad lit a cigarette.

I stood there, arm in arm with Tessie. I could feel the warmth of her skin against mine, we didn't have a sweater or a jacket on because a few minutes ago we were inside, warm around the electric griddle on the kitchen table.

When the fireworks were over, Mom, then Dad, turned around and went back into the house.

"We're still alive," Jolan said. "No nuclear meltdown."

"Yeah," I said. "That's good."

Tessie didn't say a word. I saw Jolan look at her, look away, then look back. I noticed his discomfort first, then I saw the reason for it: there was a tear rolling down Tessie's cheek.

"The computer survived," I said.

"I know," Tessie replied.

I didn't understand why she was crying. Maybe she was right to be disappointed. We would crawl into bed, and tomorrow everything would be back to normal.

Jolan pulled his watch out of the glass of water, dried it on his shirt, and wrapped it around Tessie's wrist. Even on the smallest hole, the strap was still way too big. The clock read three minutes past midnight.

"It's not a real G-Shock. Mom bought it at Aldi and threw away the box," Tessie said.

1:00 p.m.

I DIDN'T COME here for nothing. Right above my head, through the wood floor in the master bedroom, I hear someone shuffling around on my dad's side of the bed. He's just sat up on the edge of the mattress and is searching around for his slippers with the tips of his feet. He waits a half a minute for the morning stiffness to settle before pushing himself up on the corner of the bed.

It'll take him a total of six minutes to reach the kitchen table—to roll out of bed, shuffle down the stairs while leaning on the banister, sit on the toilet, wait for the dizziness to subside, squeeze out a dark yellow puddle of piss, forget to shake off the dribble, and—with drops of urine on his pants—stumble into the hallway, cough up his lungs over the bathroom sink, try to flush down the brownish clots and walk through the dining room to the workshop to smoke his first cigarette. On the way, he'll pick up the empty beer crate so it can be refilled with fresh bottles.

I have six minutes to make up my mind. Do I want to see him, or do I want to leave? And if I leave, should he know I stopped by or should I make it look like I was never here?

Behind the row of Christmas trees, on the other side of the untrimmed hedge, a heavy gray cloud moves across the sky. The sun lights up the snow on the lawn. The backyard is like a blank sheet of paper.

I used to draw here sometimes. The glass tabletop was a perfect surface, the tip of the pencil never pricked through the paper. We were only supposed to draw on scrap paper, but when no one was looking, I'd take one of the clean, white sheets of expensive printer paper, even though it wasn't allowed.

One time, Dad came home from work earlier than usual. He saw me sitting at the table with my pencil ready to mark on one of his fancy white sheets.

"Draw me," he said in a last-ditch effort to save the paper. He sat down across from me at the table.

His request made me anxious, nauseous even. I knew—this is not a happy man. And I didn't want to look at his unhappiness for too long; I didn't want to have to draw it.

I carefully studied his face, all the details I hadn't studied for a long time: his crewneck T-shirt, the stiff, wiry hairs in his eyebrows, the white hair that he made the same joke about at least once a week—that someone had forgotten to color him in.

After half a minute, I didn't see the facial features anymore, only the stories, the things people said about him in town: that he walked his bike home from the bus stop after work to put off coming home. When I heard that one, I decided to check and see if it was true. And there he was, off in the distance, rolling his bike down the bridge, his white head bent over as if he were walking into a strong headwind. There, from a distance, I wished with all my heart that he was the one who had a secret trapdoor in the backyard with a second family behind it, that there was more to his life than the things I knew about.

My pencil remained frozen on the paper. All that was left was pity, an oval whose lines didn't merge at the top. I handed Dad the portrait. He took it, looked at it, and said nothing.

A few minutes later, I heard him open the printer and put the sheet back in the paper tray.

It's now three minutes past one. Above the fruit bowl is one of the sketches I made of this very same fruit bowl, tacked up next to the two drawings of the house. The bowl contains almost exactly the same fruit as in the drawing—a pear supported by two soft apples, a discolored banana, a couple of tangerines. Over time, the drawing has come to serve as a guideline.

It's four after one. Everything in this room has remained intact, even the appliances have stood the test of time. The colon between the hours and minutes on the digital clock on the microwave blinks every two seconds. Thirty blinks, then the minute changes. The dots used to remind me of eyes. As long as they were watching, everything remained the same. But as soon as they blinked, as soon as time closed its eyes for a split second, that's when we got older, that's when it hit us.

July 21, 2002

It's been two hours, and Pim and Laurens still haven't called. Not to check whether they're still welcome in our chicken coop, not to ask where I am. I offer to help Jolan turn over the garden. As long as I'm doing something useful, it'll seem like the radio silence was my choice.

"Fine, but don't whine if you get blood blisters," Jolan says.

His eyes rest briefly on my ribs. He's noticed the difference—this morning I put on two padded bras to make my breasts look bigger. I had to do it today, so I'd have time to get used to having the two bumps with me everywhere I go, at the lower edge of my field of vision. Soon I'll have to face Laurens and Pim again, and I didn't want them to notice that I still don't entirely believe in those bumps yet myself.

"Give me a job too," says Tessie, who has just come outside. She doesn't notice my new cup size, but that doesn't mean anything—she doesn't know to look for it yet.

"We've only got two tools," Jolan says. He's got the heavy digger in one hand, and in the other, what Dad calls the "truffle" or the "shuffle", a collapsible spade with a wooden handle and an iron blade that he bought at the American army surplus store. There must have been someone behind the counter who couldn't pronounce the English word "shovel".

Jolan pushes it into my hands.

"Tes, you're on earthworm duty. If they're still intact, you can save them for the compost pile. They help keep it aerated."

"And if they're not alive anymore?"

"Then throw them back."

Tessie nods. She pulls out a saucer from under a flowerpot with a wilted plant in it and sits down cross-legged in the dirt.

These kinds of activities are good for her. The last time we turned over the garden was five years ago, back when her behavior was still normal, and she hasn't had the opportunity to develop any bizarre, compulsive sequences around collecting earthworms since then.

In the last few months, she hasn't created any new rituals, but she's been carrying out the existing ones more regularly.

I've walked in on her typing on the keyboard of the Windows 95 more often lately. Jolan spilled a glass of lemonade on it last year and it was transferred to the sideboard in the hall. For days, the keys didn't work at all, but eventually they all came back to life except for the A. Nobody except the Little Runt considered it worthwhile to buy a new keyboard for such an outdated system, so Dad bought a second-hand laptop with Windows 98 on it from a company that assembles computers from donated parts so we could throw out the 95. But Tessie wouldn't have it. She insisted that we give the old dinosaur a decent resting place, that we first "retire" it for a few months before tossing it out with the trash.

There was no talking her out of it. She threatened to sleep out in the garden next to the computer and refused to eat anything.

"Just for a little while." Mom gave in. Tessie was already way too skinny.

Against our better judgment, Jolan and I moved the heavy computer from the table in the living room to the sideboard at the bottom of the stairs. Over the years, the old piece of furniture had become nothing more than a storage chest, a place for decorative gifts from old people who would have to die before we could get rid of the stuff.

What we were afraid would happen did. Tessie's room-entering rituals didn't go away. She simply moved the little iron swing figurine from the sideboard to the table where the computer used to be. Since the hallway connected practically every room on the ground floor, I caught her hunched over the keyboard several times a day. When she saw me, she would stiffen like a nocturnal animal in headlights and act like she hadn't been typing at all, like she was just looking for something.

A few days ago, I was determined to talk to her about it. On the way to the bathroom, I found her in the hallway in her usual position. At first, I just ignored her. I slipped into the bathroom, quietly closed the toilet lid, sat down on top of it and listened to her punch the keys. She typed at lightning speed, using only her thumb, pointer and middle finger—that was how she'd taught herself to do it.

Was she making some kind of confession? And if so, to who? Who did she need forgiveness from? How many sentences did she type over all those months that never reached anyone? Typing on a disconnected keyboard is as bad as telling a joke that nobody bothers to listen to.

"Tes?"

She immediately stopped typing. The time had come. I had to say something. We couldn't go on pretending that nothing was going on.

"Yeah?" she said. Her voice was suddenly coming from the other end of the hall; she'd tried to distance herself from the computer. In all likelihood, she'd have to pay penance for this interruption later on, perform the ritual over and over again, typing even longer sentences even faster.

"What are you typing?" I tore off a few squares of toilet paper and wrapped them around my finger. I could tell by the stubbornness of her silence that she'd heard me.

"Tes?" I asked again. "What are you writing? Are you working on a story?"

Again, no response.

"I'm gonna stay here until you tell me."

"You better be careful," she said. "There are old people in nursing homes who have to wait so long for the nurse to come wipe their butts that they poop out their intestines."

"I'm not pooping," I said. "I'm sitting on the lid."

At that, she was gone.

Jolan draws lines in the dry, sandy soil with his shovel, dividing the patch at the foot of the cherry tree into smaller squares. Ten by ten.

"If we dig at the same speed, we'll meet right in the middle. Fifty squares each."

We start shoveling at opposite ends of the garden, silently digging towards each other.

Every time I bend my knees and bear down on the little shovel, I think of my two friends, about what they're doing right now, whether they've decided to meet in the hayloft or in the vacuum shed.

I wonder if they're doing something more fun, if they're still mad about the money, if ignoring me bothers them as much as it hurts me.

Today, it's Amber's turn. She's one of the few girls at Pim's school, and the only one who can operate the laser cutter, which according to Pim "increased her market value to a nine" during the school year.

"But," he added recently, "the summer's different. In July and August, girls have to do more than work a laser cutter, which is why she's only a seven and a half now."

Pim was right. The girls with the highest scores weren't necessarily the prettiest. They were the hardest to get. Buffalo Ann, for example, is really no uglier than the average eight, but she used to have a crush on Pim, which made her too easy.

It was Laurens's mother who once explained to me how it worked. "If you put the whole log of apple pâté in the display case, nobody wants it. Customers aren't interested until there are just a few slices left, too small to look unpopular, but too big to be seen as unappetizing leftovers."

After half an hour of digging in silence, stabbing our shovels into the ground, we've each turned over about thirty squares. Jolan picks at a large purple blister in the palm of his hand and wipes the ooze on his pants. He waves to show me the flapping piece of skin. I don't have any blood blisters, but all of a sudden, I feel my second period coming on. All the blood my body can spare starts seeping into my panties. At first, it's warm and liquidy, but the more I move, the stickier it gets. As it dries, it starts chafing my inner thighs.

"I think you'd better stop shoveling," Tessie says. The saucer is already full of worms: the squirming ones on the left, the dead ones on the right. "That dirt is full of tree roots. They need those roots to suck up water, you know, and now you're chopping them up." The tears are already welling up in her eyes.

"A tree's roots grow as long as its trunk. That's why you have to plant them so far apart, and far away from houses. Chances are these roots aren't from our cherry tree. They're probably from one of the neighbors'," Jolan says.

"So? The neighbors' trees are living things too, aren't they?" Tessie says. She keeps on sorting the worms. In the meantime, some of them have crawled to the wrong side of the dish.

I look down at the dirt I've just shoveled. It's full of half-rotten cherry pits and thousands of tiny roots, as thin as veins.

"Are they searching for each other underground?" Tessie asks, pulling two loose roots out of the dirt and pushing their ends together.

"Okay, we'll stop. Enough digging," Jolan concludes, even though he's halfway through his last row. He's at fifty-five squares, I'm at thirty-seven. In the middle of the garden patch is an island of solid ground covered with tufts of grass. On top of it is the bowl of worms. "We can start planting now."

"Tessie, why don't you go get the seeds?" he asks, holding up his dirty hands. "They're in the laundry room."

"I'm not done with these worms yet," she says. She holds the saucer out in front of her and carries it to the compost pile on the other side of the yard.

I look at Jolan. He doesn't get the message right away: as long as we're watching her, Tessie can't go in through the back door.

I wipe my hands on the grass and head to the laundry room to get the seeds. Before going back out to the yard, I duck into the workshop, quickly, without looking up at the rafters, in search of new equipment. I return to the yard with a small rake and a pointy steel tool for making deep, narrow holes.

Jolan coordinates the planting operation. He stretches out a string over the ground to align our holes. He reads the instructions on the package to find out exactly how far apart the seeds should be planted and measures the distance with the soles of his shoes.

"We'll plant a little bit of everything," he says.

Tessie gets the pointy steel tool because she was the only one who had a name for it: "the hole poker". She punctures the earth where Jolan tells her to, and I drop in the seeds. Sunflowers, radishes, carrots, leeks. There's amazing strength in her skinny wrists. I can barely keep up with her. Jolan scoops potting soil over each hole. In a small notebook, he sketches a map of the garden and makes a note of where we planted what and when to harvest what.

Mom's awake by now, standing at the porch window watching us and talking on the phone. She keeps the receiver pressed against her ear and sticks her free hand nonchalantly in her pocket. I can tell by the way she's standing that she's on the phone with Grandma, that they're speaking West Flemish.

Mom can switch effortlessly between standard Dutch and dialect. She rarely speaks to us in her mother tongue. It always reveals a part of her character that we're not allowed to talk about, a certain strength, a rare optimism.

She's not on the phone for very long but remains on her feet for the entire conversation, smiling—a daughter no mother could regret having. As soon as she hangs up, she slumps her shoulders, pulls her hand out of her pocket and goes back to being the regretful mother.

That night, I go to bed on time so the day will be over faster. I've dug too much, thought too much. My body hurts down to the tiniest muscles, my thoughts are ringing in my head, I'm nothing more than holes. It feels like that time in primary school when we were playing hide-and-seek, and I hid behind the trash cans next to the bike racks only to realize later that the other kids had gone off to play football—no one came looking for me.

What riddle did Pim and Laurens use today? Did they just keep using mine, assuming no one would get the right answer, or did they flip through magazines in search of a worthy replacement? I wonder if my name was ever mentioned, if they even thought of me today, if they decided who would call me tomorrow, what they'd say to make up for what happened.

Just as I'm about to drag my stiff calves up the stairs, I run into Tessie, bent over the keyboard in the hallway. The evening hasn't fallen yet but the sky is tilting; it's half dark in the hallway. I feel as caught as she does. But this time, she reacts differently. She doesn't freeze.

"I can't stop," she says without being asked. She hits the Enter key hard. For a moment, she looks me straight in the eyes.

"I want to, but I can't."

I sit down on the stairs. For the first time, Tessie finishes what she's typing while I watch. The buttons on the old keyboard are caked in dirt and resistant to her touch.

Her hard keystrokes show off the muscles and tendons around her joints—she reminds me of an old cat making a valiant attempt to catch a few mice. New freckles have appeared on her face today. Her eyelids are trembling. When she's done, she lays her bony fingers on the keyboard. Her hands surrender, the rest of her resists. I want to take her in my arms.

We all know it—Tessie has made her body the secretary of her mind. The worse she feels, the more overtime she has to work. Even from where I'm sitting, all the way up on the third step, I can smell how hungry she is.

"Come to bed," I say.

"I'm not ready for bed yet."

"You can read another one of those Gaston comics."

I wait. She types a bit more. I let her count her steps as she walks up the stairs in front of me. From the looks of her, she doesn't have any aches or cramps at all. Each foot lands on exactly the same lines on the cardboard-covered steps. On the evens, she steps with both feet, and on the odds with only one. I try to copy her movements until she notices. Halfway up the stairs, she stops.

"No, this isn't right. We have to go back down."

"And what'll happen if we don't?" I ask.

"I can't tell you because then it'll happen for sure."

With small, backwards steps, we make our way back down the stairs.

Swallow

"I HAVE A plan," said Pim in the tone he always used to announce ideas that would turn out badly. It was exactly ten o'clock, the first summer night of the twenty-first century. The church bells sounded louder in the flimsy tent than they did at home in my bed, even though our house was closer to the church than Laurens's backyard was.

"Are they ringing the end of nine o'clock or the beginning of ten o'clock?" I asked.

"Who cares," said Pim. "It's the same thing."

The evening officially kicked off at seven o'clock with Pim and Laurens counting their pubic hairs in the back of the yard. When they came back, they lay down on their backs on their air mattress and, with contracted abs, started debating where the scrotum stopped and the ass began in the hope of minimizing each other's pube count.

This summer would be significant—we all knew it. July and August marked the end of primary school and the beginning of high school, and everything we knew, including ourselves, was about to change.

It was the same tent we'd used to convince Laurens's mom that camping and troublemaking didn't necessarily go hand in hand. There was as little left of that plan as there was of the tent itself. The outer shell was worn and tattered and the camouflage colors all but completely faded, which actually made it less noticeable in the trees.

Shortly after midnight, the lights went out in the house. It was finally dark enough.

Pim's plan was to poop in Elisa's Mimi's mailbox. Really, she didn't even have a mailbox, just a slot in the front door. But in Pim's eyes, this just made our plan "even bolder than that of the average mailbox pisser".

"What did Mimi ever do to us?" I said, walking as sluggishly as possible in front of the boys, hoping to slow them down. "There are plenty of other people with a mail slot. Why does it have to be Mimi's?"

"Elisa shouldn't have had to move back to Hoogstraten," Pim said.

"But if this whole thing is about Elisa, can't we just look up her dad's address?"

"Mimi will make sure he gets the message." Laurens and Pim tiptoed across her yard to the front door. I stayed at the edge of the street to keep a lookout. Pim held up his flashlight for extra light and stifled a laugh in his T-shirt. Laurens's giant shadow stretched across the entire front lawn, revealing that the plan wasn't as easily executed as they'd thought. The mail slot was low, and the flap opened outwards. Laurens had spinach-colored diarrhea—he'd been bragging about it all day—but apparently this wasn't such an advantage with a mail slot that opened outwards. He picked up a flyer on the porch and used it as a funnel.

I kept my distance so I wouldn't have to smell it. I watched with one eye open, that way I wouldn't miss the spectacle but could still say later that I wasn't really there.

It was the youth priest, of all people, who told Laurens's mom about it in the butcher shop. He didn't know who did it, but he said that Mimi now had a note on her door that read "Next time, please use envelope." Her sense of humor had compelled the priest to write off our exploits as "mischief".

"Mischief is for kids who tape episodes of *Hey Arnold!*," Pim said when Laurens told us. He didn't want to talk about it anymore.

On the last night of the summer, Pim showed up with a gigantic spotlight. The tent had been set up in Laurens's yard for two months so we wouldn't have to pack it up again after every use.

"If my dad finds out I took this, I'm in big trouble," Pim said with a swat alongside his head.

"How's he gonna find out?" Laurens asked.

"If a cow decides to give birth in the middle of the night, he'll need it himself. Then we'll hang."

For a while, it wasn't clear what Pim planned to do with the spotlight. We started the evening by going over the old scores—which girls had gone up a cup size and thus gained an extra point? Then I had to make sketches of different types of breasts, and they wrote the girls' names in columns under each one. It was all just speculation.

Just after midnight I went out in the yard to pee, at a safe distance—where I could still see the tent but they couldn't see me. I squatted down, lifted up my nightshirt and looked at the brightly lit dome with their two perfectly outlined silhouettes inside. They were secretly flipping through my notebook. I never let them look at it. Not just because I wrote down the wrong scores for the prettiest girls, but because their blind trust in me was the only thing I had left, because my own score would never come up.

I hurried back to the tent. The grass was damp under my bare feet. As soon as I got there, someone unzipped it from the inside. Laurens and Pim crawled out, shining the bright lamp straight in my face. It took a moment for my eyes to adjust to the darkness again.

Pim climbed up the swing set behind me. He fastened the spotlight to the top of the monkey bars with the beam pointed towards the vacuum shed. The light was so bright that the crickets in the yard behind it took it for the sunrise and stopped chirping.

Outside of the spotlight, the night was blacker than before. In that darkness, there was something more dangerous about Pim's face. His eye sockets became two black saucers.

I sat down in the damp grass, far enough away from where I had just peed.

Laurens and Pim climbed up on the swing set and started making shadow puppets with their hands. Two wolves appeared on the wide, flat wall of the vacuum shed and gobbled each other up. Then came butterflies, then two-headed birds.

For each animal, I gave a little round of applause, until all of a sudden an elephant appeared. I looked at the wall, not at the swing set. As long as I only looked at the shadow, I didn't owe them anything, I thought. But in the end, I turned around anyway—why, I don't know. Maybe I was looking for an explanation. And there was Pim with his pajama pants around his ankles. He folded his scrotum around his shaft, forming two ears. Projected on the wall of the shed, it actually looked like a pretty credible elephant.

Laurens pulled down his pants too and wiggled his limp willy back and forth. His pubic hair was scarcer but thicker; in the giant shadow I could see the flecks of crud stuck in it.

The possibilities turned out to be more limited than with their hands. After a little elephant war, Pim and Laurens pulled their pants back up.

I didn't clap. Pim jumped down and came over beside me. "Your turn, Eva," he said, "Surprise us."

He ducked into the tent and came out with my sleeping bag. Then he spread it out on the grass and sat down on top of it.

I slowly rose to my feet, climbed up the swing set, next to Laurens. His pants were securely fastened. I made a few animals with my hands but couldn't do anything that hadn't been done already. There was no applause.

After a few minutes, Pim shouted, "Come on, it can't be that hard to make a clam."

"Or a swallow!" Laurens said. "You've got the goods to make that too." He climbed down and sat next to Pim on the sleeping bag.

All the nights out in the tent had led to this. I had something they didn't have. If we were stamp collectors, this would have been a huge advantage, but in my case it was anything but.

I stood there in the spotlight trying to figure out how to get out of it, how to not have to take off my pajamas. I could jump down, land wrong and break something. My ankle, for example—I snapped it once before so maybe it would cooperate again.

"I don't know what a swallow looks like," I say.

"Long wings. Little head. Should work." Pim made himself more comfortable. "Come on, nobody can see you."

"You guys aren't nobody," I said.

"Well, somebody's gotta watch. Otherwise it never happened." It sounded like something I could have said myself. It didn't really help.

"Okay, but you guys keep your eyes on the wall." I positioned myself in front of the light.

"We promise."

I waited for them to turn their heads. Crouching over the lamp I pulled up my nightshirt and lowered my panties. On the wall, right next to the door of the shed, I used my labia to model some kind of creature.

All I could think about was the inside of Mimi's hallway. How we'd soiled it at the beginning of the summer. Laurens and Pim couldn't imagine what it must have looked like. But I could. I knew exactly what was behind the mail slot: a narrow hall with a mat, a stool with a cactus on it, piles of unopened mail, Mimi's Sunday shoes that she always put on with a shoehorn and polished every month.

Since I was the only one of us who knew what those shoes looked like, how they were neatly lined up with the heels against the wall, I was the only one who felt guilty about Laurens's shit.

The lamp was hot and created a pleasant glow between my legs. I looked at the wall, at the shadow of my fiddling hands. No matter what I did, my labia were too tight and hung too close to my body. I couldn't make a bird or any other kind of animal with them. The best I could do was a stingray or a flatfish.

I stopped. In the distance, I could see the tops of the surrounding houses. There were families sleeping under those roofs.

"What kind of animal is that? Pigeon roadkill?" Pim started giggling loudly. Even Laurens let out a feeble chuckle.

Of course, they weren't just looking at the shadow anymore. I immediately dropped my nightshirt and turned to climb down the

ladder, but I forgot about the panties still hanging around my ankles.
I tripped on the top step and slid down the side of the swing set
like a plank with my back bouncing down the round wooden poles.
I landed on my feet with my nightshirt rolled up around my neck.
All I could feel was the burning of my chafed skin.

For a split second, I didn't know where or who I was. It felt like
the best possible option: being nobody, being nowhere. Then the
pain hit me.

"Eva, are you okay?" Laurens's voice sounded far away, as if it
was coming from inside a closed bag. But he was still sitting next
to Pim in the grass.

Against the back of the house, in the courtyard, was a leather
chair. Laurens's father liked to plop down in it after a day of cutting
steaks. I sat down and discovered a giant splinter in the back of my
forearm. It didn't bleed when I pulled it out.

Laurens and Pim asked if I was coming back to the tent to sleep.
When I didn't answer, they didn't ask any more questions. They
silently retreated into the tent with the lamp, leaving my sleeping
bag out in the grass. I saw their shadows flop down on the air mattress without a lot of gesticulating. Maybe they didn't know what
they'd done wrong. They did leave the spotlight on in case I wanted
to find my way back.

But I didn't want to go back into that tent. Going home wasn't
an option either. Dad always locked the back door from the inside,
and I didn't want to wake Tessie.

Suddenly I heard nervous, irritated murmurs coming from the
upper floor of the house behind me. Laurens's parents were still
awake. The window in their bedroom looked out over the courtyard, and they had a good view of the vacuum shed from their bed.
A light was turned on, its yellow beam cut the backyard in half.
Then the window was closed, the curtains were closed, and the
light went out again.

Had they watched me make the shadows on the wall like I had
watched Pim and Laurens at Mimi's—not wanting to look but still
wanting to see what would happen? The boys had stood on top of the

swing set together. They'd get away with it because it was impossible to say whose elephant was whose. I was the only one with a flatfish.

The scrapes on my back didn't burn as much as the shame.

I sat there for hours. I saw the night sky disappear layer by layer, as if it were slowly being erased. The church tower stood in the background. The hands moved around the clock. But I couldn't say exactly when the sun came up.

Somehow, I found it comforting. Another eighteen hours and it would be night again, and the blackness would return the same way it left, layer by layer. This moment would gradually fade into the past, under countless layers of darkness, until Laurens's mom had forgotten what she had seen.

The first light of dawn made everything in the garden visible: the rustling leaves, the dandelions and poppies sprouting up in the grass, the first bees. Of course, there were just as many bees as the day before, but now everything seemed like too much.

My damp nightshirt clung to my skin. There were no tears, no raindrops. I was sitting so still, so stiff with shame and regret, that the morning took me for a plant and sprinkled me with dew along with the rest of the garden.

A little after six, I heard the first sounds in the house. Laurens's parents always got up early to get the shop ready. The bedroom window opened. Two minutes later the shutters on the back of the building were rolled up.

Laurens's mom appeared: first her sandals, then her shorts, her swollen knees, her neck. The more of her that became visible, the more I shrunk. Looking at her knees didn't help this time. I was weaker and uglier than she was. I looked away before we could make eye contact. I was going to lose her special smile.

She came out and stood beside the chair, without laying a hand on my shoulder. "Why are you up so early?"

"I couldn't sleep," I said.

"That can happen," she replied. She glanced at the half-camouflaged dome in the back of the yard, turned around, walked back inside and slammed the window screen shut.

For a second, I thought: she didn't see us last night, she closed the window from her bed, she didn't see the shadows on the wall.

The rest of the morning she putzed around the house. She didn't come outside. She kept her lips pursed, didn't bring out any of the usual breakfast stuff—no bowls, no spoons, no milk, no cereal, no plate of sandwiches under a basket against the flies. With every item she didn't bring, I became more certain that she had, in fact, seen my shadow performance.

When I heard the sound of forks clinking on plates from inside the house, I knew that Laurens's parents had started having their own breakfast. I couldn't help but think about what Laurens's mom had said when she heard the story on the news about the speed demon who caused a deadly accident, fled the scene of the crime and then crashed his own car into a tree: "God either punishes immediately or within fourteen days."

The remark played over and over again in my mind. I walked back out into the yard, shuffling my bare feet through the wet grass. Laurens and Pim were still asleep. All was quiet in the tent. Inside, it was hot and smelled of sweat and bad breath. The spotlight had left a dark burn mark in the fabric. Pim was lying diagonally across my air mattress. I grabbed my clothes and put them on in the middle of the garden, over my pajamas. Laurens's mother was standing at the window on the first floor, looking down at me.

I decided to stay away for at least fourteen days, to disappear from her sight. I wouldn't come back until the scratches on my back had healed. Two weeks, that should have been doable.

1:45 p.m.

IT'S STOPPED SNOWING. From the doorway, the backyard looks quiet—not just quiet, silenced. As if the trees were just talking about things that can't be discussed in my presence.

Before I go, I make a quick stop in the workshop. I lift the latch and push open the door, giving myself a few seconds to take it all in. The space looks small. On the right is the ladder and a giant rack laden with jars of screws and washers.

These last few years, I've caught myself wondering about my parents more often. When I think about Dad, there's only one question that comes to mind: is that noose still hanging there? Though to be fair, he too deserves a more complex kind of concern.

I want to look up into the rafters for the answer to my question, but I scan the ground instead, then the gardening tools.

The only one that's not in its usual spot is the American shovel—Dad probably used it to bury the dog the other day.

I walk down the garden path, taking giant steps in an effort to make as few footprints in the snow as possible. I notice the low-hanging branches of the cherry tree too late; the snow ends up in the collar of my jacket. It melts the second it touches my skin.

In the top of the tree, hanging between the thick branches, is a ragged T-shirt. Attached to one of the strongest boughs is a black radio strung up with bungee cords that was once used to chase away the crows. The antenna has broken off. The plug is dangling a meter from the ground, waiting for an extension cable.

Never did we have so many cherries as we did in the summer of '97.

That year's spring had met all the conditions of a good harvest. Warm, but not too dry. By early June, the branches were already groaning under kilos of fruit.

Dad put a sign out front that read: FREE CHERRIES, LADDER IN YARD.

He was delighted by all of the sudden attention from the neighbors, who came over to pick to their heart's content. All summer long, moms and dads would take the dog out for a walk and come home with a pair of cherries dangling around their ears so they could make the same joke with their kids—look at my new earrings.

Mom was the only one who complained about the ladder under the tree and the unexpected arrival of cherry pickers. To her, it was all in the way, the tree had always been in the way. Whenever somebody she knew showed up, she'd run into the house.

Maybe it was the cherry tree that had heard all her griping or maybe it was the neighbor who dug up his blackberry bush, sending the birds our way—but every year after that, the cherry harvest only got smaller.

More and more crows descended on our backyard to eat our fruit. They'd swoop down and snatch up everything they could. Sometimes they'd pluck a cherry from its branch, only for it to fall out of their mouths a few seconds later. The damaged fruit shriveled in the summer sun. After a storm, the garden paths were covered with cherry guts.

Mom hated having to trudge through the rotten, sour fruit in her sandals on her way out to the chicken coop. This didn't have so much to do with the strange crushing sensation under her soles, but with the bloody footsteps left behind on the kitchen floor that betrayed the frequency of her trips.

At the beginning of the first summer of the new millennium, Jolan and Tessie came up with a plan. Jolan was the mastermind; Tessie just carried it out. I wasn't there. I was off somewhere with Pim and Laurens. If I had been there, I probably would've put a stop to it.

Jolan crushed a cherry in Tessie's ear. Then he dragged her on her belly through the rotting fruit under the tree and laid her on the path between the back door and the chicken coop. She was wearing a short beige summer dress.

It must have looked pretty credible, as if she had fallen from the top of the tree and landed on her face. And it actually could have happened—Tessie climbed up the trunk all the time trying to reach the T-shirts that Jolan tied to the ends of branches to scare away birds.

All I remember is that when I came home for dinner that night, one of Dad's old T-shirts was hanging in the tree. The cotton was too heavy; there wasn't a breath of wind, the T-shirt wasn't fluttering. Mom was nowhere to be found, not in the kitchen, not in the armchair. Nothing had been laid out on the counter for dinner, just a frozen pig's snout for the dog.

I found my mom in the garden lying in the gray hammock strung up between two of the stronger Christmas trees. She'd wrapped the sides over herself and held the edges together from the inside. She hung there like a grain of rice, completely impenetrable. Under the hammock, lying askew on top of her sandals, were her glasses, the temples folded.

"Mom?"

"No," she replied.

Afterwards Jolan told me what happened. He had been hiding behind the tree, waiting for her to go out and check on the chickens, which happened pretty much every hour.

She walked out of the house and saw her Little Runt lying there in a contorted position under the highest branch of the cherry tree with a puddle of blood in her ears. Mom screamed her name, patted her back, turned her head to the side, but Tessie didn't make a sound. She hadn't been crowned Dead Fish champion at school for nothing—she was able to lie motionless on the floor for an entire gym class, even after she'd won the game and the other kids were allowed to break the rules and tickle her.

Tessie played dead until the ambulance siren could be heard off in the distance, and Mom had mustered up enough courage to call

Dad at work. Only then did Jolan understand the seriousness of the joke. He made a few owl sounds, and Tessie sprang back to life. They ran into the corn field and hid from Mom for the rest of the day. When the ambulance quietly drove away, Mom tore all the linen off the clothesline in big, exaggerated motions so the neighbors waiting around on the sidewalk would know there was nothing to see. After everyone had disappeared, she crawled into the hammock and kept returning to it for three days. She didn't make a single hot meal, didn't run a single machine. She only went out twice a day with the dog, and they took even longer walks than usual.

It was her best and only attempt at detox.

I walk down the Bulksteeg to my car. I can see the house through the hedge. There are no lights on. Maybe Dad doesn't care that it's so dark all the time anymore. How old is he by now? Early seventies? An age when logic isn't quite gone yet, but it's definitely in decline—when you have to think about how to tie a tie, have to start hauling out instruction manuals, have to search longer for the ON-OFF switches on simple devices. An age when you can't really talk people out of life anymore, because you've almost lived it out yourself, and that would make you about as credible as a dairy farmer who only drinks sterilized milk.

I'm sure that if he's standing in the kitchen gazing out the window right now, he wouldn't dare to hope it's me off in the distance. You have to see to believe. And the older he gets, the less he sees.

I unlock the car from a distance. The ice block hasn't shrunk a bit. There's just a tiny bit of slush at the bottom of the plastic tub. I get in the car.

In my rear-view mirror, I see the crown of the big tree peeking out over the house.

July 22, 2002

PIM AND LAURENS rarely set foot in our house. Today, as usual, they politely wait in the doorway for me to get my shoes on, as if they're afraid of being swallowed up or infected by something inside.

I called Laurens this morning. His mom answered. It sounded like she was in a hurry. She put down the receiver and shouted, "Laurens, phone!" and went back to her customers. The phone is on the wall in the shop, between the helicopter photo and the roll of meat-packing paper. I listened to the sounds in the shop from the other end of the line, the hum of the machines, the fraying of meat, the murmuring of customers, the cheerful ding of the cash register. I closed my eyes and felt like I was there, part of it.

"Pim and I are pissed." Laurens's tone was abrupt, not unfriendly, but it didn't sound like he missed me. "What do you want?"

"How was Amber yesterday?" I tried.

"Amber was a lesbian." That's all he said. For a moment, there was silence on the line, and all I could hear were the sounds of the shop.

"Are you coming today?" he asked.

I nodded immediately, but Laurens couldn't see that. "What's the plan?" I asked, my voice betraying how happy I was.

"We can't skip your house," he said. "Everyone's equal before the law."

"Okay, come over then," I said.

I squat down to tie my shoelaces. The padding in my bra presses into my stomach. So far, Laurens and Pim haven't noticed my larger cup size; not once have I caught them staring at my chest. To be fair, I am wearing a pretty loose shirt. It's all part of my plan: wear baggy shirts for a couple of weeks and strike at the end of the summer with a tight top and two better assets.

"Where are your parents?" Laurens asks.

"They just left for Top Interior."

Pim looks knowingly at the cracks in the stone facade, at the piles of dishes on the kitchen counter, at the stained curtains serving as cabinet doors.

He's right. What are my parents looking for in a showroom full of sparkling kitchens, faucets that you never know where the water will come out and coffee tables with goat legs? People who don't come to buy, who are just there to browse for inspiration for a better life, are quickly driven out of the store. They don't get offered espresso or free samples.

I lead Laurens and Pim out to the chicken coop, past the turned-over vegetable patch. Clumps of grass are drying in the midday sun. Nothing has sprouted yet—it takes time for the seeds to germinate.

Today, it's Leslie's turn. An eight-pointer. Chances are Laurens and Pim will be on their worst behavior now that they're not on their own property. It's always been like that—we only ever dared to make dirty hot dog jokes at other people's birthday parties, never at home, where the walls had eyes.

"Leslie's parents are going through a divorce. That's good for us—girls like that don't have a solid foundation anymore. You can do all kinds of stuff with them and still get away with it afterwards," I hear Pim explaining behind my back.

Halfway through the yard they stop for a moment, not for the view, but for what they hope to see: Elisa riding her horse. She usually wears tight black riding pants with two shiny stripes that run up from her ankles, along the inner sides of her thighs.

But Elisa isn't out there, only her horse. The lean, muscular animal rubs his head on his trough. Laurens and Pim quickly lose interest.

I rush to tidy up the chicken coop before they walk in behind me. I slide the hay bales against the wall, close the chicken-feed bin and toss a few logs into a rusty barrel.

"Watch your head," I say, only after I hear Laurens bang his forehead against the low doorframe. He rubs his knuckles over the bump. They both take a seat on a bale of hay.

I remain standing. In a few minutes, I'll recite the riddle, with the same intonation, the same pauses for breath. The more I repeat it, the dirtier I feel.

As long as Laurens and Pim can't solve it, they still need me, and I won't betray them, which is why they've never asked me for the answer.

"Have a seat, Eva," Pim says, slapping the bale beside him.

This is it. I shouldn't have given away the two hundred euros. Now there's no money left to manage. My role as secretary-treasurer is about to be dissolved. They're going to demand the answer to the riddle. Then they'll send me away, or they'll leave and never call me again. I don't sit.

"What exactly happened with Amber?" I ask quickly.

"Amber was a lesbian," Pim replies.

"So, she didn't solve the riddle?" I ask.

"No. She wanted to see the two hundred euros before she started guessing."

"And then?"

"Well, we didn't have it, of course," says Laurens. "So we said, 'We don't want to see if your boobs are real anyway.'"

"I said that, not you."

"Pim said that."

"And?" I ask.

"Amber just stood up and showed us her tits," Pim says. "It turns out lesbian boobs aren't all that different from man boobs."

"She did bring beer."

"Yeah, it was pretty good actually."

"We made the best of it," Pim concludes.

"Yeah, we made the best of the situation," repeats Laurens.

They shrug in unison. Now that they're sitting here in front of me, I feel guilty about the fact that this is exactly what I'd wished for all day yesterday—for their plan to fail.

"Listen, Eva. Our rules aren't watertight, especially now that the money's gone," Pim says in a strict tone. "But we still want you there. Laurens and I tweaked the rules a bit after Amber left. They're more or less the same. You tell your riddle. But now all the girls get eight guesses. If they can't figure it out, they have to do us a favor, whatever we ask. If they get it right, we have to do something for them."

"So, it's not for money anymore?" I ask.

"Nope."

"And they don't have to take off their clothes?"

"No," Laurens says, "it's like Truth or Dare. If you can't figure out the riddle, you get Dare."

I nod. Eight guesses. So far, no girl has shown up wearing more than eight items of clothing, even if shoes did count for two.

In a way, Leslie should thank me. Her chances of success have just been increased due to a lack of funds.

"And what if one of the girls gets it right and dares you to eat chicken shit?" I ask.

Laurens and Pim exchange quick looks, unimpressed.

"As long as you provide us with a good riddle, it won't come to that," says Pim, bumping fists with Laurens.

Easy for them to say. They didn't make up the riddle, they don't feel guilty about anything. I'm just bait. I'm not here because I'm Eva, I'm here because I'm a girl and my presence makes the other girls feel more comfortable.

It's hot under the black roof of the chicken coop. The elastic in my underwear itches in my sweaty groin but I don't want to scratch it while they're looking.

I sit down on the hay bale. We wait.

Next to us is a chicken that won't leave the coop. Her skinny head is pointed straight at Laurens and Pim; she doesn't take her eyes off of them for a second. Patches of bare flesh shine through her feathers.

I stand up, walk over to the chicken-feed bin and run my hands through it. In the cool, fresh kernels, my hands land on the neck of a wine bottle. I push it down deeper, then toss a handful of feed to the bird in the straw.

The chicken jumps up and starts pecking around. Pim grabs a stick and jabs her wounded wing. At that, she scurries out of the coop, forced to face the flock she was trying to hide from.

"Chickens don't have feelings. They're cannibals," Pim explains. I don't respond.

"You got anything to drink?" Laurens asks.

"Apple juice or fruit juice?" I suddenly realize how thirsty I am too. We keep the juice in the basement, where it's cool.

"You got anything else? Beer? A half pint?" Pim sticks his pinky in the air.

There's plenty of beer, but Dad will need all the cold ones.

And there's wine—it's all over the place, but nowhere officially. Mom will notice if I dip into her stash. She wouldn't care if I drank some, but it would mean that she could no longer pretend I don't know about it, and that she'd care about.

I can't leave and come back empty-handed. I walk over to the bin, whisk away the lid and conjure up a bottle of chilled wine as if it were a minibar.

"Well, well, look what our little Eva's got here," says Pim, almost proud.

He unscrews the bottle of cheap German wine and presses it to his lips. I watch the bouncing of his Adam's apple as it goes down. Then he passes it to Laurens, who gulps it down like fruit juice. He leaves plenty for me. I plop back down on the hay bale.

"Come on, Eva, are you a musketeer or not?" Laurens pushes the bottle in my face.

I'm not a musketeer here. I'm an umpire. My job is to remain completely neutral. I take a few tiny sips of the wine. It tastes like sour, rotten apple juice.

Laurens and Pim split the rest of the bottle.

Even though I didn't drink very much, I instantly feel fuzzier. Just then, we hear the tingling of spoke beads approaching outside.

"Sure you don't wanna just pretend?" Laurens asks.

"Pretend what?" I ask.

"That you didn't give all our money away to a retard," snaps Pim.

"No."

He staggers to his feet and walks out of the coop.

A few seconds later he returns with Leslie. She has brown skin and is wearing a thin yellow sweater with three-quarter sleeves.

"It's not my bike, it's my sister's," she says. She's sucking in her belly. Her high-heeled sandals make her walk like a duck, with her pelvis tilted forward. She stands there like that while Pim explains what's going to happen. It takes her as much effort to maintain this posture as it does to listen.

"With eight guesses, it'll be a cinch," he concludes. "And Eva, is there any wine for Leslie?"

I nod before I've figured out which stock I can tap into this time. For a moment, all eyes are on me, and in my half-foggy state, I can't remember any other hiding place than the bin of chicken feed.

But before I know it, I'm walking down the garden path, past the cherry tree and into the basement. The hinges on the door creak just like they do when Mom goes down there.

I go down the stairs, grab a box of wine from the back of the shelf, tuck it under my arm and hesitate about which random snack I should take.

I hurry back up the stairs with a box of Kinder Surprise Eggs, close the door and head back out to the chicken coop. I hurry, not because I don't want to miss anything, but because I don't want anyone to notice how miss-able I am. There are only three surprise eggs left in the package.

Leslie has already sat down and is thinking about which eight questions she's going to ask to try to solve the riddle. It's quiet in the coop. The chicken is back—she's just sitting there, looking at us.

"I've already told her the riddle. But you can still say whether her guesses are right or wrong," Pim says.

Laurens immediately opens the box of eggs. The surprise inside his is a little light-up ghost with a hat. He doesn't even put it together.

Leslie's egg contains a little car. Pim gets a Smurf on a skate-board.

He removes the bag of wine from the cardboard box and pours it directly into Leslie's mouth to wash down the chocolate. Then he pours it into Laurens's mouth, then into mine. It streams down my chin. Pim keeps pouring. All I can do is swallow.

After that, Leslie starts guessing. Every time, I answer with a yes or no. Since she doesn't have to give up any clothes, she thinks differently.

I roll the little car back and forth over my hands, thinking about how I'm going to cover my tracks: I can put the empty bottle and the winebox back where I found them, or toss the bottle in the glass container and act like I don't know anything about it. I can go to the Corner Store with my allowance and try to convince Agnes to sell me a full box of wine, pour half of it in the empty bottle, bury it back in the chicken feed and then put the half-empty box back in the basement.

"Was he a frog that transformed into a person and landed in the room?" That was Leslie's eighth guess.

"No, wrong," I say.

"Now what?" she asks.

Outside it's starting to rain. Fat drops plop down on the corru-gated metal roof. I stand up and look out in the yard. One half is still dry. In the other, it's pouring.

"Check this out," I holler. By the time the others have gathered at the door, the clouds have shifted, and it's raining in the whole yard.

"What?" Laurens asks.

Pim sticks his hand outside and flings rainwater on Leslie. She screams, nearly tripping over her heels.

"Now you have to do us a favor," says Pim.

"Who gets to pick the favor?" Leslie asks. With this weather, she won't be leaving any time soon.

"Who do you want?"

Leslie looks at each of us, one by one.

"I want Eva to choose."

"All right then, Eva," says Pim.

I think about it. I have to come up with something that'll make Pim and Laurens happy, but I also have to do that thing girls do, meet each other halfway.

"Laurens and Pim each get to touch you for three seconds," I say.

"Okay," she sighs. It's hard to say whether she's relieved or disappointed. She mostly looks drunk. I hope my face doesn't look as numb as hers does.

Laurens gets to go first. He stands in front of Leslie and gingerly places his hands on her sweater, where he assumes her breasts must be. He squeezes with his fingers, but he's standing just a little too far away, making the motion clumsy and cautious at the same time. It reminds me of how Tessie tests fruit to see if it's ripe.

I count three long seconds.

"Okay, enough," says Pim. Laurens steps aside, and Pim takes position. First, he looks at Leslie from head to toe, sizing her up.

I count.

In a smooth, quick motion he whips up her skirt and pushes the elastic band of her underpants to the side. He raises the middle finger on his other hand, holds it up to the light like a doctor with a syringe and wets it with saliva. Then he lowers it to her crotch and pushes it in, slanting it upwards with the line of her lower body. Leslie spreads her legs wider apart and loses balance. I can tell by looking at Pim's forearm that he's holding her upright, his wrist muscles contract. She is now pinned on his finger, which is inside her as deep as it will go.

"The three seconds starts now," Pim says. "Now that I'm really touching her."

Laurens is watching in awe. He's sorry he didn't think of this himself.

I count three quick seconds.

On three, Pim moves his middle finger in and out three times. When he withdraws his hand, the elastic on Leslie's panties jumps back between her labia. She pulls them back into place. Pim smells his finger and sticks it in Laurens's face.

"Come on. Better than any pâté from your shop. You can taste it if you want."

Laurens hesitates, then clumsily licks Pim's finger, mostly because Leslie's watching.

After she's left in the rain, Pim declares: "That, boys, is what they call middle-fingering." She must still be within earshot. We haven't heard the sound of her spoke beads riding away yet.

He cracks his knuckles and passes around the bag of wine again. The grin on his face seems wider than usual.

At what point did he start believing he was good at this, and was that before or after he got good at it?

An hour later, the whole family's gathered for dinner. Mom is the last to join. She accidentally slams the cast-iron pot down in the middle of the table, having miscalculated the distance. Jolan checks if there are cracks in the tabletop.

My skin and muscles are burning. I don't think the wine has left my system yet. I carry out each motion deliberately. I pass the potatoes, lift the fork from my plate to my mouth.

The contours of my body don't feel sharp, but blurry, like the skin of a shadow. My movements stick to my body, my arms feel like sponges. Mom sits down beside me but doesn't notice a thing. We're two people drawn into the twilight, blurred photographs.

But Tessie does notice. She follows the movement of my fork closely. Unfortunately, we're having peas.

The Treatment

MAYONNAISE. MOM HEARD it helped get rid of lice. She wanted to wait until the start of Easter vacation so Tessie wouldn't have to go to school with greasy hair.

"If this doesn't help, I'll have to use the clipper," she said. She banged on the bottom of the 1100ml jar of Devos & Lemmens lemon-flavored mayonnaise, in an effort to loosen the lid. Jolan and I were setting up the Mastermind game on a nearby table so we could keep an eye on the kitchen. The mayonnaise hair treatment didn't seem like a good idea to us. But we didn't have any better ideas, so we kept our mouths shut.

Tessie stood reluctantly in the middle of the room. She was wearing her favorite frilly pink Barbie nightdress, which she had long outgrown. The ruffled seam ran straight across her nipples. I had the same one—an aunt had given them to us along with a matching mini-version for our dolls. Only Tessie still believed that as long as she made Barbie look like her, she looked like Barbie.

Mom draped an old bath towel over Tessie's shoulders, pulled the hair-tie out of her silky hair and ran a comb through it.

We felt nervous and knew we shouldn't laugh—both me and Jolan understood that.

All three of us had had head lice, but the Little Runt was the only one who couldn't get rid of them, because everything she contracted was worse and lasted longer.

"I don't want Jolan to watch," Tessie said. Her head bobbed back and forth from the strokes of the comb like a snowflake in the wind.

"You heard her, Jolan. Turn around," Mom said.

Fortunately, I was on the right side of the table, so I didn't have to turn my head to see what was going on. Still, I looked away.

The walnut tree on the patio was covered in buds. Some of the other trees were blossoming already, and one small shrub had tiny sour berries on it. Even the rhubarb was full of leaves. A bird landed on the swing in the back of the yard. Jolan fetched his binoculars from the counter.

"*Erithacus rubecula*. A robin." He was picking up new Latin words every day.

"Even if you were making it up, we wouldn't know," Tessie said.

We watched the robin pick a few seeds off the suet ball in the birdhouse and listened to Mom stirring the mayonnaise in the jar. It made the same squelching sound as the wallpaper glue she'd once made.

She carefully rubbed the goo into Tessie's roots and spread it down to the ends. Once a section of hair had been fully smothered, she pushed it over to the other side of Tessie's head and patted it down with the rest of the strands plastered to her skull.

When two thirds of Tessie's head had been thoroughly greased, Mom paused to pluck a stray louse from her shoulder. Tessie had been standing there for a while by then. She lifted one foot off the ground, twisted her ankle, and lost her balance for a second.

"They're falling off your head. That's a good sign. They're surrendering," Mom declared. She squished the louse in the open handkerchief on the table with palpable irritation.

Jolan examined the black dot with his binoculars.

Mom took the red spoon with the long handle and plopped another glob of Devos & Lemmens on Tessie's head. She spread it out with the rounded side of the spoon.

Blobs of mayonnaise dripped down Tessie's head and onto her shoulders. She wanted to wipe it away. Her fingers fiddled with the corner of the towel around her shoulders.

"Don't touch it," Mom said. "That's their struggle you're feeling. These are the final convulsions."

By six o'clock, there was enough mayonnaise on Tessie's head

for a school-wide hamburger party. The shadows in the backyard
had disappeared. For a spring evening, that only meant one thing:
dinner time. Jolan packed up the Mastermind game. He didn't even
ask me what the winning color combination was.

"What now?" he asked, turning on the light in the kitchen.

Tessie was squirming, shifting her weight from one leg to the
other. She was tired. Mom read the label on the mayonnaise jar.
There was no answer on it, only the ingredients.

"It needs time to sink in. She'll have to sleep in it."

"How am I supposed to sleep like this?" Tessie moaned, pressing
her hands between her knees.

"Standing up. Like the cows," said Dad, who'd just walked in
and was waiting for someone to start setting the table.

He decided to intervene. He took a roll of cling wrap out of the
cupboard and started wrapping it around Tessie's head. Then he
pulled it down under her chin and secured it on the other side of
her head so it wouldn't slide off. Only thing left uncovered was her
face.

"Not too tight! I can't breathe," Tessie wailed. She jammed her
fingers under the plastic so Dad would have to leave more room.

"Don't touch it! A person doesn't suffocate that quickly," Dad
said. He yanked it even tighter. I could see the skin on her neck
wrinkling under the pressure of the plastic.

I looked away so Tessie wouldn't be able to see on my face how
bad this looked.

We ate a baguette that had been warmed up on top of the radiator, but the thermostat had recently switched to summer mode so
the crust wasn't very crispy.

After Dad had finished his first sandwich, he went to get the
mayonnaise that Jolan had deliberately forgotten to set on the table.
He plopped it onto his bread in the same motion he uses to drip
Maggi seasoning into his soup—three flicks of the wrist. Tessie's
plastic hat rustled every time she turned her head.

Dad opened his mouth and took a giant, greedy bite. The mayonnaise squished out on the other side of the bread. His second bite

was slower, more emphatic, because now everybody was watching. He dabbed up the drips on his plate with his finger. All of a sudden, he started coughing.

"See, Tessie, that mayonnaise is pure poison!" Jolan said. "It'll knock out those lice for sure." He gave Dad a nod—he could stop now, the point had been made. But Dad jumped up, his face red, his arms flailing. He wasn't joking. I smacked his back until the bread came flying out of his windpipe.

I went to bed early with Tessie. Mom handed us four cut-open garbage bags to protect Tessie's mattress.

"Are you asleep?" Tessie asked in the middle of the night. The sweet, lemony smell had permeated the room.

"Yeah, I'm asleep." Normally, this would have made her laugh, but she didn't make a sound. "Hey Tessie, should we just go wash it out? I think that stuff's been on long enough."

"It's on there now, we might as well let it soak in," she said.

Because of the friction against the garbage bag, the cling-wrap turban had sagged to one side, pulling her mouth crooked.

"You want to try sleeping in my bed?" I ask. "It's cozy up here under the slanted ceiling."

"No, that's not necessary," Tessie said.

But a few minutes later, she brought it up again.

"Maybe I would be able to sleep better up there."

We switched. Her bed consisted of four low cupboards pushed together with a mattress on top. Due to the lack of ventilation in our room, there was mold seeping out under the edges of the mattress. "I can do it," she said, as I tried to help her up the ladder.

From the lower bed, I watched Tessie climb up into my bed with her head wrapped in plastic, dragging the garbage bags behind her. She carefully spread them out on top of my mattress, even more carefully than she'd done on her own bed. Then she lay down on top of them. The plastic crinkled with every move she made.

"You can start saying goodnight now," she said. She whispered the names of everyone we needed to say goodnight to, one by one.

"Goodnight, God, goodnight, Tes," I ended.

"Goodnight, Eva," she said.

I woke up before dawn feeling nauseous. The mayonnaise had curdled during the hot night. Tessie was still asleep. Her body was covered in oil and thick, greasy clumps of hair stuck out of her hat. There was melted mayonnaise everywhere, in her ears, on my pillow, dripping down her neck. The plastic-wrap turban had loosened in the night. She was lying on top of the garbage bags, stiff and motionless.

I woke her up and took her into the bathroom. I told her to lean over the edge of the tub, so I could rinse the stuff out of her hair. Pearls of grease formed on the surface of the water. I washed her hair twice with shampoo. Tessie gave me specific instructions. Both sides of her head had to be massaged exactly the same way. Afterwards she shampooed herself one more time, to wash off me washing her.

Two days later it was Easter. There was a noticeable increase in the number of chocolate eggs from the Easter Bunny that year. Tessie's hair still hung down in heavy strings beside her head. When you tried to run a comb through it, the greasy spikes just shifted position. The short strands, which always broke off before they were long enough to put in a ponytail, left a shine on her forehead. Between them you could see her scalp—and the little black bugs wriggling around on her head.

When Easter break was over, she returned to school with the side pockets of her bookbag full of Easter eggs to hand out on the playground. She wore one of Dad's old caps to cover her bald head.

2:00 p.m.

WINDSHIELD WIPERS SOMETIMES move like arms and sometimes like legs. I have no idea what this depends on: the type of car, how fast they're moving back and forth or the state of mind I'm in when I crawl behind the wheel.

For a long time, heavy rain reminded me of Jan, the way the wipers sputtered and struggled, no match for all the water. I wondered whether Pim ever thought about Jan when he was in his car or on the tractor in the same rain. Whether he ever pulled over to the side of the road like I did just so he could turn them off.

I look down at the invitation on the passenger seat for the thousandth time. The party still starts at three o'clock.

I could just drive back to Brussels, make myself a cheese sandwich, finish a drawing, listen to the kids next door playing on the other side of the wall. With every noise in the hallway, I'd hope it was the downstairs neighbor. Eventually, he'd come knock on the door—not because he's reliable, just predictable. Tomorrow there would be yet another envelope from Jolan. I'd drop it in the shoebox with all the other ones I've received. At some point it would become too much money to keep in the house, and I'd have to decide what to do with it: keep it or not.

I shouldn't have left so early this morning. The farm is only a three-minute drive from here, five at the most in the snow. Even if I took the longest detour in town at ten kilometers per hour, zigzagged up and down all the main streets and parked backwards in every free spot I find along the way, I would still arrive well before the party starts. Only people who are worried about the nuts running out—people like Laurens—show up early to parties.

Waiting in front of my parents' house isn't an option. I turn my car down the most obvious street, the one leading to the church. I've taken this route countless times. I don't think there's a route in Brussels I've taken as frequently as I've taken this one, not to the school where I teach, not from my front door to the nearest supermarket, not to the gym on Rossinistraat where I row for an hour every morning, not to the school where I took the figure-drawing class, not even the twenty meters to my neighbor's door. As long as this town is the place where I've spent most of my life, I'm more at home here more than I'll ever be in Brussels.

There must be exact numbers—how many times I've biked past the church, how many times I stood in front of Laurens's house watching his mom in the shop, how many slices of meat she passed me over the counter because she thought I looked pale, how many times I pedaled away with the taste of cheap sausage in my mouth wishing everything around me would freeze, everything except the kids, and we'd all have to rotate, without protest, to the next house on the right, because families are nothing more than systems to be passed through.

Life is no more than a sum of numbers, but few people manage to keep track of them, to start counting in time. Those who try end up making themselves sick or crazy. They start calculating in advance how many chews it should take to grind down a certain piece of food and then subtract each jaw movement from there. Their life is not a sum but a difference, and eventually they bring themselves to zero.

I slowly steer the car through the center of town. I let the places I don't want to go determine the roads I take. I don't want to go to Miss Emma's house, but I have to. I owe it to her. Ever since that goodbye party at school, I owe her everything.

The party was on a rainy day. It wasn't the last day of the school year, but it was the only day that we, the side class, could take over the classroom: the fifth-graders were sent out with the fourth-graders.

We pushed all the benches and chairs to the side. Miss Emma had invited her sister to work the dance floor. She was well known around the school. With her stocky build, short curly hair and negligible breasts, she was always asked to play Black Pete at the Sinterklaas party in December.

Halfway through the festivities I went to the broom closet in search of extra chalk and an eraser because the dancing had degenerated into drawing rebus puzzles on the blackboard. When I turned on the light, I found Miss Emma and her sister, tangled up in each other's arms. Miss Emma was startled, but she didn't let go of her sister.

"Eva," she said. "This isn't my sister. This is my fiancée." She placed her right hand on my back and her left hand on the back of the woman about whom all certainty had been lost in the space of a few seconds. "This has to stay between us. Promise?" she said.

Her hands were warm. I couldn't feel her fingertips, all I felt was the one that was missing. I nodded and did that thing Black Pete always does to silence a gym full of ecstatic toddlers: I zipped my lips and swallowed the imaginary key.

I really didn't plan on telling anyone, but as soon as we were on our way home, the lock on my mouth broke open. Finally, I had something to tell Pim.

"You guys wanna know something?" Jolan said a few days later when we were all seated at the table. He waited for Dad to respond.

No one was that interested. We all expected him to say something about the difference between single- and double-lobed plants.

"I do," I said. He gave me a faint smile.

"Miss Emma is a lesbian. Somebody saw it with their own eyes," he said. I felt like I'd been stung by a wasp. The burn spread across my entire chest.

Dad didn't react. I bent over my plate like he did and fished out the little pink bacon bits between the slimy macaroni.

Jolan wasn't the type of person who was privy to this kind of gossip, unless someone was trying to coax him into helping them with their math or physics homework. The fact that even he knew about Miss Emma was proof that Pim had spread the news all over town.

"A lesbian. Crazy, huh?" Jolan repeated. "Rumor has it they were fooling around in the broom closet." He looked up at Dad again to see if he cared.

"Why don't you just focus on finishing your plate, Jolan," Mom declared.

Jolan stopped talking and ate.

It took everything in me not to react, not to reveal that what he said mattered to me, that it was true. But for the first time I wasn't able to offer any support.

The story about Miss Emma in the broom closet spread like wildfire. Within a few days, it had reached the school board. Parents were demanding an explanation.

The news of Miss Emma's resignation came two weeks later. They made up some other reason for it.

Throughout the fall of 2000, I stood in this exact spot, behind the linden tree where I'm now parking my car. From here I could see Miss Emma's house without her being able to see me. She wasn't my conscience anymore. There'd been a changing of the guard.

I watched her trim her hedge, how she clumsily tried to balance the shopping bags on her handlebars in front of her house, how every time the handles got caught on the bell. Once she snarled at them and rang her bell three times in a row. I was the only one who heard it. It sounded like a question that no one wanted to answer.

Even though it cost me my hiding spot, I rang my bike bell three times back, at exactly the same intervals.

Miss Emma whipped around, looked at me sternly, marched into the house with the heavy shopping bags and slammed the door behind her.

That year, before the winter settled in, her house went up for sale.

She only returned to Bovenmeer twice: once in 2001, for Jan's funeral, and once in 2004, to become the first lesbian to get married in our town. Word had it that only those who had openly supported their relationship would be invited to the ceremony. But anybody could come out to throw rice afterwards.

I checked the mailbox seven days in a row. Pim was the only musketeer who got an invitation. Jan's death brought him endless privileges.

In the end, he didn't go. That didn't surprise me. When I first told him her secret, he replied, "She doesn't have some other orientation, she's just disoriented."

At first, I wasn't planning to watch people throw rice either. The summer of 2002 had already happened, Tessie didn't live at home anymore, I made as few plans as possible and did everything I could to avoid Laurens and Pim.

When the day came, I went anyway and watched from afar. A lot of people showed up out of curiosity. They all wanted to see if it actually worked: two white dresses promising to love and cherish each other forever.

I mostly wanted to see if Miss Emma looked happy. If quitting her job at the school had changed her life for the better. If it had made her even more remarkable.

No turtle doves or balloons were released.

Miss Emma wore a white skirt suit with a plunging neckline and her hair in a tight dot. Her brand-new wife wore a beige linen suit with straight legs and a purple breast pocket. They strolled out through the wide gates of the town hall. There were a few people, including Laurens's mom—who hadn't even bothered to take off her apron—who made sure to hurl the coarsest type of rice right in their faces.

July 24, 2002

I SHOW UP at Laurens's house the old-fashioned way, without calling first, hoping to convince him to stop "the sampling". I'm ready with a short speech and just enough money in my sock for a few slices of ringwurst, so I won't have to go home empty-handed if Laurens refuses to listen to my plea.

ON VACATION UNTIL NEXT WEDNESDAY reads the sign in the shop window. The display case is completely empty, except for a garland of dry sausages. Under a kitchen towel are a few jars of preserves that couldn't possibly go bad in seven days.

Laurens's dad, who is almost unrecognizable in sunglasses and without his butcher's apron on, is out in the open garage trying to squeeze the last few things into the car.

This happens every year. First, they don't have any holiday plans, then they rush off in a big hurry. They always go to the same campground in the South of France with two beaches: one sandy, the other for nudists.

Laurens is already in the car reading a comic book with one hand in the giant candy jar meant for on the road. He rolls down the window.

"Indira will have to wait a week for your riddle," he says hastily, even though they're not ready to hit the road yet. His mom is leisurely watering the plants on the windowsills. He passes me a sour fizz ball through the open window and fishes out a milder piece of candy for himself.

"Don't worry, we'll save Indira for when you get back," I say.

He rolls the window back up.

Five minutes later, his mother locks the front door.

Ever since the shadow-puppet incident in the summer of 2000, she hasn't trusted me with the spare house key. Before that, the same three people had access to the butcher shop during the holidays: Laurens's dad's brother, Laurens's mom's friend and me. I always accepted the key gratefully, without knowing what I might need it for. There were no live animals in the house, they had a fire alarm and I had no idea how to operate the power generator next to the fridge. I never carried the key in my pocket, I kept it in the sock box in my closet instead. Not only because I was afraid of losing it, but because, with every move I made, the metal reminded me of the hours leading up to their departure, and of how much I'd hoped they'd ask me to come along.

I sit on the cemetery wall with a sour, tingling tongue and wait for them to drive out of town in their packed car.

Laurens knows I won't meet up with Pim without him. The overloaded blue BMW passes by the church. Even though I've already made up my mind not to draw any more attention to the fact that I'm the one staying behind, I start waving wildly. Because Laurens doesn't see what I see—that, surrounded by all the heavy camping gear in the back seat, his head looks smaller and clumsier than usual. It's hard not to feel sorry for him.

I try to imagine what kind of vacations go with all that camping gear. For most items, it's easy enough to picture. The three coolers, for example, contain leftover meat that they'll throw on the grill tonight and then give away for free—that way they'll be able to borrow other people's equipment for the rest of the holiday without feeling guilty about it. The water tank will have to be refilled regularly, and they'll spend much of the day lugging it around the campground. The Nordic walking poles will prove to be nothing more than a good intention.

I'm able to picture almost everything perfectly, even the board games and air mattress, but there's one thing I can't imagine: Laurens's mom lying naked on the beach. Here in town she's the most reassuring person I know. At any given moment during the day, I know where she is, what she's doing and how she's doing it, which knives she's using, which meat she's cutting.

The fact that she always covers her body for us but dares to expose it on some beach in France isn't just remarkable, it hurts. Apparently, she can be more herself with strangers. This town, the familiarity of it, is somehow failing her.

The car disappears. I stop waving and look up at the church tower. The clock doesn't have a second hand, and that's a good thing. It's not even noon yet.

It's been nearly two weeks since the carnival trailers left town. By now, they've been gone longer than they were here, yet their absence is still noticeable. All the grandparents who urged their grandchildren on the merry-go-round to catch the *flosh* and win a free ride. The operator who dangled the tassel just out of reach of their grabby little hands. The one kid who, without resorting to any drastic measures, actually caught the thing—and not because anyone complained that the kids didn't stand a chance, but because he had brothers, sisters and cousins who'd all want to join him on his free ride and have to buy another ticket.

Not long after the car is gone, something else appears in its place: Elisa's Mimi on her way to the bread-vending machine in the parish square. As she comes into focus—glasses, clogs, capri pants over her bathing suit—I notice her hesitation when she sees me. First, she buys her loaf of bread and then she walks towards me with the paper bag clamped under her arm. She's looking more and more like a grandmother.

"Elisa's in town this summer," she says.

She looks me straight in the eyes. I don't dare to smile.

"I saw her riding her horse the other day," I say.

"I think she's bored," Mimi says. She breaks off a piece of crust and gives it to me. Back when I used to have lunch at her house, I always ate the crusts because she said they made your breasts grow, and by the looks of Elisa, I had no reason not to believe her.

"How is she?" I ask, chewing the bread.

"Why don't you come with us to Lille Mountain today? You can ask her yourself," she says. "Or do you have other plans?"

I crawl on my knees under the barbed wire and stand at the edge of the field, watching Elisa ride her new horse in circles, how she moves dramatically up and down in the saddle.

When she came to town the weekend of the carnival, I didn't dare to speak to her, because I didn't have any reason to. Now that Mimi has asked me to try to convince her to come with us to Lille Mountain, it's different. This time I'm here on assignment.

I just went home to put on my swimsuit. It took me a while to find a system that would allow me to keep my breasts. In front of the bathroom mirror, I put on one of the padded bras and tucked the straps under the swimsuit. The round forms weren't as big as Elisa's, but at least they were something.

It takes a few minutes for Elisa to notice me. She stops rocking back and forth on the saddle, grips the sides of the horse's neck and pushes herself up straighter. With loud clicks of her tongue, she steers the animal in my direction. This stallion is bigger than Twinkle was, and he's got a white patch around his left eye.

If he were a cow, he'd be one of those black ones with the white head. Those were Jan's favorites—he told me once.

Elisa climbs down from the horse. She's a head taller than I am. The first thing I notice are her eyebrows. Two perfectly shaped arches. I don't think she tweezed them herself. There's probably a beauty salon in Hoogstraten where they can do it for you.

The horse snorts impatiently. Elisa clicks her tongue again and walks in front of me to the water trough outside the barn.

"Mimi wanted me to ask you if you'll come with her to Lille Mountain," I say. "She asked me to come too."

Elisa frowns with her sharp eyebrows.

"If I say no, will the two of you go together?"

She leads the horse into the barn. Inside, she hoists the saddle off his back. She takes her time, performing every step emphatically.

The sight of Elisa's back irritates me. As long as I'm looking at her back, I'm not being seen by her. With most other people, Dad, for example, I feel the opposite. His back is the only part of his body I dare to look at, that I don't hold against him—it's his blind spot.

It takes her an hour to get ready to go. I don't really believe she's coming until she's sitting beside me in the back seat of the car showing off the neon yellow bikini under her clothes.

"Sorry it took so long," Mimi says.

"No worries," I say—at least we've killed some time.

I try to relax. Now that Laurens is on his way to that sandy beach in the South of France, where he'll suck in his belly every time a group of Dutch girls walks by, I don't constantly have to wonder whether he and Pim are off having more fun without me.

A half-hour later, we arrive at Lille Mountain.

For a recreation area in a small Belgian town like Lille, it's a pretty strategic name. Every year, at least a hundred lost tourists show up at the swimming hole with hiking boots or a map of France wondering how on earth they ended up here. Most of the time these are the people who rent the jet skis, so at least they can say they didn't come all this way for nothing.

We find a spot away from Mimi and spread out our towels in the opposite direction of hers, that way the boys up ahead won't think she's with us.

"You didn't get so fat after all," is the first thing Elisa says as we take off our clothes to reveal our swimwear. She squirts twice as much sunscreen into my hand as the amount she claims to need for her own body.

Once I've got it all rubbed in, I lie down on my belly and turn my head away from her. Elisa takes a magazine out of her bag and starts flipping through it. I should've brought a comic book.

The last time Elisa and I read a book together was in the fourth grade, the night before a language arts test. I was the best sentence dissector in the class, but I needed a good excuse to knock on Mimi's door so late in the evening. I said I forgot how to identify a direct object.

"First you have know what the subject is, then you can find the direct object," Elisa explained in a teacherly tone. "For example, in the sentence, 'Elisa explains sentence analysis to Eva', who is performing the action? Elisa. She's explaining something. She's the subject. Who is Elisa explaining something to? To Eva. So Eva is the direct object."

Based on her explanation, I concluded that she hadn't understood very much of the grammar lesson, but I didn't correct her. On the contrary—I let her get the answer wrong on the test the next day, because either way she still understood the basic relationship: as long as she and I were in the same sentence, she was always the subject.

Finally, around three-thirty, when the sun is no longer high in the sky, Elisa decides it's time for a dip. She stands up from her towel and jumps around in the sand to loosen her muscles. The line from her neck to her tailbone is covered with pointy vertebrae. It reminds me of how sloppy kids draw dinosaurs. The weight of her breasts is supported by a tiny yellow string tied behind her neck. We have about the same amount of fat on our bodies, hers just hangs in the right places.

Her belly is flat with one deep wrinkle just below her navel, like pants with a crease. When she sits down, it rolls only there, nowhere else.

It was something I'd already noticed on that field trip to the swimming pool. Even back then, I already knew that the things I admired about her were the same things I would later come to hate. Now I think the prettiest thing on her body is her mole, especially how she artfully manages to keep it tucked under her top. She must have had to try on a lot of bikinis before she found one that would cover it.

"I don't feel like swimming," I say. When Elisa doesn't respond, I stand up and follow her down to the water, taking cautious baby steps.

"Okay, fine," I say. "But I'm not going in past my waist." Otherwise, the padding in my bra will fill up with water. Everybody knows that wet circles under a dry bathing suit are an easy way to tell which girls are cheating.

Elisa ducks under the water. A few seconds later she grabs me by the ankles, pulling me off balance. I fall forward into the shallow pond.

With my nose full of water, and even afterwards—while we're plodding through the sand back to our towels—I can't remember why I ever liked her, why I even came. It must have been the same for the sand: there was a time when all the grains were fused together in a single rock that had no intention of ever crumbling, but over time, the water decided otherwise.

We plop back down on our towels. Elisa keeps turning over so each side will dry evenly. I stay on my belly so she won't see the two wet spots on my chest.

Elisa's bikini bottom is one of those ones with little strings on the sides. She catches the attention of a couple of guys behind us by sucking in her stomach and tilting her pelvis so her hipbones stick out and the fabric floats from one bone to the other like a bridge. Even I can see right down to her crotch. Her pubic hair is in one big, uncompromising wet curl.

Only after the boys have turned over on their stomachs one by one to conceal their excitement from each other does she lower her pelvis again.

"Are you still a virgin?" she asks, just loud enough for the boys to hear.

"Are you?" I ask. That's exactly what she wants—the opportunity to answer her own question.

"Of course not," she says. "But you don't know the guy. He's from Hoogstraten. He was pretty sweet, actually, it didn't hurt at all. Did it hurt for you?"

"No, it didn't hurt for me either," I say.

We lie there in silence for a little while. The boys get up to play soccer. As they walk by, they grope Elisa from head to toe with their eyes.

I think about Tessie. About how I left her at home earlier. She'd already put on her bathing suit under her clothes when she got up this morning, hoping to convince someone to go swimming with her. I could've taken her to the Pit. I could've finally set the pool up in the backyard so Dad could stop using the promise of it to get her do all kinds of chores.

Mimi shows up between our towels.

"I'm going for ice cream," she says. "What kind do you girls want?"

Elisa shakes her head. "We're not hungry."

We watch Mimi walk over to the ice-cream cart, dodging the dried pinecones in the sand as if they were landmines.

"One time, I came on my horse," Elisa says after Mimi is out of earshot.

It's the first time she's brought up her horse all afternoon.

"There's this little bulge on my saddle. It's in just the right spot, if you know what I mean." She articulates slowly as if she expects me to take notes. "After Twinkle died, I got rid of all her stuff. But the one thing I kept was the saddle."

Mimi hurries back with an ice-cream cone and two Calippo push pops. She tosses them down between us and goes back to her towel to eat her vanilla ice cream.

If I wanted to shut Elisa up, I could just tell her the truth: it'll be her own dumb fault when her vagina gets all gray and saggy from rubbing on the leather saddle. I unwrap one of the Calippos.

"Want me to teach you how to ride?" she asks. I shrug.

She takes the other push pop, places it between her thighs and rubs her hands up and down it until the frozen ice flops out of the tube. Then she wraps her lips around the top and licks the sticky syrup off with her tongue.

Most of the boys are completely absorbed in the soccer game; only the goalkeeper sees what Elisa is doing. On the second lick, someone kicks the ball into his goal.

By six o'clock, it's getting chilly. The smell of burnt meat hangs in the air, though there's not a single barbecue in sight. Elisa isn't sucking in her stomach anymore. The boys are all gone. The sand is covered in wet-towel prints. "We're going to leave soon," Mimi hollers. She's waist-deep in the pond, not far from a group of kids splashing around in the water.

"Bet she's peeing," Elisa says.

I put on my T-shirt and sit up on my towel. We look out at two little boys stuck on a pedal boat in the middle of the pond. A half-naked lifeguard swims out to save them. Even when we're looking at the exact same thing, Elisa and I always see something different. That's not going to change. Pretty soon, I'll lose her again. After today, we won't talk for a long time. She sits down on my towel so she can use hers to wipe off her feet.

I want to give her something, a few words that can be kept between us, a secret, but I can't tell her about what we've been up to this summer, about Laurens and Pim's plans, about the scoreboard with her name at the top, her nine-and-a-half—she won't take it as a secret but as a compliment.

"I've got a riddle for you," I say. "It's a good one."

"Tell me," Elisa says.

I recite the riddle with chattering teeth. Elisa listens attentively. Her skin glows against mine. For a moment, I suspect she already knows the answer, that she was the one who told it to me in the first place, the one whose pauses and intonation I forgot. But she looks at me, slightly perturbed, and says, "I have no idea. Just tell me the answer, I hate guessing."

Without hesitation, I tell her the answer.

"You know, once you know it, it makes perfect sense," she says.

She stands up, unties the strings on her bikini bottom on each side, one by one, and tightens them again. Then she loosens the fabric between her crotch, so her camel toe isn't showing anymore.

Fifteen minutes later, we're back at the car, parked between the rows of evergreens. Mimi suggests we sit in the back seat together, but Elisa takes the front. She rolls down her window. Her back is nicely tanned, and as soon as we pick up speed, her ponytail starts blowing in the wind. I can still feel her skin glowing against mine.

Encarta 97

I NEVER REALLY asked for world peace. I didn't ask for a rosary either, but I got one anyway from my grandpa for my First Communion. Instead of the standard donation to my new bike fund, he handed me a little leather pouch. Inside was a chain with fifty-five beads—between every ten white beads was a blue one.

Praying the rosary was so second nature to Grandpa that he didn't think to explain to me how to do it. Then again, he didn't explain how not to do it either.

I started in the morning in the bathroom, on my bare knees. I ran the beads through my fingers like I'd seen him do. On every white bead, I repeated the same wish—to win the annual interschool field-day race. On the blue ones, which were a little heavier and felt like they shouldn't be used for selfish purposes, I asked for world peace.

I didn't know what world peace meant in practical terms, but I assumed it was a big job and hoped that God, either out of laziness or pure compassion, would go for the easiest, most profitable option: victory in a national field-day race.

In fourth grade, I stopped praying the rosary. Four interschool field days had come and gone, and I hadn't won any races—my legs weren't going to get any longer.

That winter, we didn't get a TV, but we did find Encarta 97 under the Christmas tree.

"First-aid for school projects," Jolan called it. He got a microscope for his birthday that year and was still in the phase where he'd only accept information that he'd observed firsthand. While he was out digging up insects in the garden so he could squish them between two glass plates and examine them under the microscope, Tessie and I pulled up an extra chair at the computer and inserted the educational CD-ROM. We scrolled through dozens of articles, took a quiz where you had to match pictures of strange-looking musical instruments to their sounds and cultures of origin and watched video clips. The one we watched the most was a clip about the earthquake in Kobe, Japan. Not only did it show a two-mile bridge falling to the ground, it also explained what to do in the event of a landslide: steady yourself in a doorway or crawl under a sturdy desk.

Finally, I was able to form a clearer image of the world that I hadn't wished peace for in years. A gold medal for the eight-hundred-meter dash had never seemed so trivial.

Instead of praying the rosary that night, I opened the bedroom window all the way and lay down on my back on top of my duvet with my arms and legs spread out wide. I tried to take in as much of the cold air as possible so I could feel what people in other countries must feel, people in areas devastated by earthquakes, children who didn't have their own recorder and had to make do with a hollowed-out tree branch.

My first act of solidarity lasted five minutes. The only parts of my body that were affected by the cold were the extremities: the ends of my toes and the tip of my nose.

Soon Tessie joined in too. I tried to stop her, but she wouldn't listen. She kicked off her thick duvet and copied my position.

Since we were now sharing the misery between the two of us, I extended the duration of our solidarity acts to ten minutes. Tessie didn't have a clock radio. She depended on me to keep track of the time and wouldn't pull her duvet back up until I said it was okay.

There was a trick: lie on top of the duvet instead of tossing it over the foot of the bed—because the body, like a cat sleeping next to you on the bed, warms the blankets underneath. After half an hour, you can crawl back into a warm bed.

But I didn't say anything. I already knew that Tessie would rather keep the duvet completely off the bed to make it as grueling as possible.

Cold suffering became a biweekly ritual, practiced on Tuesdays and Thursdays. We'd always decide beforehand which culture we were doing it for, which picture or video clip our solidarity was intended for.

"Has it been ten minutes yet?" Tessie would ask after five. She was closer to the open window and skinnier than I was. Most likely, she didn't just feel the cold in her extremities, but deep down in her bones too.

There were many times when I lied. Just because I could. Not just because I liked being able to punish both of us, but because I wanted to know what it was like to manipulate time, to hold it back.

Sometimes we lay shivering on top of our sheets for more than half an hour. Tessie always chattered harder than I did. I think she knew I was adding minutes, but still she obeyed—she probably thought we deserved this.

When I looked at her pale, bony butt and the purple varicose veins all over her body, that's when I knew: I was destroying her.

By the time I told her we should stop, it was already too late. That was a few months before the air salesmen showed up on our doorstep. Tessie had already started performing her own acts of solidarity.

Much to the annoyance of everyone, but especially of Jolan— who liked being able to calculate exactly how long it was until his birthday—she started flipping the calendar in the bathroom back to February every time she used the toilet.

The calendars were Mom's project. She bought one every year to support an international charity organization. They were expensive but contained colorful, high-quality photos from developing countries. Each year, she hung them in different places around the house so they could just stay there, if only for the faces: people who, despite their hardship, still looked happy.

The oldest calendar, the one from '98, was hanging in the

bathroom across from the toilet, which meant that every time you sat down to pee you were less than fifteen centimeters from a third-world country.

Tessie started using that bathroom more often. So often that one day Mom started listing the symptoms of bladder infections and asked me if I thought Tessie might have one.

Sometimes I heard Tessie whispering on the toilet, but I could never make out what she was saying.

"Were you talking to yourself?" I asked her when she was finished.

"No I wasn't." She sounded hurt. I understood the defensiveness in her tone. It was an insulting question. Mom talked to herself sometimes, too.

It wasn't until she came out of the bathroom, and I saw that the calendar had been flipped again, that I knew for sure. The month of February had a photo of a black woman with flies on her lips sitting on a giant tub with a clump of steamed rice in her dark hand.

"You were talking to the calendar," I said.

I stood in the doorway and put my hands on either doorpost, so she couldn't pass. She just stood there.

Carefully, Tessie explained how it had come to this. The month of January had a picture of an ox in a wide-open landscape and a man scowling into the camera. She had to sit on the toilet sideways for a whole month so the man wouldn't be able to see her privates.

Finally, February came. The rice-eating lady in the picture came as a huge relief. Tessie didn't feel embarrassed in front of her. She started telling the woman things about herself. It was a good month. They became friends.

But then came March. Somebody flipped the calendar, the lady disappeared and Tessie missed her—there was no one to watch her anymore, to listen to her.

"It would be like if someone covered all our windows in cardboard until it was our turn to look outside again," she said. "We wouldn't want to spend eleven months in the dark either, now would we?"

I understood Tessie better than she knew. I could have told her about the face of my conscience. I tore out the month of February for her. We hung the picture in our bedroom, over the foot of her bed.

2:15 p.m.

IN SEARCH OF a driveway to turn my car around in, I drive a bit further and turn down Vlierstraat. There are two kinds of houses on this street too: horizontal and vertical.

I grew up in a vertical one; our house was one step up from workers' housing. Pim's white farmhouse, on the other hand, was horizontal, curled up beside the barn like a cat by a noisy furnace. Laurens's butcher shop, with its wide panoramic windows on both floors, looked as if it wanted to stretch out and make itself comfortable too.

Ever since I made the distinction, I can't help but notice that most village houses are horizontal, and most city houses are vertical, so the saying "a city that never sleeps" doesn't really tell us much about its inhabitants.

Miss Emma's old house is vertical. Next to it is "the forest of the forest", and behind that are Pim's parents' fields, and beyond that a vast nature reserve.

The forest got its name because there were two forests in town, thus we needed two names. There was our forest, the one by the Pit, with benches and trash cans and sagging docks built by locals, and then there was this forest located on private property that we didn't discover until much later because of the wide, boggy creek around it. Here, no nails had been pounded into the trees to hang hammocks; no tree-houses had been built in the boughs; nettles and hogweed grew wild up around the trunks. This forest belonged to no one but itself.

In the winter after Jan's death, I often walked along the creek with the dog. This wasn't just because there were no cars and hardly any people, but also because Pim's parents' fields were on the other side. I came to inspect the pastures, to judge how the family was doing by looking at the cows. The animals received very little care. No one brought them in at night or bothered to brush them. They spent the entire winter out in that field, first in snow, then in rain, huddled together, with nothing but frozen or otherwise green water in their trough.

Every time I walked by, they lumbered over to greet me, with their sunken bellies and matted fur. But like everyone else in town, I didn't do anything about it. I didn't look them in the eye.

It wasn't until the end of March 2002 that someone lodged an animal cruelty complaint with the municipal authorities. It came from a bird-watcher who'd been out with his binoculars in the nature reserve behind the fields—he was from out of town and didn't know anything about the farm. Pim's dad was still grieving, and even the city council could understand that. The complaint was dismissed.

After nearly half a kilometer I still haven't found a driveway to turn around in. I know who lives in each and every one of these houses, or at least who lived in them nine years ago. I know which households recycled, how often they drove off their grass, how they received their wafer at Communion, whether they used to be teachers. In some houses, I even recognize the Christmas decorations.

I don't want any of them to know that I'm here. I don't want their dogs to start barking and them to peek out from behind the curtains suspiciously because they weren't expecting any visitors today and see me. I don't want them to come out for a chat and, after testing the water with a few remarks about the bad weather, to ask me how Tessie is doing, to look curiously at the contents of my trunk.

I just keep driving straight. After about a kilometer, I'll come out on the gravel road again and turn left. I resign myself to the fact that I'll have to pass by the butcher shop after all.

I steer the car down a slight curve.

In the distance, I see it—the building the shop's in. The facade has been plastered dark orange. That's new.

I drive up to get a closer look in the shop, but the aluminum shutters have been rolled down. There's a sign on the door with something written on it. I pull up as close as possible so I can read it. WE WILL BE CLOSED ON DEC. 30, 2015. ORDERS CAN STILL BE PLACED BY PHONE. 03 475 64 32. The message is in large handwritten letters across two sheets of paper.

In the front yard is a big new sign on high poles. Two spotlights shine lost light up on it. Under a simple cartoon of three smiling piglets are the words THREE LITTLE PIGS BUTCHER SHOP.

I already knew that the butcher shop had a new name. It was changed in 2004, while I was still living at home, right after a brothel opened nearby on the other side of the canal. It was owned by a Dutch guy with a white Mercedes. He decided not to name his business the Whorehouse (even though there were no other brothels in town so there'd be no chance of confusion). Instead, he named it the Lucky—to fit in with the Welcome and the Night, hoping that his establishment might become equally legendary in town. Neither of the two bars were very happy about this, and nor were the Bakery, the Butcher Shop, the Corner Store and all the other family businesses in Bovenmeer. But since none of them wanted to go door to door with a "NO to the whorehouse" or "NO to the Lucky" petition, they just followed the example and came up with more original names for their businesses, Laurens's parents included.

I'd heard through the grapevine that there'd been a lot of discussion about the new name at Laurens's house. Three Little Pigs must have been Laurens's idea, because his mom could have come up with something better than that. Even the Pit got a new, big sign: THE FISHING HOLE.

Maybe they did it for all the dads who needed a place to say they were going to—"I'll run by the Three Little Pigs" or "I'm off to the Fishing Hole"—something less ambiguous than "going out for ground beef" or "a quick dip at the Pit".

In the spotlights shining up on the new sign, I can see it's started snowing again. I drive as close to the parking lot as possible, so I can get a better look at the scribbly handwriting on the sign—it's Laurens's.

I can picture exactly what's going on inside, the flurry of activity as they rush around filling orders. Me and Pim helped Laurens's parents prepare the tinfoil platters many times. They'd be neatly spread out all over the ground floor, on every free surface—on the cupboards, the counter, the chairs, the windowsills, everywhere except the toilet seat.

Laurens's dad would pass us the trays of freshly cut meat, one by one. Then we'd walk around the shop, dividing them evenly across the platters—the good customers got an extra lamb chop, less good ones got fatty pieces of chicken.

Laurens's mom would make the first round to cover each platter with a layer of lettuce and the last round to check the overall presentation, adding a sprig of parsley or a handful of chopped onion here and there. Then, we all watched from the sidelines as Laurens's dad made one last round to add the finishing touch: toothpicks with little Belgian flags on top.

The whole evening was imbued with a sense of elation that I'd never seen in my own house, an efficiency that would have never occurred to my parents.

Once, at the end of the work day, Laurens's dad held up his meat-smeared hand in front of me, and even though it wasn't clear to me that he was trying to give me a high-five, the way he wrapped his big fingers around my cold hand and pressed it into a fist made me feel like he wouldn't have minded if I were his daughter.

To avoid being seen, I park my car a few meters away in front of Laurens's neighbors' driveway—they're probably away skiing, all the shutters are rolled down. From here I have a perfect view of the butcher shop door and the sign with the three pig heads on it. In addition to the time, the sign also tells the temperature outside: it's exactly two degrees below freezing, sixteen minutes past two.

I've still got at least forty-five minutes to go.

I call Tessie. I let the phone ring. There's not much she could be doing right now. Why doesn't she pick up?

The phone rings three times. I hang up right before the fourth. I don't want to leave a voicemail. Voicemails are always listened to at the wrong moment, after their content has already become irrelevant.

July 31, 2002

"THAT HOWLING IN the backyard is just a cat," Dad reassures me when I come down the stairs an hour after bedtime to check on him and Mom.

"That kitty's got a bunch of burrs stuck on his penis," he says, forming sharp claws with his fist. "You'd be howling too."

Back in my bed, I reassure Tessie that the shrill cries that've been echoing through the yard for the last forty-five minutes aren't coming from Mom.

"Cats have to defend their territory," she says.

"Yeah," I say.

It's two minutes after eleven. I'm almost used to Laurens being in France. Maybe that's because I know he's coming home tonight.

As usual, Tessie starts bidding everyone and everything goodnight. The wardrobe, the children in the third world, objects in the room, the teachers she likes, Nancy Soap, Agnes from the Corner Store, Nanook, the nearest stars and planets, her rabbit, Stamper. The whole thing takes about a minute and a half. She ends with God and me. It's been like this for almost two years now, every night, without exception. She recites the prayers as if she were playing "I'm-going-on-a-trip-and-I'm-going-to-pack . . ." In the past, she would tag new names onto the end of the list, but now the goodbye has taken on a definitive form.

I look at my clock radio. It doesn't tick away the time but adds every passing minute to the rest, as if it's still owed to us.

". . . goodnight, God, goodnight, Eva," Tessie finally says at four after eleven.

Now it's my turn. I have to wait exactly two seconds before I can start.

"You have to count two CROC-A-DILE," Tessie told me once. "It takes exactly two seconds to say 'crocodile'."

After the crocodiles, I have to end the ritual by replying on behalf of everything and everyone with "goodnight, Tes", and then I can only hope that no plane flies overhead, no car honks, no dog barks, no cat meows, or that I don't accidentally say "Tessie" or "Sis" instead of "Tes", because that would lead to a sigh of irritation, and she'd have to start all over again from scratch, wishing everything goodnight again in exactly the same order.

One CROC-A-DILE. Two CROC-A-DILE.

"Sweet dreams, Tes."

For a moment, all is quiet, both in the bedroom and out in the yard.

Did Dad ever show Tessie his noose? Did he ever try to talk her out of life like he did to me?

The crying starts again, shriller this time. It's coming from the back of the garden. Of course, Tessie hears it too. The whites of her eyes shine in the dim light. One of her hands emerges from under the sheet squeezing a juggling ball with calculated rhythm: thirty squeezes, two-second pause. I wait for her to start the goodnight ritual again, but a few minutes later, at fourteen past eleven, I hear the little bean-bag plunk to the floor. It lands on the vinyl-covered parquet. This is exactly what the juggling balls are for. It's a trick I invented at the start of the winter—when she was already having trouble sleeping.

It's simple: you think of something in the back of your mind, a relatively unimportant task that's even more tedious than falling asleep itself, like holding that little ball, for example. Then, you let your wrist dangle just over the edge of the bed and close your eyes. Slowly the sleep will begin to creep into the task, until somewhere far away, between sleep and memories, the thought of holding on slips away, your muscles slacken and the ball falls to the ground. The task becomes a duty, sleeping becomes a right. A body lying flat is more inclined to choose what's allowed over what's required.

At first, Tessie took to it easily; the sound of the stress ball plopping to the ground came shortly after her final goodnight. To me, the sound was like a starting gun for my alone time.

Lately, however, she's been kneading the ball more furiously, more rhythmically, as if she were giving it a heart massage. It's taking longer and longer for her to let go. When the thud finally does come, all I feel is relief—we're done. I can sneeze, cough and move again without having to worry about the consequences.

It's a warm evening. I lay my own ball down beside me. The sheet sticks to my lower legs, my arms, making my skin feel heavy. I yank the blanket down to my waist and pull up my knees like a frog preparing to jump. Then I let them fall open to either side until they're resting on the cool mattress, peeking out under the blanket. It must be a ridiculous sight for whoever is looking down at me from above now—the sheet wrapped around my waist like a diaper.

Under my pillow, jabbing into my shoulder, is a colored pencil. It's there because I told a lie to Elisa, and now the lie has to be undone. I have to do it before Laurens and Pim get back. The longer I wait, the more obvious it will be that I'm still a virgin.

Normally I keep my pencils in a metal box with multiple shades of each color and Bruynzeel printed on the top in gold letters.

Last Thursday, the day after I came home from Lille Mountain, I took the box out of my backpack. I carried it up to my room as inconspicuously as possible, though there was really no reason to sneak around. Nobody was even looking and even if they were, they wouldn't have thought anything of it. I drew at my desk in my bedroom all the time.

It wasn't until yesterday that I finally decided which color to use: the reddest shade of brown—no one at school will ever ask to borrow that one because it's so ugly. Which is the same reason why it still has its original, factory-sharpened tip.

I pull out the pencil from under my pillow, cover the sharp point with the palm of my hand, and move the blunt end down my navel, under the crumpled sheet, to the inside of my thighs.

There's a noise downstairs, probably Dad.

I freeze. He's headed out to the yard to holler for Mom. She shouts back. The low-pitched tones seem to come from outside, through the open window. The high-pitched tones come from inside, through the bedroom door. The voices cross exactly in this room.

I wait with the pencil against my thigh. I don't want to look back and feel like one of my parents was in the room.

Tessie is sleeping soundly enough. The headlights of passing cars scan the entire room, over her spiky hair, the calendar photo on the wall. Then, all is dark and quiet again.

I push the blunt end of the pencil inside.

Red-brown. Somehow it feels less wrong than yellow or green.

I don't think about any boys. Instead I imagine I'm some other girl, that my vagina isn't mine. This is important. As long as this isn't my body, the shame doesn't have to be mine.

Slowly I push the pencil in deeper, exactly the way Mr. Rudy moved the chalk across the clam drawing on the board while the class named the parts he was pointing at. Labia majora. Labia minora. After a couple of centimeters, the pencil won't go any further. As I push harder, the pain spreads. The tip of the pencil is jabbing into my palm. Maybe this is the hymen. This is where I have to apply force.

I turn the pencil around and point the tip inward. Then I thrust my palm against the top end. The path is cleared. The pencil shoots in deep. Slowly, the pain fades.

It's done. I've no longer told a lie. I could stop here.

Instead, I push the pencil in even further, just to see how deep it will go. It's too thin, I hardly feel anything, only the prick of the pointy tip.

A pencil floating in an open cavity, is that all this is? I want it to fill me up, for it to just barely fit, for it to have to wriggle its way in. I jerk around a bit, but I still don't feel much of anything.

It's not for nothing that dicks are big and blunt. How thick is the average penis? About six or seven colored pencils, I guess.

I pull the pencil out from between my legs. The wood is as warm as it is after coloring in an entire sheet of paper. It doesn't smell like anything; there's no blood on it. I wipe it dry on my blanket and tuck it back under my pillow. I lean out of bed and try to grab the pen pouch on my desk. Just as I've got the corner between my fingers—the little juggling ball beside my pillow falls to the floor with a loud thud.

I stay as quiet as I can. Tessie rustles under her blanket and turns over so we're face-to-face.

"Tessie?" I ask.

Her eyes flutter but she doesn't hear me. She turns around and falls back asleep.

I decide to finish what I started. I empty the pouch's contents onto the mattress.

Inside is a glue stick; it's round and smooth. It glides in easily but is still thinner than the fingers Jan used to nudge me along underwater at the Pit. The ruler fits in beside it. I'm able to push it in deeper until it hits the top of my uterus. I move fast and hard. For a second, I imagine I'm Elisa, that I have a long ponytail swinging back and forth, that I'm riding on the back of a galloping horse, but I like thinking about Jan better.

I make figure eights, press my crotch into my hand. There's enough room for a finger in there too.

The poking starts to make a soft, squelching sound. I wipe off my fingers on the blanket.

Suddenly Tessie sits up in her bed.

She looks at me strangely. I stop wriggling, pull the blanket up and push my legs together.

"What's the matter?" My voice sounds startled.

"I have to pee," she says.

I lie there motionless. Tessie crawls out of bed and into the hallway. The light from the landing shines into the room and reminds me of what a small, clumsy, ugly person I am.

I have a uterus covered in red pencil marks. And there's no way to erase them.

Tessie is gone longer than it takes to pee, which means she's typing on the keyboard again. She shuffles back down the hall, turns off the light, climbs into bed and checks that her blanket is hanging down evenly on both sides.

Then, she starts saying her goodnights.

I still don't dare to move. I have to throw away the red-brown pencil tomorrow, along with the glue stick and the ruler. I can't take them back to school after the summer.

Tessie would be angry if she found out what I did with the school supplies. She would find the thought of it unbearable: a pencil separated from its family forever, me creating a hole in my beautiful Bruynzeel collection purely for my own pleasure.

I look at my clock. Two after twelve. It's Wednesday. Maybe Laurens is asleep in the back seat while his parents drive home. Maybe they'll stop at a roadside cafe at the crack of dawn for fresh baked croissants.

One CROC-A-DILE. Two CROC-A-DILE.

"Goodnight, Tessie." I can tell by the sound of my own voice how nauseous I am.

"Not funny, Eva!"

"What?"

"You said Tess-ie."

The muscles in my lower abdomen tighten. I don't know if my vagina is shrinking or the wet ruler is swelling.

"No, I didn't."

"Yes, you did."

Tessie immediately starts saying her goodnights all over again, in a tone more nagging than before. It no longer sounds like a routine, more like a reproach.

At six past twelve Tessie says her final goodnights, to God and to me. I count two crocodiles, and make sure to do everything right this time.

I turn my head as far away from my body as possible, with my cheek against the soft mattress. The sheet smells like sweat.

Only after I'm sure that Tessie's asleep do I dare to remove the glue stick and ruler from between my legs. It hurts, like a hair-tie that's been tight around your wrist all day.

I hide the school supplies under my pillow.

I lie awake for hours and feel myself losing something. I'm no longer compatible with the image Tessie has of me. I'm an even bigger liar than I was before. I definitely don't deserve to be last on a goodnight list.

Confirmed

IN SIXTH GRADE, we had to make our Solemn Communion. It wasn't really any more solemn than the First Communion, but it was an extra opportunity to collect money—not for a starter bike like the first time around, but for a larger model to take to high school.

Our town was full of moms who jumped at any opportunity to do crafts in the parish hall. Some joined the parish voluntarily just so they could help with the confirmation preparations. Every other Tuesday, me, Laurens and Pim would go make pottery with them, paint our names, nail together little wooden crosses, pour candles—square or round. It didn't matter, as long as the whole time we kept in mind "what it means to be confirmed".

The last two months we shifted into high gear, practiced our posture, worked on the texts we'd have to read aloud. We were reminded of the proper wafer-receiving etiquette—which hand goes over which, which one should be used to make the sign of the cross, not to say "thank you" but "amen".

To avoid taking any time away from the fifth-graders, whose class we'd been tagged onto that year, we mostly rehearsed during lunch. Odette, a lady from town who was particularly involved in the church and had an extremely high voice, came in to teach us the songs. Once a week during recess, we met with her in the gym, where we had a panoramic view of the playground and the adjacent football field.

"Until seventy times seven, I shall forgive thee, until seventy times seven, the Lord hath forgiven me." We sang it as fast as we could, hoping we'd still be able to catch the few last minutes of recess.

"You know, four hundred and ninety chances might sound like a lot, but you'll run through them quicker than you'd think," said Pim. For the rest of the school year, he'd bring it up every time somebody missed a goal.

Since we were incapable of harmonizing, we were allowed to pick an instrument from the box of musical objects. Me and Laurens got two coconut halves, Pim claimed a toilet-paper roll filled with rice and Odette took the triangle.

"All eyes will be on you," Principal Beatrice said. "So don't strut to the altar like you're walking down a catwalk. When you get the wafer, swallow it immediately. It's the body of Christ. It's not a toy." She came by to check on our dress rehearsal when she heard all the coconut clapping—she said it sounded like a stampede of wild horses. She was wearing tiger print, as usual. I think it made her feel like she had a secure position in the pecking order.

Despite all the preparations, the church was far from full on Solemn Communion day. Though they did spread out our three families across the empty chairs.

I wore a dress that Mom made from the fabric we picked out together. In the fabric shop, surrounded by rolls of colorful prints and corduroy, she insisted I wear something girly. I felt naked the whole day because at any moment the skirt could be blown up by the wind.

Because of the church's size, the gigantic crucifix and the oak confessionals, our coconuts sounded less like a herd of horses and more like two nervous, newborn calves. No matter how hard we clapped and shook, the sounds of our instruments were negligible, and we remained invisible. Until the top of Pim's toilet-paper roll flew off from all the heavy shaking, flinging rice all over the confessionals.

In an attempt to save the ceremony, Odette raised her voice so high that it gave me an uneasy feeling, like watching the ballet girls showing off their splits on the playground.

The Mass was over sooner than planned.

Out in the parking lot, a photographer was there to take pictures of each family. I wanted us to be the first ones out, so the others wouldn't see my family being photographed, but first initials didn't count, and my surname came last in the alphabet, so I had to pose in my skirt with everybody watching. The photographer tried to make sure that Jolan, Mom, Dad, Tessie and me all looked good in the photo.

"Okay, look happy everybody!" he said at least three times. Just before the flash went off, I saw Laurens covering his mouth behind the principal's back to show Pim "the travesty in his mouth"—he hadn't swallowed his wafer.

That's when I knew it for sure—Laurens would never be confirmed.

According to Jolan, people were more inclined to give money when they knew what it was for—that way it's not a gift, it's an investment. So I made a big piggy bank out of an old shoebox and stuck a cut-out picture of a black ladies' bicycle on the top.

I shoved all the envelopes and cards I collected during the party into my collection box without opening them—all except one. When I walked out of the church, Laurens's mom handed me an envelope. I put it in my closet when I got home without checking how much money was in it. I didn't want to know exactly how much I meant to her. I wanted to treasure it, but I also wanted to hide it out of shame—my parents hadn't given anything to Laurens.

The next day I opened the other cards in the shoebox at the kitchen table and counted the money. It was a lot—hard to believe it was only enough for one bike.

There used to be a bike shop in Bovenmeer, next to the gas station with one pump. Both the shop and the station went out of business. Maybe the owner got rich on all those Solemn Communions. He moved to Nedermeer to open a shop with a showroom there.

Following his advice, I chose the bike with the softest saddle—22,000 francs.

"You're not just buying a bike, you're buying a Gazelle," the owner said as he counted my stack of bills a second time.

It seemed strange to take a Gazelle home in the back of a car, so I was allowed to ride it home. I left on the two big wheels all by myself.

As long as I was still in Nedermeer, it biked great. What a powerful feeling. I'd never felt anything like it. It reminded me of diving into the water with flippers on during the free swim at school—every kick had more effect.

I assumed I'd get used to it quickly, that after a few minutes I wouldn't be able to feel the extra power anymore, like with flippers—it wasn't until I took them off that I noticed how tiny, pointed and inefficient feet actually are.

But I didn't get used to it. Back in Bovenmeer, biking along the houses I passed every day, I no longer felt powerful. I didn't even feel tiny. I just felt strange, awkward—the fat handle grips barely fit in my hands. I could peek over the firs and hedges into other people's yards. Now I could see everything—the trash, the piles of wrinkled clothes on kitchen tables, a hamster cage on the counter, women forcefully pushing the vacuum back and forth. All of a sudden, I saw the world I grew up in from a different perspective. I didn't fit in like I did before. I was a Duplo man in a Lego house.

After buying the bike, I had two options, same as Laurens and Pim. Either I could bike twelve kilometers a day to the high school in Vorselaar or I could go to the vocational school in Nijlen, less than three kilometers away.

It seemed like a good joke—me wanting to study languages and Laurens wanting to study economics and the two of us having to bike twelve kilometers in a strong headwind to do so, while Pim— who wanted to do something with his hands, screwdrivers and brute force—could practically walk to school, and yet he was the one who learned how to fix up a moped in his first year.

To learn the route to our new faraway school before the year started, we did a practice run with Laurens's brother, Jan Torfs, who just went by "Torfs" because there were two other Jans in town.

Torfs had gone to school in Vorselaar a few years earlier, but then he joined the army and only came home when he had to, and always in camo. He promised to show us the best shortcuts.

In Laurens and me, he saw an unactualized version of himself. He filled our backpacks with rocks to simulate the weight of all the textbooks we were going to have to carry. We weren't allowed to sit down on our seats for two kilometers, and if either of us complained that that's what a seat was for, he'd make us crank up our gears. At the end of the day, reeking of sweat, our calves hard as stone, we knew the order of the towns we had to pass by heart, in both directions, including their postal codes.

He showed us two routes. The first was the canal road, a straight shot along the dike with a steady headwind—good in the morning, when you aren't quite awake yet and would rather not think.

The second route ran through the fields. It was a poorly paved road full of deep holes, but in the straight stretches, you were protected from the elements by one Spanish-style villa after another.

"If you're planning on getting a flat tire, you'd better go for the second route," Torfs said. "That way, you can ring the doorbell at one of the houses."

Laurens and I chose the spot where we would meet every morning at 7:30 sharp. It was halfway between our two houses, under the E313 bridge. We were going to have to travel this road every day for the next six years, passing exactly the same villas. So, following Torf's recommendation, we devised a clear plan. If one of us was sick, we'd call the other at a quarter past seven. If we hadn't heard anything and the other person was just running late, we'd wait five minutes tops.

Most of the time it was easy enough—unless there was a strong headwind, raindrops pelting against our foreheads like grains of rice, strands of hair getting stuck in my mouth. On those days, Laurens and I dared to call Pim a wuss.

"One day, we're going to graduate from university and live in one of those big villas with a swimming pool," I said.

"Then we'll hire Pim to come over and clean the gutters in the rain."

In reality, it wasn't twelve kilometers. The distance had been exaggerated by our predecessors, by all the other kids who had travelled this same route every day. Laurens and I had just taken it over.

Even though I generally preferred to be honest, sometimes, when I stopped by the bike shop for a repair and the owner asked me how many kilometers I biked to school each day, I'd say: "Twenty-eight. Fourteen there, fourteen back."

It was a lie, but part of it was true. Those meters were a lot longer with Laurens at my side.

During our second year, it got even worse. The shortcuts didn't bring any relief, because it wasn't the monotonous landscape that was starting to get to me, but Laurens himself, who moved with it beside me like a fly on a car window. He talked about his mom a lot, about how unbearable she could be when she was on a diet. His pedals were rusty. The right one was jammed and made an audible crack with each rotation.

Slowly, without ever having to say it out loud, we dared to admit it: biking to school together had never been about us. It was about the summer, when school would be out for two months and our new friends wouldn't want to come all the way to Bovenmeer to hang out, and we'd be forced to fall back on our hometown, on the three musketeers, on each other. Our friendship was bait for Pim.

After Jan died, we weren't ashamed to bring up the topic of Pim anymore. We were constantly trying to outdo each other: who understood Pim best, who had managed to get something out of him, who knew how he felt when his brother died, how his life was unfolding far away from ours, who his new friends were, whether they were better than us.

Laurens claimed that his brother was taking Jan's accident extremely hard.

"Losing a namesake is worse than, like, just losing somebody you know," he said. He acted as if having a brother with the same name as Pim's gave him more right to grief than me.

I bit my tongue. Of course, I couldn't tell him what I knew about Jan. As long as Laurens didn't know the truth, he'd always be a step behind Pim and me.

"Pim got a moped. A blue Honda," shouted Laurens when I biked up in the morning on the day before the last day of school in 2002. I had my German and biology exams that day. I'd written the cases on my hand so I could study them along the way.

For the first time, I was repulsed by the sight of Laurens waiting for me in the distance. I knew he'd waited there for me hundreds of times, that he would do it for four more years. I wanted to erase him.

A moped. The chances of Pim wanting to spend time with us next summer were getting slimmer and slimmer. As far as we knew, he hadn't made any friends at his new high school who'd want to hang out in a hick town like Bovenmeer, but if what Laurens said was true, the empty streets and the wide-open fields would grow on them eventually, and pretty soon there'd be a row of mopeds in front of the farm.

"I've never seen him go by on a Honda," I said, though I didn't know what a Honda looked like and hadn't seen Pim for a while.

"It's blue. A PS50K. I know these things. Guy stuff," Laurens concluded.

"Wanna play 'Don't say um'?" I asked. The narrow bike path widened out again. We could've easily ridden side by side, but we only sort of did. I started reviewing the German cases.

"Okay. Give me a theme." I didn't care that Laurens was good at this game, if anything it was a reassurance—he was good at talking without thinking.

"The theme is Carnival. The word you can't say is Pim," I said.

Laurens started telling about the year the town parade was cancelled because of rain, and Pim fired the confetti gun in the classroom.

I hardly listened to a word he said, but I couldn't help but notice that my name was barely mentioned in the key sentences, that my presence at the Carnival festivities sounded even blurrier than I'd felt that day. I fired that confetti gun, not Pim.

Suddenly, it was clear: Laurens got to choose who he focused his attention on and that choice determined how his memories were shaped. He had always chosen Pim. If he had chosen me from the start, maybe I wouldn't have grown up so out of focus.

I started to pedal slower. Laurens kept talking. It was hard for him to stay behind me, but still he didn't pass.

The exams were held in Zonnewende, in a block of portable classrooms that were supposed to be torn down five years earlier to make room for a new school building. On the right was the big, empty playground, which always filled up as soon as the bell rang.

It was an oral exam. I got a question about the pituitary gland.

While I was explaining how it determined the body's hormone production, I made a decision: I would walk out, get my bike and leave—no more waiting for Laurens. It would be a statement, one that he couldn't just shrug off like it was nothing.

After answering all the questions, I hurried outside. Laurens was already waiting for me at the bike rack. He was holding a cup of chocolate milk from the vending machine.

"My exam was a piece of cake. But I still waited for you," he said.

When we got back to town, we parted ways a little earlier than necessary, at the dog hotel-slash-crematorium. The manager was out training one of her favorite dogs. She shielded her eyes against the bright sun with her hand so she could watch us wave goodbye to each other, as if she too had noticed that something had changed between us.

On the morning of my last exam, I left home ridiculously early, at a little after seven. I cycled under the highway. Without us, the empty bridge just stood there awkwardly. There was nothing about it to suggest it was a meeting point.

My limbs were tired but still I picked up speed, racing down the narrow bike path toward the road to school.

As I rode up one side of the canal bridge and down the other, I still felt like I was doing the right thing, that I had to break free from Laurens.

I looked back, hoping he would suddenly show up behind me and, at the same time, already annoyed that this could actually happen. But it didn't. I passed the bridge, and the town slowly disappeared from sight. Laurens had no idea I'd left without him; he was probably still at home eating veal sausage on toast for breakfast.

I thought about the phone hanging on the wall of the butcher shop and considered ringing the doorbell of one of those Spanish villas and asking to use their phone so I could at least give him a heads-up.

But with every rotation of my pedals, it became too late for that.

It was 7:30. Laurens would be waiting for me under the bridge by now, the cars and trucks racing by overhead, his shoulders slumped, his eyes glued to the horizon I wasn't going to appear on.

I thought about Carnival, about the Pink Panther suit Laurens wore to school every year. One year, Pim ripped off the tail. Laurens had announced with tears in his eyes that his grandma would sew it back on. The tail hung on the coat rack in the corridor for the rest of the day. The following year he came dressed as a butcher.

I thought about the clicking of his right pedal.

It was as if I didn't feel guilty about Laurens as a person, but about every detail that made him whole.

When I got to school, my legs felt exactly like they did the day Torfs had made us haul rocks in our backpacks.

I wasn't relieved, but I knew the worst was over. Laurens would be on his way by now. I started thinking of a good explanation as I parked my bike in the bike shed and waited for him to arrive.

The bell rang. The exams started. He was nowhere to be found.

I finished my test as fast as I could, filling in just enough answers to pass. It wasn't until the end of the morning that I saw Laurens walking out of the Zonnewende block. I followed him out to the bike racks.

Without a word, he tied his backpack on his luggage carrier. Summer vacation had officially begun. Normally, we would have celebrated this with candy and chewed jawbreakers until our teeth ached.

All of a sudden, the elastic around his baggage rack snapped off and hit him in the face. He staggered, held his hand on his cheek, and stood there frozen for a moment, eyes closed. I forced myself to keep watching. It wasn't blood that oozed out of the cut on his face, but a murky juice. He didn't cry, but that didn't mean anything.

I biked home, roughly a hundred meters behind him. He didn't notice me. Or maybe he did but didn't say anything. His pedal clicked at a faster pace than usual.

That's when I understood that Laurens was the best friend I would ever have.

3:00 p.m.

I CLOSE MY eyes for a few minutes. I won't fall asleep. I've been warming my fingers in my lap for half an hour. I left my mittens at home. They're hanging on two separate hooks on the coat rack, waving to a deserted apartment that must be sweltering by now. I forgot to turn off the heat this morning.

I study my lips in the rear-view mirror. They're bleeding here and there. This always happens when I'm nervous. I gnaw on my lower lip with my front teeth until the skin starts to fray, and I start peeling it back piece by piece, until finally, like now, my lips are covered in patches of raw shiny flesh. Because of the cold, I don't feel it so much. They're just the scabs of old wounds. Lips recover quicker when you don't smile.

Right before I turn on the windshield wipers, the aluminum shutters over the Three Little Pigs start to roll up. Someone steps out from underneath them before they reach the top. I roll down my side window to get a better look. It's Laurens. He turns a key and the shutters lower again behind him. He's so fat. I guess that's what happens to people who think it's okay to soak sugar cubes in their tea and then press them against their lips to suck out the luke-warm Earl Grey—for the taste without the calories.

I mainly recognize his gait—legs that would just refuse each step, but, once they're hoisted up, have no choice but to land. His shiny shoes crunch in the snow.

How many times had Laurens said he never ever wanted to be a butcher, that he didn't want to grow up to be like his father? After he graduated high school—not in Vorselaar but somewhere else—he tried to study engineering, or that's what I gathered from his public photos on Facebook. He was studying in Leuven, at the university, and living in student housing.

When his father died two years ago, he moved home to help his mom with the business. Dad emailed us about it: the guy just collapsed on a meat delivery, right next to his truck. Coronary artery rupture. Dad also included a link to an article about the impact of red meat on cholesterol levels.

At the side gate, another person appears: Laurens's mom. She's carrying a transparent bag with the shop's logo on it, filled with what look like little plastic containers of leftovers. The handles are too long, so the bag drags in the snow. She takes small careful steps, holding her broad shoulders as straight as possible—the slightest jerk and her upper arms will pop out of her winter coat.

She hasn't aged much. She's just a bit fatter around the middle, or it might just look that way in the dim light.

They pause in the driveway for a moment to discuss something. They point at the road, the sky, the car. Based on their gestures, I presume they're debating the best way to travel the short distance in this weather.

Suddenly, my heart skips a beat. What if Laurens and his mom aren't going to Jan's party at all? What if they're going to some other family gathering? What if I'm the only person crazy enough to show up to remember Jan today? I need Laurens to be at that party.

Laurens starts scraping the ice off the windshield. His mom is already sitting in the car with the bag in her lap.

Less than two minutes later, their BMW pulls out, leaving behind tire tracks and a snow-less rectangle in the parking lot. I slowly turn my car and follow. We drive to the end of the street and turn left. This is the way to the farm.

I hardly look at the road. My eyes are fixed on the rear window in front of me, at the back of the two heads sticking up above the seats. The empty spot in the back seat on the right-hand side that was once mine. I used to love to rest my chin on the passenger seat and watch Laurens's mom's tremor-free hands take us somewhere. When she was driving, the car never drifted across the median.

For the entire route, I keep a close eye on the distance between my and Laurens's car. I follow the rhythm of his brake lights. The lighting up, the going out. I don't want to skid in their tire tracks. I don't want this trip to end with me bumping into the back of their car. If I were going to hit them, I'd do it at full speed.

Right across from the entrance of the church, in front of the glass bins by the cemetery, we turn onto the Steegeinde. If I had any doubts before, now I'm positive—they're on their way to Pim's. Our destination is at the end of this road.

Laurens's brake lights go on. He turns onto the property in front of me. The car comes to a stop by the fence around the old goose pen, which is still fenced off with poles along the sides of the driveway. I drive on a bit. I choose a spot under a fir tree with big, dark green needles where I can see who shows up without anyone seeing me. Wherever the darkest shadows fall in the summer must also be some shelter from the cold in the winter.

Laurens steps out of the car. He glances over his shoulder, looking for the car that was just behind him. From where he's standing, I'm invisible. The plastic bag full of plastic containers of salad dangles between him and his mother as they walk towards the back to the barn. That's where the party is. Every once in a while, the faint red and blue spotlights send a stray beam across the courtyard, like the shadow of someone constantly tracing his steps.

I will stay in the car until all the guests have arrived. Even those who show up fashionably late.

For the first half-hour, people trickle onto the property one by one. When I see the shadows of a few women approaching, my heart starts beating faster. Elisa! I think at first. Until the figures come into focus and transform into other women with Elisa's curves.

Even though there's a clock on my dashboard, I check the time on my phone three times.

It's way past three o'clock now. Elisa isn't going to show.

This can mean one of three things: she got here before I parked under this tree, she wasn't invited and therefore won't come or she was invited but has finally figured out that there's nothing here for her.

No one has arrived for several minutes. No old acquaintances, no shadows of the past.

I step out of the car so I can look over the hedge to the other side of the yard. In the back, next to the barn, is the giant mound of silage, covered with car tires, just as I'd hoped.

All of a sudden, another person shows up, walking towards the barn in a hurry. I try to duck out of sight, but I bang my knee against the bumper of my car. I buckle over in pain. The person sees me and looks my way. It's Anne, my old babysitter.

"Hi, Anne," I say.

Anne gives a friendly nod, too friendly, in fact. She has no idea who I am. She walks by, shivering on her stilettos. I remember when she switched from wearing tennis shoes to these kinds of high heels with short skirts. According to Jolan, she didn't always wear underwear. By that time, she didn't come over to "babysit" anymore, but to "kidsit".

The last time she came to kidsit, she showed up with a Colorado beetle skewered on her heel. With every step, it left a trail of yellow-brown blood on the kitchen floor. Jolan helped her remove the insect from her shoe.

That night, before bedtime, she wanted to show us what she did with her boyfriend when her parents weren't home. We'd just brushed our teeth, but she insisted we sit on the couch to drink a glass of *lait demi-écrémé*. The milk tasted bitter.

She took off all of Ken and Barbie's clothes. She'd already fished out everything she needed from our Barbie gym bag. On the kitchen floor, she set up the hair salon, the Barbie car, the living room, the kitchen and some loose furniture and began laying out the floor plan of her life. Then she showed us all kinds of positions, twisting the dolls into one unnatural pose after the other.

"One person is the nine and the other's the six," she said. "It all comes down to making numbers."

She kept making numbers until one of the dolls' heads popped off. It rolled across the kitchen floor and came to a halt against a table leg.

"It's way better in real life. You'll see. Now it's bedtime."

I followed Tessie to the bedroom, in as straight a line as possible. Jolan stayed behind to show Anne his beetle collection.

Today, she's wearing an oversized brown winter coat that hangs over her back like a shield. She pricks her heels into the snow so she can hike up the slightly sloped driveway, until she reaches the group of men smoking under the awning in front of the barn. The smoke from their cigarettes alternates blue and red.

I keep watching them, hidden behind my car. All around me is the smell of the past, manure mixed with hay. I take a deep breath. It makes me nauseous but, at the same time, more determined.

The cigarettes are extinguished one by one. The demonstration is starting. The milking robot is ready to put on a show. I watched a few video clips last night, so I can imagine what's going on inside, exactly what this robot is going to do. I don't need a front-row seat to see that it's not very exciting.

The barn door closes. Now it's my turn. I've got to hurry.

August 1, 2002

LAURENS CALLS ME the morning after they got home. I stand there winding the phone cord tightly around my index finger until he asks me how my week was.

"Too bad for Indira," he says, without even saying hello. "I just went by her house. All the shutters are closed. We'll have to skip her. We can't wait, she's probably with her dad in Asia for the month."

The comment is followed by a short pause.

"Too bad she's got those slanted eyes," he adds.

I nod.

"You still there?" Laurens asks.

"Yeah, too bad," I repeat.

Laurens is right. Girls like Indira are the melon in the fruit salad, and in small towns like Bovenmeer there's never enough of them to go around. It's just her and her dad, who came to live here after Indira was born. They built a house, a big wooden cube on four high wooden poles, diagonal to the primary school. Even though the school was right across the street, her dad still sent her to another school, closer to where he worked. That was too bad too.

Laurens and Pim sometimes pissed against the wooden poles under her house on the nights we camped out. They called it a future investment: in ten years the wood would rot, the cube would come crashing to the ground and Indira would end up out on the street in her pajamas in the middle of the night, helpless. It sounded like revenge, but I didn't know what they had against her, except her skin color.

"How was France?" I ask. The tip of my finger turns a darker shade of purple.

"It was sunny, and they renovated the swimming pool. Other than that, it was a shitty vacation. Next year, they won't want to take me with them. I made sure of it."

"Nice."

"No, it really wasn't."

"I meant nice about the pool."

The weather's changed. Outside, the sky has turned gray. Through the window that Mom's covered with a sheer piece of fabric tacked up with four pushpins, the clouds move like freshly poured concrete, following their own path. Cars pass by, first making the mailbox tremble, then the makeshift curtain. Their tires rumble over the seams between the asphalt slabs.

"Eva, you still there?"

"Yeah."

"Can you come to the vacuum shed tomorrow?"

"What time?"

"Two o'clock," he says. "Oh no, wait . . ."

He pauses. I can hear someone gesticulating on the other end of the line.

"Two-thirty is better."

"Why not today?"

"I still got to unpack."

I hear the sound of a wrapper crinkling in the background, but for once, Laurens isn't talking with his mouth full.

"What are you eating?" I ask.

"Chips."

"What flavor?"

"Barbecue." Now I'm sure Pim is standing next to him. Pim always eats barbecue chips.

"Well, enjoy. See you tomorrow, Laurens." I hang up and let go of the cord around my finger. The blood drains down from the swollen fingertip.

I head out, not on my bike, but on foot. Sitting on a bike seat would hurt. I can still feel the glue stick. My vagina still feels stiff when I walk, like new shoes that need to be broken in.

At every corner, I look down all the streets to see if I can spot Pim rushing home. It's quiet at the butcher shop. There are no cars or bicycles in the parking lot. Most of the neighbors are either on vacation or they haven't heard that the Torfs family is back from France.

Laurens's dad needs time to ease back into his role. The display case is still half empty, but not for long: the side gate to the garden is blocked by a roaring refrigerated truck, and a hefty delivery guy is unloading animal carcasses.

Laurens's mom waves at me, signaling that I can cut through the shop. As I walk by, she passes me a spoonful of salad across the counter.

"It's new. What do you think?"

The salad consists of threads of something, fish or meat, and some kind of slimy, salty base.

"Yum," I say. I swallow without really tasting it.

"The boys are out back, in the shed," she says.

"How was the vacation?" I ask.

"Camping was wonderful. I'm sure Laurens'll tell you all about it."

"Yeah."

"Actually, would you do me a favor?" She passes me another spoonful of fish salad. "If the boys are planning to smoke again, will you come tell me? I can trust you, right?"

She pushes the spoon closer to my mouth. I lick it clean. My flatfish shadow puppet has been forgiven and forgotten.

Other than the rustling of a chip bag, there's not much going on in the shed. Through the small windows, I can't see where Pim and Laurens are, what they're doing or who's with them. They're in a corner, exactly out of my line of sight.

I wait outside, trying to think of some news or an anecdote to deliver.

"No, don't look away, man," Pim commands suddenly.

It sounds like an invitation.

I gently push open the door and slip inside. Because of the dreary weather, it's even darker inside than usual. In the corner is a small screen emitting a warm glow.

Laurens and Pim are standing right in front of it with their underpants around their knees. The color of their butts blends in seamlessly with the flesh of the bodies on the little screen. Laurens is exceedingly tan, except where his swimming trunks were. Pim looks as pale as ever.

The rhythm of their movements is perfectly in sync with the pumping of the black hips against the two white butt cheeks on the screen. They're standing about thirty centimeters apart with a low coffee table between them. On the table is a bowl of chips, a mix of barbecue and regular. They're holding the empty bags out in front of them.

They didn't see me come in. I take a few steps back, sink down with my back against the wall, next to an old chair. I need to know what they do when I'm not here. I want to be able to simulate every activity they try to exclude me from.

All they have to do is turn around, and they'd see me. But given the nature of the footage, there's little chance of that happening.

Pim is the first to ejaculate. I can tell by the way his butt cheeks expand and contract, like the nostrils of a galloping horse.

"No!" he roars, when it's all over. Oddly enough, he sounds disappointed. He smacks his hand on Laurens's shoulder, creating a thin, snotty thread that only breaks after they've restored the distance between them.

He takes a handful of chips, sits down on the coffee table with his trousers still around his knees, and stares at the screen, not at Laurens.

I want him to notice me, to stop the game, so I won't have to see Laurens come in the chip bag, but I don't dare to interrupt.

Laurens checks his watch without stopping. He does it differently than Pim, patient but frantic, like someone searching for the end of a roll of tape.

"Fourteen minutes and still counting," he says, in a bad attempt at English. Dutch people on campsites are so good at this.

Finally, he ejaculates with the happiness of a last-minute penalty shot. He pulls his pants halfway up, wipes off his knob on the inside of his pocket and finishes getting dressed. Then he pushes his bag of chips under Pim's nose.

"Look how much. That means I didn't cheat and jerk off before coming here."

Pim takes the evidence from Laurens's hands, weighs both bags out in front of him, between his thumb and forefinger. He acts as if his own bag is clearly heavier.

"Mine contains more semen, yours is just mucus and air," he says.

"Learn to take a loss, man." Laurens gives him the middle finger.

In the background, the black butt cheeks are now making clumsy, swirling movements, faster and harder. Then, the man flips the woman over, still swirling like you do with egg whites—hoping it's almost done.

"It's not how long you last, it's how you do it." Pim taps his limp penis against the screen, between the lady's breasts. It immediately starts getting hard again.

"Top up the salt level and go again?"

Laurens grabs another handful of chips and fishes out the saltiest ones.

"Let's take a breather."

"Can I ask you something, dude? Man-to-man. What's your tactic? Who do you think about when you're trying not to come?"

I push my face deep against the armchair beside me. It smells musty, like wet dog. I brace myself, following the example of the lady on the screen in front of me.

"You don't want to know," says Laurens.

"Yeah I do. Come on, tell."

"You first."

"No."

"Do you ever think about my mom?" Laurens asks, almost rhetorically.

"Jesus." Pim presses the chip bag against his lips, blows it up as big as it will go and holds the opening tightly closed. He approaches Laurens with the puffed-up bag, his pants still hanging around his knees. Then he pops it right next to Laurens's face. Cum flies everywhere; a big blob plops on the floor in front of my feet.

Suddenly all eyes are on me.

"Eva? What are you doing here?" Pim pulls up his pants. He sounds more shocked than embarrassed.

Actually, I've seen their penises before. I remember them very vividly—it was during those weeks when we had to put our bathing suits on beside the pool because they were renovating the changing rooms. Pim's penis was long, slim and sturdy, like his hands. Laurens's penis was brownish-gray and already had all the characteristics of a beef stick.

"Nothing," was the only answer I could come up with.

"Well, you're a little early," Pim says.

"A little? Like a whole day," Laurens corrects him.

The room falls quiet.

"What kind of chips are you eating?" I ask.

"Pirato." Pim holds out the other, not-yet-exploded bag in front of me. I refuse to stick my hand in.

"You shouldn't take this too seriously."

"We're just getting ready for August," Pim says.

"We don't want to disappoint Elisa."

I nod. I don't mention my own preparations.

"Where'd you get that movie?" I glance down at the plastic case, which is being used as a coaster for the bowl of chips. The price tag is still on it. Nineteen euros.

"I bought it at a gas station on the way home from France while my parents were napping in the car," Laurens says.

"You could buy seventy-four jawbreakers or three hundred sour bears for that money," I say. The thought surely didn't cross Laurens's mind as he surveyed the gas station's collection of films and magazines.

Laurens and Pim both give me a sheepish look.

I walk home. Pim bikes slowly next to me, a few meters ahead. He's waiting for me to say he doesn't have to stay with me. Since I'm on foot, I don't make the usual detour past his house today.

We don't talk. There must be an uncomfortable feeling in his pants. Sticky.

I think back on the night Dad tried to explain the difference between men and women. He called me out of bed. Since my eyes were small, he poured me a glass of Coke. His eyes were smaller than mine, but he wasn't drinking soda.

He waited until my glass was empty and proceeded to trace the bottom of his empty beer can with a pencil. Two even circles on a sheet of paper. Breasts, I thought at first.

Then he drew a cross under one of the circles and an upward arrow on the other.

"Do you know what this means?" he asked.

It was two minutes past two.

For some reason, that seemed more important to remember.

The Club Quiz

A FEW DAYS before the Millennium bug, we were given a choice: either come to the club quiz or stay home. I wanted to go. Tessie and Jolan wanted to stay home. For the first time, my parents didn't bother to call a babysitter.

"You guys are old enough to stay home alone, aren't you?" Mom asked. She headed down to the basement, and rather than coming back with the usual can of tomatoes or a bottle of sparkling water, she brought up a big bag of NicNac snacks.

Most of the time, Mom looked as if she'd been folded up the wrong way and shoved into a box, but not that night. That night, she looked as good as new. She put on make-up and brushed her hair. She wore her square-rimmed glasses. The clicking of her heels on the tile floor made every step sound like a confident decision.

She plopped the whole bag of NicNacs on the counter and reached for her sleeve garters hanging above the sink.

"Don't eat them all," Dad said as we were heading out the door.

The Millennium Quiz, like all the other quizzes, was organized by the local clubs and held in the parish hall across from the church.

"You better keep your mouth shut, because you're not registered to play," Dad said.

Mom put on her coat. He didn't.

"It's warm for this time of year," he said.

Pretty much everyone in Bovenmeer lived within walking distance of everything, which is why "far away" activities were generally described as "far enough that you need a coat"—a definition that didn't say anything about the actual distance, it was just a measurement of your own resistance.

The hall was still practically empty. The tables were set up two by two, ten squares that could seat eight people each.

Right in the center of each table was a plate with a precise number of cheese cubes. In the middle was a little flag on a wooden skewer. If you got thirsty, all you had to do was wave the flag to attract the attention of one of the waitresses circulating with a tray and a notepad to take the players' drink orders.

I only saw one other kid. Mathias, a shy boy adopted from India. He was sitting next to his dad at an empty table, twirling the little flag faster and faster between his fingers. For the first time ever, there were slices of sponsored salami next to the cheese cubes, and nobody had thought to wrap the sharp tips of the skewers with tape. Somebody could get hurt.

I asked Laurens and Pim at school if they were coming to the quiz. They both said they thought it was stupid and that they didn't want to go. I nodded in agreement.

It was quite possible that they, like me, were lying, that they'd still show up tonight anyway.

Mom and Dad each played for a different club. I sat down at Mom's table and watched the room fill up with neighbors. Most of them looked like they'd just gone out with the trash and somehow ended up here at the parish hall. Only a few of them, Mom included, had noticeably tried to spruce themselves up a bit.

In the middle of our table was a drink flag representing the Catholic women in agriculture organization. Laurens's mom was one of the first to join us. Laurens's dad didn't come. He didn't like clubs, unless they were for fellow meat entrepreneurs. He had stayed home with Laurens to eat chips and watch a weekend movie.

Slowly the table filled up with rural women, all different shapes but all with the same sleeve garters. That was what was so rural about it: they'd all agreed to wear them as if they were fashion accessories. On Laurens's mom they didn't go up very far—halfway up her lower arms they were already stretched out to the max.

The only person who looked out of place, despite having the right equipment, was Mom. The sleeve garters had been a present from Dad, but she never wore them to do the dishes. It wasn't that she had a problem with the things themselves, it was more the attempt to belong to something that didn't suit her. She must have felt that too. At first, when she was still alone at the table, she sat there sipping her first glass expectantly, shrinking at the sight of anyone who barely noticed her, who forgot to say hello. Until the room filled up, that is. Then she ordered another drink and fell into another behavior I recognized: shrinking after she actually was being seen.

The quiz was set to begin at eight o'clock sharp.

True to their word, Pim and Laurens didn't show up. The few kids who did, including Mathias, retreated to the beer corner in the back, where they'd set up a mini-TV with cartoons.

There were eight question rounds of about fifteen minutes each.

For an hour or so, I sat there wondering whether I should've just stayed home like Laurens and Pim. I tried to imagine what I'd be doing at home but the only image that came to mind was me sitting there wondering what was going on at the quiz, whether my mom was sitting next to Laurens's mom.

At the back of the room were two big green swinging doors cut into a white wall; all the other white walls had windows with beige curtains. They were all closed, clumped in strange pleats. They kept the cigarette smoke from escaping through the open windows. It was getting hotter in the hall, but I didn't want to take off my long-sleeved sweater. Then everyone would see my chubby arms.

Between nine and ten o'clock, Mom waved the flag three times.

Meanwhile, as they called out the quiz questions, she stayed in her seat and occasionally closed her eyes for a few seconds. Other people, like Laurens's mom, might have thought she was just trying to think of the answers to the questions. But I knew—she wasn't trying to think of the name of the guy who invented the Zeppelin. Most likely, she wasn't thinking anything at all.

As long as her eyes were closed, I kept my eyes on her. I owed her that; somebody had to do it, to record her in the moments when she couldn't see herself.

At eleven o'clock came a question that I knew the answer to before they even finished reading it: "What was so unusual about the year 1988 in Bovenmeer?"

All the teams began thinking out loud. Mom leaned forward and started to speak.

"There was a huge thunderstorm that year. The clouds just burst—forty centimeters of rain. We lost a couple of shingles on our roof," she concluded. "I remember sending Karel up there to look."

It was the first thing she'd said all night. The table got quiet and people exchanged looks. Laurens's mom was holding the ballpoint pen—even she didn't dare to question it. Mom's answer was written down in the corresponding box.

The theater club, Dad's team, thought it had something to do with the brothers who lived in the castle up by the brewery. It was a well-known fact that two of these brothers owned so much land that they could walk all the way to the Dutch border without leaving their own property. Just about every run-down farm in the Noorderkempen region belonged to them. They were both single and had lived together their entire lives, on either side of the castle. They had no electricity or central heating, bathed in an old washtub and patrolled their property with shotguns.

"Wasn't '88 the year of those famous city council elections?" someone on Dad's team asked.

It was during these elections that the older brother formed a one-man party to change the collection scheme for household waste. In the end, his party only got one vote, which is how he found out that his own flesh and blood hadn't even voted for him.

"He tried to put a bullet in his head—what was that guy's name again?" I heard Dad roar.

The answers to the questions weren't read out until the end of the round.

"Question number nine: What was so unusual about the year

1988 in Bovenmeer?" In the microphone, the quizmaster's voice sometimes sounded far away and other times dangerously close by. "You were all way off on this one. Unfortunately, we can't award the three points to any team."

At midnight, the quiz ended, and it was time for the raffle. The grand prize, a color TV, had been on display under a white sheet at the front of the hall all night. It wouldn't be raffled off until the very end.

The little kids were ushered out of the beer corner by the youth priest to help draw the winning numbers. Some of their eyes were misty from sleep, others from grief—Pocahontas had just been forced to say goodbye to her beloved.

"We got the question about the year you were born wrong," Mom said. She scooched back her chair, stood up and gulped down the rest of her Tripel so no one would clear the half-empty glass in her absence. She pushed the sleeve garters up on her forearms; they slipped back down again.

"It's not Eva's fault we got it wrong," Laurens's mom said to the other ladies, "we should have made more babies."

People laughed. Under the table, she placed a hand on my knee and gave it a little squeeze.

The littlest kids skipped around the room, delivering the prizes to the winning tables. They gave out the worst stuff first—bags of balloons, ballpoint pens, cactuses. The second to last prize was a beer basket.

The daughter of one of the judges carried it around the room. I saw Mom glancing down at the number on her ticket. The child brushed past her and handed the basket to Laurens's mom. One of her neighbors offered to trade it for a set of Tupperware, and she immediately accepted.

Mom waved her flag in the air, ordered another Westmalle Tripel from one of the passing waitresses and gave me a handful of coins to pay for it.

She staggered behind the first person to get up to go to the bathroom. As she stepped out of the hall, the swinging door swung back and hit her in the face, just as they were about to announce the winner of the grand prize.

I saw it happen. Still it took a second to sink in—the loud thud and the silence that followed—before I realized how much it must have hurt. It made a loud clunk, like an apple falling from high up in a tree and smashing open on the ground.

Several people turned around to look. Mom lost her balance and fell backwards on the tiles. For a few seconds she just sat there, too miserable to even reach for the spot that hurt the most. Then she scrambled to her feet. Her glasses had landed somewhere farther away, behind her, she didn't see them. Her face looked fine. No scratch, no blood.

But having taken plenty of penalty shots in the face, I knew what it felt like: your nose feels swollen and ridiculously huge, but everyone keeps saying you look fine.

Mom didn't seem to remember why she wasn't sitting in her chair, why she walked through the door in the first place—or maybe it didn't even matter anymore. She stood there motionless for about ten seconds. I realized she was about to pee her pants. I'd seen her do it before. I knew how it looked. Then, sure enough, the dark spots appeared, gradually moving down on the inner sides of her thighs. Nothing happened.

Her immobility lasted for about three more seconds. Finally, she took a few staggering steps, searching for the right configuration, for the right balance, and turned around to face the hall. And that's when it all came out. The vomit spewed from her mouth with a final bow.

The entire hall went quiet, even the people who had tried to ignore the incident altogether for the sake of their grandchildren.

Then somebody started applauding, three claps. Women's hands. Probably some lady taking advantage of the situation to put her own drunk husband in his place. Before I could see who it was, the clapping stopped.

Mom's eyelids opened slightly at the sound of the applause. She moved in a more controlled manner; that too could be explained—the adrenaline that came with the shame. But her stomach still hadn't quite recovered. She turned back towards the wall and puked again. Against the white background, you could see the blood clots in the beer flakes.

No one stood up to help her. Even Nancy Soap didn't hurry over with a bucket of water.

For the first time, I didn't have the reflex to jump up and rush to her side either. I'd never seen my mother embarrass herself like this before. I didn't dare to look at Laurens's mom. In the end, it was Dad who stood up and tapped me on the back.

"Run home and get the wheelbarrow," he said. In his hand was the winning raffle ticket.

The church bells weren't ringing when I walked out of the hall, but it was exactly half-past midnight—high time for criminals, but the darkness was the least of my worries.

I broke into a run, not so I could get back quicker, but so I wouldn't have to listen to the swelling murmur of the audience. I ran past the mailboxes on the Kerkstraat. The full moon cast a faint glow on the front yards, like an energy-saving light bulb still warming up.

On the way back with the wheelbarrow, I walked under the same moon and along the same flowerbeds, slower now, out of breath. It wasn't until I reached the end of our street that I saw their shadows.

Mom and Dad were just starting to make their way home. She was crawling on her hands and knees on the sidewalk. He was carrying the color TV. The box was heavy and bulky and didn't fit in his arms.

The closer I got, the more I hurried.

Mom didn't want any help.

"I'll get myself home," she barked. In her hand were her glasses, the lenses cracked. Every time she leaned on her hand, the temples bent under her weight. Her knees were all scraped up. I tried to position the wheelbarrow in such a way that all she'd have to do was fall backwards and she'd land right in it. But she crawled away from me, out into the street.

Dad set down the TV. He pulled Mom up by her armpits and pushed her into the wheelbarrow. She bumped the back of her head against the rim and dropped her glasses. I picked them up off the ground. Dad laid the cardboard box on top of her. She didn't flinch.

"It's not too heavy?" I asked. She didn't nod, but she didn't shake her head either.

Staggering, Dad heaved the back end of the wheelbarrow off the ground and lurched it into motion. It took him a second to get used to the uneven weight distribution.

"This TV is heavier than you'd think," he said. He'd probably had a fair amount to drink as well, but his body was bigger, which did something to the density of the beer.

From the parish hall, there were still voices coming through the microphone. The final sponsors were thanked. The mayor had just become a grandfather and called for "one last round on the house", which was met with more applause. Men's hands, women's hands.

Our house was straight ahead, barely four hundred meters away. There wasn't much I could do to help; my one hand was clutching the glasses, the other hand was on the edge of the wheelbarrow. Dad shouted whenever I tried to help steer or moved to let go.

We weren't sharing the burden; we were sharing the shame.

Mom's arms were wrapped around the television. She didn't react to a word we said.

"We got a lot of use out of that freezer," she mumbled as we pushed her the last few meters down the Bulksteeg and into our junk-filled yard.

Dad pushed the wheelbarrow around back to the big walnut tree, where he finally set it down. He carried the television inside, leaving Mom to fend for herself.

"If she can get herself into a pair of clean underwear and find her way upstairs, she can come to bed," he said right before he let the back door slam shut. Mom closed her eyes. I could see the wet spots on the inside of her pants. All of a sudden, I smelled them too.

I walked in behind him. The house was dark and quiet, except for the light over the stove. Tessie and Jolan had already gone to bed, probably on time. On the kitchen counter, I found the evidence: the untouched bag of NicNacs.

While I waited for Dad to finish in the bathroom, I stared out the kitchen window. I was still holding my mom's glasses. Without them, she'd never make it—she'd have to feel her way up the stairs.

At first, I didn't dare to go back out to her.

Then the dog started barking in her kennel. The spotlight turned on. I opened the door, went out, pulled off Mom's shoes and covered her shoulders with the first blanket I could find. I placed her pretty high heels next to the wheelbarrow with the glasses on top, temples neatly folded, just as she would have done herself.

Halfway up the stairs to my room, I stopped on the landing and looked out the window into the backyard. Mom was still there. I knew she threw up blood sometimes, but I'd never seen it on a white wall before. As long as I kept paying attention to the details, I wouldn't be able to get used to anything.

I struggled up the ladder into my bed. I felt exhausted—though I'd barely even helped with the wheelbarrow. Tessie sat straight up in her bed. She'd been waiting for me to get home.

"Did you see the NicNacs on the counter?" she asked.

Outside the dog started barking hysterically again. The spotlight turned on.

"Of course," I said.

"Who won the quiz?"

"Nobody."

"Was it a tie?"

"No," I said.

"But isn't there always a winner?"

"We won a TV."

Tessie jumped out of bed. Only after she'd turned on the light to make sure I wasn't joking did she understand that Mom and Dad didn't even notice the unopened bag of NicNacs.

For the rest of the night, we kept watch behind the window on the landing to make sure Mom was okay, hoping that our gaze might change something.

"She doesn't really look like Mom without her glasses," Tessie said.

I said nothing. I'd never really looked at the wheelbarrow before. I wouldn't have been able to pick it out in a row of ten. Every detail needed to be thoroughly examined—the red handles, the half-flat tire. We stared at it all night until we could have picked it out of a thousand wheelbarrows.

Every so often I saw Tessie open her eyes wide in an effort to stave off sleep, to force the sun onto the stage.

"What do you think would be worse?" she asked. Nanook stopped zooming back and forth for a second; Mom was still out there in the dark. "If the dog died, or Dad died?"

I could tell by the way she asked what her answer would be.

Although I felt sorry for the dog—like us, she'd done her best to bring a little sunshine into Mom's life—I still said "Dad". That way I was sure he would at least get one vote.

We didn't say a word about the scene outside, which was becoming increasingly visible and pathetic as it got light.

Finally, the sun showed up to relieve us of our post, but we didn't leave. It wasn't until Mom turned around to shield her eyes from the first rays of light that we went back to bed. We owed her a chance to crawl out of sight, to slip into the house barefoot, to pass through the rooms she'd walked out of in high heels, to search around for a dry pair of underwear and her weekday glasses. The chance to sit down at the breakfast table and act like nothing was wrong. At least she could still have that dignity. That, and a color TV.

4:30 p.m.

It's getting dark. Halfway up the driveway, across from the goose pen, is the dog cage. There's a new sign attached to the bars with metal wire. Beware of dog. Under the words is a picture of an aggressive-looking dog baring its teeth. I hadn't noticed it before. Lying on the ground under the sign is a docile Labrador that doesn't even lift his head when I walk by; he watches me with about as much energy as a concierge in Brussels who works for his keep instead of a salary.

There are a couple of cars parked out in the yard next to a big yellow tractor. Tea lights in empty Nutella jars lead the way up to the barn. The feeble flames struggle against the freezing temperature. I put the remaining candles out of their misery.

The last Nutella jar is less than ten meters from the entrance to the barn. I could just walk in. Greet people, shake hands, tell them what they want to hear, how much their children look like them.

"Why did you do that?"

I turn around to find a little boy standing behind me. He's about five years old, all bundled up, wearing gloves that are way too big for his hands. I have no idea how long he's been watching me. He's pulling an empty sled on a long, thick rope. It slides towards him until it comes to a halt against the back of his legs, knocking him off balance and sending him toppling into the thin carpet of snow. Attached to the sled is a neon bicycle flag flapping in the wind.

I have no idea where he came from. Kids are like mice. It doesn't take much for them to wriggle their way in.

I pull him up by his hood.

"Why aren't you wearing any pants?" he asks. At first, I don't understand what he means, then it dawns on me how it must look from his perspective—my winter coat is longer than my short skirt.

"I'm wearing tights," I say and pluck at the flesh-colored hose on my legs so he can see them. The little boy comes closer; he wants to touch them. I allow it. He caresses my thigh with the limp, empty fingers of his glove.

Other than the big sled, everything about this kid is small and sweet, which somehow makes his touch more pleasant.

We just stand there for a moment.

"Don't you want to see the robot?" I ask.

He shakes his head. "That robot can't even talk. All it does is milk."

"What's your name?" I ask.

Before he's opened his mouth to reply, a sharp, high-pitched screech blasts from the barn. Someone's holding a microphone too close to the speaker. Nervous animal sounds reverberate across the farm: tongues scraping on salt licks, hooves stomping on grates, heads banging against troughs.

"The party is about to start," the little boy says, motioning me to follow.

"You go ahead. I'll come later," I say.

The child leaves the sled behind, walks back into the barn, into the commotion.

I duck behind the tractor and creep around the outside of the building towards the mound of silage. I climb up the side without puncturing the plastic. It's not easy. The cold has shortened all the muscles in my body, except the ones in the leg that was just touched.

At the top, I peek down through the wide gap between the roof and the wall of the barn, which provides ventilation for the cows. I now have a bird's eye view of the party. The tops of people's heads. A heat blower. A modest disco bar. A table with a tray of Melba toasts covered with spreadable cheese and bowls of chips. Somebody makes a beeline for the refreshments, then turns around. Maybe the toasts are already soggy. Next to the tray is the plastic bag Laurens was carrying. His mom isn't talking to anyone. She's just standing there with her arms clasped against her stretched-out waistline, like a child holding an inner tube ready to jump into the pool.

The longer I watch, the clearer it is that the party is well under-way, and no one is wondering where I am. My presence wouldn't make any difference.

I search the room until I see Pim. His face looks cheerful, though that might just be the contrast with his sober, dark-blue shirt. His shoulders aren't broad, but narrow and sinewy. An auto-mated farmer from head to toe.

I stretch my gaze all the way to the corner of the barn, as far as my eyes will go, to where Pim's arm gives way to a hand that's clutching something—the child I was with a few minutes ago. He's falling asleep against Pim's leg. Pim's firm hand is the only thing keeping him on his feet.

Two heads with the same curls. How is it possible that Pim has a son, and no one, not even my dad, told me? It's hard to guess who the mother might be.

Just then, I'm struck by the same realization I had when I saw Laurens: I'd been expecting the fourteen-year-old version, the ver-sion I had a vendetta against, not this man with sloped shoulders holding up his little boy.

I climb over the tires to the other side of the mound. From here, I have a view into the stalls. Now I see what everybody's looking at. The photos they collected are being projected onto the wall. They roll from one to the next with the help of vintage effects, casting a warm glow over everything and everyone in the room.

Most of the photos were taken with the vacation cameras. They'd been scanned, edited and arranged in chronological order. There's a photo from Pim's birthday party with Pim, me, Laurens and Jan—four boys in a row, wearing red scarves with white pom-poms knotted on their heads. Then the picture splits into strips and weaves into another picture I'm not in: Jan and Pim in the garden with bathrobe sashes around their waists and washcloths over their loins—two Indians around a bedsheet teepee.

After a few seconds, this image melts into a picture of Pim's First Communion. Jan, Laurens and I are standing beside him, wooden crosses hanging around our necks. I'm wearing a colorful outfit; they're dressed in beige. Jan's got his arm around me and Pim. Laurens's mouth is open wide to reveal a carefully preserved wafer stuck to his palate. You can see the pride on our faces: we've just let Our Lord and Savior into our hearts. All of a sudden, I distinctly remember Jan pressing his arm into my neck.

Before I've finished studying the photo, it splits and zigzags into the next image: the lip-syncing show at a parish party. Jan is standing sideways on stage with his face turned towards the photographer. Legs bent, thumb tucked into his belt, a white hat—his best imitation of "Smooth Criminal". Every year he did a song by Michael Jackson; the lip-syncing competition was the only event that he and his dad came into town for. He never won first place.

The two heads at the bottom of the picture catch my eye. Tessie and I are sitting in the audience, sharing a bag of chips. We seem more interested in the snacks than the performance. Tessie is wearing an overall dress. I'm the red, sweaty head sticking out of a turtleneck, the only person in the whole room wearing long sleeves. We both look fairly happy. Though chances are the problems were already brewing at the time these pictures were taken.

I look away and scan the rest of the farm in search of a good spot to set up. All the barns and stables are exactly the same. I take one last look at the photo on the wall before it switches to another one. Tessie and me. She's just shoved a handful of chips in her mouth; I'm holding the bag. If I could, I would become two-dimensional, travel through time, crawl into this picture, slip into this moment, warn Tessie about what's coming, say, "Get out of here!" To Jan, I'd shout, "Don't listen to them, you're the best Michael Jackson I know!"

Even if I could say these things, it wouldn't change much. If twenty years ago a thirty-year-old version of myself suddenly showed up and said, "I know what's going to happen, you'd better get out of here," I wouldn't have budged. Me and Tessie would've just sat there, not because we were happy, but because things have to happen before you can regret them—and because the bag of pickle-flavored chips wasn't empty yet.

August 2, 2002

I WAKE UP to the sound of the neighbor's lawnmower. Yet the first thing I think of is Laurens and Pim standing in front of the sex-filled screen squeezing their butt cheeks. Tessie's bed is empty and hasn't been carefully made. That's disturbing too. I hurry downstairs. With every step the temperature drops a little.

I run into Tessie at the bottom of the stairs. She's standing barefoot in front of the sideboard with her hands on the keyboard, wearing her favorite nightdress with the pink ruffles. It looks strange now that her long blond hair is gone. She doesn't take her eyes off the keys.

We used to have a bald Barbie, but it only ever served as an enemy or a cancer patient.

"Don't go sit on the toilet and listen to me again, Eva," she says.

I really need to pee, but it can wait.

When I get to the farm, I find Pim standing next to Laurens. There's something hidden under his T-shirt.

"What's that?" I ask before I've even parked my bike.

He glances around in all directions before showing it. His dad is nowhere to be found. The farm is empty; the cows are out to pasture. He pulls out a videotape from under his clothes. "I think there's a blowjob in this one."

Laurens has just arrived too. He's still clutching his handlebars. I didn't see him biking down the Steegeinde, which might mean he took a different route than usual to get here.

I glance down at their shorts and the hair on their calves. It must have sprouted when I wasn't looking, because I hadn't noticed it at the start of the summer.

"I found it in Jan's room." Pim says the word "Jan" softer than the rest of the words in the sentence.

Pim didn't find this tape, I did. I stumbled on it one time when I was hiding in Jan's room while we were playing. I took a quick look at the cover and put it back exactly where I'd found it, so no one would notice I'd been in his room. I can't tell them this now. Nor can I tell them that on the day of Jan's funeral I saw this tape again: exactly where I'd left it two years earlier.

"Didn't you promise your mom not to touch anything in Jan's room?" I ask.

"Jan should thank me for destroying the evidence. My mom'll be home in a few days. They're going to empty out his room, box everything up. You wouldn't want her to see this, would you? Let alone my dad."

"Why would you do that?" I ask.

"So your mom's coming back?" Laurens asks.

Pim doesn't answer. He walks ahead of us, towards the farmhouse. We follow him inside, and he locks the back door behind us so his dad won't walk in. It's suspiciously clean for a house occupied by two men. The living room is in the back. There's a big cabinet made of dark wood and two armchairs with wooden armrests and leather-covered cushions.

Laurens and Pim sit down on either end of the three-seater couch. Without a word, I plop down on the smaller armchair. It's oddly positioned in the room, not in front of the television, but diagonal to the other armchair.

Only after sitting down do I notice that the chair is facing the wall with the aerial photo of the farm. It had belonged to Pim's mom. She used to sit here knitting socks and scarves, not because anybody would ever wear them, but because it was the perfect spot to admire her family watching television.

For some reason, I've never sat in this chair before. We've watched TV in here plenty of times, but we always fit in the three-seater.

"I'll be this one. Which one do you want to be?" Pim asks. He shows the video cover to Laurens. On it are three men and a busty actress in sexy nurse uniform. Pim taps his finger on the actor on the left, the darkest and most muscular of the three. He takes the tape out of the box and pushes it into the VCR.

Laurens points to one of the other characters on the cover. "I'll be this one."

Pim sits back down. They give each other a high-five.

No one asks me anything.

It's Penny's turn today, but she won't be here until later. Laurens heard she had to go to the dentist, and it'll take at least another hour with teeth like hers.

Penny used to be in Jolan and Jan's class, but then she got held back in fifth grade and ended up in the class we'd been tagged on to. She's the youngest daughter of a woodworker and has six older brothers. People used to say that her parents had six sons and just kept on going—one more wouldn't make much difference. They assumed it would be their seventh son in a row and, as per Belgian tradition, King Albert II would be named the child's godfather and the queen would present them with a monogrammed silver bowl.

They weren't disappointed when it was a girl. Nevertheless, they always dressed her in boys' clothes—it's not clear whether this was meant as a punishment or if it was just easy. Penny had a delicate face and reddish curls, which usually hung down on her shoulders like a ball of yarn that some cat got into.

Penelope was an unusual name for someone from Bovenmeer, and even though everyone called her Penny—which stuck, probably because of her copper-colored hair—she was still the girl whose name nobody could remember, who always faded into the background.

This came to an end when, at some kid's birthday party, where she hadn't said a single word, she laid down her fork and knife, stood up on her chair and shouted at the top of her lungs: "I gotta go dump a darkie!" The cake had just been cut, the aunts and grandparents were all there, there was an uncle with a camera. Sure enough, the moment was captured: in the foreground the shocked hostess almost cutting into her own hand, and in the background a blurry ten-year-old with curly red hair, standing on her chair with her hand over her belly.

After Penny had finished her business and washed her hands in the kitchen sink, she quietly returned to the table and ate her cake in frugal little bites.

"Dump a darkie" became slang for a big turd, one you really had to work hard for. The expression even caught on among kids from surrounding towns. They all claimed that one of the shy girls in their town came up with it, that it was first shouted at one of their birthday parties. We let them think that, but we knew better.

Suddenly, Penny was popular. She got invited to all kinds of things; everyone hoped she'd shout it again, or rather that she would come up with some other obnoxious statement that might become a fixed expression and make the party more memorable. But she never did anything like that again. She just nibbled on the cake that was served to her. She didn't let anyone in on the depth of her thoughts. But thanks to that one outburst, all the boys wanted her. Suddenly they saw her for the girl she'd always been, how pretty those red curls were.

Laurens and Pim turn on the movie, and I watch them from my single-seater chair. Pim feels around for the remote control and cranks up the volume; all the smacking drowns out the sounds of the farm and Laurens's heavy breathing.

I can tell by the looks on their faces what's happening. In the whites of their eyes, I see the reflection of bodies flickering on the screen; the movement of their pupils suggests the direction things are going. I can see the tension in their bodies when it's their chosen character's turn.

The end of the sampling is finally in sight; we've already tested more than half the girls. After Penny there are only two left—and we're not even halfway through the summer vacation yet. At the end of the summer, there will still be some time left for the three of us, like before.

Outside, the dog and the geese sound the alarm. Trapped, Pim lowers the volume.

"Is your dad back already?" Laurens asks.

"I don't know." Pim takes advantage of the chaos to pat down his crotch for a moment. "Go look, Eva."

I get up, turn the keys in the back door and check to see who's walking up.

It's Penny. She's early. She's wandering along the empty stalls, looking around tentatively.

I could go out to her, tell her to leave, that there's nothing to see here. I could warn her, ask her if she wants to go swimming at the Pit, or even somewhere farther away, in another town.

Just as I'm willing my feet into motion, I see her stepping up on the ladder of a tractor to check her appearance in the rear-view mirror. She straightens her hair.

This goes against Pim's theory. He claims that the prettiest girls don't know they're pretty, which makes them shy about taking off their clothes, which makes them even prettier.

"Penny's here!" I shout, and ring the bell hanging by the back door to bring everyone to attention, like a referee signaling the next round in a fight.

I walk out to meet her.

She greets me with a kiss on the cheek. She smells sterile, like toothpaste.

"The guys are coming," I say.

She looks sharper than she did in the last class photo. She's got a turned-up nose and eyes that bulge out of her head.

Together we watch Laurens and Pim walk up. They've both got these strange walks, not the ones I'm used to seeing. Pim holds his arms away from his body as if somebody's pumped too much air into him.

The rest of the afternoon is like a movie playing in the background—no one's really watching it because we all know how it will end.

Laurens and Pim are more efficient, but also more uptight than usual. It goes fast. Penny agrees to the eight guesses; I recite my riddle. Penny does her best. She doesn't solve it.

"Time for your punishment," Pim declares, cracking his fingers. "Take off your clothes."

"I have my period," she says. "I'm not taking off my clothes for anybody."

"And we're supposed to believe that?"

"Fine, let Eva check," she says.

"Eva, go check." Laurens doesn't seem to know what to do with his hands. His porn character would be fiddling with his moustache about now, but he doesn't have any facial hair yet.

"Okay, but not here. Somewhere private."

Penny and I disappear around the corner, so as not to spoil their appetite. Penny doesn't show me anything. She just smiles sweetly, like girls do with each other. There's a spot of toothpaste on her upper lip. I immediately believe her.

When we come back, Laurens and Pim have thought up an alternative, I can tell by the way they're standing.

Pim is all puffed up again. "Even girls on their period have their uses. Look at porn stars. You're not telling me those women take a whole week off every month, are you?"

"Not a whole week, but four days at least," I say.

Penny shoots me a quizzical look and brushes her red curls out of her face. I don't understand what the boys are getting at.

"So you want a blowjob," she says. "Fine. I'll do it." She kneels down in the straw.

"No more than ten seconds each," I say.

Laurens wants to go second this time, probably so he can watch Pim first and avoid looking stupid again. He stands there fiddling with his balls until it's his turn.

I count, not too fast, not too slow.

Pim drops his pants, pulls his foreskin back three times, like a cowboy loading a pistol. As soon as the skin is all the way back, he pushes the tip between Penny's teeth.

She sucks in a couple times, making her delicate face get even narrower.

"Ten. Why do they even call it a blowjob?" I ask. "You don't really want her to blow, do you?"

Now it's Laurens's turn. He doesn't answer my question.

His dick refuses to get all the way hard. It reminds me of one of those cheap sausages from the butcher shop that are mostly just fat, so they flop over when you hold them up straight. They don't really look like something you're supposed to eat, but they're good for smacking people with, so they do get sold. Penny makes the best of it for ten seconds.

"Time's up," I say just as Laurens is becoming aroused. "That's ten."

"I won't tell my brothers about this," Penny says.

She gives me another kiss on the cheek, the same kind she gave me when she walked in. The boys let her go without protest. I can smell the sour scent of their penises.

"What's the answer to the riddle, by the way?" she asks.

"She can't tell," Pim says immediately. "We've still got a few more girls coming. After they get their chance, we'll give out the prize."

He's tucked his dick back in his pants; the foreskin is caught under the elastic band and the crumpled tip is peeking out. There's a sticky trail hanging from it, like the silvery slime left behind by snails in the garden.

For a split second, I want to whack it, like Pim's dad does to moles—he lures them out of their holes and pounds them on the head with a spade.

I leave with Penny. The boys stay behind in the hayloft.

She says very little, and when we reach the edge of the property, she immediately turns the other way. She could have biked with me a lot longer, but I get it—I didn't even give her the answer to the riddle. That's the least I could have done. Her curls flap behind her in the wind.

A few minutes later, a helicopter flies by overhead. All I can do is keep pedaling and hope that no aerial photos are being taken. That the landscape isn't being immortalized at this very moment to be hung on the wall in somebody's living room, with me as a dot, Penny as a dot, both of us moving in opposite directions.

Two-Chair Restaurant

JAN DISAPPEARED TWO days before his sixteenth birthday, on December 28, the last Friday of 2001, not long after Laurens asked me which superpower I wanted.

Christmas break was almost over. Laurens and I were in his backyard, hanging out on the swing set. He was sitting one step lower than me. His hair had grown longer. I looked down at the crown of his head. Laurens had always had the same part, but now that his hair was longer and heavier, the line down the middle of his head was wider, more pronounced. The split made him vulnerable, revealing the exact spot where I could break him. Those last few days, we'd hardly done anything but sit on the swing set. The living rooms contained balding Christmas trees, still decorated with lights and pompoms.

For the first time, Laurens's parents had more orders than they had neighbors. They were very proud of this fact. Customers were driving in from all over the place—there weren't enough parking spots in front of the shop.

"I'd pick teleportation," Laurens said, answering his own question before I did because I was taking too long to think about it.

"Where would you want to go?" I asked.

"An island," he said.

"What island?"

"Any island."

People who want to go to an island don't necessarily want to go anywhere, they just don't want to stay where they are.

The church bells rang three o'clock.

"I'm hungry," he said.

Every time the shop bell jingled, he would look out into the courtyard, hoping it was Pim. He'd promised to come over at two o'clock. We were going to set up the old restaurant.

"Two-Chair Restaurant" was a game Laurens had invented. It combined the best of his two worlds: food and competition. We placed two kitchen chairs in the middle of the room, where Pim and I would sit blindfolded. Laurens would play the chef. He would concoct a strange, never-before-seen combination on a teaspoon and feed it to us. Whoever guessed the ingredients correctly was appointed the new chef, switched places with Laurens, and created the next item on the menu. The restaurant went bankrupt the day Pim served us a raw rabbit kidney with chocolate and cayenne pepper.

Now, looking down at the part in his hair, I remembered the look on Laurens's face and felt sorry him all over again.

I tasted the blood and immediately spit it out.

"It's a kidney," Laurens guessed, but Pim wanted to know from which animal. So Laurens took another bite of the organ, chewed it slowly, but he couldn't quite put his finger on it.

"Rabbit?" I guessed. I won.

It was quarter past three. "Come on, let's go call Pim." Laurens got up and walked towards the house. I followed him so I could press my ear against the phone.

"Where are you?" Laurens asked, turning away from me. He frowned as he listened to the answer. "Should we come help look? Or can we help you with the cows?"

He sighs, says goodbye and hangs up the phone.

"Jan left this morning without milking the cows and now Pim has to do all Jan's chores *and* help them look for him," he said, summarizing the conversation. "He doesn't want our help."

I doubted whether Pim had really suggested that having to take over Jan's chores was worse than his disappearance.

We went back out to the garden; this time I sat on one of the lowest steps. I missed the view I had before, being able to look down on Laurens.

"Don't you think it's unfair? Pim's the one who didn't come, but he's the only one who knows what to do," he complained.

I nodded. "Where do you think Jan went?" I asked.

"Beats me," Laurens said. "My stomach's growling."

He tapped my head with the top of his shoe. Was I supposed to say I was hungry too, so he could suggest we play One-Chair Restaurant?

"Go eat something then," I said.

Laurens sighed, got up and dragged himself through the backyard again. I watched him get smaller and smaller, until he was swallowed up by the back door. That's how easy it was to disappear. Sometimes a sudden hunger attack was all you needed. One time, there was a story in the newspaper about a man who went out for French fries one day and was found years later at a holiday park in Sweden working as a gardener. He was wearing glasses with fake lenses in them.

"Mom, what's for dinner?" I heard Laurens yell from the garden. I knew what kind of answer she'd give. It was busy in the shop, so she'd say something like "shit with stones" or "bear puke". Laurens had never seen the value of a mom with a sense of humor.

He marched all the way back with a bag of shrimp crackers and a leftover chocolate Santa. He set the bag of chips in his own lap and tossed the chocolate figurine into mine.

I bit off Santa's head—a quick decapitation—like Tessie always did. "People who start with the feet—they're the ones you've got to watch out for," she said.

The shrimp crackers crackled and crunched on Laurens's tongue.

At half-past four, Laurens's mother walked out into the yard. The bag of shrimp crackers was almost empty. Laurens quickly hid it in the hood of my coat. Laurens's mom was carrying a large, thinly sliced sirloin steak on her arm. Her face was as pale as the ring of fat around the meat. Her hot breath should have formed little clouds around her this time of year, but I didn't see any. Her panting didn't match the aimlessness of the rest of her body.

As she came closer, she reached out her arms to grab us, and only then did she realize she was still carrying the piece of meat. She looked around and balanced the steak on one of the steps of the swing set, then she put her hands around Laurens's knees and hugged his legs. When she saw me, she hugged me too. She pressed my head into her chest; it was the first time she'd held me since the night I made the flatfish on the wall. I inhaled the sour smell of her apron. The almost empty bag of chips crinkled in the hood of my coat. She didn't say anything about it.

"Children, my sweet children," she said. "They found Jan."

I knew right away what this meant. Why hadn't I picked a superpower a few minutes ago, when Laurens asked?

"He's gone." We said nothing. "Dead," she added, as if that somehow made it more specific.

"How?" Laurens asked. I was wondering the same thing.

"The priest didn't say. Most likely an accident."

The shop bell rang intrusively. Laurens just stood there.

It wasn't the words sinking in that hurt per se, but everything else, everything that was still there, all the futile things that would simply have to go on.

"Pim needs us," Laurens concluded. He was already on his feet.

"If I were you, I'd leave him alone for now. We can give him a call later. Are you coming inside?" she asked. "I'll warm up some milk."

She walked back to the house with firmer steps than the ones she came out with. She wasn't going to heat up milk. She had to help spread the news, that's what had to happen now—there were so many more people to inform.

I wondered who she'd call first. Events like this had a way of revealing how people in this town were connected, how the social structures worked, like the way heavy storms revealed the root structures of trees. Who would call my parents? Would anybody think to tell them at all?

I stood up. The fatty steak was still hanging on the swing set. I sat down on the swing so Laurens wouldn't see me crying. He just sulked, but maybe that was already a lot for him, more than enough.

I looked down at my shoes and then back at the steak. It wobbled back and forth as I swung. Laurens stood up and came over to me. He pulled the bag of chips out of my hood, took another shrimp cracker and sat down in the grass. I couldn't speak. The chocolate Santa was melting in my hands. I bit off the feet. Now he couldn't run away.

"What do we do?" Laurens asked. He sank down in the grass.

My stomach instantly rejected the chocolate feet. I threw up in my mouth, just a little bit—it tasted sour and bitter. I quickly swallowed it again. Now was not the time to barf. People were going to die, people I knew a lot better than Jan, people I saw every day, and I'd have to be a lot sadder than this. I had to leave a buffer, for Jolan, for Tessie.

"Monopoly?" Laurens suggested.

I nodded only because I wanted to get out of the backyard, away from the steak.

We went inside, not into the shop, but upstairs. I hadn't been up there in a while, and under different circumstances, I would have liked nothing more than to sit on the soft couch next to Laurens's mom and watch TV.

Now all I could think of was Jan, but I didn't quite know what to think about, which details. What kind of accident it was, how it happened, who found him, where.

I didn't know who to feel sorry for either. Jan—though it's not like he was suffering, not anymore at least—or the people who found him. Maybe it was Pim's parents, they'd always refused all forms of help, and today was probably no different. They probably went looking for him themselves.

Laurens unfolded the game board. I just sat there. He distributed the pieces, the Chance cards, the money. He counted it all out quickly, sloppily.

Should we be doing this right now, playing? Wasn't there something else we should be doing? But I couldn't figure out the right response, so I just kept rolling the dice.

The store was right below the living room. Every few minutes, between doorbell rings, I could hear Laurens's mother spreading the news, the cries of disbelief, the dinging of the cash register.

There was a big chance that at the moment Jan died, Laurens and I were sitting on the swing set in silence, that the cash register was dinging then too. We might not have been able to prevent the accident, but we could've at least done something besides sitting on a swing set.

I rolled double sixes three times in a row. Laurens sent me to jail. I leaned back in my chair for a moment and thought about the furniture in Jan's room.

It was easier to picture that room than it was to picture Jan's face. Ever since I found out he thought I was pretty, I hadn't really looked at him. One time, I hid in his bed while we were playing hide-and-seek. For a half an hour, I just lay there, next to a couple of hard tissues, under his boyhood bedspread with a tractor on it. There were ironed sweaters on a chair and an unused candle on his bedside table. Never had I been so close to a boy that I knew liked me. I pressed my face into his pillowcase, pushed my tongue out of my mouth and left a kiss for him.

After a few turns, Laurens lets me out of jail.

How much was going to change now? It would start with the little things: the rags around the farm, most cut from Jan's old shirts and used to wipe off greasy hands and mop spilt milk off the floor. Those rags had been around for years and never had any value—I took one home once so I could smell it—and now everybody would cherish them.

By the sixth round, I couldn't afford the rent for Nieuwstraat anymore.

"Count your money," Laurens ordered. He fanned himself with his five-hundreds even though it wasn't even hot.

Was it because of people like him that, in times like these, when grief ought to be shared, people like me feel obliged to feel everything twice as intensely?

At home that night, we didn't have dinner until eight o'clock. The timing of the meal had nothing to do with Jan's death but with the meat that had been set out not wanting to defrost.

I wasn't sure whether the news about Jan had reached my house or not. I didn't think so. When Mom came home, she was no more drunk than she usually was around that time. The moon was small and high in the sky. Our reflection in the sliding door in the kitchen was crystal clear. Eventually the meat was thawed in the microwave, which just made it tough—since Christmas, when she had to eat dinner with the dog, Mom hadn't been putting much effort in her cooking.

I could tell by Jolan and Tessie's silence, the way they held their forks, that they'd heard the news. It didn't feel right to eat. Someone had to say it.

"It might snow," Mom said. Behind her, the lights were flickering on the last Christmas tree we'd ever have.

I chewed my meat very slowly. The bite lasted forever.

"Jan drowned in the slurry pit," I said after I finally got it down.

On the counter to my right were Tessie's untouched chocolate Santas, standing in a row. She'd turned all four of them to face the wall. It still felt like they were staring at me too.

5:00 p.m.

I RECOGNIZE JOLAN right away, even with his face hidden behind the collar of his winter coat against the icy wind that occasionally whips between the stalls. Siblings, you can always pick them out immediately—whether you want to or not—because you see part of yourself in them.

He walks past the base of the mound I'm standing on, dawdling in front of the barn doors before walking in, in a way that only he can. He closes his eyes; for a moment he's the insect waiting to be examined. He turns around, looks back in the direction he came from, at his brand-new Range Rover parked in the driveway. Then he straightens his tie, smooths his vest and enters the barn.

The last time I spent the holidays with Jolan was two years ago, in 2013. That year, just like the years before, we had our Christmas together—Tessie, him and me—not on Christmas Day itself but a few days afterward because Tessie celebrated the holidays with her foster family, and Jolan had a girlfriend at the time. It was some girl from his lab who he had stolen a bicycle from and then played the romance card with to save his own skin.

Jolan picked up Tessie first, and then they came to Brussels together to get me. We drove to a restaurant in the city center that I'd picked out. Along the way, we made a major detour around the Atomium, mostly because Jolan liked to drive, Tessie liked being driven and I liked telling them which neighborhoods I liked. I always picked the same restaurant—a place where a lot of people ate alone. That way we'd feel more whole.

This year and last year, we didn't celebrate Christmas together.

Tessie decided she couldn't do it anymore. "I'd rather have no party than one behind Mom and Dad's back." She couldn't stand the thought of them sitting at home alone without us, not knowing they weren't missing anything.

On Christmas Day, I got a text message: "Merry Christmas, Eva." Jolan sent me an online Christmas card with two singing reindeer. After that, the envelopes of money started showing up.

I've received more than thirty of them by now. None of them—except the first one—came with any kind of message. No letter, no explanation, it was supposed to be self-explanatory. Inside was just cash with a Post-it note folded around the first and last bill stating the amount: "200 euros" or "100 euros".

The first time he sent me an envelope, Jolan wrote: "To be used wisely (and sometimes not). No need to pay me back." What he meant by "wisely" and "sometimes not" still isn't clear to me. I also don't know what to call it. Is it a donation, a contribution, an allowance, a compensation? I decided that as long as I'm not sure, I won't spend it.

Sometimes we message each other on WhatsApp. A while ago, I scrolled back through our chat, trying to figure out who initiated contact the most. I saw that, in one year, I had started a conversation with exactly the same question seven times.

"How are things there, and how are the grasshoppers?" The "there" referred to Tessie, to her new house, her new sister, her new mother, and "the grasshoppers" were meant for Jolan; he runs a lab where they research something related to the digestive system of insects. Sometimes both Tessie and Jolan replied, sometimes only one of them did.

I couldn't help but regret that I hadn't asked other questions, more original ones, and more often.

I saw that they asked me questions too sometimes. "How's it going in Brussels?" "How's your apartment?" They always asked me, same as I did them, about my relationship to certain places, never how I was doing as a person. I think they were afraid I might tell the truth.

I didn't know Jolan was coming today. He hadn't marked himself "Going" on Facebook.

I guess it makes sense that he was invited though; he knew Jan better than I did. They were in the same class. He was one of the few kids who actually liked going to Jan's birthday parties. They both had a fascination for animals. But unlike Jan, Jolan managed to keep the bullies at bay. Not that he got much credit for it later—he steered clear of anything that didn't have at least four legs, and even to them he wasn't always friendly: one time, he smoked a walking stick after it died. He held it between his fingers like an elegant cigar.

Through the gap between the stalls, I see him milling through the crowd. He stands off on his own, takes a few chips, rubs his hand over his head and pats down a few more hairs to hide the fact that he's going bald.

I never had the same relationship with Jolan that I did with Tessie, maybe because we never shared a bedroom. There were times when our sisterly bond cost him dearly, like when the poodle vase got broken.

Dad called us all down to the living room.

"Who did this?" he demanded, pointing to a cabinet he'd made himself. On it was an ugly little vase, broken on one side. It was this color that there's not really a name for, something between blue and brown, not khaki. It wasn't meant to hold flowers. The edges were fragile and thin and bent outward.

It was a failed version of a vase, like a poodle is a failed version of a dog. Some friend of theirs had made it before eventually disappearing from their lives. That made it even more fragile. Now, the time had come—we were about to pay for the lost friendship.

"It's just a vase. That's what I had to get out of the bathtub for?" Jolan said shivering, wearing nothing but a towel around his waist. Dad slapped him on the head. A few drops of water flew from his ears and splat against the wall. The white drywall that had never been painted, so the splatters turned light gray.

"The truth always comes out," Dad said.

Mom didn't do anything, she didn't even nod. It was one of the rare moments when they didn't try to undermine each other's authority.

"All three of you will stay right here until you've figured out who's responsible for this," she said. She left the room without looking back.

"I didn't do it, I swear," Tessie whispered.

"Me either," Jolan said.

"Well, it wasn't me," I said. That was the only thing I knew for sure.

The cat weaved between our legs, rubbing against us. Jolan started to dry. We didn't look at each other—we were all afraid this would incite suspicion.

Around six o'clock, we heard Nanook whining in the kitchen. Mom had started making dinner, maybe she'd thawed a piece of lamb for the occasion. A little while later, we heard the sound of knives and forks clinking on plates. We saw the dog pass in front of the doorway to the living room, greedily pushing her bowl out in front of her.

For the first time in months, we heard Mom laugh.

"You should break a vase more often," Jolan said to Tessie.

Tessie bit her fingers and showed him the teeth marks.

"But it wasn't me, I promise."

Not biting would be a confession. Jolan and I bit our fingers too.

By eight o'clock, no one had come forward, and we were sent to bed without dinner.

"Sleep on it. If you don't know by tomorrow, all three of you can help mow the lawn."

From our bedroom, we listened to the crickets chirping in the garden.

"It really wasn't me," Tessie whispered. "Really."

"Somebody must've done it," I said.

"So it was Jolan."

"Probably."

"It was the cat," Jolan told us the next day, but it was too late—we'd just told Mom that he did it. We helped him mow the lawn, but we were still traitors.

My hands are frozen from the inside out. I can't feel my lower body anymore. I could stand, I could sit—it wouldn't make any difference. The cold has cut through my panties and into the skin on my butt. I worry that my legs are dying without me noticing. I need to move. Not just to get out of the wind but to stop staring at Jolan. The longer I look at him, the less courage I have to take that ice block out of the car.

I carefully climb down the silage mound, along the back side, so no one can see me, and head back to the car. The ice block has barely melted at all. The Curver container is harder to lift. One of the handles is broken. Suddenly, I remember how that happened: it was that sharp turn off the exit into town. I can just barely lift it out of the trunk; gravity helps. For a moment I think of the neighbor. Of his arms and hands.

The other day, while I was sucking him off, he grabbed my head. He didn't understand why I bit down on his cock until he let go.

I carefully flip over the container next to the car and hit the bottom a few times. The block comes loose and plops to the ground.

I gently lift off the plastic mold.

The water runs out, over my shoes, melting the surrounding snow.

I put the empty Curver back in the trunk and close the door. I leave the car unlocked, with the key in the ignition.

It's hard to move. I open the trunk again, take out a red checkered blanket and spread it out on the ground. I hoist the block onto the middle of the blanket, gather the four corners and drag it behind me like a knapsack.

The last few meters, the block is easier to slide because there's snow stuck to the blanket.

When I reach the old milk house, I look back at the wide, winding trail I left behind. It could've just as well been made by a sick, dying animal that dragged itself through the snow.

August 5, 2002

RARELY HAVE I seen such a doubtful look on Pim's face. Laurens and I press our noses against the hayloft window so we can see what he sees: two strange forms waddling up the driveway. One of them must be Heleen, an eight-and-a-half-pointer on the cemetery wall. The other one we can't quite place.

Pim had warned us as soon as we got there that Heleen was bringing somebody with her. He blurted it out before we'd even reached the ladder to the loft. From where I stood, I could see straight up into his nostrils. There were grains of brown dust stuck in the snot.

"Is that good news or bad news?" I asked. Nobody answered.

Pim had wanted to meet in the hayloft again today, which went against our rotation system. He hadn't given any specific reason, but I suspected that if we met at his place today, there'd be no reason not to meet at my place next time, where the walls didn't have eyes—better for Elisa.

We watch the girls enter the barn and climb up the ladder, which isn't easy because they're wearing so many clothes. We can't tell whether Heleen's friend has a good body or not—at least it's not another mongoloid.

"This'll never work," she says, with both hands gripping the bottom of the ladder.

"Try harder," says Pim. "Come on, you've got plenty of padding. It's not like you're not going to break something if you fall."

They must have heard what they were in for. Who knows, maybe Melissa or Ann—the four girls hang out together a lot—told them to wear lots of clothes, that this was the only way to solve the riddle. Apparently, the previous contestants hadn't heard that the rules had changed.

"Can't you just come down here?" the other girl asks.

"This is April, by the way," Heleen says.

I look at Pim. He shakes his head—a clear no. "Okay, April," I say. "We're coming down."

Grudgingly, Pim leads us across the yard, past the cesspit, to the area behind the milk house, a tiny barn where they store sawdust for the calves under a sheet of black roofing. Heleen stumbles in her five pairs of pants. It's three times hotter down here than up in the loft. Pim explains the new rules very slowly.

"I hate to tell you this, but you girls are out of luck," he says. "Eight questions, that's all you get."

"Then you guys are out of luck, 'cause we're not playing." Heleen turns to leave.

"Yeah, why would we even want to?" April says.

"Because if you win, we have to do whatever you say," says Laurens.

"So I could make you piss in the milk tank?" Heleen asks Pim.

"Yep," he says.

"Or make you give us free meat every time we come to the butcher shop?" she asks Laurens. "For a whole year?"

"Yep," he says.

"One guess per piece of clothing, take it or leave it," April says, crossing her arms in front of her chest, which doesn't really work with all the layers of sleeves.

Pim and Laurens exchange nods.

"Okay," Pim declares.

Heleen quickly pulls a pair of mittens out of her pockets and puts them on too.

They start out with a couple of decent guesses, but it's so hot that all the clothes end up working against them. In the sweltering heat, all they want to do is shed their layers. Their guesses become sloppy and less tactical. At one point, they even guess the same thing twice.

Heleen removes the beanie on her head. The long curls that had won her extra points are now stuck to her forehead in wet strands. Pearls of sweat are forming on April's temples. If they had come in bathing suits and flip-flops and only had two guesses each, they might have given the riddle more thought.

By the time they're stripped down to their underwear, they seem more relieved than ashamed. Between us are two big piles of clothes lying in the sawdust.

For a second, I worry that this is just a diversion tactic. Who knows, maybe wearing a lot of clothes wasn't the only tip they got from Melissa and Ann, maybe they gave them the answer to the riddle, maybe they looked it up at the library or on the internet. What if April happens to be friends with Elisa, and Elisa told her the answer and now they're just messing with us?

Heleen and April exchange looks.

"That's it. We quit," April declares. "This riddle is unsolvable."

I let out a sigh of relief.

"Of course it's solvable," Laurens says, "and you can't just quit. That would be like ordering a steak, eating half of it before paying and then trying to give it back. Right, Eva?" He looks at me.

"I've never eaten a steak before paying for it," I say.

"Who are you, by the way?" April asks.

Nobody responds, so I don't either.

"What do you think we should do, Eva?" Pim asks.

Then he turns to the girls and says, "Eva always calls the shots. She'll decide what we're going to do with you."

"Okay, so it's going to be Duck-Duck-Goose, then," Heleen retorts, pointing to the teddy bear on my sweater.

Pim bursts into laughter.

"Do you want to keep guessing? You've still got a few chances left," I say with a glance at their bra and underwear.

"Just tell us what we have to do, Eva. We'll keep our underwear on, thanks. It's not like we're going to solve that stupid riddle of yours anyway."

"All right then, you have to jerk them off, each of you, two times in a row," I blurt out. Heleen whips around to face me.

"Excuse me? What do you mean?"

"Two times each." My hope is that the girls get sloppy the second time around, and it'll start to hurt. "You need me to demonstrate?" I ask.

It gets quiet. Laurens and Pim stare at me in amazement.

"Fine. Who goes with who?" Heleen pulls down her padded bra so it pushes her breasts up even higher. "Who do I get?

"You guys can fight it out amongst yourselves," I say. Her areola is peeking out over the edge of her bra.

No one says a word. They exchange glances, sizing each other up, trying to figure out who belongs with who. Eights don't go with sixes—that was always the boys' rule. But no one dares to say this out loud now.

"Okay, Laurens. I think Heleen and Pim should go together. You're better off with April," I say.

Laurens looks as if he's just been punched in the face. He turns to Pim and Heleen for help, but they're smiling at each other with satisfaction. Then he looks back and forth from April to me.

"How about I start with April, and then we switch?" he says.

Pim shakes his head vigorously behind Laurens's back.

"No, no switching," I say.

Head down, Laurens kicks at the pile of clothes on the floor.

"You're one to talk, Eva de Wolf. You know, it's not for nothing that you were always the fastest wheelbarrow," he says.

With his foot, Pim sweeps the scattered clothes back into a pile so the girls will have some padding under their knees.

I don't stick around to watch. I hurry off to my bike and head home.

I knew what Laurens was getting at about wheelbarrow. Back in primary school, we used to do wheelbarrow races in gym class. The girls automatically dropped to their knees and wriggled across the floor like question marks. The boys would rush to grab the nicest pair of calves they could get their hands on and push them around the gym.

Pim always grabbed my calves immediately, otherwise he'd have to push Laurens, who weighed twice as much as I did. He didn't put me down until we'd gone back and forth across the gym. We won every time.

At first, I attributed our victories to Pim's muscular strength and my ability to move my arms quickly and keep my body as stiff as a board. Until I realized what it was really about: wheelbarrow races were the perfect opportunity for the other boys to peek into the loose legs of the girls' gym shorts and catch a glimpse of their underwear.

Pim had always preferred to keep his eyes on the prize.

"It smells like sweat in here," Dad says. "Can you pass the croquettes?"

He must have decided to bike home from the bus stop for a change; it's the first time he's been home on time in a while.

"Maybe it's you," Mom says.

He sticks his nose in his armpit as he reaches for the croquettes. I hold the bowl up to his nose.

"I think it's Eva," he says to Mom. "That's what you get with those elephant feet."

It takes a lot of effort to keep the bowl in the air while he selects his croquettes, but I do it because it's Jolan's birthday. The bowl is lined with a sheet of baking paper. If I were a mom, I would've chosen a more festive color.

Tessie leaves the table to fetch another knife. She cuts open her croquettes lengthwise one by one, scoops out the filling with the tip of the knife and pushes it to the edge of her plate. She does the same thing with the excess butter that needs to be returned to the butter dish.

She lines up the six hollowed-out shells on her plate. She orders the peas to send three men to every ship and adds a teaspoon of gravy to each vessel.

No one asks her to eat her artwork after she's done.

That night I can't sleep. It takes an hour for Tessie to decide that the room is finally ready for bed. She stands next to her mattress the entire time, shifting things a few millimeters, flattening the sheet at the crease. Every night her bed is a different wild animal whose trust has to be earned.

I ask her if she wants to come up in my lofted bed.

"Do you want to switch beds again? Or do you want to share your bed?" she asks.

"Whatever you want."

Tessie does the unexpected. She climbs up the ladder and lies down beside me, leaving just enough room between us so we don't touch. She starts her list of goodnights, the words occasionally distorted by the lump in her throat.

"Goodnight, Tes," I say. I want to do something, say something sweet, ask her a question, curl up closer to her, but I don't want to break the silence and force her to start all over again.

She doesn't fall asleep right away, but at least she's lying down. That's a start.

The next morning it's clear that we both fell asleep at some point. For the first time in months, I wake up before she does. I carefully slide out of bed without touching her. She's lying on her back with her hands at her sides on top of the sheet, just like the dad in the Don't Wake Daddy! game who can pop up at any moment, his nightcap flying off his head, and force all the players back to start.

I head downstairs, the rest of the house is still asleep. The hallway is chilly, damp, not the kind of place you'd want to hang out in for very long. The monitor and keyboard are on the sideboard. The air smells like mildew and sleep.

No one but Tessie stays in this hallway longer than necessary. And, strictly speaking, neither does she—for her the typing is necessary.

Instead of going straight to the bathroom, I stop in front of the sideboard and place my hands on the keyboard. I press a few random keys, then I type "Hey Tessie! What's up?" It feels silly because anything I type will be lost on the spot, no one will answer. All of a sudden, without having to mull it over for months, I come up with a fully-fledged plan.

I cautiously slide the heavy sideboard away from the wall. Its small, pointy legs screech on the tile floor. I wait a moment, listening to make sure no one's woken up. All is quiet.

In the back of the cabinet are round holes. Dad cut them out before we were born, back when putting the finishing touches on things still mattered, so the stereo cables could slip discreetly out the back.

The old computer tower has been inside the cabinet on the top shelf ever since it was retired. There wasn't enough room behind the doors for the monitor and keyboard. I wriggle the power cord through the hole, insert the plug into the socket so you can barely see it, and push the sideboard back against the wall. I turn on the computer. It boots up reluctantly but with the devotion of an old dog who still gets up when he hears his name.

The huffing and puffing of the machine can still be heard through the cabinet doors, and eventually it will start giving off heat, so I cover it with a towel. This dampens the blowing sound, so you'd really only hear it if you knew to listen for it.

I close the cabinet doors. Slowly but surely, the old monitor comes to life.

The desktop is empty. We deleted everything, all the programs, folders and documents, everything except an old version of Word, a few games and the folder called "fun stuff".

I tinker around with the computer's settings, turn off the screen saver and deactivate sleep mode. Then I open an empty Word file and save it under the name "TES.doc". The cursor flickers on the blank white document. I switch the monitor off again. At the top of the stairs I look back one last time: it looks exactly like it did before. Only the fluorescent light bulb reveals how long I was there; its bright, cold light is now completely swallowed up by the first summer sun.

Lying Fallow

IT WAS SUPPOSED to start at ten. I'd never been to a funeral before, but I still recognized all the clichés. Rows of people stayed outside the church, even though there were plenty of empty chairs inside. Most of them were parents who preferred not to sit down at a funeral for a teenager, people from other towns who'd heard the rumors, or people who just happened to be walking by and considered themselves too underdressed to go in. The crowd was parted by the arrival of a black car—a cross between some kind of wartime vehicle and a giant beetle crawling down the street. Behind it were Pim and his parents, walking not quite slow enough. They kept having to stop and let the car carrying the coffin get ahead. Pim's mother had her hand on the shoulder of her remaining son—it was hard to say whether she was clinging to him or trying to slow him down.

Tessie came with me to the funeral. We shuffled into the church. I told Mom and Dad that Laurens's parents weren't going to be here either, and they didn't have any trouble accepting this as an excuse not to come.

We sat down beside Laurens in the third row of the nave, next to a statue of Mary with a weird look on her face—a broad smile that somehow still looked sad. Maybe the sculptor had started with the smile and changed his mind halfway.

Laurens's mom sat to our right, next to Tessie and me. Behind us was a whole row of teachers. Miss Emma had come back to town for the funeral, but she and her Black Pete sat off to the side, as far away from the other teachers as possible.

Jolan was there too, somewhere. I hardly saw any of Jan's other former classmates. Those who did come sat with their parents, hoping that this would somehow change things, that they'd no longer be the classmates who had collectively decided not to show up at Jan's birthday party.

Pim sat in the front between his parents. As the church bells rang, Jan's casket was carried in by four young men. They were followed by a lady wearing a ridiculous black hat, black gloves and a tight skirt suit. Her gait, although not cheerful, clearly said: this is somebody else's grief.

Then came a wave of coughs. It started with an old man. His cough infected other people with the idea that coughing, like yawning, might bring some relief. It took a long time for the church to get quiet again.

Jan's casket was carefully placed on a special stand at the front of the church. The master of ceremonies motioned to the four pall-bearers that they could go. They tried to look mournful, but I knew they were just going to go outside to smoke until they were called back in. It would've bothered me less if they'd just been honest about that.

The priest stood up from his chair and lit the giant candles beside the altar. Everyone knew they were fake. Only the outsides were made of wax, inside was a little oil tank that could be refilled.

The priest waited for it to get quiet.

"Dear family of Jan, dear parishioners," he began. "We are gathered here today in the presence of God to remember Jan and to say farewell. It is heartwarming to see how many of you have come." He cleared his throat, the sound of which was amplified in the microphone, just like his voice. "The way I see it, people are like farmland. Occasionally they have to go quiet, lie fallow, so later they can move on."

He was doing his best to make the concept of mourning tangible to Pim's family. I wondered whether he had written the text himself, whether Pim's parents actually wanted all these bizarre metaphors and stories about reaping and sowing. Wasn't the priest worried about ruining the only thing these people had left, their entire livelihood?

I barely listened to what was being said. My eyes were on Pim, two rows in front of me.

He was wearing a black shirt and shiny black pants—he looked like someone who still had something to lose. His father sat hunched beside him, wearing an old suit that exaggerated the broadness of his shoulders. On the back of his neck was an unruly patch of hair.

This was the church we were baptized in, where we had our First Communion together, where we were confirmed. For this ceremony, there had been no rehearsals, but it all went off without a hitch. After about fifteen minutes, the offering basket went around for the first time. I didn't have any change in my pocket.

I didn't want to cry. I knew that I was perfectly capable of not crying, that I could control my tears.

Pim's mother was asked to come forward. She unfolded her notes. She was wearing black pants that were narrower at the bottom than at the top and chunky heels about four centimeters high. Her notes were the only white thing in the entire church. She walked slowly, using her heels as picks.

Was there a word for it, for what she had become? A word like orphan or widow, but for mothers who have lost a child. Would it help that there was no name for it, or would it only make the grief wild, harder to tame?

Her voice sounded hoarse. Her hands were shaking. Before she even opened her mouth, I was in tears.

I felt sorry, for Pim, for his father with the two broad shoulders that nobody dared to lay a hand on. Pim and his parents were all alone, and I was too far away to offer any comfort.

Nobody in that church visited the farm as much as I did, nobody could imagine how horribly empty it was right now. Laurens wouldn't think to do it, so I did. I thought extra-hard about the big white mound, the stalls where the cows were chained up to give birth, the camera connected to a screen in Pim's parents' bedroom so they could keep an eye on the pregnant mother from their bed.

Pim's mom read the sentences she'd prepared very slowly. She stuck to the script.

As she spoke, I thought again of that camera, the view of the barn playing on the screen in their empty bedroom.

Tessie started to cry too.

I wasn't surprised. She had bottled up a lot of grief over the last few days—Christmas was always hard.

Laurens's mom was stroking Tessie's forearm, not mine. I didn't know why she was crying for Jan, she hardly knew him. She didn't go out to the farm. She'd never received compliments from him or kissed his pillow.

I didn't look at Tessie and didn't offer her any comfort either. Laurens's mom was already taking care of that. And maybe that was a good thing—Tessie needed to empty her tanks.

Laurens's mom gave us all a coin for the second collection. Laurens took the money and slipped it into his breast pocket.

I was afraid I might burst out laughing. When it comes down to it, there's not much difference between laughing and crying. It was like leaving home and coming back—it all happened in the same house.

The funeral lasted about an hour. Pim didn't read anything, though there was a folded piece of paper in his shirt pocket. He didn't look at us, not even as the casket was being carried back out— the four pallbearers had switched sides to avoid uneven shoulders.

"Yes! Sammies!" Laurens whispered as we entered the parish hall.

I smiled, though it was a pretty depressing sight, the rows of little sandwiches. No matter what happens, people will always eat.

We sat down at the front on the edge of the stage. From there, we had a good view of the entire hall. Other than the white napkins, there was very little decoration to speak of. Only neutral things that anybody in the parish could use, objects that were suitable for weddings, funerals and quiz nights: wicker baskets, lace tablecloths, chrome bowls, ashtrays, fire extinguishers, cake forks, sponsored coffee cups. The tables had been pushed to one side, in a long row. The chairs were stacked in such a way that they looked like they were sitting in each other's laps.

On the salmon-pink walls were faded landscape prints, the banners of local clubs, a few trinkets, a bow and arrow from the archery association, pictures of baptisms, communion parties, celebrations. There were a few kids wandering around who were under strict orders not to have too much fun.

I kept watching Pim. He was accosted by people, some of them shook his hand. From where I was sitting, it almost looked like they were congratulating him for something.

"Do you remember that time Jan's clothes disappeared from the locker room during swim lessons?" Laurens asked, finishing off a sandwich. He shot the rubber band that had been wrapped around it into the room, trying to hit somebody in the back. There was a leaf of garden cress stuck between his front teeth.

"No." I didn't want to have to think about it again, about Jan having to take the bus home from Verhoeven barefoot, wearing an oversized bathing suit borrowed from the lifeguard, with the wet print of his swimming trunks on it—he had refused to take a pair of underwear from the lost and found. Weeks later, his clothes and towel were found in the sinks of the men's bathroom.

"I'm going to go find another rubber band," Laurens said. He jumped off the stage and waddled through the hall.

As soon as Laurens was gone, Pim came over to me.

"Eva," he said. "Do you want to read this?"

He handed me the folded note that had been in his breast pocket all day. My fingers were almost too weak to open the paper. I read through it, twice. The first time I scanned it quickly, to judge where it was going. It wasn't what I was hoping for: a message from Jan to me, a declaration of love found in his bedroom, a poem with my name in it, nothing like that. It was just Pim's handwriting, a few short sentences, starting with the words "Dear Jan."

I read the message Pim had written for his brother a second time.

Suddenly, I thought back on that day we all went swimming

together at the Pit and wondered whether Jan would've gone after me if his mom hadn't put him in charge of bringing us home safely.

"Nice," I said. "Very appropriate." My lungs contracted around the air I inhaled. A lump rose in my larynx, slowly but surely, climbing up with an ice pick.

Pim put the note back in his pocket.

We watched Laurens in silence. He had already passed on three cheese sandwiches. Clearly, he was looking for one with meat salad, though he kept insisting that he was only after the rubber bands.

5:45 p.m.

CLOCKS SHOULDN'T BE able to just stop. They're supposed to keep the pace of human hearts.

Hanging over the entrance to the milk house is an old Mickey Mouse clock, frozen in time. Mickey's arms make up the minute and hour hands. He stands there stiffly, the big hand on eleven and the little hand on two, cheering unconvincingly. I step away from the ice block for a moment and tap on the glass in an attempt to nudge the second hand into motion. Nothing.

The milk house used to be the heart of the farm, but no one comes in here now. The front area has been completely dismantled. For years, it housed a giant cooling tank for storing milk until the big tankers came to town. They showed up every few days, maneuvering down the narrow streets like the trucks in the Coca-Cola Christmas commercials, giving little kids something to stare at. It only took a few minutes for them to pump up all the milk—"to rob us" as Pim's parents would say, because milk prices were only getting worse each year. Then the trucks took their load to the factories, where the milk was sterilized and bottled, and eventually found its way back to the Corner Store via wholesalers. Jolan once calculated that the odds that the milk on our breakfast table came from "our own cows" were about the same as the odds of finding a perler bead in the garden.

Jan must have looked at this clock a lot. To stay on schedule, four cows had to be brought in, set up and hooked to the milking machines every ten minutes.

The milk tank used to be right in the middle of the room, in the exact spot where I'm now setting up the ice block. There are still six holes where the humongous thing was bolted to the floor. To the right, behind the door, there used to be a kind of trench. It was a meter and a half deep and a couple meters wide, kind of like a manhole in a garage. From there, Jan and his father could attach the suction cups to the udders without having to get down on their knees every time.

Nowadays, the trench contains six igloos. In five of the white domes are calves sleeping on a bed of straw, each one under its own heat source. Attached to the bars on the front of the cages are buckets full of yellowish milk. At the bottom of the bucket is a rubber teat that looks more like a phallus than a nipple. I take the one heat lamp that's not being used. The calves don't stir.

I haul it back to the front of the milk house.

Carefully, I step up on top of the block of ice. I toss the lamp's cable over one of the roofbeams in one go and position the lamp so it hangs just above the ice. I do the same with the rope I just nicked from the sled. I make sure there's enough left over so I can reach it.

There are a lot of tools you can't get in the city because nobody ever needs them; there are no neighbors to come borrow them. I was sure I'd find everything I needed here. But that Pim's little boy would supply the rope—the odds of that were about the same as the odds of finding a hot bead in a garden.

The music next door dies out. I hear voices in the yard, just a few meters away, there's shouting and mooing, little kids who want to scare the cows by trying to talk to them.

Was Pim's son out there? What if they come in here, to have a look at the calves in the back? What if they find me here?

The music starts again, it's a country song, probably chosen by Laurens's mom, or by somebody else from the Catholic women in agriculture organization who still dons their checkered shirt every week and hauls the portable CD player to the parish hall for line-dance practice.

I give the rope a little tug. The knot's tight enough. I call Tessie one last time. Her phone rings. Once, twice, three times.

Just as I'm about to hang up, the phone already away from my ear, I hear a voice—not Tessie's. Probably Nadine's. I hang up immediately.

When I heard that Tessie's new foster mom was named Nadine, I looked her up on Facebook to see if she had any kids of her own. I went through all her photos. After that, I looked up where the term "foster mother" even came from. Who was being "fostered"— the mother or child? A lot of things can be fostered, including illusions, I thought, but then I met Nadine. She was kind and helpful. She ran a bakery and looked kind of like Laurens's mom—round and independent. She just showed up too late with her good intentions.

Tessie was placed with Nadine at her own request, and with my and Jolan's approval. I had just moved to Brussels, and until then, I'd worried about her day and night. I'm letting her go, I thought, then she can stop wasting away in that group home where she lived for the first two years after she was hospitalized, where she only stayed because she didn't want to go back to Mom and Dad in Bovenmeer. She could have dinner with another family, around another table, with normal brothers and sisters. At first, I found the thought of it reassuring. I was living in a new home myself, surrounded by other students. I could focus on my own life, make friends, be a bit more carefree. There was a force that stopped nagging at me for a little while. I assumed that Tessie was the reason I had always kept myself invisible—that I'd only wanted to be there for her.

It wasn't until a while later, when I started hearing from her less and less, that I began imagining what kind of bed she slept in, who she shared a room with, whether that person knew about the crocodile rule and ended with "Goodnight, Tes," how the food was served, who her new friends were, how she was doing in high school, whether she, like me, would bike the many miles back and forth with somebody at her side, whether she too would run out of things to talk about with her friends, whether she would ever have the guts to turn her back on those people, whether there was someone who came up with little tricks to help her fall asleep, whether she could curl up with her foster mom on the couch in the evenings.

Nadine said I was always welcome to visit. When I told her I didn't want to be a fifth wheel, she didn't really insist I wasn't, which is why I never knocked on her door again.

I struggled with it the most during the weekends when my roommates all went home. I wasn't even a fifth wheel—I was the spare tire hidden at the bottom of the trunk that people hoped they'd never have to take out. I waited for Monday, for the time to pass, for the city to fill up again.

After I'd finished my schoolwork, I started designing houses I could live in myself. With a bedroom for Tessie, an extra guest room for Jolan, room for a big kitchen. I made the design so minimalistic that it was almost impossible to create rituals in it.

I decided to stop studying architecture right before the end of my second year, a few weeks after I got a phone call from Dad.

He had tried to call me seven times during class without leaving a voicemail. After half an hour, he sent a message: "CALL BACK. URGENT. KIND REGARDS, KAREL DE WOLF, FINANCIAL ADVISOR DEXIA, ANTWERP."

Dad had never bothered to change the automatic signature on his messages after he retired. Every email and text message he sent us was proof that he had been useful elsewhere, that he had once been appreciated by other people, that he used to be fairly functional.

"Eva. Nadia called, an hour ago," he said when I called back. "Tessie, your sweet little sister, our sweet little girl, she tried to kill herself."

By emphasizing our relationships to her, he was trying to make up for his years of disengagement.

"Who's Nadia?" I asked.

"Nadine, I mean," he said. "She found a bottle of drain cleaner under Tessie's bed."

I thought about how Tessie would have swallowed the acid.

How it would've burned through her mouth and lips on first contact. How it would have run down her esophagus, destroying everything in its path. I could feel my intestines burning.

"Do you realize what this could've done to her?" he asked. "Do you need me to spell it out for you?"

"How bad is she?" I ask.

Dad pauses for a moment, to postpone the truth that would end the tragedy. I could hear Mom screeching things in the background.

"Nadia got there in time," he said.

I took a deep breath in and blew the air out. I leaned against the wall in the school hallway. Around me, classmates were walking out of the classroom, off to have a drink together in the cafeteria.

"Is Mom there? Put her on the phone."

"Okay, here she is." I could hear the disappointment in his voice: he had lost my attention, I wanted Mom. It was this very sense of disillusionment that compelled him, time and again, to put his own need for drama over the well-being of others, over us, over the truth.

He passed the phone to Mom.

"Eva?"

There was a tremor in her voice. I hung up without a word.

Afterwards, I never asked Tessie about it because I didn't know whether Dad had been telling the truth, and if she hadn't really hidden a toxic substance in her room, I didn't want to give her any ideas.

The milk house feels empty, but that's just because the corners of a room are always the darkest, and that's exactly where all the unused stuff is kept—sink frames, disconnected water pipes, empty built-in cabinets. In the background was the incessant twang of country music.

Was that PowerPoint still going? Would those pictures of me, Pim and Laurens projected on the wall, playing over and over again— each time repeating the wrong account of history—reveal how our friendship really ended? Or would they stop short, at the last photo of Jan, taken roughly six months before the summer of 2002?

I check Facebook again.

Jolan is online too, on his phone. There's a green dot next to his name. I've turned off my chat to everyone except the people I want to know are online, so I can see how often they sign on, so I can assess how well they are doing, whether they too spend their days wishing they had someone else's life. Neither Laurens nor Pim has been on for three hours. They don't want to be anywhere but at this posthumous party. Tessie is online too, not on her phone, but from a fixed connection.

All three of us are looking at a screen right now. Tessie in Nadine's big white villa, Jolan less than twenty meters away from me. He's hearing the same music I am; he's probably thinking about the same things. Maybe he stopped by Mom and Dad's house earlier today too.

They should all be able to see that I'm online too. So why aren't they saying anything?

I open an old group chat.

"Hello Tessie, hello Jolan," I write. I hit Enter. The way I've written it makes it sound so official. That wasn't my intention.

On a new line, I add a smiley.

August 7, 2002

FOR THE PAST two days, I've been acting like one of those fisher-men Laurens and I used to see on the dike along the Albert Canal when we crossed the bridge on our way to school. Unless there was tension on the line, they'd never pull it out to check if they might have caught something anyway. They didn't want to scare away the larger, approaching fish.

The best fishermen are never the ones with the most expensive raincoats, or the ones who cast their lines the most gracefully. The best fishermen are the ones with the most patience. Every time they cast a line and the bait goes untouched for a while, they have to convince themselves all over again that there's a big, fat fish on the way, that it will bite in the next few minutes, that it's worth it to wait just a little bit longer. All they see is the water sloshing against the dike, the mouth of the beer bottle they press against their lips.

That's exactly what I'm trying to do—just get through the day. By not looking at the clock, not watching the hours slowly passing by, not noticing how little happens. I sit in a spot overlooking the backyard with a comic book in my lap. Every time Tessie goes out into the hall or I have to go to the bathroom myself, I force myself not to check whether she's typed any words in the empty document.

Yesterday, I had these strange cramps in my lower abdomen all day. Only then did it truly hit me, what I was actually doing. By setting up that empty document, I was using Tessie's most trusted confidante as bait, as a double agent.

I was sure Tessie had typed something by now. It was the first thing she did every morning—she had to pass by the computer to get downstairs. And when she went from the bathroom to the kitchen to fix herself something for breakfast, or got up to go to the bathroom, she must've had to type something. She must have taken the bait.

I avoided her all day. I was afraid she would notice, by the way I moved, by the way I looked at her, that I was the one who was trying to trap her. I had no idea if the document was still open, if the computer had crashed, if she had figured out what I was up to and disconnected the keyboard.

Again today, I hope the computer will continue recording everything. Running into Tessie in the hallway is harder than usual. Maybe I'm afraid these last few hours will be too much for her, that my help will arrive just a little too late.

I think of Elisa almost as often as I think of Tessie. It's possible that she's already over at one of the boys' houses, that they're having the big summer finale without me, that they don't need me there to tell the riddle anymore.

Would Elisa remember the answer? Would she play dumb at first and then suddenly realize just how valuable the information I'd given her at Lille Mountain was? Would she call to thank me? Would her gratitude lead to something new, a friendship that could eventually replace Laurens and Pim?

Every time I think of Elisa, of how she could be with Pim and Laurens at this very moment, of how beautiful she is, I feel the double bras pressing into my chest. I'm pulling a fast one on everybody.

At the end of the afternoon, I finally have the chance to check the document. Tessie and Mom have gone to the supermarket. Mom has been letting her tag along lately in the hope that she might actually eat the food she picks out herself.

As soon as the car is out of the driveway, I dash over to the sideboard and lay my hand on the tower. It's red-hot under the blanket, but it's still churning. I turn on the monitor. The document is still open. The white page is covered in writing.

I use the arrows to scroll through the pages and bring the cursor back to the top. It takes a half-minute to get all the way back to the beginning. At the bottom of the document it says: "Page 26 of 28".

I don't read anything yet. I just let the letters pass through the ascending cursor.

Tessie and Mom won't be gone long. There's no way I'll be able to read the whole thing before they get back.

I go get the printer. After a lot of fiddling with cables and shuffling around clutter, I manage to print the whole document. I click on double-sided. That way the paper will reflect how it looks in her head. Hundreds of lines, divided across the two sides of her brain.

I tidy everything up and make sure to clear my tracks. I take the stack of paper outside and search for a place where I won't be disturbed. I sit down under the pear tree in the back of the garden, where I used to sit with the 3Suisses catalog and check off certain pictures in pencil—not of the clothes I wanted, but of the women I wanted to be.

I've brought a few comic books to bear down on. I lean back against the tree trunk. For a few minutes, I look out at the landscape in front of me, the driveway and the fields. Elisa's grazing stallion has no idea that there was once a more beloved horse than him.

The white papers in my lap reflect the sunlight. It's not that I want to start reading. The letters are both repulsive and attractive at the same time.

A cardiogram is to a heartbeat what this printout is to Tessie's thoughts. I'm not supposed to see this. I'm not a doctor; I can't help.

But I don't have a choice, just as I have no choice but to look at flattened pigeons on the street for at least ten seconds, to examine their crushed skulls, their twisted intestines, because the only thing that would make it worse would be if their death didn't horrify me at all.

On the first pages, everything is written in lowercase letters, Arial, size 12, exactly as I set it up myself. I start out reading very slowly, to let it really sink in.

But within seconds, I realize it's not written in any decipherable language. There are no recognizable words, no content. The only thing that makes a bit of sense are the numbers; sometimes counted up to ten, sometimes alternating between even and odd.

Since the keyboard was never fixed after Jolan spilled lemonade on it, the A-key sometimes gets stuck. Halfway through the first page, the A's start creeping in, more often and longer. By the sixth page they count for about a third of the letters. From there, the entire message reads like one long scream.

After fifteen pages, the Caps Lock is switched on. Judging by how far along in the document we are, it must have happened last night. Tessie couldn't have possibly noticed this herself; nothing lights up when Caps Lock is turned on. The transition from small to large letters forms a clear separation between what was written on the first day and what was written on the second. But it remains meaningless. No concrete sentences, no message, no information, no explanation for her odd behavior.

But the capital letters do create a strange tone, angrier, more powerful. I look up from the sheet.

The stallion has his tail high in the air; he's taking a piss. As long as Elisa isn't out there with her horse, she could be with Pim and Laurens.

I get up, walk back into the house and grab a notebook and a highlighter. I have to decode whatever there is to be decoded. I need to know how bad Tessie is. Because whatever is wrong with Tessie could've been wrong with me; we've been through the same things. And yet, I'm not the one typing like crazy on a switched-off computer every day. Somehow, I've escaped this, but I can't remember how, which way out I took.

I start highlighting all the letters between the many A's, until only the original, intended ones emerge. I look for meaningful terms, names. I write down all the words I encounter, one by one, in my notebook. In the margin, I keep a tally of the ones that appear more than once.

It's mostly articles, a few simple words that could have been typed deliberately or by chance—stand, lamp, sip, till, cut, crab, oreo.

On page two, there are three letters that jump out at me. Eva. My name is repeated more often than any other combination of letters. Every time I add a tally by my name, a sharp pain ripples through my lower abdomen. Twenty times. Jolan isn't mentioned once.

Maybe there's something about the layout of the keyboard that makes the E and the V two letters that are often struck by random typers, and the A, well, it's all over the place. My name is simply a matter of all the letters being in the right place. "Jolan" would be a much greater coincidence.

Halfway through the stack of papers, the car pulls into the drive-way. Mom and Tessie step out and start unloading the groceries from the trunk. Tessie carries a crate of beer to the workshop and sets it down in front of the door, next to the empty crates. Her shoulder blades are sharp and jut out of her back, as if she needs to let them puff up with air.

Mom grabs the least heavy shopping bags first.

Tessie walks back to the trunk to get the second crate of beer. Only then does she notice my presence. I hide the stack of papers under the comic books. She waves, but I don't react—she can't come over here right now.

With a straight back, she hauls the next crate of beer to the back of the house. Her pants are too big, and she doesn't have a free hand to pull them up. With every step, they slide down, exposing her crack.

I turn back to the pages. There must be something to distill from them: a message, a secret, an escape plan, a series of goodnights like the one she has to recite every evening.

The old Windows isn't an authority that Tessie has to report to, it's become her very operating system.

I've been sitting out here for half a day. I don't realize how much time has passed until I notice that the long, skinny shadow of the tree trunk that was on my left when I came out here is now on my right.

All of a sudden, Tessie comes running towards me. I quickly stash the papers between the comic books.

"Look," she says, opening her hand. It's empty.

"Oh, well, I caught a grasshopper. But he escaped."

She sits down next to me. We both look out at the fields. All of a sudden, there she is, in the pasture in front of us—Elisa. She saddles up the horse and climbs up effortlessly onto his back. There's a good chance she hasn't met up with Laurens and Pim yet.

"You know what I heard?" Tessie asks.

She looks straight at me. Her eyelids flutter above the thick gray circles under her eyes. It looks as if her face has just decided to accept the dark, saggy skin. She'll never be able to get rid of the bags, no matter how much she sleeps.

"What?"

"Mimi poisoned the last horse."

"How do you know?"

"Because she bought rat poison from Agnes a few days beforehand."

"Agnes sells rat poison?"

"She used to."

"Why would Mimi do that?"

"You'll have to ask her. Maybe Twinkle was too expensive to take care of and nobody was riding her anymore anyway? All I know is she didn't want the vet to do an autopsy. That says it all."

"I think we have to go in and eat," I say.

"I'm coming," she says so I'll go in first, and she can use the back door without anybody watching.

We've already started eating by the time Tessie joins us at the table. She took advantage of the fact that we were all gathered in the kitchen to type, to make up for the passages she missed today.

She looks at the carefully arranged sandwich fillings on the cutting board. Mom has layered the cheese slices like scales to make them look fancier than they really are and added a few slices of cucumber as garnish. There is also a plate of smoked mackerel topped off with chopped onions. Dad slaps a piece of fish onto a slice of bread and starts picking out the bones. He sets each one he finds in the corner of his placemat—penalty points for Mom.

"What'll it be, Tessie?" Jolan asks.

For a while, Tessie says nothing. She's considering her answer.

Dad starts counting down from five. When he gets to one, Tessie snatches up a slice of cucumber.

Dad's favorite threat used to be: "I'll give you a swat on your bare behind in front of the whole town." He used to say this a lot to keep us in line, weekly almost.

Every time, I imagined it what it would be like—my bare butt bent over on Dad's knee on the church steps. I wondered who would come to watch.

He almost did it once too, with Tessie. She was still just barely small enough to be carried. She had done something wrong at the table, I don't remember what, knocked over a glass of milk maybe, or said something rude. Dad got up, jerked down her pants, swung her over his shoulder and hauled her out of the house.

"Don't move," Mom snarled at me and Jolan. The dog whimpered with her nose pressed against the window on the sliding door.

We stayed in our seats and listened to Tessie cry and scream all the way down the Bulksteeg towards town—with every step, we could see Dad's white hair and Tessie's bare behind spring up over the top of the hedge. We were sure he wouldn't really do it, but we weren't sure if Tessie knew that. The screaming didn't stop until they turned off the street.

It happened on a Saturday. We were eating mackerel then too.

"Can you pass the butter?" Dad asks. Tessie hands him the butter dish. The slice of cucumber is still on her plate. Nothing on the table matches. I've recently learned a few rules of color combination: yellow doesn't go with green.

"Can I put the Nutella on the table?" I ask. I know this is against the rules of this household—no sugar in the evening.

"I won't have any tomorrow morning. I'll eat cheese. It's all the same in the end, and that way Tessie can have something sweet now," I say.

"This has nothing to do with the amount of chocolate," Dad says.

Maybe that's one way to recognize the families in which even the most basic things aren't right—they try to compensate with all kinds of ridiculous rules and principles.

I stand up, walk over to the cupboard and take out the store-brand chocolate spread. I slam the jar down on the table. Jolan lowers his eyes. Mom and Dad keep eating in silence. As long as they're not sober, we've got stronger counterarguments.

I see Tessie hesitate. She wants to honor my rebellion, but she also doesn't want to cross Mom and Dad if she doesn't have to. She looks at me. She looks at Mom. I smile encouragingly.

She spreads a thin layer of gooey chocolate on a piece of bread.

For the second time in the history of this family, Dad doesn't ask whether she's having chocolate-covered bread or bread-covered chocolate.

The Gnawed-off Foot

AFTER THE PERIOD of nighttime solidarity rituals, Tessie started asking me for a story every night before bed.

"Aren't you a little old for that?" I asked.

"Never," she said.

She didn't really care about the plot. All she wanted was for me to use as many diminutive words as possible, for the world around us not to matter anymore, to be cut off from the arguing voices around us. The stories were mostly variations on the same theme: someone ending up safe and sound, there was a threat of a natural disaster, but everyone was saved.

The day Elisa was transferred to the sixth grade and I refused to finger the blackberry jam in front of all the girls, it was particularly cold. I remember this because I had lent Elisa my mittens that morning and my hands were freezing on the way home from school. That evening we ate pea soup. Mom always made pea soup in that kind of weather. She'd always say she was going to invite the postman in for a cup, but in the end, all the leftovers went in the freezer.

That evening Tessie begged me for a story, but I couldn't think of one.

"You can choose. One story or two," she concluded.

I always thought Tessie was a good negotiator, but it suddenly occurred to me that I was just a bad refuser.

So, I started telling a super-babyish story about two little bunnies, hoping that she'd say, "That's enough, you can stop." But she clung to my every word.

"The little bunnies hopped and hopped, but they had no idea what was brewing off in the distance."

I paused dramatically and sat up straight in my bed to emphasize the severity of the looming threat.

"A big, huge tidal wave. Higher than our house!"

Another pause.

"Well, to make a long story short—the two little bunnies were just about to hop back down in their hole when the bigger bunny got his foot caught in a hunter's trap. The little one wanted to help, but there was no time. The big bunny was stuck, and the tidal wave was getting closer and closer. 'Bite my foot off!' the big bunny squeaked, but the little bunny didn't dare. He'd never bitten into anything but carrots. The big bunny begged and begged, but the little one had no choice but to leave him behind. He hopped down in the hole in the nick of time and shut the watertight door so the tidal wave couldn't touch him. Outside, the water washed away everything in its path."

Another long pause.

"And then?" Tessie asked.

"What do you mean, and then?"

"What happened to the big bunny?"

"That's it."

"Are you sure?" I could tell by Tessie's tone that there were tears welling up in her eyes.

"Yep," I said. "That's the end."

"The very very end?"

She asked twice, just to be sure.

"Yeah, Tes. That's the very very end."

"But maybe there was a really hungry buzzard that swooped down and yanked the big bunny free and accidentally dropped him somewhere the tidal wave couldn't get him?" she asked. "Couldn't that have happened, Eva?" Suddenly she sounded more like a six-year-old than a nine-year-old.

"Come on, Tessie, that's not possible."

"What about the hunter, where was he? Couldn't he have freed the bunny and carried him off in a burlap sack?" The more unlikely her ideas were, the more irritated I became.

"No," I said. "Think about it. The hunter wouldn't have been able to escape in time either."

"The little one could've just bitten the foot off though, right, Eva? Isn't a gnawed-off foot bad enough?"

"No," I snap. "A gnawed-off foot isn't enough."

She didn't say anything else. It took more than an hour for her to fall asleep. Little by little, the lump in my throat disappeared.

After that night, Tessie stopped negotiating for stories. Every so often, she'd ask for one "with a happy ending", but I'd tell her I couldn't promise that anymore, for her own good. I thought I was toughening her up a bit, preparing her for something.

It was around that time that, in the absence of fairy tales, the goodnight ritual became more elaborate, and my name was bumped to the end of the list, after God.

At the end of 2001, the night after Laurens's mom came out to the backyard to tell us the bad news about Jan, neither me nor Tessie could sleep. My head felt fuzzy. I couldn't get a single thought to take shape.

"You want to know something about Jan?" she asked.

6:30 p.m.

It must be as cold in the milk house as it is outside. Under the heat of the lamp, the ice block is finally starting to melt. The soles of my feet create imprints on the surface, two little dips, like the top of a mattress slept in by the same two people for a very long time.

It won't be long now. The water is seeping into the grout and moving down the uneven floor. The little streams run into the wide, deep gutter at the side of the room, where the spilt milk used to collect, along with the cats and flies.

I check the clock again. I have no idea how many minutes have gone by. If only the thing would spring back to life, if the hands could at least let me believe I'm not alone, if Mickey Mouse could stop cheering and lower his arms. Now all this is happening outside of time. Eighteen songs have played in the barn since I've been out here. If each song was three minutes on average, I've been here about fifty-four minutes.

I could have been back in Brussels by now. I probably would have gone down to my neighbor's apartment, knocked on the door and asked him if he wanted to spend New Year's together.

"At my place or your place?" he'd ask.

"I don't care," I'd say, although I would prefer to celebrate in his apartment, because there's nothing there to remind me of myself, not even a toothbrush.

We could smash the block of ice with a hammer, store the ice chips in his giant freezer and use them to chill our drinks for years.

At least the local paper will write a story about me. I'll become an anecdote, the subject of local rumors.

A rumor because it will become yet another a story about some-one who's had something happen to them. Rumors are just stories about acquaintances that people around here like to spread because they feel like they set them apart, allowing them to belong to the group of people who escaped something.

Anecdotes are different. They're the non-time-sensitive gossip. The stories you have no problem passing along because you don't know the subject in question personally. Stories like the one about the drunk guy who was pushing his wheelbarrow down the street when he accidentally bumped into two cops who made him blow into a tube and suspended his driver's license for ten days.

If I had the choice, I'd want to be both.

One thing's for sure, the snow's not going to melt tonight. Which means there's always the chance that tomorrow morning, at the crack of dawn, someone will bend down to inspect the meandering trail I left in the yard.

If Pim's little boy is as curious as Jolan was at that age, he'll want to know what kind of animal made those tracks. He'll follow the trail, in the wrong direction at first, down through the yard, until it ends at my car a little further down the street. Then he'll turn around and go the other way. He'll end up in front of the milk house, push open the door, see the water.

After that, they'll start piecing it together: the car that was parked in front of the butcher shop for a long time with the head-lights on and later abandoned on the street with the key in the ignition, the neighbor who helped freeze the block of ice, the shoebox full of envelopes under my bed.

People will wonder exactly what happened, how it came to this.

And then Laurens's mom will finally talk, because she won't be able to stand the thought of spreading a false rumor a second time.

I'm sure she's wondered how I've been getting on since the summer of 2002. One time, she accidentally liked one of my photos on Facebook and immediately unliked it, but I had already received the notification.

She even stopped by Jolan's place one time to ask him how I was doing, how Tessie was doing. He told me that two years ago, at Christmas.

What happened at the end of the summer never became the subject of a rumor or an anecdote, and that's only because she didn't spread it. It took me too long to figure that out, that she was the linchpin in the entire gossip mill, that all the stories in this town, all the rumors about Tessie, about Jan—they all came from her. She determined what the reality, and ultimately the memory, would become.

After the summer of 2002, Laurens didn't go out much. He spent most of his time in the shop, taking refuge at his mother's side. When a customer would ask how he got the deep cut above his eye, she'd say: "He bumped into the edge of the counter while cleaning the display case." Then she'd point to the sharpest corner in the shop, and people would nod silently.

She even told the story to Jolan when I sent him into the shop to buy meat—he hadn't even asked. The discount she gave him was proof that she was lying, that she knew exactly what her son was capable of.

August 10, 2002

YOU CAN TELL it's boiling outside from the way Nanook is acting. Without batting an eye, she watches a bird take a leisurely bath in her water bowl. Tessie and Mom are out. They both have an appointment with the same doctor, a specialist in varicose veins.

I sit at the kitchen table going over my notes. I've been studying them for a long time but still don't know what I'm looking for. Without a pencil or a marker in my hand, it feels like I've given up trying to understand Tessie. My eyes keep coming back to the many tally marks by my own name.

Eva. It starts and ends with the same letters as Elisa. I take a pencil from the jar on the counter and write her name next to mine. "Elisa" is a lot more work, almost twice as many letters. Mine is just an abbreviation, an answer to a problem. A word that was never finished.

There's a smack on the kitchen window behind me. I hide the papers and turn around. It wasn't a bird smashing into the window, it was Laurens. He's trying to get my attention. The plastic bag dangling from his wrist hits the window, making the smacking sound I just heard.

I stuff the notes into my pocket. The back door is only two steps further away, but I prop open the window instead. Pim's there too.

"Can we come in?" Laurens pushes his face into the opening.

"If you wanted to come in, you should've knocked on the door," I say. It's still early, the sun is low. The light is shining in my eyes.

"Hey, Evie, sorry about last week." Pim steps closer to the window.

It's the first time in my life he's called me Evie. Only my dad calls me that.

"Sorry for what?" I ask. I want to know if we're thinking about the same thing.

"Listen, Eva—it's Elisa's turn today," Laurens says.

"And she's coming here," says Pim.

"She's coming to solve your riddle. She said she'd only come if we did it at your house."

"She's the last one on our list." The sun dips behind Pim's head for a moment, only to blind me again the next.

"I mean the first on the list, not the last, you know what I mean. Our top scorer."

"We have to finish this together, Eva."

"C'mon, you get that."

They stop talking and wait for me to respond. Beads of sweat are pearling on their heads. They biked over here together, which means they rehearsed all this beforehand. In the plastic bag around Laurens's wrist are a couple of cans of soda. Cokes. Not two, but three.

I pull the window shut and slip on a pair of my mom's clogs, so I won't have to walk barefoot over the cherry pits in the garden.

Laurens and Pim lead the way out to the chicken coop. When we reach the cherry tree, they stop and look out into Elisa's field. The horse is grazing. There are braids in his mane and tail. Elisa is nowhere in sight. This could mean she's already on her way.

The cans in Laurens's bag swing back and forth now that he's stopped. His fly is open, his underwear is sticking out. A small white bulge. I don't tell him.

It's pretty hot outside, but I'm still startled by the heat coming out of the shed. The small wooden structure is right in the sun and has a flat black corrugated metal roof. It's so hot inside that the air has weight. The longer you stand still the heavier it gets.

Laurens and Pim sit down on either side of the hay bale. In the corner is a brooding chicken.

"That egg is gonna come out hardboiled," says Laurens as he

opens the first can of Coke. The foam fizzes all over his hands. Startled, he drops the can. It lands in the straw.

"Way to go," Pim says.

"Bring your own drink next time," says Laurens.

He lets the other two cans settle for a while.

Pim's wearing cut-off jeans. I think I saw Jan wearing them once. Or maybe I imagined it. All three of us sit with our knees the same distance apart. Our own body heat is too much to bear.

Pim pulls the bottom of his T-shirt up through the neckline and ties the fabric in a knot, exposing his abdomen. Laurens does the same.

I sit across from them on a log. Laurens's fat rolls, the pearly sweat in Pim's navel—they suddenly seem easier to talk to again. I already feel sorry about what they've got coming.

In this heat, it takes more effort to stay silent than to talk.

Laurens opens another can of soda, hands it to Pim and keeps the other one for himself. Between gulps, they press the cool sides against their foreheads. Every time I want a sip, I have to ask. Before long both cans are empty.

"Diet Coke is gross." Pim offers me the last sip of lukewarm cola without me having to hold out my hand for it. "It tastes like Coke that somebody drank and spit back out."

"Mom's on a diet again. She won't let regular Coke in the house," says Laurens. "Everything with sugar costs points. She keeps track of every meal in a little book. But every night she eats a can of fruit and drinks the syrup because fruit doesn't count." He puffs up his cheeks.

"What kind of diet is that?" I ask. "Weight Watchers?" I can picture her standing in the kitchen drinking out of a can of fruit cocktail.

"No idea."

"It all comes down to the same thing—the better it tastes, the more points it's worth," Pim grins.

Laurens lets out a forced laugh.

"Man, Eva, it stinks in here. Like fried chicken shit," he says.

"Who called Elisa?" I ask.

Pim raises his finger. "She said she was coming."

"You sure?"

"Yeah." Pim sticks up his nose, then lifts his shoulders, leans back and closes his eyes.

I can tell he's having second thoughts. I see it, because I know what it looks like. I invited Elisa over here plenty of times before. She never came once.

The chicken looks nervously back and forth from her nest, her eyes shifting from the hay bale Laurens and Pim are sitting on, to me. Her head almost makes a complete circle. It takes her a moment to figure out which way to turn it back.

"Can't we wait outside?" I ask.

"No," says Pim.

He looks at his watch and keeps trying different poses, not sure how he wants to look when Elisa walks in.

Whenever he finds the perfect pose, he can't hold it for more than two minutes before having to wipe the sweat from his brow.

"So this is it then, the end." Laurens leans back so his belly has one less roll of fat. "What are we going to do tomorrow?"

Pim thinks about it for a moment and opens his mouth to speak.

I'm curious to hear what he has to say, but just as he's about to say something, there are three knocks on the door of the coop. I can tell by the way it sounds—resolute, commanding—that it's Elisa and that she has been out riding all morning.

Only the lower half of the split door swings open. It slams against the chicken-feed bin with a loud bang. We stare out into the blinding sunlight.

Slowly my eyes adjust. Elisa is still wearing her riding clothes. They accentuate her curves. The lines of her inner thighs make a sudden curve inwards just below her groin. Even when she stands up straight with her legs pressed together, there's a gap under her crotch wide enough for an entire fist. She's wearing her tight black riding pants with the shiny piping down the sides. Her labia are packed in tightly, revealing none of their secrets. Framed by the sunlight, her lower body alone is worth the full nine and a half points.

Elisa opens the upper half of the door. Only now can I see her face. Her long hair is pulled back in a tight ponytail, so tight that it almost corrects her eyelids. Her eyebrows seem even sharper than they were last week. Her firm, muscular breasts are high on her chest.

Laurens licks his lips.

"Ew, it stinks in here," Elisa says.

"That's what I said too." Pim quickly unties the knot in his T-shirt.

"Can't we do it in some other shed?"

I want to say there is no other shed, but Elisa has already turned around and is heading for the workshop. Pim and Laurens follow her. I collect the empty soda cans and put them in the plastic bag. Right before I shut the door behind me, I see the chicken, winking at no one.

"Your dad is ridiculously well equipped," Elisa says when I walk in behind them. She looks up in amazement at the tangle of tools hanging from the rafters. It's damper and cooler in here.

"Yeah. Thanks," I say, though I'm not sure it was a compliment.

The noose is dangling just over Laurens's head. If you don't know what it's for, you might think it's just for hanging tools. Dad's had the whole summer to carry out his plan. In the meantime, the limp rope has gone from shocking to annoying. Yet another unfinished project.

"Okay, let's hear it. What am I doing here?" Elisa spins the blades on the grass trimmer hanging on the wall. Pim is standing behind her, eyeing the gold piping running down her thighs. He makes maneuvering gestures—if these were the lines of a parking lot, he'd have no trouble parking.

Laurens and Pim exchange a few excited glances to decide who'll do the talking. They try to catch Elisa's eye, but she's looking only at me.

This is what Laurens and Pim have been working towards all

summer. They think that when this is all over, they'll be real men, that they'll be able to bike home, triumphantly parading through the streets. I already can see the victory dripping from their faces— they're about to score a nine-pointer.

The sun shines down on the crown of my head through the broken window.

Pim explains the rules of the game, which have changed again. They've gone back to one item of clothing per guess. That's what's proven most effective.

"For every wrong guess, you have to take something off. When you're naked, you lose. Then you have to do something for us. If you solve the riddle, we have to do something for you. Whatever you want."

"What if I don't want anything from you two?"

"C'mon, there must be something." Laurens rubs his thumb and index finger over his upper lip and sniffs his own sweat.

"So you guys would clean my horse's stall for the rest of the summer?"

"Of course!" Laurens and Pim answer in unison.

"What's the riddle, then?"

"We'll only tell you if you agree to play."

"That's not really fair."

"We could just tell her," I say.

Pim hesitates, weighing the pros and cons.

I take advantage of his indecisiveness to tell the riddle. Then I know Elisa will stay.

I try to repeat it exactly as I told it to her at Lille Mountain.

"A man is found in a room with a noose around his neck, hanging over a puddle of water, dead. There's nothing in the room but him, the rope and the water. No windows, no furniture. So the question is, what happened? How exactly did the man die?"

No one says a word.

The hanging man isn't just some random image anymore. I see him in front of me, suspended fifty centimeters above a puddle of water, his two legs dangling, his jeans bulging at the knees.

"That's the riddle?" Elisa asks. She looks at me.

"Yep," I say.

Elisa lets out a deep sigh. She's putting on a show. There's not the slightest sign of relief on her face.

"No way I can figure this out."

"Sure you can!" Laurens and Pim exclaim, again almost in unison. "Just think about it."

"Okay, I guess I can try."

Pim sticks his hand down his pants and makes a quick adjustment. Elisa looks me straight in the eye and smiles faintly.

"Swear," Pim says to her.

"Swear what?"

"That we'll stick to the rules."

"I swear. On my horse." She holds up two fingers, scout's honor. "You have to swear too, then."

"What do you want me to swear on?" Pim asks.

"On Jan's grave."

Laurens and I exchange looks. This is the first time an outsider has said Jan's name out loud. Pim looks away at the rakes, the shovels.

"Do we really need to swear?" I ask. "We can all trust each other here, right?"

Pim cuts me off. "I swear," he says. "On Jan."

"And you," Elisa asks Laurens, "who do you swear on?"

Laurens looks around in desperation. He doesn't have anything of the same significance.

"Just swear on something, your mom if you have to," Pim commands.

"Fine. I swear on my mother," Laurens declares.

"Good. What about you, Eva?" Elisa shoots me a conspiratorial look. I smile back hesitantly.

"Just say the first thing that pops into your head, Eva." Laurens's face is red from the heat.

I can't think of anything.

"Come on, Eva, just pick something," Pim insists impatiently.

"On Tessie," I swear. The sun dips behind a cloud. Suddenly the temperature drops. A shiver runs down my back to my tailbone.

Moments later I'm having second thoughts. Should I have given Elisa the answer to the riddle? Couldn't I have gotten back at Laurens and Pim even more by just continuing as planned? Then they could see for themselves how ugly her vagina is, and that she's got a big mole on her back. Then they'd have to face the truth: they spent an entire summer working up to an anticlimax. They'd finally realize how inaccurate their scoring system had been all these years.

"You're wearing six pieces of clothing, so you've got six guesses," I say.

Elisa thinks long and hard before asking the first question.

"That water on the ground . . . is it urine?" She does her best to make it sound like a real guess, like she's not sure, without falling out of character.

"No," says Pim.

He knows it's wrong—that question has been asked a bunch of times. "Take something off."

Elisa bends down and pulls off one of her riding boots. The tight pants are crumpled around the calf.

"Do shoes count for one point or two?" she asks.

The way she's dragging this out, the confidence with which she undresses—it's reassuring and, at the same time, terrifying. I didn't expect Elisa to be such a good liar.

"Do you ever go out with one shoe on?" Pim asks. "No way, shoes go together."

"If you say so, Pim." Elisa takes off her other boot and sets them upright next to each other, between us. They hold the shape of her calves.

She stands up, thrusting out her chest again. Before she pulls her fleece sweater over her head, she blurts out the next question. It's almost as if she wants to lose the game, to be dominated by a couple of dimwits. I see Pim balling his fist behind his back.

"Did the guy do it himself, or was there another person

involved?" Her ponytail is charged with static electricity now; the hairs start floating up in all directions. Pim reaches to smooth them down for her, but she quickly does it herself.

"You can only ask yes or no questions," I say.

"Was he alone?" Elisa rephrases her question.

"Yes," I say.

"Did he fall down through the ceiling from upstairs?"

Pim looks at me. I shake my head no.

"Nope," Laurens repeats triumphantly.

Elisa looks me dead in the eyes as she removes her T-shirt, exposing her upper body. Her firm breasts pop out from underneath. The non-elastic stitching around her lacy bra presses into the round flesh. She winks at me.

Then, she stands there in silence for a few seconds, in nothing but her bra, socks and riding pants. She lets Pim and Laurens grope her body with their hungry eyes. I'm the only one who seems to be wondering why she didn't take off her socks first.

"Okay. Another guess. Was it an accident or on purpose?" she asks.

"It wasn't an accident," I say.

Elisa bends down. With her hands on the cuff of her sock, she stops; her fingers glide up to the little hook behind her back. She unfastens it. For a split second, as her ponytail falls to the side, the thick, grape-shaped mole on her upper back is visible. Laurens and Pim don't see it; their eyes are locked on the straps sliding down her shoulders. Even when she bends forward her breasts stay as round as ever.

She straightens up again. The mole disappears back under her ponytail.

Elisa's breasts are the most beautiful we've seen yet. They've grown fuller since the last time I saw them in the changing room.

I shouldn't be jealous. She's doing this for us, for herself, for me. The more she lets Laurens and Pim salivate now, the more disappointed they'll be when they don't get to touch these two prime specimens.

"Were any other bodily fluids involved besides urine?" Elisa guesses.

"No," I say. Finally, she takes off her socks, first the right, then the left. Her breasts hang to the side as she leans sideways. She crumples up the socks and shoves them down into the riding boots still standing upright in the middle of the workshop.

"Was the room full of water, so the man could float up and slip his head through the noose, and did it empty out afterwards?"

Pim's posture changes. Laurens crosses his arms. It's the first guess in the right direction.

"Is that right, Eva?" Pim practically squeaks.

"No," I say.

Now Elisa has no choice but to peel off her tight riding pants. They are so tight against her skin that she has to pull down on each leg one by one. Her thighs are pale and covered in a thin downy layer of hair. She's wearing a light blue thong, which is stuck in her crotch. Her labia hang there like the droopy leaves around a head of cauliflower. She pulls the panties out of her crotch. There's not much left of it for the boys to see.

"Okay," she says. "Let me think for a second."

Slowly, she reviews her previous guesses. "It's not pee, no ladder, no second person, not an accident, no swimming pool."

She scratches under her left breast, massages it, just for a second. Laurens and Pim look at each other proudly. And that's when she gives her final answer.

"Could it be that this man stood on a chunk of ice with the noose around his neck and waited for it to melt?"

A deep, long silence falls over the workshop.

Laurens and Pim are looking at me. No one has ever guessed this before. The stallion whinnies in the distance, probably at a passing cyclist.

"Is that right?" Elisa asks.

"Eva, say something." The arousal in Pim's body turns into desperation. Laurens wipes the sweat from his forehead and smells his fingertips again.

I take a step back. For a second, I hesitate.

Of course, I can still say it's the wrong answer. I'm the riddle-keeper after all. I can say whatever I want.

"Eva!" Pim shouts. "Did you swallow your tongue or what?"

I look at him, then at Laurens. In the corner of the shed is the big shovel, facing the corner, as if it's being punished for something.

"That's right," I say. "The man was standing on an ice block."

Laurens and Pim look from Elisa to me, and then back to Elisa in dismay.

"How can you stand on a block of ice? Isn't it slippery?" Laurens squeaks.

"So the guy had shoes on, shouldn't you have mentioned that?" Pim says.

"What that man had was a lot of patience," I say.

"What a stupid riddle, Eva. This is bullshit." Pim snorts loudly through his nostrils even though there's no snot in them.

Elisa puts her bra back on. Pim and Laurens watch as she lifts each breast one by one and drops it into the preformed cups. This is as good as it's going to get for them—watching helplessly as their present is wrapped up again.

Once the hooks are fastened behind her back, she pulls out her ponytail, holding it up in the air longer than necessary.

"So, if I'm not mistaken, I just won, right?" She wriggles her tiny butt cheeks back into the narrow legs of her riding pants, inching them up on one leg after the other.

Pim looks at Laurens. They both swore. He shrugs his shoulders and nods. If cleaning the stables is the only way left to please Elisa, that's what he'll have to do.

"I know what I want from you. Take off your clothes, guys."

Laurens and Pim straighten up.

"All three of us?" Laurens asks.

"No, just you and Pim," Elisa commands.

Once Pim and Laurens are bent over untying their shoes, she gives me another wink.

I try to relax as much as possible. It's time. It's my turn to humiliate Laurens and Pim a little bit, just enough to bring them back down to earth, to make them the boys they used to be.

"These aren't the rules," Laurens mumbles. Pim motions for him to shut up. He must think something good is coming; he takes off all his clothes.

"You chose this yourself," Elisa says to Laurens. "You can't complain now."

Reluctantly, he starts removing his clothes too. It doesn't take long—all he's wearing is a pair of shorts and a baggy T-shirt. He looks over at Pim to see if he has to take off his underwear. Laurens is the more embarrassed of the two. Now that I see them standing next to each other almost completely naked, I understand why.

"How about I buy you a membership at the tanning salon?" Laurens asks before dropping his underwear.

"Who's going to pay for that?" Pim jeers.

"My mom. She's got a bunch of money under the cash register; it's all off the books, she only counts it once a week."

"Why didn't you say that before, when we needed the money?"

Laurens and Pim are facing each other, thrusting their chins higher and higher in the air.

Elisa grabs a stray paintbrush and waves it to call them to attention. "If I wanted money, I'd just ask my dad. Everything off. Underwear included," she demands and flings the brush off into a corner.

Pim tugs down his boxer-briefs, first sliding them down his butt, until the fabric gets caught on his penis. It flops out, half erect.

Elisa casts a quick glance at Laurens's penis, which is hanging sheepishly in his lap. Her gaze lingers longer on Pim's. The longer she looks, the harder it gets. Elisa takes a step closer and pushes her index finger first into Pim's firm pecs and then into Laurens's flabby tissue.

Last week, they were still acting like men. But when it comes down to it, men are just boys who've been overpowered by something.

Elisa takes a few steps back so she can get a good look at them.

"Okay. Now you have to do whatever I tell you," she says. "No whining. That was the deal."

The hairs on Laurens's arms are standing on end. I look away, at the two heaps of clothing on the workshop's dirty concrete floor.

"What about Eva?" Laurens sneers. "Shouldn't Eva have to do something?"

"Eva didn't do anything to me."

"And we did?"

"You guys invented this game. Not Eva."

"Eva came up with the riddle," says Pim.

"So what if she did? What's in it for her?"

"We taught her something. She should be thanking us."

Laurens nods in my direction. "You should be thanking us."

Elisa forces a loud, emphatic laugh. "What do you guys even know about it anyway? How many girls have you slept with?"

Laurens looks down at his toes. For just a second, during a quick glance, I think of our last day of school. This is exactly how he must have stood at our usual meeting spot when he realized I wasn't coming.

"Didn't Eva ever tell you she poisoned your horse?" Pim asks. He looks Elisa straight in the eyes. His penis is now fully erect. A boa constrictor, ready to attack. If the thing had eyes, I'd swear it was staring at me.

I shake my head. "It wasn't like that."

Elisa looks at me. "Is that true?"

I try to shake my head more convincingly, but all of a sudden, I'm not sure whether I should be nodding yes or shaking no.

"She told us when we were playing truth or dare at the beginning of the summer. She fed the horse candy. Poor Pinkle."

"Twinkle," I correct him. "She didn't die because of the candy." I look each of them in the eye one by one. "I know what really happened."

Pim won't even let me finish the sentence. "Elisa, do you remember all that shit in Mimi's mailbox?" He nods in my direction. "Her idea."

"Not true," I say, twice as loud. It's my word against theirs.

Elisa's eyebrows are now straight lines above her eyes. She turns her back on us. I can't see what she's thinking. She brings her hands to her ponytail, pulls out the elastic, and shakes her hair loose.

Denying it should be enough—after all, I've been friends with Elisa longer than the boys have, and I've known the boys way longer than she has. I have selflessly predicted their future countless times, I'm the link that holds them together. They can't just ignore that.

"All for one and one for all, Evie," Pim scoffs.

Musketeers. It doesn't mean anything anymore; it's a remnant of the past, a name we shared when we still knew how to bring toy soldiers to life in the sandbox.

"It was Pim's idea and Laurens's poop," I say. "I was just there."

Elisa pulls her hair back up into the same ponytail as before, only tighter. She whips around.

"It doesn't matter. You were an accomplice. You take off your clothes too, Eva."

I back up against the wall; both my feet are standing on an old paint splatter on the floor. The white spot has always been there, but only now do I notice it's in the shape of a clover.

"I did give Twinkle candy, but it couldn't have killed her," I say. "Lots of sugar over the long term can sometimes make dogs and cats go blind, but a horse can handle a lot more. Big animals are a lot stronger."

I turn from Elisa to the boys. "Did you ever see Twinkle up close? She was huge. It would have taken a lot to kill her. Jolan looked it up on the internet."

"What does Jolan know about it?" says Laurens. I'm sure he's heard the gossip about the rat poison too—if Tessie's heard it, Laurens probably has—Agnes most certainly told his mom.

"Come on, you know it too, Laurens, admit it. I'm not the one who poisoned her."

"What are you talking about?" Elisa asks.

Laurens gives me a quizzical look too, but he doesn't ask any questions. I believe he really doesn't know what I'm talking about.

"Don't be such a prude, Eva," Elisa says. "Stop lying."

Can I just tell them all to go home? Would they ever want to come back? I'm not taking my clothes off. This is my property. This is my dad's workshop. I make the rules here.

"Can't I do whatever you want me to do with my clothes on?" I say.

"Sure. In that case, we'll wait for Tessie and ask her the riddle." Elisa picks the dirt out from under a nail and flicks it away, not at the boys but between my feet.

I look at Pim, then at Laurens. It's up to them to intervene. They both know that Tessie's not much to look at, she's skin and bones.

"Or better yet, we can tell her how her big sister lured all those girls into a trap," says Pim. Elisa laughs.

Without accomplices, I don't have any arguments left. I start taking off my clothes. I have no idea who I'm trying to satisfy the most.

I slide my sweater off my arms, unbutton my pants, and pull them down. I don't know which way is better—to strip down slowly, like Elisa did, or fast and sloppy, like how you unwrap a present from Aldi so you don't have a chance to get your hopes up.

I keep my panties on for now. I suck in my belly and lift my T-shirt over my head. I can feel their strange looks, and that's when I remember: I'm wearing two padded bras on top of each other. This is how I've been training myself for larger breasts.

I want to unfasten them both at the same time but that's going to be tricky. If I stand there fiddling with the hooks, I'll only draw more attention to the bras. So I unclip them one at a time as fast as I can. Just removing the first bra cuts the volume of my breasts in half. After the second one comes off, there's barely anything left. I stash the two bras away under the pile of crumpled clothes. Elisa looks at my two little cupcakes with amusement and thrusts her cannons forward. Laurens and Pim look down at the T-shirt I've just stuffed the two bras under—four little hills on the concrete floor, my breasts. They don't quite understand what just happened, or worse, they don't care.

"Your panties too," Elisa says.

I stay as close to the wall as possible, my feet firmly planted on the white clover, for some kind of cover at least.

These are my friends. This is just a game that's got out of hand, that's all.

For the record, my labia look way better than Elisa's; I've got a nice tight package. I lower my panties, fold them up immediately and stuff them into the leg of my crumpled pants, hoping to hide the white skid mark. I comb my pubic hair with my fingers, two quick strokes, just to make sure it's not matted together.

I don't have enough hands to cover everything I'm ashamed of. I let my arms hang at my sides like Laurens and Pim.

"So, are you satisfied, Elisa? Seen enough?" Pim asks. He pronounces her name strangely. He's holding his hands in front of his penis, which has grown limp at the sight of my naked body.

There are three piles of clothes between us, clothes I could recognize Laurens and Pim in from a distance. When I think of all the afternoons they wore these T-shirts, all the holes in them . . . Now that we've taken it all off, stripped ourselves of our masks, why bother submitting ourselves to what we swore, why keep our promise, like good little musketeers?

Elisa looks around the shed, scans the rafters, studies the tangled tools with narrowed eyes. Then her gaze falls on the tool rack on the wall.

"Do you guys know how long a drill is actually used in its entire life?" I ask.

"Ten minutes?" Laurens guesses. He's the only one who responds.

"Eleven," I say.

Annoyed, Elisa raises an eyebrow. She shifts her eyes to the corner of the room and reaches for the American shovel leaning against the wall. It's covered in dry dirt. Half an earthworm is stuck to the back of the blade.

"What would Twinkle do to Eva if she could avenge herself?" Elisa asks Laurens and Pim.

"No idea, I've never talked to a horse," says Pim.

They look at me—Elisa is going to have to decide this one for herself. They don't want anything to do with this. Elisa holds the little shovel upright between the two boys, trying to balance it.

"Eva is still a virgin," she says without looking at me. "You two can either fix that for her, or she can fix it herself."

I want to tell them I'm not a virgin anymore, that I already took care of that lie, but before I get a chance, she lets go of the shovel.

For a second, it stands upright. Then it falls in Laurens's direction. He doesn't try to catch it. I know what Elisa wants, she wants me to do the dirty work. I take a step towards Laurens. Pick up the shovel and go back to where I was standing. Laurens and Pim each take a step back, so they're practically on the other side of the barn, standing there like a penalty wall, their hands over their crotches, eyes down.

I stand up on my tiptoes. The handle fits right between the floor and my pelvis. I hold the handle with one hand and use the other to spread my labia. I try to look as experienced as possible. The wooden handle is varnished. At least I won't get any splinters.

I carefully sink down through my knees. At first, it won't go in, the tip of the handle is thicker than the glue stick and ruler combined. It doesn't fit, it's too dry. I spit in my hand, rub it on the handle in circular movements, just like the lady in the movie did before she got down to business. I spit again and rub it between my legs. I try again, pressing down a little harder than before. Reluctantly, the handle goes in.

I look at Elisa. This is the only chance I'm going to get. I can't let Laurens and Pim down either. This will determine how they'll remember me, what part I'll play in their stories, the woman or the klutz.

I wet my lips with my tongue.

It's hard to hold a smile when I think of the holes we dug with this shovel. I can feel the notches in the wood made by Dad's wedding ring over years of angrily planting Christmas trees.

I gently move up and down the handle. I moan, not too loud,

not too soft. I try to imitate Elisa's posture on her horse, her graceful riding. I'll never be as elegant as that, I know. Laurens and Pim look as far away as possible, their eyes on Elisa, hoping she'll put a stop to it soon.

I'm not a woman, not a girl, but I'm not one of them either. I'm the merry-go-round horse that goes up and down, always on the same pole, every year the same track, the same carnivals, the same children.

I count the blue Maes Pils ball caps stacked on top of each other in a corner. That way I don't have to count how many times I move up and down.

Elisa is the only one looking on with amusement. Laurens and Pim just seem embarrassed for me.

I don't dare to look at their penises. It's the most honest part of a body—the limpness would tell me what they really think of me, whether they'll ever find me attractive, whether they'll ever be capable of seeing me as a girl.

Pim is keeping his penis hidden behind a sock he just picked up.

"Are you about to come, Eva? Can we start the countdown?" Elisa asks.

I nod, even though I don't feel a thing. The more I move, the drier it gets. The wood absorbs the moisture and swells. The grain expands. Elisa already has her hand in the air, fingers raised.

"Five more," she says. She lowers a finger with every downward movement.

When she gets to the fifth and final finger, two others shoot back up again, like trick candles.

Elisa laughs. Pim laughs too. It's not clear whether Laurens is closer to laughing or crying.

I catch a glimpse of what's hidden behind Pim's sock—his balls, not hanging down all the way, but higher and tighter than usual. It could mean he's not completely limp.

Instead of two, I do five. Just to stay ahead of the humiliation. Elisa lowers her hands again.

Only after I can't feel anything anymore do I step off the shovel.

My knees are trembling, my abdomen is burning, I feel dizzy, but I stay on my feet.

I drop the shovel down between us. All eyes are on the tip of the handle. You can tell by the moist, dark wood exactly how deep it went in.

I squeeze a smile onto my face, bend down to wrap my bras in my T-shirt and pick them up.

Elisa kicks the clothes away.

I stay standing. It can't get any worse than this.

"Okay. Now it's these guys' turn," Elisa says. "They're not going to get off easy either."

I nod.

"What shall we make them do?" she asks.

She looks around. Blue spots flicker on my retinas, a mix of dizziness and blue Maes Pils merchandise. I feel cold. The muscles in my calves and thighs are knotting up. I push my legs together and sit down on a chair. Maybe sitting will help the pain, stop the burning.

Behind the ladder is a bucket of wallpaper glue. It's been there for a while now, ever since Mom decided to re-wallpaper the bathroom but ended up being too tired to actually do it.

"Something with this?" My voice sounds very soft. I point at the bucket. The glue is practically unusable anyway.

Elisa takes a few steps back and stands with her back against the door.

"Okay, Laurens and Pim. You heard what Eva said. Something with the wallpaper glue."

Laurens and Pim look at each other, then at the bucket.

"But they don't have to do anything for me," I say. Tessie and Mom will be home any minute. "How about everybody just go home."

Elisa laughs.

"You know what?" she says. "You two are going to give Eva an orgasm. She really deserves it after all that hard work. Prove that you can do it. If it works, you'll each get a chance to fuck me."

Pim gets hard the moment he hears the word fuck.

Elisa gathers a few of the tools standing in the corner by the door. She throws them down at the boys' feet. A roll of iron wire, a rake, the hole poker. She casually brushes her hand along Pim's cock. Then she goes and stands by the door. "Of course, you guys can just use your hands, too."

Pim immediately reaches for the sharp metal tool. Laurens tries to catch my eye, push Pim away, make him see reason.

"Come on, it's not worth it," he says. He smacks Pim on the shoulder, but not hard enough. Pim won't be deterred.

"Work with me, Eva, and it'll be over before you know it," he says. "I know what I'm doing."

Should I get off the chair, go stand between them, so we're no longer physically separated?

"Be happy your dad never bought an ax," Elisa jokes. Pim's the only one who thinks it's funny.

I stay on the chair, that seems safest to me. I wrap my feet around it.

"You gonna help me, Laurie, or are you gonna be a pussy?" Pim says.

He approaches me, holding the hole poker out in front of him. In his hands, it fits perfectly, unlike in Tessie's when she used it to dig holes in the garden. His erection swings back and forth in his underwear.

Laurens breaks eye contact with me and looks back and forth between me and Elisa. I can see him hesitating. Does he really want to stand up for me? Or does he want the chance—probably the only one he'll ever get in his teenage life—to fuck a nine-and-a-half pointer?

Then Elisa starts massaging her breasts in front of him through her bra, exposing her right nipple.

I refuse to lie down.

Pim sics Laurens on me. He kicks over the chair. I let go of the backrest to break my fall. Laurens grabs me by the shoulders, forces me to the ground with all his weight and sits down on top of me, one leg on either side, facing me. He holds down my wrists.

Gravity is working against me.

Pim pushes my legs open. I kick and flail, hoping to hit his head, his balls.

"Can't you just use your fingers?" Laurens tries again. "You can put these on if you want." He tosses a pair of work gloves into Pim's lap.

"Get your fingers dirty and you can forget about sticking them inside me later," Elisa breaks in. "I don't want to get some fungus or plant virus."

"Just let it happen, Eva. Then we can put it all behind us," Pim says. He lays down the hole poker, puts on the gloves and picks it up again, holding it firmly in his hands.

This is our punishment for their actions this summer. I am their punishment.

I assume they didn't picture it this way, that they would have preferred to use someone else. I'm just a substitute. The Diet Coke of sexual experiences.

Elisa picks up a level and balances it so that the bubble is between the two dashes. Her hands are shaking. Then she places it on top of her breasts and tries to make it level there. For a moment Pim stops moving, his eyes fixed on the scene, but as soon as she puts down the level, he becomes even wilder, even rougher than before. Laurens presses my wrists against the ground.

I stop resisting. I don't want to make it worse for them, for myself. The more I struggle, the more I deserve the rough treatment.

Laurens is getting hard now too; his little sausage inflates in front of my face, its shiny tip pointing straight up.

It's so close to my mouth I could bite the tip off.

"Sure you want me to do it, or do you want to?" Pim asks Laurens, holding up the hole poker.

"Man, just do it." Laurens stays firmly planted on my abdomen even though there's really no need to hold me down anymore. He just doesn't want to get dirty. Maybe he wants to save his strength for later, for Elisa.

Pim curses. I can't see what he's doing, because Laurens is

between us, but I can feel it: he tries to push the hole poker inside me, wriggles the rounded tip against my crotch and butthole, like dogs sometimes do with their wet snouts when they catch a whiff of menstrual blood, trying to locate exactly where the smell is coming from. I tense up, tighten my muscles, just like I used to do when Mom would shove a suppository up my butt—it doesn't help. There's nothing I can do to stop the tip from sliding in with ease. At first, I don't feel anything, this tool is thinner than the handle of the shovel. All I can feel is the scraping of sand, the point hitting my abdominal wall, where it causes a sharp pain, like a menstrual cramp but worse.

"Does it feel good, Eva?" Pim asks.

I say nothing. Every time he pulls back, I go over the order we planted the seeds in. Carrots. Leeks. Mint. Wildflower mix. A few poppies, because Tessie wanted them. The seeds had been in the laundry room for a few years. With a bit of bad luck, they'll never bloom.

"Here, I think it's too dry." Elisa pushes the bucket of wallpaper glue towards Pim.

Pim hesitates for a moment, then dips the tip of the hole poker in the slippery leftover slime.

I contract every muscle in my body, but it doesn't help.

Laurens looks away. For a split second, I make eye contact with Pim; he's down on his knees with a focused look on his face, the same look he had at the funeral. He looks through me. Elisa seems lost in her own world for a moment too, they both have the same excited look on their face.

I've never lain on my back in this workshop before. I've done it in almost every other room in the house. The roof is made of mossy tiles. Spider webs are strung between the mushrooms. A fat spider crawls out to see where all the tremors are coming from and scurries for cover again. The hedge clippers are dangling right over Laurens's head.

I hear a squelching sound between my legs, the sound of races in wet rain boots.

I hope the clippers will break loose and crash down on Pim's head, leave Laurens slightly wounded, put an end to all this.

The chances of that are slim. Almost as slim as the chances of Miss Emma watching us right now. There's no one in here but us. And there's less and less of us left.

The wallpaper glue is starting to dry; it's getting grittier and more abrasive. It's not just burning, it's itching now too.

"You know why scars can be so itchy? An itch is the mildest detectable form of pain," Jolan once told me. I don't know if I believe him anymore. Maybe an itch is the body's way of telling you the pain threshold has been reached, the warning light for a power failure.

Pim thrusts the pointed tip in more violently, checking my face every now and then to see if I want him to push harder.

"Come on, Eva, try. You can moan if you want." He dips the thing in the glue again and pushes it up my ass. I've got more muscles down there, or better control. With my last remaining strength, I tighten everything up. He pushes and twists, trying to get the thing in as deep as possible, stretching my sphincter as far as it will go. First it's cold, then it burns, then both. I scream, kick my legs into the air. The metal won't yield; it's as unrelenting as Laurens. The unprecedented pain triggers new reflexes. Someone puts a hand over my mouth. I bite into it.

Laurens screams. Pim pulls out the hole poker and sticks the tip back into my vagina. I can smell my own ass.

"Come on, Eva. Imagine I'm Jan if you have to," he whispers.

How Pim found out, I have no idea. How could he possibly know I've fantasized about Jan? Who told him? I want to say something, but the words don't come. My mind is a vacuum, I can barely remember what Jan looked like, what I look like, I can barely remember language.

I look at Laurens's chin, at his nostrils. He must smell it too, the smell of old feces. He keeps his eyes closed. Sweat pearls on his forehead and drips down in my face. I taste the salt.

What's he thinking about right now? About Elisa? About that

Christmas we had to stuff sixty turkeys, fill their butts with plums, smash them down in there with the bottom of a glass? We joked about it for months—"fucked fowl" anyone?

Pim keeps poking. My labia become stiffer, so dry that they're dragged inwards with the metal. It feels like they're about to rip off, like they're just barely hanging onto my body by a thread. The throbbing of the pain alternates with the beating of my heart, swelling with every thump.

What's my best option here? I could go on like this. Or I could pretend to orgasm so they'll stop. But I don't know how to make it believable, what sounds to make, how long it usually takes for girls to come. And then I'd be letting Laurens and Pim have their way with Elisa.

I want to close my eyes, but I can't. If I stop watching, I'll be all alone. There'll be no more witnesses, only offenders. And without a reliable witness, it'll be like this never happened.

I hear car doors slamming. Pim does too. He freezes, tells Laurens to cover my mouth. I can smell the sweat on his hands.

I had no intention of screaming. I wouldn't want Tessie to see this, Mom either.

They're talking, walking around to the front door. Tessie's shoes appear behind the crack under the workshop door. She sets the beer crate on the ground, then the grocery bags. Mom disappears into the kitchen. Tessie begins her ritual—we hear her tapping, spitting, humming. Elisa and Pim exchange mocking looks. The back door clicks shut. All goes quiet. The coast is clear.

Pim starts jabbing again, faster, harder. If it were a fireworks display, this would be the grand finale, the point in the show when, after a dramatic pause, the loudest, most expensive explosives are detonated all at once. The final push for the ooh's and aah's.

"Come on, Eva. Work with me," Pim begs. He passes the tool into his left hand so he can stretch out the fingers on his right and jams my leg under his armpit to give himself more power.

All the color drains from Laurens's face, he looks at Pim petrified.

Elisa steps back too. I call out her name to make her look at me. I want the image of me seared into her mind when she's showing Pim and Laurens her clam. She needs to know that my labia were once more beautiful than hers.

But she just looks down at the tops of her shoes. Her cheeks have gone completely pale, accentuating her lips.

Now Laurens is shouting. "Pim! Stop! Enough."

He clambers off me. Now I can see why they've gone so white: Pim's hands are covered in blood. It's running down his wrists. His bare chest looks like Laurens's dad's apron after an afternoon filleting meat. Pim slides back but stays there on his knees. He drops the metal tool; it clangs down on the concrete floor beside him.

I scramble to my feet. Without Laurens's weight on top of me, my body feels light, as if only half of me is left. Sticky globs are dripping down my inner thighs, leaving a trail of pink glue behind me.

I don't dare to look down.

Pim looks up at Elisa. Has he earned the right to fuck her now?

She unbuttons her pants.

My hands reach for the shovel, which is still lying in the middle of the barn. The handle has dried by now.

I want to whack Pim in the crotch with it, but I can't. He's still sitting down, and he's still Jan's brother, the one who's already lost so much. So I draw it back and aim the tip of the spade right between Laurens's eyes. But as I thrust it forward, the blade snaps shut, and the blunt end of the shovel hits his eyebrow, not quite hard enough and with a dull thud.

Laurens sinks down to his knees, clutching his eye. He pulls back his hands to see how much blood is on his fingers, what kind of screams he can lay claim to.

The shovel has left a deep gash in his forehead. For the first few seconds, nothing comes out of it at all. I can see right down to the bone of his eye socket. The flesh is pink and juicy. A few seconds later, the wound gets organized and starts sending out blood in the appropriate amounts. It oozes out in two streams from the deepest parts of the wound, bright red.

I drop the shovel.

On my way out, I grab a few items of clothing. I need my pants. My Tessie notes are in there. Outside, in front of the workshop door, I throw on the clothes I picked up. My own pants, Laurens's T-shirt. I quickly wipe the tears off my face. I leave the two bras and sweater behind.

Laurens's whimpering has turned into cursing.

My bike is leaning against the porch. I jump on it and race out into the street. I grip my bare feet around the pedals so I can go faster. The soaked crotch of my pants sticks to the saddle. It burns. It's okay, I tell myself, it's just sand.

My tires leave a trail in the hot asphalt. I race down the Bulksteeg, not sure where to go. I pedal and pedal. I feel something in the right leg of my pants, a bulge around my shin. It's my crumpled panties. They sink further and further down with every rotation. A few hundred meters on, at the pollard willows, they fall out of the leg of my pants. They hang there on the pedal for two more rotations until they fall down and land on the side of the road. I don't want to leave them there, but I can't stop and get off either.

I have to go home and wash up. At the canal, where the water level is low from the relentless sun, I can't go on anymore. One of the fishermen, sitting under a raincoat propped up on bamboo sticks for shade, waves at me. Only then do I realize that home is where I came from. In the whole town, there's no place left for me to go.

Slurry Pit

NEVER BEFORE IN Bovenmeer, or in the entire surrounding region, had three hundred grams of horse meat been cut into such thin slices as in the week after Jan's funeral.

"People just start telling me stuff while I'm slicing their meat," Laurens's mother replied when I asked her how she knew so much about the accident. I knew she was lying, that it worked the other way around. She moved the hams slowly and carefully through her razor-sharp blades so the people waiting would either have to start talking or keep listening. It was as if she had swallowed a cassette tape. She talked to customers about nothing else these days, their only choice was whether or not to press Play.

Unlike the meat she sold—which was always weighed down to the gram, even if it meant breaking off an edge on the cheese or a corner of the pâté—the stories she gave away for free were a little less precise. As long as the overall storyline made sense, and the decades and surnames were correct.

But Laurens's mom wasn't the only one to blame for the fact that there were twenty versions of what happened to Jan going around, each one more spectacular than the last. Everyone who came in to buy ringwurst or pâté in the weeks after his death so they too could hear the stories was at fault, myself included.

I didn't dare to ask Pim how exactly they'd found Jan and brought him up. I knew he would just repeat what had been printed in the local paper, in the hope that one day this brief summary would be all that was left of his trauma, three simple sentences under the headline "Farmer's son (16) drowns in slurry pit".

Right after closing time, on the first Saturday of 2002, January 5, I walked into the butcher shop. It was really cold outside for the first time that winter. There was smoke rising from almost every chimney. Laurens's mom let me in even though she'd already closed up shop. She handed me a cube of sharp cheddar after carefully cutting the edges off it first.

It had been a good day. Almost everything in the shop had been sold. The stories about Pim's family were still playing a role in that—while talking about tragedies and death, people are quick to order a few hundred grams extra, out of a sort of gratitude for the fact that they could go home and consume it with their unbroken family.

I knew that Laurens's mom had a particularly loose tongue when she was emptying the display case. The version I'd get from her would be peppered with untruths, but that was exactly what I wanted—not the truth, but for someone to talk about Jan again, to sing his praises, under the assumption that it was all just an accident.

"Did you know that on the day he disappeared, Jan came by the shop?" she asked.

Saying "no" at this point was the same as pressing Play.

"He looked so good that day, so full of life. I was even surprised that he didn't have a girlfriend. Behind all those pimples, he was a really nice, polite young man," she continued. "Little did I know that less than a half-hour later, he'd be gone."

She told me how he bought at least thirty euros of meat—veal sausage, head cheese, pâté, bologna and even some of her delicious homemade onion confit.

Her stories always contained a little advertising for her meat products.

They were probably planning to have a family breakfast that morning, in between all the daily chores.

"Actually," Laurens's mom said, "I should mention that his parents had wanted a dozen children, preferably sons, though a daughter or two couldn't have hurt. That's why they had that long kitchen table—they bought it before they knew there'd be complications. Shortly after Pim was born, they found cysts on that poor woman's fallopian tubes and had to remove her uterus . . ."

She paused for a moment and wrung out the rag over the bucket of dirty water.

These dramatic pauses were becoming more frequent. She had already told this version of the story so many times that she knew exactly where they were needed, where the listener would need time to process, where there would be sighs, where handbags would be shifted from one arm to the other. I didn't have a handbag with me, so every time she paused I nibbled off a corner of the cheese.

Pim and his parents had no idea what they were waking up to that morning. They found the rolls and cold cuts on the table and sat down to breakfast, assuming that, like always, Jan would join them after he was done milking the cows.

He never came.

They didn't wait. The breakfast table was cleared; the meat and cheese were put back in the refrigerator.

Two minutes after Pim's father had gone out to start his chores, he came back into the kitchen. "The cows haven't been milked," he said, alarmed. Pim's mom needed to see it with her own eyes. She knew Jan was up already—she'd heard his alarm go off that morning, he'd gone to the bakery. But still, she went to check his bed.

"The sight of that empty, crumpled bed—that must have been when she realized, that moment when you, as a mother, think, 'No, it can't be . . .' " The last words came out higher pitched so that it didn't sound like anything Pim's mom would say.

Jan's boots were missing. Maybe he went for a walk, his parents must have thought.

But after a few hours, they were losing hope. Their son hadn't taken anything with him, no bike, no car, no money, no tractor. He should've been back by now.

"If you're planning to be gone for a while, you'd leave a note, wouldn't you?" Laurens's mom pulled the little sign out of a lump of pâté, wiped the stick clean and stuck it back in exactly the same hole.

"True," I said. The cheese left a sharp taste in my mouth, as if I hadn't swallowed my saliva for three years.

"And Jan wasn't the type to sneak out or plan surprises. He was just your average guy with no secrets," she said.

"True." My chin was quivering. I clenched my teeth and followed the movement of her rag, of her eyes.

"Isn't that how you picture him—blond, skinny, with braces and pimples?" she said.

"Yes." I tried to imagine it, Jan standing in this very spot, how his voice must have sounded. I conjured it all up in my memory—his boots, the shape of his nose, his muscled arms.

"If my son had that many pimples, I would've taken him to see a dermatologist. A splash of lemon juice is no match for that kind of acne. But anyway—between you and me—those farmers aren't much for beauty products, if you know what I mean. They probably think they're too expensive, not that it matters, if they'd sell off some of that land, they'd be the richest people in town."

I nodded faintly.

Laurens's mom pronounced "pimple" as if there were a whitehead on the tip of the word that she could pop with her mouth—the way she articulated the syllables, it sounded like he had way more pimples than he actually did.

I wish I'd had the nerve to challenge her on this.

"After a few hours, Pim's parents had looked everywhere—the stables, the hayloft, the grain silos, the milk tank. That's when they saw the loose grate at the edge of the yard, above one of those pipes that drains the animal waste into—what's it called, there's probably a word for it—oh yes, a slurry pit," she said.

Pim's dad poked around in the pit with a stick but couldn't rule out the possibility. So they immediately called a company to come drain the pit.

"They'll do that for a hundred and fifty euros nowadays, but that's usually excluding tax and travel costs, which they don't say on their website, of course. They didn't say anything about having to pay in cash either."

The guy from the pit-draining company came all the way from Brasschaat. He wanted to see the money first, so Pim's mom had to jump in the car and drive to the nearest ATM in Zandhoven.

Every time Laurens's mother embellished the naked facts or deviated from the original story, she glanced in my direction. She started talking faster, more furiously.

Pim's dad didn't warn the guy that there might be a teenager's body at the bottom of the pit. He just kept telling him to hurry. They inserted the suction head, turned on the pump and let the tank fill up with muck. Then the machine stalled.

"It must have sounded like a vacuum getting jammed on a sock or a tissue—you know what sound I'm talking about?"

"Yes," I said.

It was a shovel, one that had been missing for a while, but no one was very happy to find it.

"Pim's father was always so fond of his tools. He was usually more careful with them—that's just how we entrepreneurs are."

They turned the suction back on, the level of slurry went down a little more. Halfway to the bottom of the pit, the machine started malfunctioning again. Pim's mom was back out there too at that point, holding the wad of cash in her hand.

"That can't be," she said, "we're not missing two shovels."

Laurens's mom took a deep breath, looked over my shoulder at a point somewhere behind me on the wall, the jars of jam.

"The first thing they pulled up was his left boot. That's when the guy from the slurry pit company realized what they were really looking for. He stopped, said they should call the emergency services, but Pim's father wouldn't have it. He grabbed hold of the suction head and tried to suck away as much of the dirt as possible. He had to step back a few times though. Those fumes can be deadly—they'll get you before you know it."

"Two minutes later," she continued, "they found a body at the bottom of the pit. Pim's father went down with a rag over his mouth. It was Jan all right. Pim pulled his own brother out of that pit with bucket hooks."

Pim's mom shouted at them to only attach the hooks to his clothes, not to his skin, she wanted him in one piece. Once they got him out, they carried him to the edge of the garden and laid him out on his back in the grass. Jan's father knelt down coughing over his son's corpse and immediately began resuscitating. With every push, a bit of cow shit bubbled up in the throat.

Pim's mom fetched a towel and used it to wipe off Jan's face, so she could be sure it was her son, her gangly boy with the long legs, big feet and head full of hair. Then she just started screaming, loud, in a way that only mothers can. Afterwards, the whole farm went deathly quiet.

I could imagine the silence perfectly; even the geese stopped honking. And Pim's father—I had no trouble picturing him either—knees in the grass, a brown circle around his lips from the CPR. Jan's ribs cracking under the force of his weight.

Pim—the man testified later—remained quite calm. As if he had just helped deliver a stillborn calf. After the first responders confirmed the death, he pulled off Jan's other boot, cleaned them both and placed them next to the barn door, exactly where they would've been if Jan hadn't put them on that morning.

Laurens's mom walked over to the roll of cling wrap and gave it a jolt. She pulled off about three meters. Together we covered all the salad dishes in the display case. I wiped up a splatter of cherry sauce on the counter with my finger, just to get rid of that sharp cheddar taste in my mouth. When I finally headed for the door, she grabbed me by the shoulders.

"Didn't you come by to see Laurens?" she asked.

I didn't dare say no.

"He's at his grandmother's, but we can call him if you want."

I shrugged. As I turned to leave, she finished her story.

"In the end, the guy with the suction head was kind enough not to take their money."

She must have noticed the state she was sending me home in. Hence, the positive note.

Jan was lifeless in a giant pit of manure, while I was sitting with

Laurens on the swing set doing nothing—the thought of it kept whirling around in my mind, occupying my entire body. Of course, he was unconscious when he died, we all knew that, Pim's parents repeated it often enough: the fumes were enough to knock anybody out. But unconscious or not, the body must have sunk to the bottom. The slurry must have seeped into every cavity; he must have gone down like a teapot in the kitchen sink. His lungs, esophagus, ear canals, every hole completely filled.

Legs trembling, I headed for the fields between the boggy wetlands and the forest of the forest, towards the grassy meadow where the cows grazed.

There were about twenty of them out there, huddled close together, with hardly any grass left to graze on.

Standing there, gazing out into the field, I saw several of them lift their tails and relieve themselves. They just let it all out, totally unaware of my presence, or of the fact that I—along with a lot of other people—couldn't just let Jan go.

Pim's mom and dad had spent most of their lives working the fields to grow corn, grass and grain just to feed these animals. If they wanted to go on selling milk, they had to keep these cows alive even after Jan was dead. As long as they kept feeding them, they would keep on shitting, and that shit would be used to fertilize the fields so they could keep on growing enough corn, grain and grass to feed them.

His parents had no choice. I would have done the same thing— give the cows just enough food to survive but not more.

A few days after that first Saturday in January, Laurens called. He was back from his grandma's and had something to tell me: Pim's mom had left the farm with a big suitcase full of clothes. She'd gone to live with her sister's family in Lier. They had a guestroom for exactly these types of situations.

This was good news for the butcher shop. The story about Jan's accident had been told and retold too many times. They needed some new gossip. Farmers getting divorced, now that was a big deal—who would run the business?

One day, Pim's aunt stopped by the butcher shop. She ordered a few slices of cheese, and as she was paying, she dropped a few details in an attempt to find out for herself what kind of rumors were going around about her sister.

"No one said anything about a divorce," she said. "Pim's mother just needs a different environment so she can grieve. She's not going to leave Pim or Pim's father, she just needs to get away for a while."

It wasn't until later that all the juicy details came to light: Pim's parents had gotten into an argument in bed one night. His father swore he'd never leave the farm, said they owed it to their son, together, that Jan took care of those animals with all his heart. How could they just give it all up?

Pim's mom got out of bed and left the room. What happened next must have been fully witnessed by Pim's father from the bed. Pim's mother appeared on the screen. She grabbed the shovel, which had been leaning against the wall of the barn since the day they found it, and stabbed it into the belly of a pregnant cow.

7:00 p.m.

I LOOKED IT up on wikiHow. At the top of the article was a disclaimer: "To be used as a scary Halloween decoration or for fishing or boating. If using for decoration, make sure to check your local laws first. In some areas, displaying a noose is regarded as a threat, and thus illegal. Never tie a noose around your neck, not even as a joke."

I didn't try it out step-by-step at home. It seemed insulting, but to who I wasn't sure. I read the instructions on the screen out loud until I was certain I wouldn't forget them.

I tied the knot right. When I let myself hang on it for a second, my breath is instantly cut off.

It's getting dark, but the night still hasn't settled in yet. The children playing in the barn are gone now. I miss their voices. Actually, I'm surprised how quiet it is. The only sound is coming from the party next door. After years of living in the city, I guess I forgot: cows get tired too.

People are starting to leave. Cars drive away, voices die out, the sound of motorbikes fades into the distance.

If I stand on my tiptoes, I can see which cars are still out there through the window.

Laurens's is still there. Jolan's is gone. I saw him walk out. I could tell by the way he opened the door that he was hoping to disappear unnoticed, but Pim's mom came running out after him. They chatted for a minute. I couldn't hear what they were saying. Jolan got in the car and started the engine, but he didn't leave right away. My phone's going to ring, I thought, he's going to call me. Slowly the snow started to melt off the hood of his car. I watched him fumbling around with something under the reading light. It was a waffle. He wrestled it out of the wrapper and took a bite.

I've never asked him what he hopes to find with all his research in Leuven. I don't think it can be explained in layman's terms anyway. He once told me that when he removes the locusts from their terrariums, they poop on his gloves out of fear of death, and when the experiment is all over, he snips their heads off with scissors.

Every time I see him, I can't help but picture it: a worktop full of convulsing, decapitated insects.

I never told Jolan what happened at the end of that summer. There was no gossip, so he didn't hear about it through the grapevine either. Elisa, Laurens and Pim never breathed a word about it to anyone. The only rumors flying around were about how Laurens got that gash on his forehead. But it was enough to explain the visible damage.

Those first few weeks of the new school year, I left home as late as possible in the morning, later than Laurens, so he wouldn't have the chance to make a show of catching up to me, or—even worse— try to bike next to me. I knew that he would try to make things better by talking, by asking how Tessie was doing now that she'd been admitted. But I had nothing to say to him, and definitely not about her.

Every day, I biked past those blue panties with the white skid mark on the inside slowly disintegrating on the side of the road.

Once I'd passed them, the twelve kilometers left to school seemed to last an eternity. I used my savings to buy a Discman and forced myself to reach my destination before the end of the CD. As long as I was able to do that, it would be an okay day.

Of course, I wanted to ask Pim why, while he was jabbing me with the hole poker, he mentioned Jan. Was it just a coincidence or had Jan told him he thought I was pretty?

But I never spoke to him or Laurens again after that summer day. Nobody thought anything of it. In our town, it wasn't that unusual for old friendships to end without a lot of discussion. I hoped they'd at least find me a little bit hard to ignore, but even that was in vain. We were already drifting apart before the summer even began.

Every day, I saw Laurens at school, somewhere in the distance, usually in a sea of hundreds of other kids. He had a new backpack and had stopped parting his hair down the middle. He still had a Band-Aid on his forehead on the first day, but eventually he stopped covering the thick scab. One time, a bunch of kids gathered around him on the playground to cheer him on as he pulled a strand of red licorice out of his nostril. I moved closer too, not because I wanted to watch but because I wanted to see just how ugly that scar was. Laurens's mom didn't take him to the emergency room for stitches, she just glued the open flesh back together herself with a few strips. I saw it as a gesture to me: she had seen the blood on the floor in the butcher shop in the exact spot where I'd passed out. She must have had her suspicions about what happened and wanted to punish Laurens by making sure it left a scar on him too.

Sometimes I biked past the butcher shop just to watch her serving customers from a distance, sometimes helped by Laurens. Often, I'd be clutching a cobblestone in my hand. The choice was mine: throw the stone through the shop window or slowly disappear into the back of her thoughts.

Three months after the first day of school, the panties on the side of the road disappeared, well before they'd reached their estimated decomposition time.

My guess is that I've been standing here for about an hour and a half now. There's a lot of stuff I could've done in that amount of time. Water the plants in my apartment. Answer all the emails Dad's sent me over the last few years. Respond to his comments on the family website. Suck off the neighbor fifteen times in a row. Walk from my apartment to the Marolles, give money to every vagrant I pass along the way, take the elevator up to the top of the Palace of Justice. Clean the mold in the corners of the bathroom.

But I wouldn't have done any of these things if I hadn't come here. I'm deluding myself. I would've just been sitting at home by the window, watching how the snow sticks to other people's balconies better than it sticks to mine.

Maybe I should have looked up how long it takes for a block of ice to melt. Obviously, I had no way of knowing that today would be the coldest day of the year, that I'd only have one small heat source. I can already feel the rope tightening around my neck, but maybe that's just because my legs are getting tired from standing, and I'm starting to sag a bit.

I try not to picture myself from above, to see what Miss Emma would see, but I can't help it—here I am. A young woman in flesh-colored hose, standing on a block of ice under a light bulb with chattering teeth, hoping to become a riddle once and for all.

August 10, 2002 (2)

IT COULD BE seen as a bold move or a statement, showing up at Laurens's mom's butcher shop not wearing any underwear. But in this case, it's nothing more than a chain of events, driven by a lack of alternatives.

Something switches on inside me that allows me to record everything I encounter with extreme precision—fishermen, trees, houses, mailboxes, clothes lines, garden sprinklers—without any of it becoming a permanent thought; my brain refuses to make memories.

There are no customers in the shop. Laurens's bike is nowhere in sight. I park mine right in front of the display case. The kickstand sinks into a mossy crack between the cobblestones. The handlebars clatter on the ground. The little bell rings. I want to pick it up, park it neatly, but the pain in my abdomen won't let me. I just leave it there. Laurens throws his bike on the ground all the time.

Slowly, I inch closer to the shiny veal sausages on display. They're strung up like bunting in the shop window, tied three at a time.

I have to walk slowly. The ground beneath my feet is like a sponge. The sound of the doorbell lasts longer than usual. I can see the spots of blood on my crotch reflected in the window.

Laurens's mom is standing with her back to the counter when I walk in.

"Hello," she says after the bell's gone silent. Her voice is neutral, suitable for all ages, for open houses and funerals.

When no one replies, she glances up. But her eyes are fixed on the log of cheap pink bologna wrapped in bright red plastic casing that she's gliding across the sharp blade.

"Oh, Eva, it's you," she says over the sound of the machine and the radio.

Was she hoping it was somebody else? Would she wonder why my breasts have suddenly disappeared?

On her moving hand, she's wearing a white latex glove that's a few sizes too small. As the hunk of meat gets smaller, the pile of plastic casing gets bigger.

The soft, processed meat doesn't make a fraying sound when it's cut. It's the cheapest kind there is. It's not made of real flesh, not from thousands of threads.

When there are no customers listening, Laurens's parents have a different name for this stuff. I can't think of it right now. It's irrelevant, but I keep searching for it. Somehow it makes my thoughts less volatile.

I read the names on the little signs in the fancy salads. Martino, Spring Salad, Meat Salad. Each black plastic tray is filled with a different pastel color. I can't retain these names for more than a few seconds either. The name tag for the cheap sausage on the slicer is lying on the counter.

I want to know what it says, but I can't quite make it out.

The cold air in the display case is leaking out through a crack in the glass; it smells like all the stuff it's touched along the way—teddy bear sausage, chicken wings. The air blows straight between my legs. It seeps in through the zipper on my pants, fanning the flame underneath it. My labia are pulsing. The wallpaper glue is starting to harden. My pubic hair is drying up in tangles, pulling at my skin.

"Here you go, Eva, sweetheart."

Laurens's mom hands me a rolled-up slice of the suspicious-looking meat. I can smell it. It's sour-sweet. Offal with flecks of pork in between. My mouth fills with saliva. It runs out the corners of my mouth. I wipe it away with the top of my hand. I lay the sausage back on the counter. It rolls open. Laurens's mom looks at it, surprised. Then her gaze sinks down through the glass display case, stopping at the height of my crotch. Maybe she's trying to figure out whether the blood belongs to me or to the reflection of the tenderloin.

I've hardly eaten any solid food today, but I'm not hungry. The only thing left in my stomach are the few sips of sugar-free soda from this afternoon. The Coke comes up first, lukewarm and grainy—lubricant for the throat.

The rest of the vomit comes from much deeper. It had already followed previous orders to exit via the other end of my body, and it didn't have time to return to its liquid state. I start gagging and take two steps backwards as I cough it up. The puke, solid and sausage-shaped, gets caught in the prolongation of my body, like it does with cats who eventually end up eating it afterwards for the sake of tidiness.

You can't tell what kind of food it was originally.

Laurens's mom stops what she's doing. The blades on the meat slicer come to a halt. All that's left is the sound of the radio, far away, in the back of the shop.

"Eva? What's all this?" At the sound of my own name, I bend over and start gagging again, but there's hardly anything left in my stomach. Now comes the real lump in my throat. I burst into sobs, but there are no more tears.

Laurens's mom dashes out from behind the counter with her fat knees sticking out under her shorts. She grabs a bucket with a couple inches of cleaning solution sloshing back and forth in the bottom. She shoves it under my face, to catch the tears maybe. She dabs my forehead with the rag that had been sitting at the bottom of the bucket.

"Come here, sweetheart." A piece of eggshell lands on my eyebrow. She plucks it away. She leaves the unrolled piece of meat behind on the counter, helps me up and leads me out of the store. But I refuse to move. My knees buckle beneath me. I clamp my legs together under my body. I want to sit here until I'm dry, with my butchered flatfish stuck to the floor. She can't know that I'm not wearing any underwear.

She walks over to the shop window and tilts the wooden blinds down halfway. I keep an eye on the driveway and hope that Laurens hasn't lost too much blood. If he shows up now, he'll snatch his mother away from me. Then he'll leave a trail all over town.

Laurens's mother scoops up the vomit with her gloved hand and, as if it were a dog turd on the street, pulls the glove around it inside out and ties it in a knot at the wrist. Since there's no trash can within reach, she throws the glove into the cleaning water.

"Is there any left?" she asks, pointing to the space between me and the bucket.

"No," I say, rubbing my eyes.

She squats down beside me, caresses my neck, and looks down at the blood between my legs. I didn't know she could squat. Her bent knees are almost as wide as my thighs. You could fit two of me in her. She gently rocks me back and forth. She must be able to feel that I'm not wearing a bra. She's got to be wondering.

"Could it be that you're having your first period?" she asks. "Don't cry. I've got all the supplies in the house."

She places her hand on my forehead. Then she stops rocking and looks at the T-shirt I'm wearing. Only now does she recognize it.

"Why are you wearing Laurens's shirt?"

I don't respond.

"Where is he, by the way? Wasn't he at your house today?"

Again, I don't respond. That cut on Laurens's head might be pretty big. Who knows, maybe he needs stitches. I start feeling nauseous again. I lean back and rest my head against the cool display case.

Laurens's mom is the only person in town with any idea about how bad things are at our house, but she'll never intervene, not as long as my parents are alive, she's too polite. If I were to tell her about this summer, about all the girls I humiliated with Laurens and Pim, she wouldn't be worried about me anymore, she'd be worried about all those other girls.

"Did something happen at home? Do you want to tell me about it?" She pauses dramatically after each question. But I shake my head.

"Some people have a hard time talking about their feelings, Eva. Maybe we can work it out together. Let's try another way: if the answer is 'no', you don't have to say anything, if it's 'yes', squeeze my arm," she says. "Should we give it a try?"

I squeeze her arm.

"Did something happen at home? With Jolan? With Tessie? Or was it your father?"

At the word "father", I grip her arm almost automatically.

"Did he do this?"

A half squeeze isn't an option, so I clear my throat. In one long sentence, I blurt out that Dad's already got a noose hanging over a ladder at home. I make it sound like it's not such a big deal, which it really isn't to me anymore now that my vagina is on fire.

"Eva, a father who does something like that needs help." She keeps stroking my neck.

"Not from you, not from me, but from a professional," she adds.

I feel her heart beating against my cheek. I can't remember if I've ever heard my mom's heartbeat like that. The detergent in the water smells like lemon. There are little bits of minced meat floating in it. My skin softens under her repeated strokes.

In the distance, I hear the clatter of a bike chain. It's Laurens. I can tell right away that it's him by the creak of his broken pedal. He races up the driveway and tosses his bike down on the cobblestones, next to mine.

His mother hasn't heard anything yet. She's sitting with her face towards me and her back to the shop window. The more I let my shoulders slump, the faster she moves her hand back and forth.

I lay my head against her chest one last time.

Laurens, divided into spaces behind the blinds, freezes at the sight of me. Between the wooden slats we make eye contact. There's blood running down his temples. He's wearing Pim's T-shirt and holding mine against his eyebrow. It's full of bloodstains. His eye is thick and blue. He walks with a slight, but still exaggerated, limp.

"Laurens? Son? What happened?"

Laurens walks into the shop. He points at me, shaking his finger until his mom is looking at me too.

"Whatever Eva told you is a big fat lie."

Laurens blinks his damaged eye, which sticks in the corner from all the clotted blood.

"She did this. She abandoned me at school at the start of the summer, and today she hit me with a shovel. Pim saw it. Ask him."

Her eyes jump from the blood between my legs to the blood on Laurens's temple, then back, as if she's playing eenie-meenie-miney-moe. But she's not impartial. Her eyes will always land on Laurens in the end. I can feel the spot where she was stroking me just now. She takes a step towards Laurens.

"Is this true, Eva?"

I shake my head. I don't know what else I can do to make her believe me.

I pull myself up on the display case and try to stand, so she can see my blood too. It hurts even more than before, like muscles that only really start to hurt after you've allowed them to relax. Maybe the wallpaper glue hardened while I was sitting still for so long, maybe I tore something loose.

As I clamber to my feet and search for my balance, it all comes back to me, starting with the things revolving around me right now.

Suddenly I remember what that cheap bologna is called. Monkey head.

That's the one thing I won't miss.

Laurens lowers his finger and wipes away the snot under his nose. He doesn't look at me. His blood mixes with the mucus and tears, taking on the same pink color as the trail of wallpaper glue I left behind. He leans against the display case.

We're both in pain. Neither of us got to have Elisa. Neither of us have Pim. Maybe none of this would have happened if we had just settled for each other.

Laurens's mom wipes his hair to the side, inspects his eyebrow and makes soothing noises.

"This is going to leave a scar if we don't get it taken care of."

She kisses Laurens just above his wounded temple. He looks at me over her shoulder. There's a yellow clot in the inner corner of his eye. I grab the bucket beside me, though I don't have to puke anymore.

"Monkey head," I say. I aim straight for his face, but right before the dirty water hits him, he lowers his eyes and I'm already wondering whether this is really going to help my case. The water splashes against the glass case, all over his mom's sandals. The puke-filled glove bounces off of Laurens's chest. His mother looks sheepishly at the empty bucket in my hands. Is she wondering where all this water suddenly came from? Then she looks at Laurens. The blood has been washed off his face. The minced meat sticks to his hair. Next to his feet is the inside-out glove.

She grabs me by the upper arm and drags me to the door. I'm still holding the bucket.

At first, I resist. I stand in the doorway so the doorbell keeps ringing.

Then, the ringing stops, our struggle is over. We stand there for a second, facing each other, she on one side of the door and me on the other. I can't feel the spot where she caressed me anymore, all I feel are her nails digging into my upper arm.

"That bucket belongs to us. Leave it there."

I look around. Everything here belongs to them, except the things you pay for.

I set down the bucket on the doorstep in front of her. The bell rings one last time.

Was Laurens right? Was meat really just a bunch of threads waiting to be unraveled?

I turn around and pick up my bike. In this moment, my greatest source of pain is not my naked crotch rubbing against the zipper of my pants, or the wallpaper glue drying in my pubic hair and tugging at my skin, but their eyes, weighing down on my back, on my shoulders.

Those eyes will follow me until I'm gone, out of their sight. Only then will they take the bucket from the doorway and close the shop with a sigh of relief. And when that door finally closes, something will be taken from me that I have been saving up for my entire life.

I don't know if I should bike fast or slow to make this hurt less.

Pasta Tongs

THE EVENING THAT Mom and I first talked about Tessie didn't start out very well. It was in January 2002. We came home from school to find the kitchen table pushed against the wall. We wouldn't be eating meals with the whole family anymore, that much was clear.

It wasn't Wednesday, but the table was set for a typical mid-week meal. There was a pot of defrosted spaghetti sauce on the stove, a can of corn, and four deep plates.

"Look," Mom said, as she paced across the room, "now we can walk around the table to the sliding door." All of a sudden she was calling it a door. Until then, we'd only ever used it as a window, never as a passageway. "I've been craving spaghetti all day."

For the first time in months, she sounded happy. None of us dared to ask why, or where Dad was going to sit.

Less than half an hour later, the pasta tongs broke. They snapped at exactly their weakest point, where the two limbs meet. This also happens to be the weakest spot on people. Jolan and I were playing with them at the time. We laid the two pieces beside each other to try to figure out who was the most responsible.

Jolan pleaded innocent and quickly put his piece back into the strainer full of drained pasta. I did the same. We waited in silence for Mom to come back from the kitchen with the freshly grated cheese.

When she did, she reached for the tongs, and, in a wild motion, scooped up a clump of spaghetti. The tongs fell apart in her hands. Startled, she immediately started inspecting the tool to figure out where exactly it broke. She pressed the two pieces together at least ten times. That's what she always did: keep trying to fix things long after they're broken so she could look back and regret that they never worked.

The tongs kept falling apart. She slumped down in her chair.

"I paid seven hundred and fifty francs for that thing," she sighed. "Why does everything I touch fall apart?"

"It was already broken before you touched it," I say.

Mom didn't even ask who did it.

"I'm taking it out of your allowance," she barked. She looked at each one of us, then down at her watch and loosened the clasp a bit.

"From mine too?" Tessie asked.

"I did it," Jolan blurted out. He pulled out his wallet. Inside, to everyone's surprise, was a thin wad of bills. He kept it with him everywhere he went, ever since the day Mom paid the plumber with money from his savings jar. "How about we just make it an even eight hundred?"

"No, it was me," I say.

There was a bicycle coming down the Bulksteeg. You could tell by the looks on our faces that all three of us were hoping it wasn't Dad. But it couldn't be, it was still too early.

Jolan tried to scoop the pasta out of the strainer with his fork in the hopes of demonstrating that pasta tongs didn't offer any added value, but the spaghetti just swirled around in one big clump.

Mom got up, walked into the kitchen, and came back with the scissors. She started cutting the clump of spaghetti into chunks. She reminded me of the former hairdresser at Sels Hair Mode in Nedermeer who used to cut bangs and bobs unevenly on purpose so she'd get fired and be able to collect unemployment.

The first piece Mom hacked off was slapped down on Tessie's plate. It was a perfect cube except on one side.

"Who else wants spaghetti?" she snarled.

Jolan and I didn't dare to say no, but we couldn't conjure up any enthusiasm either, so neither of us said anything. We both got a small heap, exactly the same amount she'd plopped down on her own plate. Though her serving was only meant to be looked at.

The pot of sauce had a perfectly usable spoon in it, so she just let it sit there while she clumsily shook the corn out of the can onto everyone's plate.

Dad once told me that it was just her nature—to start things and not finish them. At first, I thought he was trying to say something about Jolan's twin sister, but he didn't say anything more about her. After that, however, I started seeing it everywhere: her unsorted stamp collection, the long panel of Styrofoam with only three beetles pinned on it, the dozens of unopened cookbooks, the earrings she bought and never put on, the piles of fabric for new curtains, Jolan, Tessie and me sitting at the table. With us she'd had the same good intentions, the only problem was that we couldn't be soaked or dried, folded up or stashed away—we needed clean clothes and three meals a day. We were just another collection, only in our case her failure was more noticeable.

Mom slapped down a scoop of tomato sauce on top of our corn. Since Jolan was the farthest away, he got splashed the most. The sauce left a spot on his new T-shirt. I could see him fighting back the tears.

I'd recently stopped eating corn. The other day, some kids at school had used a piece of corn on the cob to demonstrate, in front of a whole circle of spectators on the playground, the best techniques for squeezing Jan's pimples. A couple of them decided that they were going to drop a few kernels in his pockets every day at recess.

I tried to pick up as few pieces of corn on my fork as possible. In my mouth, I sorted through each bite with my tongue. If it felt crunchy and round, I swallowed it in one gulp, and the rest I chewed very carefully. Every time a kernel popped in my mouth, I felt nauseous.

I offered to help with the dishes. On the counter were two bottles of water, one sparkling and one flat, as usual. There was an opaque plastic cup too, but no water was ever poured into it.

While washing the dishes, I didn't dare to look at Mom. I just watched her reflection in the kitchen window.

In the double glass, she had two reflections: one floating about two centimeters above the other, like a dying cartoon character whose soul was drifting out of its body.

It was there, with her hands in the hot water, that she brought up the topic of Tessie with me for the first time.

"You know, Eva," she began, her back hunched awkwardly over the low sink. "You had an older sister. You knew that already, I guess. We found out I was pregnant with her seventeen years ago today. That's why I celebrate her birthday today. I don't like the thought of remembering her death on Jolan's birthday."

I understood what she was trying to say, but I didn't understand why. We could've just talked about my grades, about Laurens and Pim, about how it was possible that so many girls already had their period and I didn't. And if death was really the only thing she wanted to talk about, we could always talk about Jan.

"I'm only telling you this because you remind me of myself," she said. "What we have, it's not a gift, it's not a talent, it's a burden we have to bear. A radar for other people's grief."

She was quiet for a moment. I looked at her. It was hard to imagine she'd ever been thirteen years old. That there was a time when she could've become anything she wanted.

"It's like an infrared camera. Except we're not looking for people's warmth, but for their cold, their emptiness."

I looked at her reflection in the window again. There, facing the sink, we looked like two perfectly normal, satisfied people. The subtle details—Mom cleaning the silverware with her eyes closed, the exact shape of my chubby arms—were all a blur.

Outside, in the darkness, the branches of the cherry tree clawed at the wind. It had been too quiet for too long. It was my turn to say something.

"Why didn't you give Tessie some other name? Tessa, or something completely different?" I asked.

"What kind of question is that?" she said.

I shrugged.

If Mom was right, if we really had the same radar, she'd know exactly what I meant.

For the past few weeks, Tessie had been writing her name as "Tessa" on all her tests and in her school agenda.

Giving a child a diminutive as a name—and the diminutive of her dead sister's name, no less—implies that you want to keep that child small, half alive. Perhaps, unconsciously, they'd set it up that way: Tessie would always be the one who could have the rug ripped out from under her, and I'd always be the one she could lean on.

Mom didn't say anything.

"Why do you drink?" I asked suddenly. "Is it because of the radar, or because you know that you've burdened me with it too?"

With that, I didn't even dare to look at her reflection. I stared down into the sink. Mom plunged her hand into the water.

Out of nowhere, she smacked my face with the wet rag. The water dripped over my shoulders and down my neck. Strings of spaghetti stuck to my skin and clothes. The water was neither hot nor cold. I took a few steps backwards.

The dog looked as startled as I was. She lapped up the strings of spaghetti on the floor. Either she was actually hungry or she was trying to cover Mom's tracks. The two of them were in league together. My throat was burning, like a sharp stone was trying to squeeze its way through the tiny opening.

"Go," Mom said, "I'll dry these dishes myself."

I wiped my face with the kitchen towel and left it on the counter.

I left the kitchen, wishing we were dumber, or less sensitive, like our neighbors, like Laurens's parents. Then she would have hit me harder, with an iron ladle for example, hard enough to make me hate her, or at least to make me cry. Then we wouldn't have to feel all this. At least we wouldn't have the words to describe it.

I sat down in the living room, as far away from the kitchen as possible, and flipped through a comic book. I didn't want to go to bed until Dad was home.

It was late when he finally walked through the door, but Mom still wasn't finished with the dishes—she didn't want to leave the kitchen. With her wrinkled hands and sore back, she was ready to pick a fight. She'd been building up to it all day.

Before he even said hello, Dad lowered the aluminum shutters and reached for his beer crate. It was the same thing he always did, turn rooms into closed boxes.

"Is that really necessary?" Mom sneered. "We're not mice."

"How were things here today?" Dad asked softly.

Mom didn't say anything. She didn't say a word about what happened, where it went wrong, she didn't even mention the pasta tongs. She waited for Dad to come back from the workshop with his crate full of beer, pass through the kitchen and see the table— with his place at it pushed against the wall.

7:30 p.m.

THE BRAIN ISN'T all that different from the digestive system. It can process pretty much everything, but there a few things it can't handle. These foreign objects and traumas have a way of surfacing in unexpected moments, called up by specialized doctors who were actually looking for something else. A piece of iron wire, a child-hood crush, a ping-pong ball, betrayal—they can float around in a body for years.

I didn't expect Jan's posthumous party to last so long. In the past, his birthday parties always ended earlier than it said on the invitation because he wanted to go help milk the cows. I also didn't expect Laurens and his mom to stay this long. They have to go home. They have to roll up the aluminum shutters on the butcher shop, walk through the back room towards the stairs so they'll discover what I was up to this afternoon between four and five o'clock. Then they'll sound the alarm. Without the commotion, it could take days for somebody to come looking for me in this abandoned milk house.

I look out the window at the yard. All that looking. It's never brought any change.

In the end, it takes another half-hour for Laurens to head out to the car, arm in arm with his mother. She's had too much to drink. You can tell right away by the strange spring in her step. She climbs into the car and bumps her head. Again, Laurens takes the driver's seat. Maybe he wanted to leave earlier but she didn't want to have to waddle home on foot, so he just stayed.

When they first get home, they won't notice anything

suspicious, my footsteps in the parking lot will be snowed over, as will the rectangle where I left my car for half an hour with the engine running while I was in the butcher shop.

Laurens squeals out of the driveway despite the slippery asphalt. Their taillights disappear into the night. Now they'll follow exactly the same road they drove here on, the road I've already driven three times today.

At four o'clock, I went back to the butcher shop, of my own accord, with a bucket of slurry in the passenger seat. I found the copper bucket by the door of the milk house. I didn't have to do much searching for the long hook to lower it down into the slurry pit, I knew where to look—in the garage. That's where I found the pliers to cut through the iron wire that had been used to fasten the grate over the pit.

The sounds were almost pleasant: first, the snipping of the iron, then the sloshing of the slurry in the bucket next to me on the passenger seat. I almost forgot I was alone in that car.

Growing up, I had travelled the route from the farm to the butcher shop countless times, usually on my bike and sometimes on foot. It felt so strange to cover the short distance on four wheels, like moving a grain of rice with a forklift.

I parked in front of the butcher shop, right on top of the bare rectangle in the snow left behind by Laurens's BMW. I got out, opened the door on the passenger's side and grabbed the bucket. Only then, after having been outside in the fresh air for a while, did I notice how foul the car smelled.

The gate on the side of the house was locked. First, I lifted over the bucket, then I crawled underneath.

All of a sudden, I found myself in the courtyard. The back entrance to the house and shop was locked, but there was a window open under the awning. If I'd been a thief, I would've been put off by how easy it all was. But I wasn't deterred, I didn't come here to steal. I came to leave something behind.

When I crawled into the shop through the open window, an automatic light switched on. I jumped—that light wasn't there before. For a second, I thought I might run into Laurens's father, but that was impossible, of course.

Every inch of space was covered with disposable trays, each one piled with meat and wrapped in foil. A sea of aluminum flickering in the bright light. Each one had a customer's name and phone number on it. If the name was too common, there was a nickname too. Nancy was still "Soap". Next to the name was a toothpick with a Flemish flag on it, a black lion against a yellow background.

I saw the names of primary school teachers, the priest, Pim's parents. Pim and his wife had their own tray now; apparently, he too celebrated New Year's Eve alone with his immediate family.

The window had been left open for a reason: to keep the meat trays cool. It was ice cold inside.

I could just picture it—Laurens and his mother at the party, looking forward to coming home and admiring the fruits of their labor, to going through the books one last time to see who still owed them money, just like they used to. Then they would happily crawl under the covers, ready for the busiest, most social day of the year, the day when people didn't just come in to pick up their tray but also to gossip. Everybody wanted a juicy Christmas story to take the edge off their own suffering.

Thanks to me, there'd be no shortage of gossip tomorrow, though there would be a shortage of meat.

I set the bucket on the windowsill and weaved my way through the aluminum trays until I reached the swinging door on the other side. It had a round window in it. I stood on my tiptoes and looked out into the butcher shop. There it was, just as I'd hoped and feared: the display case, with every salad lined up in the same order as always. Only the cash register was different. I saw myself for the first time today in the reflection, a grown woman with long hair, more angular, less fleshy, yet still only suitable for men with moderate standards, for guys who wanted to aim higher but were held back by their own limitations. These included a pock-marked twenty-something in the university toilets, a model with a cleft lip from my drawing class and a balding French-speaking history teacher.

Why even bother to fix my hair? Still, I did it anyway.

I didn't know exactly how much time I had. The party at Pim's might not last very long or Laurens's mother could have forgotten something and decided to turn around.

I pulled out the Flemish flags one by one and peeled back the foil. Then I scooped a generous portion of slurry onto the exposed meat and carefully rubbed it in with the round end of the spoon. The yellow-brown liquid seeped its way between the pork chops, fillets and thighs. Whenever I recognized the name, I tried to picture the person's reaction when they found out tomorrow that there'd be no meat for their electric griddle on New Year's Eve.

Even the people I didn't know got a scoop. If only they hadn't ordered their meat from Laurens.

After a dozen or so trays, I didn't have to think about it so much. Spoon in the bucket, foil up, splat on top, preferably on the best piece of meat, and rub it all in with the bottom of the spoon. I had to make sure it couldn't be rinsed off, that there were enough chunks of sawdust and undigested cattle feed to go around.

I didn't stop the routine until I came to "De Wolf", with my mom's cell-phone number on top. I stood there for a moment, holding the spoon above the meat. It would look suspicious if I spared my own family, if I didn't tarnish my own name. I couldn't skip Mom and Dad's tray. That would just make it look like they were in on it. After thoroughly rubbing the marinade into their meat like everybody else's, I dropped the bucket and hurried outside. Through the open window, I looked out over the shiny sea of aluminum trays now bathing in the overpowering stench of cow shit. I sealed the room to make sure that none of the smell was lost. That was the most important step in any marinade: cover the bowl tight.

I jumped into the car and skidded out of the driveway. It wasn't until I was behind the wheel that I noticed how much my hands were shaking. I could've gone home, but I didn't. The slurry was only the start of the plan.

Pretty soon, Pim will get a furious phone call from Laurens—the copper bucket, the slurry, it must be from his cows, there's no other farmer in town. Pim will instantly sober up, throw down the phone and go looking for the missing bucket.

August 10, 2002 (3)

MY CROTCH IS numb. To keep it from breaking open or bleeding again, I bike home standing up. Even after I'm out of sight of the butcher shop, I can still feel the sting of their eyes.

In the field across from our backyard are a couple of cows from Pim's farm; they don't look up as I pass by. Cows are never aware of the evil around them. Maybe Laurens is right: they're nothing but millions of threads.

But what about humans, aren't we just spun together too? Every pore could be the back of a button, like a navel. That could explain why my limbs are numb. While I was being knocked around by Laurens and Pim, my threads must have come loose.

As I turn down my street, I hit the brakes in time to glance over the hedge to make sure the coast is clear.

Pim's bike is nowhere in sight. The grass, dry as straw, is swaying in the summer breeze. The swing rocks gently back and forth. The Christmas trees are the only ones that are still bright green, like Playmobil trees. The dog is lying on the ground licking herself. Her leash is tied to the stand of the closed umbrella. Tessie is sitting at the plastic patio table in the sun, her back towards me. She's just unfolded the Monopoly board.

I stand at the edge of the garden with the bike frame between my legs.

Tessie starts carefully counting the money. She arranges the orange bills into a pile, keeping count under her breath. Then she takes each pile with both hands and taps it on the edge of the table until there are no corners or edges sticking out. She lays out the money in neat rows. Then she distributes the start capital for two players; each one gets thirty thousand francs.

Just as she finishes setting up the game, she stops to scratch her head. One of the ten-thousand-franc bills blows away. Tessie sees it too. She jumps out of the chair, plucks the slip of purple paper from the grass and sinks to the ground. She lands in the middle of the yard like a beetle on its back. The hand clutching the bill falls open but there is no wind now, the ten thousand francs doesn't move. For a few seconds, she seems unconscious.

Then she crawls to her feet. Back at the table, she takes a sip from her glass of water. Without a trace of regret, she dumps all the venture capital back into the bank, along with the other money, and starts counting everything out all over again. She forms the same stacks, first orange, then blue, then beige. Everything is tapped down to the same size on the edge of the table.

Maybe she was waiting for the itch, for that sigh of wind to send the money fluttering. Maybe this is not preparation for a game, maybe this is the game.

The sun is burning down on my skin. As long as I'm watching, her behavior seems less harmful. I'm the audience that makes these steps seem sort of justified.

I keep watching until she has finished counting, but again, something goes awry. She starts over. The longer I stand at the edge of the yard watching her repetitions, the less it seems like this is really happening. Is this still the same day it was this morning? Is this still the same sun? Is this really my house, my sister, my back-yard? Nothing has changed, but nothing is the same either.

I lean my bike against the wall of the garage, heading for the patio so I can slip through the sliding door and into the house.

Without stopping what she's doing, Tessie follows me with her gaze. I can tell by the way her eyes move that I'm walking strangely. I try to move differently, but the harder I try, the wobblier I become.

Tessie stops counting and waits for me to pass.

"What are you doing in Laurens's T-shirt?" she asks right before

I slip through the fly ribbons. I keep moving. Her eyes sink to my crotch.

For the first time, she doesn't ask if I want to play Monopoly with her.

Mom is asleep in the armchair. All I can see is a tuft of hair sticking out over the back. The cat tries to play with it.

Obviously, mothers would never choose someone else's kid over their own. That's why they're mothers.

I go into the bathroom, fill up a cup from the faucet and drink it empty. The water tastes like toothpaste. I drop into the chair with Dad's shirt hanging on the back, my shoulder blades pressing back against the breast pockets. There's a pack of cigarettes in each one. Now that I'm seated, the pain shoots through my lower abdomen in quick bursts.

Without taking off Laurens's T-shirt, I look down at the big black letters on the front: JAMAICA. Beside them is a colorful palm tree. Laurens wore this shirt a lot this summer. Over the carnival weekend. The day he left for France.

My mouth is filling up with saliva again. Mom always told us we weren't allowed to throw up in the bathtub because it would clog the drain. I lean over the tub with my mouth open. There's nothing left, nothing but water, bile and tears. Teeth chattering, I take off the T-shirt, wipe my lips and pull the shirt on the chair over my shoulders. It smells too much like Dad. I shrug it off.

As long as I don't know what I'm going to do, there's no point in getting off this chair. I can't go to the doctor. Who knows, maybe Laurens and his mom are already at the hospital waiting to have Laurens's forehead stitched up. And even if they aren't, I can't just walk in and tell the nurse what happened. I'd have to confess everything that happened this summer. Then the doctor would examine me with a light and stick yet another tool inside me to assess the damage.

I push down the stopper in the bathtub and turn on the water.

I lower my pants until I can open my legs wide enough. The bloodstains are brown and dry. I can only partly see how battered it looks, I need a mirror. Pink flakes of dried wallpaper glue flutter down on the bathmat. I take a washcloth, run it under the water, and gently lay it between my legs.

All of a sudden, I'm exhausted, too tired to wash. As tired as three people combined. I can't close my eyes. This body, these arms, these legs, I can't just take them off and leave them hanging on a chair for other people to use.

There's a sound in the hallway. Before I can do anything to stop him, Jolan enters the bathroom. I'm startled, but he's even more startled than I am. He lets go of the door handle and catches a glimpse of the wet washcloth between my legs, of the blood in the pants around my ankles. I quickly pull them up and cover my bare chest with Laurens's shirt.

Jolan isn't sure whether he should leave or not, but now that I'm covered and he's released the door handle, leaving would only make things even more awkward. He decides to finish what he started. Eyes glued to the floor, he walks past me, opens his drawer and grabs a pair of socks folded by Mom.

From the black outer sock, a white one emerges. Jolan sighs, annoyed. He puts the mismatched pair on anyway. I follow his quick, almost routine movements; he could move slower as far as I'm concerned, I'm already regretting that he's going to leave soon.

"Everything okay?" Jolan asks, still not looking at me. He closes the drawer.

"Period problems," I say.

He nods gravely, as if he knows exactly what I'm talking about. "Do you want to borrow a pair of shorts?" he asks.

I don't respond at first. I wring out the washcloth between my legs and put it back on the edge of the tub. Then I nod. He hands me a pair of his shorts from the closet full of clothes that have been worn but still aren't dirty enough to be washed. They smell like grass.

Jolan picks up my blood-soaked pants and hangs them on the edge of the tub. It's already filled up with more than twenty centimeters of water, much more than what Dad usually allows. Jolan squeezes a bit of shower gel and shampoo into the bath.

"Then you don't have to scrub," he says. "That's what I always do."

He walks back to the door.

"Wait," I say.

He stops. "What?"

When I don't respond, Jolan sits down on the edge of the tub.

"Do you want me to call Mom?"

"No," I say. "It's fine."

Someone walks down the hall. We sit and listen to the tapping on the keyboard. As long as Tessie is within earshot, we don't say a word. Instead of talking, Jolan rummages around in his back pocket and pulls out an Ikea pencil and a little notebook. He hands it to me. I flip through it. At the top of each page is a header—"Croquettes", "Back door", "Calendar"—and under it a list of gestures, tallied movements, with exact times and a few corrections here and there. Halfway through the book is a crossed-out sketch of our vegetable garden, with the arrangement of plant species and their seasons.

I recognize all the rituals. I search the pocket of my pants for my own notes. They're still in there. I unfold the paper and pass it to Jolan. For the first time, he looks me straight in the eyes. Then he reads, his face expressionless. Slowly he starts shaking his head. Obviously, I don't have to tell him what he's reading.

Tessie leaves the hallway.

"It's getting worse," he says.

"Yeah," I say. "What are we going to do?"

The bath is full, the excess water is sucked down the little hole to keep the tub from overflowing. The drain chokes and makes a loud gurgling noise. Jolan turns off the water.

"She needs to see a doctor. Better today than tomorrow," he says. "I've been doing some research these last few weeks. We could take her to the emergency room in Lier. You don't have to pay there right away."

"Today?" I ask.

"Go ahead and take your bath first. An hour won't make any difference. When you're done, we'll go."

I nod. My hands are shaking. I sit on them. Suddenly, the foaming hot bath looks terrifying. The soap and shampoo will sting in my wounds. The hospital waiting room is the best option for both Tessie and me—and it certainly beats waiting on this chair in the bathroom for Laurens or Pim to call.

"Shouldn't we wake up Mom?"

"Can you see her crawling behind the wheel in her state? We'll be faster on our bikes."

"All right," I say. "Can you pack a few things for her? Toothbrush, comic books."

Jolan takes Tessie's toothbrush out of the half-built wall and walks out of the bathroom.

I pull myself out of the chair and drain the bathtub. I search the medicine cabinet for the bottle of Betadine and compresses to disinfect the external wounds. I shouldn't let them get infected. Most of the pain is coming from my lower abdomen, at a depth of about ten centimeters. That's going to be harder to reach. I dab some disinfectant on a fresh compress and wrap it around a couple of cotton swabs. Then I try, very carefully, to insert it into my vagina, just two to three centimeters. I swab the edges and dab away some of the sand. Better a bit of pain now than an ulcerating infection later.

I change clothes but don't put on clean underwear, the elastic would rub too hard against my skin. Not once do I look at myself in the mirror.

Tessie looks up when Jolan and I come outside. I'm wearing his shorts, which actually don't look that bad on me, though I did have to put a belt on to hold them up. Maybe she can tell by the way we're marching towards her that we won't tolerate any protest. Jolan is carrying her backpack, which contains a toothbrush, a pair of pajamas and two Gaston comic books. He walks up to her and hands her the jacket and shoes he's picked out for her.

"Tessie, put these on and go get your bike."

"Where are we going?"

"We're going to get help."

Without any further questions, as if it were some kind of game, she gets up, puts on her shoes and heads to the garage. Jolan and I wait on our bicycles next to our neatly planted vegetable garden.

Tessie spits on her bike seat and polishes it with her sleeve until the leather shines. Then, she rings the bell three times. She turns the front of the bike in the direction we are going to leave in and stands with her legs on either side of the frame. With her calf and shin, she maneuvers the pedals left and right with the precision of someone baking a cake, weighing everything down to the nearest gram.

Jolan nods affirmatively in my direction. These movements have all been meticulously recorded in his notepad under "Bicycle".

"Ready?" he asks once she's got her pedals equidistant from the ground.

"Wait." Almost without shame, she performs the ritual again in front of the garage door. She knows that this might be the last time she'll be able to carry it out undisturbed.

She rings her bell again, three times, and works the pedals into position.

Nanook, still tied to the swan-shaped umbrella stand, starts jumping up and down from all the bell ringing. She drags the concrete swan behind her to the edge of the patio, until the untrimmed grass makes it too hard to pull the thing any further. She whines, begging.

She didn't choose to become this family's pet.

Jolan tries to calm her down. "She's going to wake up Mom."

The dog stops whining and pulls harder. Her leash is so tight that a bird could cut itself on it in a dive.

We ride down the street. Behind the hedge I see the closed umbrella rocking back and forth.

Tessie takes off, pedaling hard. Before we've even turned off our street, she takes the lead, which she holds for a long time. Jolan and I don't pass her. We cycle next to each other in silence, Jolan sitting, me standing on the pedals. We reach the row of pollard willows that I rode past an hour ago on my way to the butcher shop. My calves are still tight, every muscle in my body aches, but all I can think about is Tessie—all of these movements are for her and therefore take less effort.

The closer we get to the canal, the stronger the headwind. It fills Tessie's jacket, making her look stronger than she really is. I can see my panties from a distance. They're standing upright in the wind. Tessie cycles by them first, without even noticing them. Jolan practically runs them over.

I could point them out to him. Tell him that they're my panties, explain how they got here, but I decide to wait until we're on our way back, until Tessie is in good hands.

We turn down the steep slope on the side of the bridge and reach the canal. The wind is fickler down here. It's a straight shot from here to the hospital—no more need to think.

A storm is coming. Dark clouds are spreading across the blue sky like a drop of ink in a glass of water. It's hard to say whether it's headed in our direction. For the first time, the thought of the same rain falling on everyone in town is no longer reassuring.

Jolan and Tessie pick up the pace. I'm in the back now.

I try not to think about what Laurens and Pim are doing, what they're going to eat tonight, whether it'll be better than whatever we'll get. Whether a doctor is tending to Laurens right now, carefully disinfecting his wound with compresses.

It starts to pour. The rain is just in time to wash the scoreboard off the cemetery wall. Elisa's days as top scorer are over.

We stop and take cover under the bridge across the Albert Canal. Heavy gusts of wind whip between the piers from all directions, leaving us hardly a dry spot to stand in.

"You want to see something?" Jolan asks. He parks his bike and motions for us to follow. In one giant swoop, he wraps his bike lock around all three of our bike frames. Then he leads the way up the steep side of the pier, his mismatched socks moving in small, shuffling steps.

Climbing is difficult, the squatting stretches my labia. I can't imagine any movement that wouldn't hurt right now.

At the top is a narrow ledge with enough space above it to crawl into. The bridge is hollow. We find ourselves in a half-meter-high crawl space between the surface of the road and the bottom of the bridge.

It's dark and muggy inside. The air is denser in here than outside, the thunderstorm sounds miles away and close by at the same time. The thunder we hear is mixed with the sound of cars driving across the tarred joints in the asphalt overhead. The sounds swell up, like they're going to hit us, then fade.

I can barely make out Jolan's profile in front of me. I follow his one white sock. It's the only thing that stands out in the dark.

Was this the hiding spot he ran away to at the age of ten, when he left home carrying a bundle of supplies—underwear, matches, rope, scissors, a juice box, all wrapped in a kitchen towel on a bamboo pole slung over his shoulder—determined never to return? I was too little to stop him, to chase after him on my bike. I did count the pairs of underwear in his drawer though—there were no more than three missing, so I knew he wouldn't be gone too long. He found his way home a little after dark and disappeared into his room, disappointed that nobody had called the police.

We waddle down the tunnel like geese. Shards of glass crunch under my shoes. Up ahead, there's light. That must be where we're going. Tessie stays close behind me, clinging to the hood of my jacket. I keep following Jolan. Crouching like this eases the burning between my legs, or maybe it's just the fact that both Tessie and Jolan are nearby. When was the last time I was so close between them like this? It must have been some time when we were playing a game, forming trains.

A few meters ahead, we come to the opening in the floor where the light is coming from. Below us is the big canal, its water open and wild.

Only here, in the lulls when no cars are passing overhead, can you clearly hear the thunder outside. The flashes of lightning reflect on the dark water.

"You can see straight down into the ships from here," says Jolan. "Look."

We stick our heads out over the hole. A few seconds later a wide freighter passes under the bridge. First the bow, then the deck, then the cargo hold carrying a mound of sand, the control cabin, a car, a bicycle, a couple of flower boxes, the living quarters. On the back are two giant propellers churning up ferocious waves. Jolan leans dangerously far over the edge.

"That ship is probably going to France. Or Dubai. Or Turkey," he says.

We nod, our eyes on the water, which remains choppy long after the ship has disappeared.

"Where exactly are we going to get help?" Tessie nudges a stone over the edge. It disappears into the waves.

"Sacred Heart." Jolan's voice sounds decisive as it echoes down the tunnel.

Tessie's whole body shrinks. "Or maybe we could just go bowling," she says, "that would do me good. And you guys would have fun too."

"We can go bowling. But first Sacred Heart." Jolan crawls past us and leads the way back out.

I let Tessie go in front of me and take up the rear.

Back under the bridge, we unlock our bikes. It's chillier than before, everything smells damp and new.

This time, I bike in front. The hospital isn't far now.

Jolan speeds up until we're almost side by side. He keeps his front wheel close to my rear wheel, making it clear that he and I are taking care of Tessie together, not the other way around.

"Isn't it hard to bike like that?" Jolan asks.

"Like what?" I ask.

"Without using the seat."

I sit down.

It burns. I shift my weight back and forth. With just the right amount of pressure the pain eases a bit, mostly when I wriggle myself over the nose of the saddle until the fabric of my shorts gets stuck. This prevents the wounds on the inside of my labia from touching each other.

We pedal through the city center. Down the main shopping street, past the municipal pool, past the bowling alley. Tessie is slowing down. But she keeps pedaling.

Within five minutes, we reach the main entrance of Sacred Heart Hospital. We leave our bicycles against a hedge.

I consider reaching for her hand, but by the time I decide it's a good idea, we're already in the waiting room.

I sit down beside her on the plastic chairs. Jolan walks up to the lady at reception. She's just tucked a cigarette behind her ear, ready to go on a break. The glass door between the waiting room and the reception desk slides shut, and Tessie and I can't hear what they're saying. I dig around in my pocket for our SIS cards and the yellow stickers from the health insurance company—they're probably going to ask for them.

I walk up to the desk and empty the contents of my pockets on the counter. The doors close again behind me.

"Why did you bring our stickers too?" Jolan asks.

"They were all in the same drawer," I say. The woman just takes Tessie's. I put the rest away. Tessie is sitting alone in the waiting room next to a giant vending machine. I go back to her.

"Are you thirsty?" I ask. "Do you want a drink?" She shakes her head no, which is good because I don't have any money on me.

We're called back by a nurse with calves you know she wouldn't have chosen for herself. She leads us through the emergency area and ushers us into a small room. Inside, she rolls a sheet of thick paper over the bed.

All of a sudden, I feel very tired again, but I don't want to lie down.

First, Jolan offers Tessie the chair, then me. Then he takes a seat on the foot of the bed, because it would be strange if we all just stood there.

The door behind us keeps opening, and every time, somebody sticks their head in, looking for someone who's not us.

I've never noticed how small Tessie's ears are. Maybe it's the neon light.

"This is just another waiting room," I say. "They'll get to us in a minute."

Hanging above the door is a plaster Jesus. One of his feet has crumbled away. The nail is still there, but it's too big for what's left of the foot. I used to think Jesus looked a little like Jan—the big head, the skinny ribs. Now, for the first time, the likeness seems sinister.

I need to pee, so I hurry down the white, sterile hallway to the bathroom. There's a handle on either side of the toilet so I can make a soft landing on the seat. The urine burns as it comes out. I try to check for splinters, but again, I need a mirror. The muscles in my butt are so stiff that I can barely lean forward.

On the way back, I peek through open doors, between curtains. I resolve to ask the first female doctor I see if she's a gynecologist or if she knows one, but the only people I see are cleaning staff and male doctors. I find a box of paracetamol in a trash can, but it's empty.

Halfway down the hall, I find Jolan back in the main waiting room.

"The doctor came," he says.

"Is it a he or a she?" I ask.

"A she. Tessie wanted to be alone with her."

"What kind of person is she?"

"I don't know. Tessie cried when she came in. The doctor asked her what her name was, and she said, 'Eleven.' 'Okay, Evan,' the doctor said, 'what seems to be the problem?' Everyone was confused."

We both suppress a smile.

"Tessie just sat there sniveling. Every once in a while, she'd say something. That she didn't want to go back home—she said that twice. The doctor told her tears were normal. That when someone finally admits that they've been struggling for a long time, it all comes out."

I nod.

"I shouldn't have gone to the bathroom just now," I say. I repeat it a few more times over the next half-hour, until Jolan tells me to shut up about it.

Every time the sliding door opens, voices rush in from all sides. Through the fake walls, everyone sounds like they have a cold.

I wonder if Tessie will say anything about me. About her failed house drawing above the kitchen table, about my bunny stories, about all those times I forced her to lie on top of her sheet in the cold.

I wonder if I should give my notes to the doctor, my name with the twenty tallies behind it.

"You need something to drink?" Jolan asks. I know he hasn't got any money on him either, so I say no.

On the table in the waiting room are magazines, comic books, a solved Rubik's cube that no one has the heart to mess up, including me.

A half-hour later a doctor comes out into the waiting room to speak to us. She doesn't beat around the bush—she tells us Tessie will be admitted immediately, that she requested this herself, but since she's a minor she needs her parents' permission first.

"Where are your parents by the way? Or who is your legal guardian?" she asks.

"Dad's at work. Mom's at home." Jolan tries to make himself as big as possible.

"And do they know you're here?"

Jolan nods, so I nod too.

"The hospital is still going to have to call them and let them know what's going on," she says. "You can wait here."

We go on nodding, standing between her and the exit.

"You did the right thing bringing her here," she says emphatically. "There's a chance she'll be transferred to Kortenberg tomorrow. There are people there who are more specialized in cases like hers."

"Cases like hers?" I ask.

"Obsessive-compulsive disorder, eating disorder, sleep disorder. In the meantime, we have a bed in a shared room for her here."

She shakes Jolan's hand, making him feel grown-up. Then she

shakes mine; I grip her fingers a little too long. She gently wiggles her hand free.

"I suggest you speak with a social worker. You don't have to do it right now. You can talk to Evan first and make an appointment. You don't need your parents' permission to talk, you know."

"Tessie," I say. "Her name is Tessie."

"Right, of course. Excuse me."

She takes a ballpoint pen from her breast pocket and then puts it back in the exact same spot. "Do you want to say goodbye?"

I go in first. Tessie is sitting on the bed with her narrow back facing the door. She scratches her scalp, first right, then left, then with both hands. I stand behind her. Her ears seem to have grown even smaller. The skin behind her ears is bunched up like the seam of a pillow that was sloppily stitched up after being stuffed.

She doesn't turn around. She's sitting upright with her shoulders slumped, but her back is still hollow.

I pull my notes out of my back pocket. On the left side of the margin are words, on the right are tally marks. I lay the paper in Tessie's lap. She stares at it for a moment.

She doesn't recognize it. She turns the paper over a few times. I give it a moment to sink in.

"What is this?" she asks, slightly annoyed. "Is it a shopping list written in code or something?"

She looks at it again, reads a few of the random words and numbers out loud, without making any sense of it.

"It's nothing," I say, "it's a word game, but now's probably not the time for it." I carefully fold the paper back up and put it back in my pocket. Anyway, it wasn't for nothing. Maybe we can come back to this later, when she's really ready to be helped.

"Will you take care of Stamper?" she asks.

"If you promise to take care of yourself." I give her a gentle hug.

"Goodbye, Eva." She says it so softly it almost doesn't count.

Jolan goes in after me. He stays with her longer than I did.

The hospital's entrance and exit are exactly the same door, but the arrows indicate a separate path for each. Arriving, leaving—hospitals have to make a clear distinction between the two. As we walk out the door, a new shift of cleaners and nurses arrives. Their hair is neatly trimmed, and you can see the color of their bras through their white smocks.

The sun beams down on the puddles through a hole in the clouds. You can always feel the sun beating harder in the presence of water, as if it's doing everything in its power to assemble an army for the next downpour.

Jolan and I look back at the hospital wing behind us.

The building is gigantic, each floor devoted to a different kind of failure—sometimes the failure of the body itself, sometimes the failure of that body's environment.

Behind each window of the psychiatry ward is a lunatic waiting for another lunatic to share the room with. Tessie is now being taken to one of those rooms.

We stand there on the sidewalk. For a moment, I'm relieved to be outside again, but the feeling doesn't last.

Who will Tessie share a room with? Will that person come to know her better than we do, now that she's finally admitted she needs help?

"Look," Jolan says proudly. He pulls a wad of gauze out of his pocket and unfolds it carefully. Inside is a bloody piece of flesh.

"I fished this out of the trash on the way out. I think it's a piece of an earlobe or a fingertip or something. I still need to examine it."

I nod. He folds the bundle back up again, practically clinging to it. Together we walk through the parking lot to our bicycles. Jolan suggests we take Tessie's home with us. We can't leave it here for days, he says, and he can pull it alongside his own bike, no problem. Not only does it sound dangerous to me, but the very thought of it makes me sad: the two of us traveling home on the exact same route we came here on, dragging an empty bicycle, as if we had lost our little sister along the way and just kept on pedaling without her.

We leave her bike in the rack in the parking lot. It's really just a gesture, since we have the key and could've just as well unlocked it. Jolan wraps his lock around her bike; I do the same. Not for extra security, but because I want to leave something of mine behind too.

On the way back, Jolan rides ahead of me. I follow close behind.

We pass the bowling alley, the swimming pool, the shopping street and soon reach the path along the canal. From there, the route is a straight line. We can cycle side by side without getting in anyone's way. Sometimes we pass through pockets of cool air.

Even now, we hardly speak. Instead of talking, I look for things that are different than they were before, that have disappeared, like Tessie. The pain in my body is the same, all that's changed is the number of slugs on the path.

I keep my gaze firmly on the asphalt and slalom between the trails of mucus. Every once in a while, Jolan says something about the feeding and mating behavior of mollusks. I could care less, but it doesn't take any extra effort to listen, so I do.

As we approach the panties, I consider telling him—everything. He would bike over to the butcher shop and beat Laurens up, then bike over to the farm and beat Pim up.

But we just bike past them, and I have no choice but to conclude that I'm not telling him because I don't want to admit that I've been wearing his shorts all afternoon without any underwear, and because I'm afraid he won't want to bike all the way back to the hospital to get me some help.

Damages

I FOUND OUT the truth about Jan's accident on the day of his funeral. The three of us left the reception together on our bikes. Pim rode on the back of mine. He couldn't sit on the back of Laurens's because his rear rack was loose, and plus, Laurens still had a meat salad sandwich in his hand.

Laurens and I had promised Pim's mom that we'd bring him home safely. We cycled down the Steegeinde, which formed an almost-straight line between the farm and the cemetery. The gravediggers stopped their little bulldozer and waited until we were out of sight.

For the first part of the route, Pim kept his arms wrapped around me. Through my thick winter coat, I felt him briefly press his face between my shoulder blades. I thought he was going to blow warm air, but when I scooched back on the saddle to get even closer to him, he let go and grabbed hold of the rack.

"Fucking Steegeinde," Pim sighed. After that, no one breathed another word. We needed the wind to blow the stale smell of coffee out of our clothes.

Actually, I always wondered where the name "Steegeinde" came from. I used to think it had something to do with geography—beyond the farm was the border of town. For years, we never went farther than the end of the Steegeinde, that's where everything ended, where we'd fall off the edge of the world. But now I knew—the dead-end street owed its name to the cemetery on the other side of the church wall, where the worms and insects were about to start nibbling away at Jan's cheeks.

Just before we reached the edge of the farm, Pim blew his nose into the hood of my coat. I didn't say anything.

Laurens and I hung out at the farm for the rest of the afternoon, until Pim's parents had carried out all their duties. Although we were intrigued by the grate over the slurry pit, which had been reattached with iron wires, and by the fluttering police tape around the yard to keep onlookers at bay, we didn't leave Pim's side. We saw this as a new beginning, a renewal of our friendship.

We sat at the kitchen table playing Loopin' Louie—it had always been Pim's favorite game before he started denying it. Laurens kicked me in the shin three times to make it clear that we were going to let Pim win, as if I hadn't already thought of that myself. Beside me was the cat that was always sitting in Jan's lap. She paced around in circles meowing, then sat down for a moment. She rubbed her belly against the table leg.

"Poor thing," I said.

"She's just in heat," Pim said.

Halfway through the game, he disappeared into the hallway and came back with a handful of Q-tips. Then he bent down under the table and pushed one of the cotton tips into her anus. It went in deep, halfway down the plastic stick. The animal growled content-edly, sank down deeper on her front legs and stuck her tail end higher into the air.

"Should you be doing that?" I asked.

"Who says I shouldn't?" Pim started poking harder. The animal meowed woefully, squirmed around on the ground, somewhere between pain and sweet release.

He kept petting her. A clump of loose hair gathered against her tail.

"Jan used to do this every day. He liked pleasuring cats so much that he refused to have her spayed." Pim gave the cotton swab one last push and let the animal go. The cat screeched and ran out through the flap in the porch door, the Q-tip still deep in her butt.

"How's she going to sit?" I asked.

"That's her problem, not ours." Pim's eyes were wide. His shirt collar was making his neck break out into a rash.

Laurens and I didn't dare to challenge him. Maybe we would have if he hadn't still been wearing his suit.

We packed up the game in silence and pushed an old Disney video into Pim's TV. *The Sword in the Stone*. Pim and Laurens stared blankly at the screen. I slipped out to go to the bathroom.

Jan's bedroom was on the way down the hall. I stood outside the door for a moment, not sure whether I should go in. If I did, I'd be no better than all those people who shook Pim's hand today, who cared more about Jan's absence than they'd ever noticed his presence.

Maybe I should have looked at Jan more often too, seen what he really looked like, studied the details. Now it was too late. I could only picture him as I did that one time in this room, with my tongue against his pillow.

I opened the door. The sheet lay crumpled on the bed, and on the pillow, I could still see the imprint of his head, little stains from picked open pimples. I stood there for two minutes, unable to remember what I'd even liked about Jan. All I could remember was the brother Pim described, the boy who rushed off the playground to tend to the cattle, who squeezed udders and pleasured cats.

I went into the room, moved around a few figurines, turned over a notebook, swapped a few pairs of ironed trousers, put on his slippers, went through his stuff, stuck a cap back on a pen. I was taking Jan back, making him mine again.

I flipped through the calendar on the surface of his desk. Certain days had been ticked off. Maybe he had marked when the cows were due to give birth. The month of December was completely empty except for three checkmarks. The last mark was on December 28, the day he died. I wrote my name on the pad in Pim's handwriting.

In the rearranged room, I lay down on the bed and pressed my face into the pillow. When I reached my arms under it, I discovered a folded sheet of graph paper. It was from the notebook on the desk. Hands trembling, I unfolded it.

The message wasn't addressed to me in particular, but it wasn't to anyone else either.

It didn't say much: a few words, no capital letters or punctuation, it might as well have been a message on a birthday card, scribbled down at the supermarket checkout. "Sorry," was the first word I read. Sorry who?

And then: "Don't come looking for me I'm already gone take good care of pim and the animals."

I turned it over. Maybe something came before this.

The other side was blank.

I pressed my head into the pillow, processing what I'd just found, trying to rewrite the memory of Jan's last days. Maybe he'd forced open the slurry pit grate with a screwdriver, looked down at the black mire below and jumped in without thinking, with the boldness of a cat strolling out into the night without a curfew. Maybe it happened without a sound, maybe he inhaled the toxic fumes without even the cows noticing what he was doing. Maybe the tick marks on his desk pad weren't birth dates, maybe they were the days he had planned to carry out this final act and then backed out.

If it was true what Jolan said the morning after Dad made us remove all the sharp objects from the house to protect Mom from herself—that people don't really want to die, they just want to find a way out of their current life—then why didn't Jan call me? It's not like he had anything left to lose.

I didn't get out of the bed until I heard Pim's parents come home. There was a good chance that his mom would come look at Jan's room as soon as she got home. I stuffed the letter back under the pillow, exactly as I found it, scratched out my name on the notepad, pulled the cap off the pen, moved the figurines back where they had been and put back the slippers and pants. Just before I stepped out, I looked around for a moment. The imprint in the pillow was the only thing that couldn't be restored to its original state.

We left. Laurens didn't ask me where I'd been for so long. He was probably glad to have Pim all to himself, or maybe he hadn't even noticed I was gone.

"See you Monday, seven-thirty, at the bridge?" he asked, before our paths went separate ways. "Call me if you're running late." He did this after every school holiday, checked that our appointment still stood.

I nodded.

For weeks, the last thing I thought about before I fell asleep and the first image that came to mind when I woke up in the morning was Jan's mother cherishing the wrong head print in his pillow.

8:00 p.m.

I ONCE LOOKED up the decomposition time for memories, just like I once looked up the decomposition time for underwear, but I couldn't find it. In any case, it can't be any longer than the time for glass, because, unlike glass, people—the containers of memories—don't last for centuries.

What I remember about those summer days is that every single moment mattered, minute after minute, how it happened, where it happened. I remember lying on my back in the workshop and seeing the hedge clippers dangling from the roof. I remember where the pebbles were on the path when I biked to the hospital with Tessie and Jolan, how careful we were not to run over the slugs on the way back. It seemed important to take note of all the details so I could forget them later, so I could wipe away the memories bit by bit.

I wasn't able to do this until I moved to Brussels, where there were other butcher shops, other streets, no pollard willows. Who said what, the color of Pim's T-shirt, which muscles had hurt the most, how exactly the sand felt scraping my insides—it all slowly faded into the background. But the fact that it happened, that it had scarred me, was undeniable, and became harder to bear over time.

Laurens should be home by now. He must've already called Pim and let him have it.

My coat pocket buzzes.

It's hard for me to look down, the rope around my neck is too tight for that now. I feel around in my pocket and fish out my phone. I hold it up at eye level so I can see the screen. My fingers are so cold they don't even feel like mine.

Tessie. One unread message. The screen goes into sleep mode. I have to feel around for the button three times to get it to light up again.

"Everything okay there? You called 16x. Tessa."

The message is so short it fits into the preview. My empty stomach is bloated, pressing against my diaphragm. It's seven minutes after eight. Later than I thought.

Sixteen times is an exaggeration. The old Tessie would have never exaggerated, the old Tessie was fond of accuracy, and always signed her messages with "Kisses", or at least with an "XO".

This was all part of it. Changing her name. Dyeing her hair.

At first, it was hard to say whether she was recovering or just going through puberty. In most cases, they're one and the same: puberty is recovering from the idea that you can be whatever you want to be, that you can choose any job you want. But not in Tessie's case—not every teenage girl ends up in a new family. Now that she's twenty-four, she's stopped bouncing around from one thing to the next. Two years ago, Nadine convinced her to train to be a pastry chef.

I have to call Tessie. Tell her it's not true. Sixteen calls—either she or her phone is mistaken.

If I call now, she'll pick up; her phone can't be far away.

I struggle to unlock the screen with my stiff fingers. It takes less than two seconds for her phone to start ringing, for the glowing line to snake through the entire town at lightning speed to connect us like in the telecom commercials.

The first ring. I can picture where her phone might be. Somewhere in Nadine's house. Or in her pocket. Maybe it's lying next to her on the bench in the bathroom where she's painting her nails. Or on the bed, while she arranges her recently opened Christmas presents in her room.

I can picture everything—the room, the wallpaper, her little toenails—but I don't know how it all fits into her life, and that makes her feel even farther away than she did when I couldn't picture any of it. It's like missing a train; the person left watching the train roll out of the station feels a stronger sense of having missed something than someone who shows up ten minutes past departure time.

Second ring.

So she's not picking up right away, that's normal. I get startled too when my phone starts vibrating. It always takes me a few seconds to understand that there's a call I'm supposed to take. That's what's going on right now. Tessie has to twist the top back on the bottle of nail polish and try to pick up the phone with wet nails or dig it out of her bedsheets.

The last time we talked on the phone for more than a few minutes was last year, two days after Christmas, right after she sent me a Merry Christmas text. Even though she told us way in advance that we weren't going to celebrate together that year, even though I'd spent days mentally preparing myself for it, when the evening arrived and nothing happened, I couldn't shake the thought that Tessie and Jolan had gone out for dinner without me, maybe even with Mom and Dad.

I went out, decided to send both Tessie and Jolan a WhatsApp photo from the restaurant we went to every year. There I was, alone at a table around midnight, beside an empty bottle of wine and a half-eaten turkey. It took me a while to get it all in one frame. The bottle was left over from the previous patrons.

Tessie called first. She left almost no pauses as she talked. We chatted for more than an hour. She brought up a few shared memories, but after a while she moved on to topics I had nothing to say about: Nadine's dog, decorating her new bedroom, the judo classes she was going to take so she'd be able to defend herself on the street, how important it is to get the proportions right when making cream-puff dough.

Her voice hadn't changed a bit. Part of me was surprised Nadine hadn't managed to change that too.

While we talked, I could hear the sound of incoming voice messages from Jolan on her phone. That's how I knew they weren't in the same room. But it didn't reassure me.

Last week, on Christmas Eve, I went to the same restaurant again. This time I didn't send anybody a photo.

The phone's rung three times now.

How was my number saved in her phone? Would it read "Evie: 17 missed calls", or "Eva", or "Eva de Wolf"?

All I can feel are my knuckles. Hard white stones. I lower my arm, slide the phone a little higher on the ball of my hand so I can swipe my thumb to hang up. All of a sudden, it falls to the floor. I don't feel it slip out of my hand; all I hear is it bouncing off the ice. It hits the ground, a few feet away from me, screen down. I can't see whether the call has ended, whether Tessie has just picked up, or whether it's gone to voicemail.

For a second, I consider stepping off the ice block, but even if I wanted to, I'm already standing on my tiptoes. The rope is stretched as far as it will go; the knot is tied so tightly that there's no way I could loosen the loop and pull my head out.

There's no turning back now. I'm heading downhill with no brakes.

I don't have to say anything. I could just wait here in silence with Tessie. Then at least someone would be with me now that the ice under my feet is really melting away.

But if I say nothing, she won't listen until the end, regardless whether she's answered the call or let it go to voicemail. Who listens to someone who's not saying anything? She'll think it was a mistake, that I just butt-dialed her or something.

"Hey, Tessie," I shout before I have a chance to consider whether this is really a good idea now that the music has stopped next door.

It's important that I keep calling her Tessie. She's never completely recovered from her diminutive birth name. As long as I say Tessie, she won't be able to hang up.

I could tell her what I'm doing, how crazy it is, that the soles of my feet are freezing from the cold, but the tops are scorched from the heat, that it's making my whole body shiver. I can tell her how the ice is melting slower than I thought, but still too fast, how I've never been so close to the edge of such a deep abyss.

Or I could keep it light, tell her about the slurry in the meat, and if she was on the other end of the line, if it wasn't a voicemail, I might even hear her laugh.

"Tessie, it's Eva," I say.

My voice sounds hoarse. The rope is pressing against my vocal cords. I try to make some spit to get them lubricated again. The last time I heard my voice out loud I was talking to Pim's little boy. My thoughts always sound different, more determined—in my mind, things aren't formulated in the standard Flemish I grew up with but in the neighbor's Brussels accent.

Should I hurry? You can't talk to an answering machine forever.

If a voicemail is recording now, I've got about another two and a half minutes. The clock in front of me is still frozen, Mickey Mouse isn't going to help me keep track of time. But I've gotten good at it. During all the sleepless nights over the past few years, I'd turn on my phone timer and let it run. After exactly two minutes, timed down to the hundredth of a second, I'd hit stop. I always knew it might come in handy.

"I'm at the party for Jan. Just stepped out to call you, I'm in the milk house."

Only now do I hear how ridiculous it sounds. The milk house. Like all the place names in this town when you really think about them. The Pit, the forest of the forest, Kosovo.

Of course, Tessie doesn't know what the milk house is. She won't be able to picture where I am right now. It's a remnant of a history she wasn't part of. It used to be the heart of this farm.

"Jolan came too. He left already. He says hello."

Maybe she already knows. Even if she does, she wouldn't have come. She never asked what happened to me after we took her to the hospital, if I'd been all right without her.

She doesn't know I started sleeping in her bed after she was gone. That I fed Stamper every day, changed his cage, pet him like she would have, with the same number of strokes on each ear.

That for the first few weeks after the summer, I kept hoping the

phone would ring and it would be Laurens and Pim calling to apol-
ogize. I waited for that phone call for four years.

Tessie spent a few days recovering at Sacred Heart before she was
transferred to a group home in Kortenberg.

I went to see her on the weekends during visiting hours, sometimes by bus, sometimes Jolan and I got a ride. We would draw
portraits, measuring each other's proportions with a pencil. I always
made sure Tessie's drawings were the best.

Mom and Dad didn't come to the hospital unless Tessie asked
them to, not because they didn't care, but because they didn't want
to impose. On their first visit, they bought her a *Cosmo Girl* in the
gift shop, because it was one of the only things with no fat or carbs.
The next few times, they filled up on liquid courage, showed up
thirty minutes before the end of the visit and said, "Don't worry,
we won't stay long." Then they'd sit in a corner of the room in
silence, waiting for permission to say something, something a parent
in a situation like this is supposed to say, but Tessie didn't speak to
them. Sometimes it seemed like all that was left of them was shame
and skin. They were like old houses, completely torn down except
for the facade, which was only left standing to comply with local
regulations. After the visit, they'd walk down the long, sterile cor-
ridors towards home, letting the oncoming traffic pass between
them.

About four months after she was admitted, in the winter of
2002, Tessie came home for dinner on Christmas Eve. Even then,
on their own property, Dad and Mom didn't dare to raise their
voices. They had removed the keyboard from the hallway and taken
all the soap out of the bathroom. There was no Christmas tree, no
flicker of colored lights in the living room. Everybody did their
best, but maybe that made it all the more painful, more obvious that
we weren't a family.

Tessie had to be back at the facility by midnight.

Everyone wanted to ride along. She sat in the back, between me
and Jolan. Dad did his best to stay in the right lane.

"You could've stayed the night," he said right before she got out of the car. I watched her disappear through the revolving door of the giant building with her backpack in hand. The further she moved away from us, the more calmly she walked. Dad stood there in the parking lot for a moment until the clock struck twelve. No other children were dropped off.

Sometime in 2003, in the presence of a psychologist, Tessie announced that she only wanted to see Mom and Dad when they were sober. After that, they kept their distance.

"It's their choice," was all Tessie said about it, and I nodded.

Shortly after that, the possibility of a foster family was discussed. By observing the contours of Tessie's body as I drew her, I could follow her healing process. Slowly, her shoulders took on different shapes, became more solid. I left all the drawings behind in her room, so she would have documentation of herself, by me, throughout the period. Sometimes I wondered if she'd ever laid our portraits side by side, if that might reveal who had made her progress possible, if she'd notice that the kilos she was gaining were slowly falling off of me.

In 2003, Jolan moved out to go to college. After that, Mom and Dad only ate at the table on the weekends, when he came home from school. While I waited for him to return, for the table to be set again, I took over his bedroom and set up my own TV in there.

I spent most of my time upstairs, eating in one room, sleeping in the other. Soon Jolan stopped coming home altogether. Whenever I called him, he told me how busy he was. I often scrolled through his pictures on Facebook—usually partying, with a beer in one hand and a girl in the other. The distance between Leuven and Kortenberg was bikeable. I had a feeling he often visited Tessie without me.

I wriggle a finger between the rope and my neck, just for a moment, to relieve my throat. I take a deep breath. A little burp comes out.

"Pardon," I say in French. "Tessie, do you remember that summer day we took you to the hospital?" I pause. Three seconds, three crocodiles. Just enough to remember our story.

In those last few meters before we got home, after we left her in the emergency room, Jolan started talking.

"We're going to take care of each other, you and me," he said. "The hospital probably already called Mom and Dad. I'm going to college in Leuven next year, and as soon as I've got some money, I'll rent an apartment big enough for two, three if necessary."

I wondered who the "if necessary" applied to, Tessie or me, but once we turned down our street, and our house was in sight, it didn't matter anymore. Clearly, the news hadn't reached anyone there yet: the aluminum shutters on the living-room window were still rolled down, Mom was still sleeping in the armchair and had probably taken the phone off the hook.

The field next to the house was dotted with color. I started pedaling faster. I knew what it was—wet Monopoly money, whisked away by the wind. The box was still lying open on the patio table. The game board, a couple of unused pieces and the Community Chest cards hadn't blown away, but they did get rained on. Only one bill remained, clamped under the edge of the lid— one hundred francs.

The rest of the pieces were under the table with the dog. One was missing.

"Did I ever tell you, Tessie, that the day we took you to the hospital, Nanook ate the Atomium? That was your favorite piece, wasn't it?" I say.

The lid was full of rainwater. When I picked it up, it fell apart. The ink had bled onto the white patio table. I think the mirror image of the top of the Monopoly box is still there.

"I'm going to tell Mom what happened, what we decided. It can't go on like this," Jolan declared, and he marched into the house with decisive steps.

I stayed behind to clean up the game. I crawled around the garden collecting all the scattered cash. I found it on the trunks of trees, on the sides of flowerpots, under the hedge and out in the field. I found a Chance card against the umbrella stand. GO DIRECTLY TO JAIL. DO NOT PASS GO, DO NOT COLLECT 4,000 FRANCS.

I put all the cards in the bottom of the wet box. It wasn't until I tried to rescue the bank that it hit me—that night, I would be sleeping in our room alone for the first time in my life. I was always the one who went camping. Tessie had never had sleepovers with friends.

Only after I'd collected all the money did I fold up the game board. And that's where I found it: a little notebook with all the scores, its pages protected under the plastic cover. The scoreboard had been neatly drawn with a pen and ruler. In the top left corner was "TES", in the top right "EVA".

I had to flip through it three times, scan the dozens of pages, read all the scores several times, before I understood, before I was able to see it: every time Tessie sat alone at that table, she wasn't talking to herself, she was talking to me.

She made sure I lost every time.

Clutching the notebook, I walked into the house. Inside it was quiet, dark. Mom was still sleeping in the armchair. Through the ceiling, I could hear Jolan up in his room. The wheels of his desk chair were sliding back and forth across the wooden floor. I'd recognize the sound anywhere—he was tinkering with his microscope, examining his latest acquisition.

"Tessie, I'm still here. You want to know why I'm calling? I wanted to tell you I went by the house today. Nanook's basket was still there, but all they have is a cat now. I didn't talk to Mom and Dad, but I think they were doing okay, or at least no worse than usual. I left them a note."

It's not a lie. That's what happened. The noise I thought I heard turned out to be a false alarm, a cat or something. For hours, I just sat there on that kitchen chair, until I heard the sound of my own thighs peeling off the fake leather. Quietly, cautiously, like a cop patrolling outside his district, I crept up the stairs. In the master bedroom, I found Mom and Dad. They were both lying face down under the covers, with only their heads sticking out.

Their faces were turned towards each other, half hidden in their pillows. The room smelled like fermenting dough. For a moment,

I thought they were dead, that they'd passed away peacefully in their sleep, but then I saw them slowly breathing. The fact that they were lying so close together made it easier to leave them behind.

I hurried downstairs to the back door. The clock on the micro-wave was blinking, winking at me.

Before leaving the house and heading out into the snow, I walked back into the kitchen and pulled my drawing off the wall, my detailed sketch of our house, with light blue clouds and a bright yellow sun and nine little birds on the electricity wire. I left Tessie's failed attempt up on the wall. In retrospect, hers had been more accurate all along.

Mom would immediately notice the drawing was gone. In the end, that was the battle cry we'd been raised with: it's better to be present somewhere than to be nowhere at all.

I better not lose track of time.

Dad used to leave me long voicemails. Usually, time would run out before he was finished. After exactly two minutes, his voice would be mercilessly cut off mid-sentence. Sometimes I didn't listen all the way to the end, not because the message was irrelevant, or because Mom was shouting in the background that he should leave me alone, but because I didn't want to hear him get cut off, the click of the switchboard giving up on him.

"You know, Tessie, it's okay you always made me lose. Then somebody else could win. It isn't good to always win. It's kind of like living in a beautiful house that looks out at a run-down facade."

It feels strange not to be able to hang up, to swipe away the call. The three minutes are almost up.

"No, wait Tessie, one last thing. I've got some money saved. I think it's enough for a new bathroom for Mom and Dad. What do you think? It's just sitting there in a shoebox under my bed. Don't let them go for the cheapest faucets, they'll start leaking again after a few months. Sound good? Goodbye, Tessie."

All I have to do now is wait. The rest will come.

This day will eventually turn out like the day Jan died. First, my parents and Tessie and everybody else will try to figure out the practical details, to understand my motives. But over time, none of that will matter anymore. It won't matter whether it was eleven or twelve o'clock when I walked out of the house I grew up in, what time I stepped up onto this block, how long I waited here, what I was wearing, how I spread the slurry on the meat, why I had the drawing of our house in my pocket, exactly how patient I must have been, or whether I wanted to be found. All that will matter is that I was here, on this first snowy day of an otherwise mild winter.

Love & thanks to Marscha, Daniel, Toine, Bregje, Lotte, Saskia, Ellen, Suus, Jeanette, Linde, Mariska, Maartje, Walter, Samuel, Mama, Papa, Thomas, Marieke and Ruth.

Translator's note

When Lize Spit's *Het smelt* was first published in Belgium and the Netherlands in 2016 by the young Amsterdam publishing house Das Mag, it was a near-instant sensation. The book received glowing reviews, won prestigious prizes and has sold more than 200,000 copies—no small feat for a debut novel from an independent publisher in such a small language area. The then twenty-seven-year-old Lize Spit was pushed into the spotlight as both a Flemish literary talent and a voice of her generation, a role that she continues to occupy today.

There is a refreshing peculiarity to Spit's writing style, a certain uncanniness that grabs you as a reader and pulls you along. She writes vividly, cinematically, with tremendous attention to detail. She uses mundane objects and occurrences to create multi-layered metaphors. She likes to turn sentences and idioms inside out, creating new, surprising—and sometimes jarring—images: two toothbrushes "standing like soldiers" in the brick holes of an unfinished bathroom wall; storm clouds that "merge like a bruise forming in reverse"; Miss Emma floating behind Eva "like a helium balloon attached to my wrist by a string"; and Mickey Mouse's clock hands on eleven and two "cheering unconvincingly" in the milk house. In these calculated descriptions of Eva's thoughts and emotions, Spit creates a complex, tragic narrator who is as believable as she is unreliable.

As a translator, my goal was to preserve Spit's idiosyncratic style—which alternates between short and long sentences, fragmented and flowing thoughts, subtle details and sweeping

reflections—and to create a translation that reads fluidly, rhythmically, that draws the reader toward the shocking climax in the same
way the original does.

I found myself fascinated by the way Spit uses Eva's perception
of small details in her environment—the aerial house photographs,
the untouched bag of NicNacs, the unraveling of meat—to con-
struct an eerie setting in which the horrific events at the end of the
book can conceivably take place. When I first read the book, I was
struck by how—as someone the same age as Spit who grew up in
the United States—so many details seemed familiar to me: Windows 95, Minesweeper, the styling of shoelaces, the boredom of
sitting on a swing set on a hot summer's day. That said, the book is
full of specific cultural references and realia whose significance may
not be obvious to English readers.

One such example is the way "the three musketeers" are separated
at the end of primary school: Laurens and Eva attend a pre-university
high school where they study subjects like German and biology, and
Pim goes to a vocational high school where he learns things like how
to fix a moped and build a swimming pool. In Belgium and the
Netherlands, children's educational trajectories are largely determined
around the age of thirteen when, based on test scores, they are put
on an academic or a non-academic track. This tracking can have a
major impact on their social circles and future prospects. One of the
reasons that Laurens and Eva cling to Pim in desperate (and often
inexplicable) ways is that, partly due to this educational system, they
know their paths are diverging, most likely forever. After their first
year at their respective schools, they are becoming more aware of their
place in society, and there's more pressure than ever to prove something to each other, and to themselves.

Another interesting and recurring detail is the symbolic role of
meat. Throughout the story, Eva observes Laurens's mom handling
different kinds of meat. She contrasts the fancy steaks that Laurens
eats every night with the cheap Aldi products she gets at home; she
marvels at the meticulous way Laurens's mom prepares her holiday
meat platters and notices a level of care that she'd never expect from

her own mother. These different meat products—pâté, meat salad, ringwurst, teddy bear sausage—are all staples in Belgium and, in addition to the carnal images they conjure up in the story, they carry socioeconomic connotations. At times, I had to rely on other ways of conveying those connotations in the translation. One of the most significant meat scenes in the book is centered around the holiday tradition of *gourmetten,* which involves grilling small pieces of meat on an electric table griddle, kind of like fondue. It's a ritual that needs no explanation for Dutch-language readers and one that conjures up cozy feelings of *gezelligheid,* or the pleasure of being together. This makes the pivotal scene at Eva's house during their last family Christmas in 2001 all the more tragic, a failed attempt at togetherness by a family in crisis. The image of greasy chunks of meat simmering on an electric griddle intended for festive purposes renders the scene even more heart-breaking: three neglected children who dared to hope for a special Christmas dinner and instead get an angry, drunk father and a mother who has to eat with the dog.

While working on the translation, I was fortunate enough to receive valuable input from the author, who was always available to answer questions and think in solutions. The few changes to character and place names, such as replacing the name "Tesje" with "Tessie", were done with her approval and only where necessary. In the case of Tessie, it was important that the English reader understand that her name was a diminutive form of Tes, her deceased sibling's name. Fortunately, like Tesje, Tessie is not an uncommon name in Belgium. The author and I also discussed images of certain objects, such as the American shovel and the hole poker, which allowed me to accurately render the horrifying images of Eva's rape.

Throughout the process, I was also mentored by two esteemed colleagues: first by Jonathan Reeder, who guided me, years ago, in the translation of the first chapters, which ultimately led to the commission of the book; and later by David McKay, who provided me with extensive feedback on my work and contributed to several solutions for difficult sentences. These mentorships were funded by Flanders Literature, which was also kind enough to support my stay at the Translator's House in Antwerp to work on this project. This experience proved immensely valuable to my overall sense of the book, its language and its setting. I am so grateful for their support and delighted to see this book published by Picador for an English-speaking audience.

Kristen Gehrman
The Hague, The Netherlands
March 2021